The Dead Chill

A Sidney Becker Mystery Thriller

LINDA BERRY

D0878229

Copyright © 2019 by Linda Berry

The Dead Chill is a work of fiction. All characters, organizations, and events portrayed in this novel are either products of the author's imagination or are used fictitiously.

All rights reserved. No part of this publication may be reproduced, stored in a retrieval system, or transmitted in any form or in any means, electronic, mechanical, photocopying, recording, or otherwise, without the prior written permission of the publisher.

ISBN-13: 978-0-9998538-3-2

www.lindaberry.net

To Mark—for three decades
of unconditional love and support.

Other books by Linda Berry

Hidden Part One

Hidden Part Two

Pretty Corpse

The Killing Woods

The Dead Chill

To learn of new releases and discounts,
add your name to Linda's mailing list:

www.lindaberry.net

ACKNOWLEDGMENTS

A wonderful community of friends and family assisted in making this a suspenseful and entertaining work of fiction.

I owe a debt of gratitude to my editors and readers, whose fearless comments kept me on the straight and narrow: Denice Hughes, Mark Fasnacht, Jeanine Pollak, Donna Berry, Trish Wilkinson, Jamie Carpenter, Cathey Kahlie, Sharon Grow, Cherie Bethe, Connie Edwards, Rob Hall, Cindy Davis, Vonnie Wignall, and LaLoni Kirkland.

I greatly appreciate the assistance of **Police Chief Rob Hall** (ret.) for his insightful counsel on law enforcement procedures.

Every day that a cop puts on his gun, he does so with the knowledge that he may have to take someone's life. Every time he puts on his badge, he does so with the knowledge that someone may take his.
~ Police Chief Rob Hall (ret.)

CHAPTER ONE

HE ALWAYS CAME at night. A soft, creeping terror surfaced in that realm between sleep and consciousness, startling Selena awake. She sensed the man's presence in the room like a force field, standing in the deep shadows, watching. In one smooth, practiced movement, her fingers gripped the hilt of the Beretta M9 under her spare pillow and aimed. She switched on the light. The shadows disappeared. The room was empty. The only sound was her labored breathing. Wide-eyed, she sat trembling until her pulse quieted, then she lowered the gun.

This behavior was irrational. The man who viciously attacked her four weeks ago was locked in a cage in Jackson County Jail. Yet his presence never faded. His shadow lurked on the fringe of her vision. His smell lingered. She felt his sour breath on her face, even when she was surrounded by students in her yoga class or barricaded here at home. The new state-of-the-art security system didn't vanquish ghosts.

Hearing footsteps scuff the hardwood floor outside her bedroom, Selena slid the pistol back under the pillow. The door opened and her sister appeared. Sidney's twelve-hour shift as Garnerville's police chief had just ended at midnight.

"You okay?" Dressed in her uniform with her hair tightly knotted at the back of her neck, Sidney possessed an aura of authority and toughness. She was born to be a cop. Duty and service were encoded in her DNA—passed down from their dad—Garnerville's Police Chief for twenty years while they were growing up. "I saw your light come on."

Selena swallowed and found her voice, which sounded calmer than she felt. "Just the usual mind-bending nightmare."

Sidney's expression softened. "Bad dreams fade with time." She was the voice of experience. A former homicide detective in Oakland, California, she had a decade's worth of grisly crime scenes embedded in her psyche. "Want some company?"

"Only if you need to talk about work."

"Nope. Uneventful. All the criminals took the day off."

"It's the snow," Selena said soberly. "Everyone's hibernating. Dad used to say a crime lull was the quiet before the storm."

"Yeah, he did." Sidney smiled. "No doubt the bad guys are gearing up for Armageddon." She glanced toward the window. "More of the fluffy white stuff is coming down as we speak. We'll have another six inches by morning."

Selena followed her gaze. The wind-driven flakes slanted past the glass on a mission to create more havoc on the roads. "Yippie. More shoveling."

"Good exercise. I won't have to go to the gym."

Selena was momentarily struck by how much Sidney resembled their father. Tall and athletic, she had his strong nose and chin, and deep-set hazel eyes. A full mouth softened her features. Though not pretty in a traditional sense, Sidney had an indefinable appeal that attracted men, and more importantly, commanded respect.

Sidney tugged the tie from her ponytail and her wavy, auburn hair tumbled around her shoulders. The aura of toughness all but vanished. "Want a cup of chamomile tea?"

"Don't worry about me, Sid. I'm okay." Selena settled back under her covers and turned off the light. "Get some rest. You'll need it for the crime spree tomorrow."

Her sister laughed as she backed out of the room.

Feeling safer with her sister home, Selena ruminated on the irony of their current circumstances. After years of separation, she and Sidney had completed a cycle of husband and boyfriends and career pivots and made their way back to each other. With their father dead and their mother in a memory care center—early onset Alzheimer's—she and Sidney now lived as roommates in their childhood home. When they were kids, Sidney had been Selena's protector, patching scraped knees and warding off bullies. That fierce instinct still burned strong. If Sidney wasn't a highly skilled detective, and if she hadn't arrived in the woods at the precise moment she did, Selena would be dead. The debt she owed her sister was staggering. Someday she would find a way to repay her.

CHAPTER TWO

SELENA'S SHOULDER MUSCLES burned with tension as her mare groped for solid footing on the icy trail. Granger Wyatt rode a horse length ahead, the collar of his sheepskin jacket turned up, western hat pulled low, his strong body swaying with the rhythm of his gelding. The horses trod on a narrow trail snaking through the Sacamoosh Forest, their breath steaming in the crisp mountain air. Snowdrifts shimmered in the filtered light. The serene beauty of this interior world didn't ease Selena's anxiety. The pungent smell of juniper was suffocating.

Granger headed into the higher elevation through towering trees. The mare snorted and her ears flicked forward and backward, listening. Picking up signals of danger? Selena touched the bulk under her down jacket and took comfort from the holstered handgun within easy reach. Granger carried his own sidearm, adding another layer of security, and at her request he'd shoved a shotgun into the scabbard on his saddle. A former Marine with combat experience, he was now one of four officers in her sister's small police department.

A wedge of ice fell from a branch and startled her horse into a quick sidestep off the trail. Selena gasped. The familiar, ghastly terror threatened to surface. With a shiver of revulsion, she fought back the memories and firmly guided her mare back on course.

Stay calm.

Granger stopped where the trail opened to a wide meadow and glanced back, waiting for her dapple-gray mare to catch up to his chestnut bay. He was all-American handsome with an angular face, square chin, and contagious smile. Raised on a cattle ranch just a few miles away, he had a country boy's down-to-earth sensibility and a cop's mental toughness. His brow furrowed as her horse pulled alongside his. "You okay?"

Selena realized her face had tightened into a mask. She cracked a smile. "Yes. Fine."

She wasn't. Since her attack, she'd felt adrift, floating in an unfamiliar landscape, as though living a life that belonged to someone else. Tears welled at the slightest provocation. Out here in the forest, she felt even more unanchored. "I'm a little nervous, that's all. Being back in the woods…"

Granger's eyes were on her, reading her emotions. He had a cop's sixth sense that could pick up any small sign of deceit. She detected a twinge of guilt in the way he clenched and unclenched his jaw.

"I shouldn't have brought you out here. It's too soon."

"I made the decision to come, Granger. Garnerville is surrounded by forest. I can't hide in town forever. I need to face my demons."

His frown deepened.

"Really. This is good for me." She took a deep breath, trying to reassure herself, as well as him. A month had passed. Granger had no reason to feel guilty. Selena should be moving on, putting the horror behind her. But she rarely left home except to teach her yoga classes. Lounging on the couch in sweats, watching endless Hallmark movies with her four cats, she had lost all sense of time—and her connection to a social life.

Granger routinely stopped by to check on her. It never took much persuasion for him to settle next to her and share popcorn—and though he hid it well, watching fluffy movies with happy endings must have been stupefying. Last night, he gently encouraged her to step out of her safety zone, come out to the family ranch, and partake in a big country breakfast with his parents and brother. On a whim, they saddled two quarter horses and set out to explore this forest wonderland. And now, here she was, quaking in her saddle.

Selena took in the wide, sprawling meadow, open in every direction, and sighed her relief. No one could sneak up on her. Cyclists, hikers, and equestrians used this trail in the summer, and cross-country skiers in the winter, but today no one was in sight. Cascading water drew her attention to the creek winding through the snow. Beneath the partially frozen surface the current moved with force and purpose. In some areas, the water was so still she could see the fine grains of sand at the bottom. "This is Whilamut Creek," she said, to lighten the mood. "Whilamut is Kalapuyan. It means 'where the water ripples and runs fast'. Kalapuya people once occupied this entire territory between the Cascades and the Calapooya Mountains."

"Some still live here. There's a small Native American community down the road a couple miles."

She nodded. "On the shore of Nenámooks Lake. One of my friends from high school lived there." The sun spilled out from behind a cloud and she raised a hand to block the glare. "She moved a decade ago. I haven't been out there since."

"I know some of the villagers," Granger said. "Visit regularly."

"To keep the peace?"

"Mostly to visit a friend. Tommy Chetwoot."

"The healer."

He tipped up the brim of his hat. His eyes, reflecting the sun, were exceptionally clear, like blue glass washed up on the beach. "Guess just about everyone in town knows of Tommy."

"And his grandmother, the medicine woman. I've never seen her, but my friend told me she's scary, and has strange powers. Supposedly, she's raised people from the dead."

"Not sure about the scary part." Granger smiled. "Paramedics raise people from the dead every day. But she's definitely not sociable. I caught a glimpse of her once. She's small, bent over, eyes black as obsidian, white hair streaming down her back. Could be eighty, or a hundred. Hard to say. I've never seen anyone so withered. Tommy learned everything about healing from her."

"Do you see Tommy to get help for your dad?" she asked gently. Granger's father suffered from Parkinson's disease. Once a stalwart pillar of the community, he'd gradually retreated from his involvement in the town's civic affairs.

"Yeah." Granger's mouth tightened for a moment. "He makes Dad an herbal concoction that eases the pain."

"Your dad looked fine this morning."

"He has good days and bad. Tommy's potion isn't a cure-all. Dad's still getting worse every year."

"I'm so sorry." A tremor of sadness passed through her as she thought of her mother, now living among strangers in the memory care center. "I'd love to talk to Tommy."

Granger gave her a long, steady stare, seeming to assess her motives.

"I know the villagers don't like outsiders rambling in without an invitation, but maybe he can help my mom."

He nodded, understanding. "I'll talk to him. See if I can bring you next time."

She smiled her thanks.

He gestured with a jut of his chin. "There's a nice view from that bridge up ahead."

They tethered the horses to a timbered post and crunched through the snow to the middle of the bridge. To the west, the corridor of water meandered through the meadow and disappeared into the forest. Far below to the east, bloated gray clouds hung over their small town, nestled in the forested hills.

"A snowstorm's sweeping in," Granger said, staring straight up the mountain. He stood close, his arm brushing hers. "It's already snowing up on top." Though barricaded in thick jackets, she felt the warmth of his presence, his instinct to protect her. "It feels good to be back on a horse," she said. "I used to ride all the time. It's been a while, though. A couple years."

"We'll have to remedy that." He turned, his face close to hers. Despite the cold, Selena's cheeks warmed. She and Granger had been spending a fair amount of time together, and his romantic intentions were clear. But she had kept him at arm's length. After the poor choice she'd made in her husband of ten years, she wasn't ready to get tangled in a new relationship. Before she lost her resolve and kissed him, she crossed the bridge to the opposite rail. This relationship needed to be a good move, not another dead-end street, which meant cooling down and thinking straight.

In just a few minutes the gauzy white clouds had taken on a harder, darker sheen. As if fleeing the scene, a flock of geese cut a lopsided wedge through the sky.

"The storm's moving in pretty fast," Ganger said, joining her. "We better head back."

Nodding, Selena lowered her gaze to the creek. The wind had cleared patches of snow from the frozen surface, revealing fast-moving water underneath. A stain of scarlet about the size of a maple leaf appeared near the bank. "Hmmm," she asked. "Wonder what that is."

They moved to the end of the bridge to get a better look. The wind excavated more snow and the leaf turned into a knitted scarf, partially frozen beneath the surface. It fluttered in the breeze then blew to the west, unfurling like a flag. Under the scarf, a human hand was exposed. A hand. Fingers spread wide.

Selena stood paralyzed, her eyes fixed to the spot. The wind continued its work, revealing the cuff of a blue jacket.

Granger lurched into motion and eased down the slippery bank, ice crackling beneath his boots. He squatted at the edge where frozen water met frozen earth. His gloved hand brushed away more snow, unveiling an arm and shoulder. A woman's face appeared, her glazed eyes wide open. Beneath her body, long black hair swirled with the movement of the water. Red ligature marks circled her slender throat. Someone had killed this woman, placed her body in this frozen creek, and abandoned her.

The realization struck Selena like a physical blow. Her eyes fluttered, then closed. When she looked again, the woman's blank face still stared up at her.

Granger climbed up the bank to his horse, pulled a satellite phone from a saddle pocket, and punched in some numbers. His urgent voice enunciated clearly, relaying the details of the gruesome discovery. He ended the call and made another. This was a man who knew how to handle an emergency, who knew how to react and stay calm. His animation highlighted Selena's inertness, which mirrored the dead woman entombed in ice. She couldn't pull her gaze from the unseeing stare.

"Selena…"

"Selena!" Granger stood close, his voice cutting though the cotton fog in her brain. He placed both hands on her shoulders and she looked into his deeply concerned face. "Are you okay?"

"Yes. I think so." Her voice sounded hollow and far away.

He led her to the horses as though she were a child, pulled a thermos from a saddlebag, and poured two inches of black coffee into the cap. "Drink this."

Selena took the cup in her gloved hands and sipped. The warm liquid glided over her tongue and down her throat. It was the sensory distraction she needed. She surfaced from a softly padded world into the snowy meadow where large snowflakes had begun to fall. Meeting Granger's clear blue eyes, she released a nervous sigh. "Thank you. I'm all right. Is help coming?"

"Yeah, but it'll be a while. They can only get so far by truck. Then they'll have to use snowmobiles. This storm could get bad, and it's likely to get a lot colder. It's too far for you to ride back to the ranch alone. I called Tommy. His village is minutes away. He's coming to get you."

"I don't want to leave you." Tears filled her eyes. "Out here. Alone."

He took both of her hands. "Selena, this is a crime scene. I'm on the job. I have to work. I also need to know you're safe. Will you go with Tommy? Will you do that for me?"

Selena nodded, hating this new version of herself. This stranger, who displayed total ineptitude, and helplessness, and had to rely on a man to help her through a crisis. She loathed the tears.

"Good," he said, and then almost to himself, "I should never have brought you out here. What was I thinking?" He pulled her into his arms, held her close, his cheek cold against her own. "And now…this."

They stood close for a long time, his body a fortress, protecting her from unknown horror, until the rumble of a snowmobile sounded in the distance. The engine grew louder and then it emerged from the forest, a black beast spraying a rooster tail of powder, gliding smoothly across the field carrying two passengers. The motor stopped and the smell of exhaust drifted in the air. The tall driver, wearing a down jacket, a wool cap pulled low on his forehead, and a knit scarf over his face, crunched through the snow to join them. Only his dark brown eyes were visible. "Where is she?"

"Just past the bridge." Granger and the man climbed down into the channel, squatted, and roughly wiped away new fallen snow.

The man gave a strangled cry. His shoulders slumped and he covered his face with one hand. After a long moment, they climbed back up the bank.

Trying to appear useful, Selena stood brushing snow from Brandy's mane. The flakes were falling like goose down—silent, mesmerizing, softening the edge of the forest and the two men who stood nearby talking in hushed tones.

"You know her?" Granger asked.

"Yeah. Nikah Tamanos. She lives...lived in the village." His voice caught, and he cleared his throat. "With her boyfriend. He's a drunk. Abusive. We asked him to leave. He moved to town."

"She have any other family in the village?"

"Not by blood. But we're all family. Nikah is...was...like a little sister."

"I'm sorry for your loss." Granger's gentle comment was followed by a respectful silence. "A recovery team is on the way. When we finish here, Chief Becker and I will need to come out to the village and talk to folks. Pick up Selena." Both men glanced toward her. It was just a look, but she thought they viewed her as an injured bird.

"Where will you take her body?" Tommy asked.

"The morgue. The M.E. is coming out."

"Dr. Linthrope is a good man," Tommy said. "He'll be respectful."

A smaller figure left the snowmobile and trudged toward them sweeping a sturdy, hand-carved staff before him, following the sound of Tommy's voice. Like the older man, he was clothed in a padded jacket and pants, his features hidden by a ski hat and a scarf wrapped around his face. He was obviously blind.

"This way," Tommy said. "You're good. Keep coming." His arm encircled the boy's shoulders. "This is my son, Tegan."

They exchanged a greeting.

"It's Nikah?" The boy's voice sounded muffled through his scarf.

"Yes."

"Someone killed her?"

"I'm afraid so."

With a choked sob, the boy pressed his face into his father's jacket. Tommy held him close.

Watching the two huddled figures in the drifting snow, Selena felt a piercing sorrow. She suddenly became aware of how chilled she had become from the sudden drop in temperature and the aftershocks of finding the murdered woman.

Tommy's voice softened as he addressed his son. "You ready to head back?"

The boy nodded and pulled away.

Tommy cast his glance to Selena. "Let's get you in front of our fireplace so you can thaw out."

"What about the horses?" Even as the words left her mouth, Tegan heaved himself onto the back of Granger's gelding, his hand deftly finding the reins of both horses.

"They'll follow," Tommy said. "We'll put the horses in our barn."

"I should ride, too," she said. How could she leave that task to a blind boy?

"Tegan's wearing snow gear, heated gloves. You're not dressed for this weather. I have a blanket in the snowmobile."

Granger's ears were red with cold. Earlier, he had stuffed a thick knit cap and scarf into his saddlebag. Selena pulled them out and he accepted gratefully, and soon his head, too, was wrapped beyond recognition, and his shoulders were turning white under the incessant powder.

Selena scanned the periphery of the meadow and her eyes froze on a copse of aspens, their mottled white trunks naked, skeletal branches raised to the sky. Something low and white slinked behind the trees and disappeared. An animal. Stalking them. Or was her mind playing tricks? "I'm worried about leaving you here," she said.

"I'll be fine. Go, Selena," Granger said firmly. It was an order. He was in cop mode. As if to reassure her, he drew his shotgun from its scabbard and held it in the crook of his arm, barrel pointing down.

Reluctantly, she trudged to the snowmobile, boots squeaking in the snow, and settled herself on the back seat. Tommy handed her a helmet, then he tucked a thick wool blanket over her legs. As the mini caravan started toward the woods, she felt warmer, but she also felt a stab of something deep in her belly and knew it was guilt. She glanced back at Granger—a white figure barely discernible behind a gauzy veil of snow.

CHAPTER THREE

SIDNEY LAID IN DAVID'S arms in a sleepy state of bliss, still damp from lovemaking, the edge taken off the desire she perpetually felt for him. The sheets were rumpled beneath them and hazy light fell though the blinds, highlighting the soft hair on his chest. Sex with David was like nothing she'd ever known, a physical conversation of intense sensitivity that words could never express.

David stirred beside her. His hand slid past the small of her back and settled on the curve of her hip. He pulled her close and his tongue teased the edges of her lips. An invitation. But it was time to get ready for work. That wasn't what she wanted to do. His warm fingers moved softly over her breast and his kiss convinced her to stay. Sighing, she relaxed and her body molded to his.

Her phone dinged on the nightstand.

David quietly groaned. He had learned that when Sidney was off duty, she wasn't really off duty. She pulled away from his arms and checked the name on the screen. It was her dispatcher. "Work," she stated with a note of disappointment, and slid her finger across the screen. "Yeah, Jesse."

"Hey, Chief. Looks like we got a homicide. Female. Probably Native American."

Sidney bolted upright in bed. "Where?"

"In Whilamut Creek, near the bridge. Granger and your sister found the body. They were up there riding. Tommy Chetwoot is picking up Selena and taking her back to Two Creeks Village."

"Granger's out there alone?"

"Yes, ma'am."

"Okay. Notify the M.E and his forensic tech. Have the fire and rescue team meet me at the station. Dr. Linthrope and Stewart will ride with me."

Adrenaline racing, Sidney pecked David on the mouth and threw the covers aside. "Gotta run. Emergency." She hurried into the spacious master bathroom, turned on the shower, and yanked on a big, floppy plastic cap that looked ridiculous. But all she cared about was not getting her hair wet. It would freeze in this weather.

As she showered, she was aware of David's presence in the room. When she stepped out, he wrapped a big, plush towel around her, and then quietly left. He had draped her uniform and undergarments over the chair in front of the vanity mirror, along with thick wool socks and snow boots.

She quickly dressed, pulled her hair into a ponytail, left the steamy bathroom, and crossed the living room with the stunning view of the lake. David's modern-style house was modest compared to others on the lakeshore, but it had been upgraded with cherry wood cabinets, bamboo floors, and a cook's kitchen with professional appliances. Extraordinary, that a man as handsome and charming as David was also a talented chef. He insisted on feeding her at every opportunity, and she was more than willing to comply. Pragmatic in nature, Sidney would have been happy to eat takeout and focus on his other talents.

She met him in the foyer.

Barefoot, hair tousled, dressed only in jeans that rode low on his lean hips, he stood by the front door holding out her bulky duty belt, which she strapped around her waist. Then he helped her wrestle into her burly winter jacket. Her gloves, scarf, and wool hat were in her vehicle. Where she was going, she would need them.

"Be careful out there."

"Careful is my middle name."

David pulled her close by her lapels. Their chests bumped and they laughed. He kissed her sweetly, then he opened the door and she burrowed down the steps through the falling snow to her Yukon parked in the driveway.

As she cranked up the heater and wipers, Sidney realized she and David had barely spoken a word since the call. They had their own means of communication, their own language, and he had left her with a smile that was meant to say, "I'm here, I understand what it means to be Police Chief of a small town, and I'll do whatever I can to support you." Five weeks ago, when she had walked into David's art studio to seek his help on a murder case, she had no idea her life was about to radically change. His expertise in art symbology uncovered an important lead in the case. Their startling and immediate attraction to each other had led to these passionate afternoons in the haven of his home.

Sidney drove with caution to the station, trying to shake off the warm glow from David's touch and morph into cop mode. She was grateful he hadn't quizzed her about the phone call. She was still trying to wrap her head around the fact that a young woman had been murdered. Aside from an occasional domestic or DUI, the tribal members of Two Creeks Village kept a low profile and rarely stirred up trouble. Granger was on friendly terms with many of the elders. That trusted relationship would be critical when dealing with folks who didn't trust law enforcement.

Equally distressing was the fact that her sister and Granger discovered the body. Emotionally fragile, her sister didn't need this shock today. It could reset the initial trauma all over again.

Sidney focused on the ice-slick road. Garnerville rarely saw more than a few dustings of snow a season, and it usually melted by afternoon. The aggressive storms that had plowed through the county in the last three weeks made October the snowiest in recent Oregon history west of the Cascades. A good foot of snow had fallen, gripping the tri-town area in a frigid chill. Everything was layered in white and deep snowdrifts rippled across the yards. Large icicles hung from every eave like dragon's teeth.

The townsfolk had greeted the extreme weather with a flurry of excitement. Bundled in warm clothing, parents towed children down sidewalks on sleds, kids built snowmen in their yards and hurled snowballs at anything that moved. The flipside to the winter wonderland was an increase in fender-benders and the small ER was jammed with patients who slipped on ice or threw their backs out shoveling snow.

As she drove through historical downtown headed for the highway, a few brave souls navigated the icy sidewalks, patronizing restaurants and gift shops. Life in Garnerville was unfolding as usual, oblivious to the woman who lay entombed in ice up in Whilamut creek.

And a murderer was walking free.

CHAPTER FOUR

THE SNOWMOBILE Selena straddled tunneled through the forest and shuddered over the rutted trail like a frightened pony. Two Creeks Village was five miles west of the highway on the opposite side of the lake from downtown Garnerville. Selena had never reached the village coming down from the mountain and she was completely disoriented. Tommy turned from the trail onto a plowed two-lane road. Through the trees she could see the metallic sheen of Lake Nenámooks under the low hanging ceiling of gray clouds. Giant oaks lined the narrow road, their gnarly branches linked at their crowns like gothic arches. This she remembered from years ago, though the trees had been leafy and the tangled canopy blocked out the hot summer sun.

Enveloped in the roar of the engine, the snowmobile glided past a general store, the Wildhorse Bar and Grill, a small school, a community center, and a few dozen houses on deeply wooded lots that hugged the shoreline. Tommy abruptly turned into a driveway and Selena spotted a log cabin that was half hidden in a grove of conifer trees. Adirondack chairs lined the covered porch, smoke curled from the chimney, and amber light wavered in one of the windows. Across a clearing, set against the backdrop of the shimmering lake, stood a two-car garage, a wood-planked shed, and a weathered barn with an empty corral. Stripped of all color, the stark-white world possessed an ethereal, frigid beauty.

Tommy parked in front of the cabin, climbed off, and offered Selena a hand. The wind came running at them from the northwest, blowing the snow and shaking the trees. Tegan rode past them and dismounted in front of the barn, then disappeared inside with the horses.

Though Selena was numb with cold and looked longingly at the cabin, she said to Tommy, "I should go help him with the horses."

"He's fine. Tegan's an ace with animals. Let's get you warm."

Marveling that the blind boy was so capable, she caught a movement at the end of the house. When she shifted her glance, something large and white darted out of sight. Crows shot up out of the trees, screaming.

"A cougar..." she gasped.

"Oh, that's just Lelou."

A dog? A big dog. She was grateful when Tommy took her arm and helped her navigate the icy walkway. They pulled off their snow-caked boots on the porch and entered the afternoon darkness of the cabin. A fire burning low in the fireplace shot flickering shadows over the floor and walls. Selena made out simple furnishings: two easy chairs and a sofa in muted earth tones, and shelves filled with books, photos, pottery, and baskets. Off to one side, a worn oak table with mismatched chairs dominated the dining room. Dishes and cups were stacked in the hutch. The place smelled of wood smoke and freshly baked bread. Irresistibly, she was drawn to the river stone fireplace across the room and stood with her back to the flames. Tommy unwrapped the scarf from his head, removed his hat and coat and hung them on pegs by the door, then turned to face her.

Around forty, he was tall and lanky, and seemed almost too big for the room. His glossy black hair fell over his shoulders, framing a long face with a full mouth, bold nose, and strong cheekbones. A nice face. A kind face. His dark brown eyes were hollow with sorrow.

"Who is the dead girl?" A raspy voice with an Indian accent came from a dark corner. Selena flinched. Someone was there, in the shadows. A lamp flicked on and an old woman materialized, sitting stoop-shouldered in a straight-backed chair. She wore a long black dress adorned with strings of colorful beads and wiry white hair streamed over her shoulders. Her deeply grooved face was expressionless, except for dark, gleaming eyes that gazed out of slits, darting from Tommy to Selena with unnerving intensity.

"It's Nikah," Tommy said.

Neither spoke, but their expressions of grief pierced Selena to the core. For a moment, a long moment, she stood utterly still, feeling like an intruder, conscious suddenly of her weight on the wooden floor.

"I knew she would come to a bad end," the old woman croaked. "I warned her."

"Yeah, you did. Many times."

Warned her of what, Selena wondered?

A long silence ensued.

"This is Selena," Tommy finally said, with a gentle wave of his hand. "This is my grandma, Elahan."

Selena crossed the space between them and extended her hand. Elahan's claw-like, bony fingers grasped it fleetingly. A token gesture. The old woman's hard stare held no warmth.

"Let me take your coat," Tommy said.

Selena slipped off her gloves and hat, stuffed them in a pocket, and handed him her parka. Tommy hung her jacket, then noticing she was shivering, placed another log on the fire and stoked the flames. Selena felt an immediate rise in temperature.

"You'll warm up in a moment," he said softly.

Selena glanced at Elahan, who sat perched in her chair like a crow on a branch, watching, unreadable.

The door opened with a burst of cold air and Tegan stood framed in the doorway, his walking stick gripped in one hand. A giant white dog with gleaming gold eyes hovered behind him. No, not a dog. A wolf!

The animal lowered his head, wrinkled his snout, and bared teeth that looked like they could rip off a limb in a heartbeat. A snarling growl sent a chill along Selena's spine. Her fingers touched the hilt of her handgun beneath her sweater.

"It's okay, Lelou. Selena's a friend," Tegan said forcefully, leaning his staff against the doorframe. The boy held the beast firmly by the collar and stroked his large, bristly head. "Down." The wolf lowered himself to the rough wooden planks, his eyes still fixed on Selena.

Tegan's head pivoted in her direction "Come let him smell you, Selena. Then he'll be your friend."

No way.

Tommy and the old lady watched her expectantly, waiting, as freezing air swept into the room. She swallowed, then slowly crossed the room and held out her fingers, hoping no one would see they were trembling.

Ignoring her hand, Lelou thrust out his neck, and she felt the heat of his moist breath on her groin as he sniffed. The wolf then sat back on his haunches and surprised her by extending a forepaw. After a moment of hesitation, Selena cupped the large paw in her hand. Tegan placed his smaller hand on top and the three made the motion of shaking hands. Lelou's mouth curled back in what might be interpreted as a grin. The boy nodded, as though they were now partners in some secret covenant. Selena's stomach muscles relaxed.

The wolf retreated from the porch, and finally, Tegan shut the door. He removed his outer garments and his knowing fingers hung them on pegs.

As he faced the light, Selena saw the boy's features clearly. Tegan looked about eight or nine. He had a slender frame and straight black hair that brushed his shoulders. He had a sensitive face and vacant sable brown eyes. Yet he faced Selena with open curiosity, apparently sizing her up using his own unique means of perception.

"Let's have some hot tea and home-baked bread," Tommy said, his tone artificially light.

"I've never seen a wolf up close before," Selena said, attempting to make conversation when she and the boy were seated at the well-scrubbed oak table. She had a clear view of Tommy in the kitchen pouring hot water from a steaming kettle into mugs. Like a shadow passing, Elahan disappeared down a darkened hallway and a wedge of light appeared behind a door. "I certainly never expected to see one as a pet," Selena continued, pulling her gaze back to the boy.

"Lelou isn't a pet. He's my spirit guide. He could have been any animal he wanted to be, but he chose to be a wolf. So he could protect me." Seated at her elbow, Tegan spoke with conviction and a level of maturity that was unusual for a child. His absolute belief in a spirit world resonated with Selena. She, too, believed in a mystical world of energy and vibration. She believed thoughts were magnetic, attracting and shaping molecular matter into everyday experiences.

"Lelou was checking you out," Tegan said. "Making sure you wouldn't hurt me. But I already knew you were okay. I could tell from your smell."

"Really? How do I smell?"

"Like a garden." He smiled shyly. "And pancakes. And your hair smells like peppermint."

Clearly, the boy had heightened olfactory perception. People with disabilities often compensated for one sensory loss by strengthening others. "I had pancakes for breakfast at Granger's ranch, and my shampoo has peppermint in it. You have a very good sense of smell."

"You have no idea," Tommy said, walking back into the room with a laden tray. After placing a dish of butter, a bowl of berry preserves, and a loaf of homemade bread on the table, he distributed three steaming mugs of tea. Gratefully, Selena lifted her cup and sipped. The tea was delicate and delicious, with a hint of cardamom and cloves. She took another sip. Lemongrass. Something else, mysterious and spicy, immediately warmed her.

"Sometimes I think Tegan is part wolf." Tommy took a seat across the table and carved the loaf into thick slices. "He can identify people by their scent before they open their mouths. He can also sense the shape and distance of objects around him, and sense color."

She smiled, thinking Tommy was joking, but his face was serious.

He liberally spread butter and berry preserves on a slice of bread, placed it on a plate, and handed it to Selena. He did the same for Tegan. The butter melted into the moist bread, which was still warm from the oven, and the aroma made her mouth water. Sampling a bite, she tasted pecans, honey and vanilla. An accomplished cook and baker herself, Selena was deeply impressed by the texture and flavor of the bread.

"What color is Selena's hair?" Tommy asked.

Tegan was busy chewing. He swallowed and lifted his face to hers. "Can I touch your hair?"

"Sure."

The boy wiped his hands on a napkin then he gently brushed Selena's straight hair from the crown of her head to her shoulder blades. He fingered a lock like a connoisseur, and smiled. "It's soft. Doesn't have much color. Your eyes don't either. You have very blonde hair and white skin."

Selena's mouth fell open.

"You're right, Son." A flicker of amusement shone in Tommy's eyes. "Selena's hair is the color of white corn, and her eyes are light green, like celery."

"I sense you're really pretty," the boy said.

"Thank you, Tegan."

"Yes, very pretty," Tommy added with a touch of humor.

"I don't meet many people with blonde hair," Tegan confessed.

Tommy addressed Selena's curious expression. "Tegan goes to school here in the village, with other Indian kids."

"Dad and Nana don't like me to leave the village." Tegan's face shadowed and he added with a touch of defiance, "They worry. But I can take care of myself."

"You bet we worry. He likes to roam around in the woods with Lelou, sometimes disappearing for hours. We don't know if he's dead or alive."

"Lelou will protect me."

"Some people don't like wolves. They shoot them, even though it's illegal." Tommy's voice was low and tense. "What would you do if something happened to Lelou and you were miles from home? A small boy, alone."

Tegan's mouth pinched. "I'm not small. I'm nine. I could smell my way home."

"Possibly. But that's not a risk we want you to take. Nikah was murdered. Her killer is still out there." Tommy's voice caught and profound sorrow softened his expression. He stared into his son's unseeing eyes, and a silent communication seemed to pass between them.

A spasm of grief passed over Tegan's face. His eyes showed signs of recent shock, wide and unblinking. Then his face went blank, but not before Selena saw a glint of another emotion. Fear. And he was trying to hide it.

Tommy saw it, too. Worry creasing his brow, he leaned forward and watched Tegan's expression closely. "I know you're upset about Nikah, Son. We all are. But if you know something…"

Tegan sat a little lower in his chair.

"Did you smell something? Hear something?"

The boy lowered his head, letting his hair veil his face.

"What aren't you telling me, Son?"

"Leave him be," came a raspy voice from the hallway. The old woman stood there leaning on a cane with both veined hands, her rounded spine thrusting her upper body forward. Her head craned sideways and her dark eyes peered at Tommy. "He's in shock. He will talk when he is ready." She said something in a language Selena had never heard before. Then she turned to the boy. "Eat. And then finish your chores."

Tommy sighed. His shoulders drooped as if with sudden fatigue but he said nothing to contradict Elahan. Apparently, she held sway in the household. The old woman scurried into the kitchen and Selena heard the clinking of pots and pans. Despite her misshapen back, Elahan moved quickly, and her mental faculty seemed fully intact. Selena made a note to talk to Sidney. She was certain the boy knew something about Nikah's murder.

"Elahan was speaking Chinook," Tommy explained.

"I've never heard of it."

"It was a common language, derived from many languages, that was used here in the Pacific Northwest in the 1800s. It allowed different tribes, travelers, and traders to do business with each other. Chinook is being revived and taught on reservations to young people. Elahan teaches it here at our school."

"Mitlite tenas, Selena," Tegan said, then translated: "Stay a while, Selena. You are welcome here."

"Thank you, Tegan."

Tommy changed the subject, focusing his attention on Selena. "So, you and Granger…are…"

Tegan swiveled his head toward her, face suddenly alert, as though all senses were open and picking up signals.

"Friends," she finished for him. "Granger works with my sister, Police Chief Becker." Selena kept her tone neutral. "We hang out. Have an occasional drink together." A feeling of tenderness warmed Selena when she thought of Granger, and she recalled how much she had wanted to kiss him on the bridge. "I hope he's okay. It's so cold out there."

"Granger's tough," Tommy said with a reassuring smile. "A former Marine. A little snow is nothing."

With the gruesome discovery of the murdered girl, emotional exhaustion was setting in. Selena longed to be home, curled up on her couch in her sweats with her four cats. And Granger. His calm, steady presence had been an anchor during the turmoil of the last month. She missed his company profoundly, and his undemanding affection. She glanced at the door, willing him and her sister to walk in. "Granger and I are good friends," she repeated, so softly it was little more than a whisper.

"Granger is more than your friend," Tegan said. "He's your boyfriend. Your body warmed up when you were thinking of him."

Selena's mouth opened. Tegan had picked up her emotional vibrations as though her thoughts were a tuning fork.

"Tegan, remember what I told you," Tommy said, casting Selena an apologetic glance. "Certain feelings you pick up from people are private. You need to turn off your sonar. No emotional eavesdropping."

Selena was struck by the gentle tone of Tommy's voice and this insight into his son's unique ability.

"I'm sorry, Selena," Tegan said, a smile tugging up one corner of his mouth.

"That's okay," she said, though she guessed the boy knew exactly what he was doing. Childish mischievousness. She felt a deepening fondness for this boy, who appeared to have an overly sheltered life, and yearned for more freedom. Like most boys, Tegan had a rebellious streak, but he also possessed a marked lack of fear, which could put him in real danger. Tommy was justified in feeling concern. The wolf wasn't invincible, and the boy seemed to put too much trust in the animal. "How is it that Lelou came into your life, Tegan? Did you find him as a puppy?"

"No. He found me. Three years ago, when I was six." Tegan brushed his hair back from his face. His eyes took on a faraway shine as he retreated into memory. "I was fishing from our dock on the lake. A thunderstorm rolled in. Fast. It rained so hard I got soaked in seconds. Thunder boomed right above me. Like a bomb exploding. The whole sky lit up with electricity. Then a bolt of lightning hit me. That's the last thing I remember. Dad told me later my fishing pole acted as a lightning rod."

Selena caught her breath in surprise.

"I was working in the barn," Tommy said. "I heard a wolf howling like it was dying. I ran out and saw Lelou standing over Tegan. Then he disappeared. At first, I thought he'd attacked Tegan. His clothes were shredded. But when I got right up to him, I saw the burns, and knew it had been lightning."

"The lightning shredded his clothes?"

"Yeah. And blew off his shoes."

"I had no idea it was so powerful."

"Very powerful. Tegan was airlifted to Portland. It's a wonder he survived." Tommy gazed at his son with unwavering devotion. Again, some invisible communication passed between them.

She sensed the strong tie that bound them. "The wolf saved his life."

Tommy nodded. "A miracle he showed up."

"The lightning burned me inside and out." Tegan lifted the front of his sweater and revealed what looked like feathery, fern-shaped tattoos, faded pink, branching out over his thin chest. "The burns left these scars. They're on my arms and back, too."

Selena felt a surge of sympathy. She couldn't imagine the suffering Tegan endured. Though horrified, she couldn't deny that the delicate scars were beautiful, as though etched by a gifted botanical artist. "I've never seen anything like this."

"These kinds of burns are common with lightning victims," Tommy said. "They're called Lichtenberg figures. Named after a German physicist who studied branching electric discharges back in 1777."

Selena was fascinated.

"When I came home from the hospital," Tegan continued, "I was blind. I couldn't walk. I hurt all over. It took a long time to get better. The doctors said the lightning changed my brain."

"In what way?" she asked.

"My new world was total darkness but I started noticing stuff right off. I could hear and smell things out in the yard. I could smell Nana and Dad when they came into the room. After a while, I started hearing and smelling things further off in the woods, and out on the lake. I could tell when the weather changed. I could smell when Lelou came into the yard. Every night, he slept under my window. When I was well enough to hobble around and sit on the porch, Lelou came and sat with me."

"Strange for a wild animal to adopt a human," Selena said. "And to be so loyal."

"Lelou is no common wolf." Tommy returned her gaze, unblinking. "He gave my son hope, and kept him going when he was in a world of pain."

Tegan chewed the last bite of his bread and jam and said out of the side of his mouth, "Lelou's been my best friend ever since."

"That's an amazing story. You went through a terrible time." Feeling a wave of tenderness for the sensitive boy, she reached out and covered his hand with hers. "You're very brave. I'm glad you're okay."

"Me, too." His shy smile returned. "I'm glad you're my new friend. Sometime, you should come walk in the woods with Lelou and me."

"I would love to." Selena leaned back in her seat, noticing that a deep sense of calm had come over her. The sharp edge of anxiety that continuously plagued her had receded. Her eyes met Tommy's. "Thank you for the delicious meal."

Tommy gave her a knowing nod from across the table.

She cradled her mug in her hands and sipped her tea. "What's in your tea, Tommy?"

He presented her with a distinctly mischievous grin. "Oh, this and that. A little bat's wool, a dash of powdered toad, a pinch of rattlesnake venom."

Selena smiled, understanding where Tegan got his naughty streak. "In other words, it's proprietary."

"Yep, you guessed it. I have to protect my family's long held secrets. Especially from you." He grinned. "I know you're Selena of Selena's Kitchen. I recognize you from your photo. I've been to your website many times."

Selena warmed with pleasure. The natural products and organic food business she started with her partner, Ann Howard, was growing in popularity. She and Ann produced all of the products themselves in a big renovated barn on Ann's farm— herbal vinegar, flavored honey, scented candles. In addition to gaining hundreds of online subscribers this year, their products were being carried by a dozen shops in town. "I hope that's a good thing."

He nodded. "I've used several of your recipes. I buy your products at the market. You didn't recognize your own honey. It's in the tea."

She blinked. "My jalapeño honey! Of course. That's the spicy heat I detected. But what's the magic potion that makes me feel so relaxed?"

He gave her a wicked smile.

She smiled back, feeling mildly euphoric. It had been a long while since she felt this peaceful. "Are you a scientist? A chemist?"

"Nothing that technical. I'm an herbalist, and a historian. I teach history at the high school, with an emphasis on Native American studies. The unadulterated version."

"Not pretty the way indigenous people were treated in the land of the free."

"No, it's not." He was quiet for a moment. "People need to know the truth, not the white-washed version, where the heroic white man fought off bloodthirsty savages. There are lots of aspects to our culture that people could learn from."

"I'd love to know more."

"I speak at the library sometimes. I'll give you my itinerary."

"Deal."

CHAPTER FIVE

THREE MEMBERS OF the search and rescue team were waiting in their truck when Sidney pulled up in the parking lot behind the station. The medical examiner and his assistant hurried out of the rear exit of the building. Dr. Linthrope climbed up front while Stewart Wong climbed into the back seat, or "the cage," which was partitioned off from the front by a steel mesh barrier. They both wore thick jackets, knit caps, and snow boots.

"Morning," Sidney said.

"Morning, Chief," Linthrope replied pleasantly, placing his coffee cup in the holder.

"Where's the body?" Stewart asked in lieu of a greeting as he clicked his seat belt. A detail-oriented introvert, Stewart was a highly skilled forensic tech and assistant pathologist who wasted little time on extraneous conversation.

"A Native-American woman was found in Whilamut Creek up by the old timber bridge," Sidney said as she followed the red Fire and Rescue truck, which towed a trailer carrying four snowmobiles. "Looks like a homicide."

"Homicide?" The doctor raised his brows.

She nodded. "Granger and Selena found the body."

Within the heated cab, the two men lapsed into silence, lost in thought, no doubt wondering how murder could have erupted in their small town again, so soon after the rampage of a serial killer a month ago. Sought out for its historical charm and stunning natural beauty, Garnerville had in recent years become a vacation destination town, and the constant flow of tourists was lifting the economy out of a decade-long decline. Art galleries, boutiques, and trendy coffee shops were replacing dusty antique shops and thrift stores. Murder did not bode well for a town that depended on tourist dollars. The pressure to find this new murderer, quickly, felt like a heavy weight on Sidney's shoulders.

Five miles out of town, she turned off the paved highway and the chained tires of the vehicle bumped over a rutted road that tunneled through the Sacamoosh forest. The wipers swiped the snow sifting down through overhead branches.

"Some weather, huh?" Wong muttered. "Can't believe this snow."

Sidney glanced at him in the mirror, surprised that he was making a stab at normal

conversation. "It's beautiful, but it sure hampers work."

Sitting next to her, Dr. Linthrope shifted in his seat. "And it's damn cold. I feel it in my joints."

She cast him a sympathetic glance. He was spry for a man of seventy-one, but at his age the cold went bone deep.

"Good weather for catching up on paperwork at the lab," the doctor said. "Which is exactly what I was doing, very happily, fortified by hot tea." The business of death rarely ruffled him, which brought a measure of calm to the gruesome task of dealing with dead bodies. He and Wong had been processing the remains of citizens in the tri-town area for two decades.

"You'll be headed over to the village later?" the doctor asked.

"Yep. Last time I was out there, a call came in about a brawl in the bar. When I got there, all was calm. A guy with a swollen eye said he ran into the proverbial door. The place was packed with witnesses but no one saw a thing.

"They don't trust cops," Stewart said.

"You need to get in good with Elahan. Then everyone else accepts you," Linthrope said.

"The medicine woman? You know her?"

"She's an old friend."

"Really? Didn't see that coming. She's an herbalist, right?"

"An alchemist, really. Can treat just about anything. Makes a special ointment for stiff joints. Stinks to high heaven. But it works. I used to drive out there to pick it up, but now Tommy makes home deliveries."

"Tommy's her son?"

"Grandson. Sits on the tribal council. Teaches at the high school. Good man."

"They say he's a healer."

"Not sure I believe in that mumbo jumbo. Sick people generally get better just by letting nature take its course."

"Or by the power of suggestion," Stewart said.

"Exactly," Linthrope said. "The placebo effect."

"I like his tea," Stewart added.

"What kind of tea?" Sidney asked.

"Relaxation tea. Takes the edge off. Helps me sleep."

"Sounds like they have a regular pharmacy," Sidney said.

"Pretty much," the doctor said. "No chemicals. Just medicinal plants."

"I could use some extra sleep myself," Sidney said. "What's in the tea?"

"Valerian, hops, mulungu, ashwagandha, catnip, skullcap," Stewart said. "And secret sauce."

"Ha. Haven't heard of half of that stuff."

"It's not bad. Give it a try."

No way, she thought. Sounded about as appetizing as cod liver oil.

When the road disappeared and became indistinguishable from the surrounding landscape, Sidney parked behind the rescue truck.

Everyone exited. The blast of icy air hit her face like a slap. She turned up her collar and pulled her knit hat lower over her ears. Ponderosa pines towered at their backs and swirling snow quickly dusted their shoulders.

The three firemen, who Sidney knew well, were bulked up in snow clothes, their breath smoking as they set to work. The snowmobiles were ready to go in record time. Years of practice. Skiers and hikers routinely got stranded in high country this time of year, and most would be doomed if not for these seasoned professionals.

Donning helmets, Linthrope, and Wong took their places in the seats behind two of the firemen. The third had a sled hitched behind his machine to transport the body. Sidney drove the fourth, which glided effortlessly over the snow at the rear of the column. After a fifteen-minute trek, the forest opened to a wide meadow and they parked by the old timbered bridge that crossed Whilamut Creek. Sidney remembered riding horses out here when she was a teenager, but it was unrecognizable under rolling mounds of white. The storm had eased up and the sun was trying to burn though a hazy sky.

Everyone started stamping their feet and moving their arms to get their circulation going.

There was no sign of Granger. Then she saw a figure emerging from the forest, head swathed in knit cap and scarf. The team watched expectantly as he approached, trudging through snow midway to his knees.

"You all right?" Sidney asked.

"Yeah," he said, lowering the scarf.

"Warm enough?" Captain Jack Harrison asked with a touch of humor. The leader of rescue team, his gaunt face was ruddy with cold, but his voice was energetic, matching his personality.

"I did calisthenics. Got overheated, if anything."

"Good. I wasn't looking forward to resuscitating you."

Everyone chuckled.

"Tommy picked up Selena?" Sidney asked.

"Yeah."

"How is she?"

He frowned. "Shaken up."

Sidney sensed his concern and shared it. But Selena was physically safe. That's what mattered. She shifted her thoughts to business. "Did Tommy know the victim?"

He nodded. "Nikah Tamanos. She lived in the village with an abusive boyfriend. They asked him to leave and he moved into town."

Bad blood there. In most homicides, a spouse or close friend was the primary suspect.

"Where's the body?" Stewart Wong asked, looking impatient.

"Over here." Granger led them to the bank and two of the firemen carefully descended. Everyone else gathered on the rise, silently watching. Snow cover was brushed away.

The woman's body was revealed, trapped in a few inches of surface ice. Her black hair and a red scarf rippled beneath her in the swirling water.

A hollow feeling filled Sidney's stomach. She was struck by how young the victim was, no more than eighteen or nineteen. Her brown eyes were glazed with ice, but she had beautiful features; prominent cheekbones, a full mouth, lips slightly parted as though whispering a prayer. Red marks encircling her throat suggested she had been strangled. Her left arm was bent, hand pressed against the ice, the other at her side.

"So young," Granger said. He hid his emotions well, but he couldn't hide them from Sidney. His eyes softened and she could see a subtle tick in his strong jaw.

"I don't think we'll need the chainsaw," Captain Harrison said. "The ice isn't that thick. Pick axes should do it."

The men got their tools and went to work, the snow squeaking beneath their boots. They spoke through the logistics of freeing the body, voices neutral as they carefully chipped away at the ice. Stewart took photos from every angle, the clicking of his camera adding an oddly mechanical tone to the sound of rushing water and splintering ice.

Wishing she'd had the foresight to wear long johns under her wool pants, Sidney moved her feet from side to side. The frigid air stung her eyes and made her nose drip. She pulled a tissue from her pocket and swiped her nose while studying the surrounding area—snow, ice, water—looking for anything out of the ordinary. It was futile. Snow covered everything.

As though reading her thoughts, Granger said, "Nothing much to go on. I searched around before this new snow fell. Any evidence is buried."

"Hopefully, her body will tell us a story," Sidney said.

"We may be in luck," Dr. Linthrope added. "The ice may have kept evidence from washing away."

It didn't take long to free the victim. The men lifted out the frozen corpse, as unyielding as a statue carved in marble. Dr. Linthrope gave the woman a rudimentary perusal, but until the body thawed, there would be no autopsy. He gave them a nod, and the men zipped Nikah in a body bag with her frozen hand poking up like a tent pole, then covered the bag with a tarp and secured it to the rescue sled.

"How long before we get postmortem results?" Sidney asked Linthrope.

"Depends. It appears only the upper half of her body is frozen. It has to be defrosted slowly in a refrigeration unit at a steady thirty-eight degrees, which can take a day or two. Go any faster, and the outside of the body will start to decompose, while the inner organs may still be frozen."

Sidney's gut twisted with disappointment. Their investigation would have to proceed without lab results. That made Sidney's job more difficult. No way to check for DNA, signs of sexual assault, or the presence of drugs or poison in the body.

"What about an estimate of time of death?" Granger asked.

"Again, depends on how frozen she is. It takes about three days for a human to freeze solid, so I'd guess she's been in the creek at least twenty-four hours."

The group disassembled quickly at that point, snowmobiles kicking out a spray of snow as they turned back the way they came, leaving Sidney and Granger behind to drive the remaining snowmobile to the village.

Granger hesitated before climbing onto the passenger seat. "Chief, if you don't mind a suggestion…"

"Sure. Shoot."

"The best way to approach the people in the village is to go to Elahan first and pay our respects." He jammed his gloved hands into his pockets. His breath was white vapor. "She's an elder. Everyone looks up to her."

"Is that the custom?" Sidney stamped her feet, trying to get blood moving.

"Pretty much. With her blessing, the other folks will be more cooperative." He gave her a thin smile. "Not willingly, but a little more receptive."

Sidney had no problem relinquishing leadership to one of her three junior officers when appropriate. After eight months on the job, working under her wing, Granger had adopted her methods of dealing with the public. Half the job was instinctual and he could think two steps ahead in a crisis situation, skills honed from his combat experience. "Why don't you take the lead on this."

"Will do, Chief."

The dull grey light changed to a deep leaden gloom as dusk descended. Swollen black clouds were racing in from the west.

Soon darkness would complicate their travel through the woods. They needed to move quickly.

"While I drive, get on the phone to dispatch. Have Darnell and Amanda meet us at Tommy's. We need to canvass the whole village."

"That's two dozen households, Chief."

"Don't I know it." Her other two officers would arrive at Tommy's within the half hour. She pulled her helmet down over her knit cap. "Hop on. Let's roll."

CHAPTER SIX

MOST EVENINGS, Tegan sat at the table doing homework, his fingers tracking the pages of books in Braille. Elahan normally occupied herself in the kitchen making bread and stews, or she helped his dad prepare remedies, measuring teaspoons of dried medicinal plants into plastic bags. The fragrance of sage, wild ginger, rosemary, and other herbs perfumed their hair and skin for the rest of the evening. Elahan labeled each bag by hand, peering through thick glasses that made her eyes look enormous, like an owl. The finished packets were placed in boxes, ready for his father's deliveries.

Tonight, Selena and his father sat at the table talking and drinking tea. Tegan couldn't concentrate. The shock of Nikah's murder overwhelmed his senses. He felt so finely tuned he could hear the melody of blood moving through his veins, the percussion of his heartbeat. Keeping his face immobile, hiding his feelings, was exhausting.

Tegan retreated to the living room and sat cross-legged in front of the fire, absorbing the heat. Tears pricked his eyes as memories of Nikah bloomed in his mind. She had always been quick to laugh, ever ready to tease him. He knew intimately the contours of her body, the feel of her hand holding his. Sitting in her lap when he was a toddler, she held him close, and her lilting, musical voice sang him to sleep. He remembered her round, pretty face, nut-brown eyes shaped like almonds, and skin that felt like silk. Nikah had the most beautiful hair Tegan had ever seen. When she loosened it from its single braid, it fell to her waist like a glossy veil. What he remembered most, what haunted him, was her smell—the fragrance of grass and leaves and herbs that clung to her clothes and misted around her like a halo.

Tegan's throat was closing up and he made harsh noises as he cleared it. *Boys don't cry.*

Before tears streamed down his face, he had to leave. "I'm going to check on Lelou," he announced, already wrestling into his parka.

"Okay, Son. Don't be long."

Elahan came out of the kitchen, as silent as a cat, but he could feel her power, her eyes studying him. He felt a muscle twitch near his mouth, betraying him. She knew he had secrets and dangers swirling around him. Elahan could read his deepest feelings as though transcribed in words on his skin. He would be shielded from her prying eyes in his safe place—the barn. With the animals who never judged him.

Forgoing gloves and hat, he stepped out on the porch gripping his walking staff. The icy breeze assailed him, cooling his flushed face and fingering his hair. He listened to the stirrings of the night, the noise of trees, the wind sighing across the sky. A certain energetic quality to the air told him it was the night of a full moon. His stick barely skimmed the surface as his internal GPS guided him in the direction of the looming structure. The sound and texture beneath his feet told him an inch of new snow had fallen since they arrived home with Selena.

A comforting cocktail of odors reached his nostrils as he entered the barn: old musty wood, sweet hay, horseflesh, oiled leather, and Lelou. Lelou bounded over to Tegan with happy growls, slurping his face with a huge, wet tongue, wagging tail beating the air.

"Okay, Lelou. Enough. Down."

They both stood quietly, listening. Lelou remained at attention near the door as Tegan made his security check, entering each of the two stalls housing Granger's horses, and running his hands over their bodies, confirming they were calm and settled. Then he approached the family's only horse, Gracie. Her rich scent and warm anatomy were familiar and comforting. The appaloosa mare provided Tegan with comradeship and long rambles through the forest, with Lelou trotting behind. He stroked Gracie's strong, sleek neck, and she neighed sweetly and gently nibbled his jacket collar.

Tegan settled in the fourth stall on a mattress of hay and the wolf arranged the upper half of his body across his lap like a huge puppy. Lelou made him laugh out loud. He laughed until his eyes welled with tears, and then he sobbed. The tears overflowed and streamed down his cheeks, his fingers tangled in the wolf's thick fur. Lelou accompanied his moans with sorrowful whines and a harmony of intense suffering filled the barn. When his last sob had been exhausted, Tegan leaned his head against the worn wood and fell into a sleepy haze. Perhaps he slept. Often times his waking hours and his dream world seemed to coexist. He could see neither light nor shadow, just a world of consummate blackness with no alteration.

When he lay all those weeks in a medicated haze recovering from his burns, memories of a ghostly man ebbed and flowed through his mind. The man appeared at the lake moments after the powerful electrical currents ravaged his body. Tegan collapsed, floating on a river of agony. The man's strong arms gently lifted and carried him from the dock to the shore. Then the wolf appeared and began to howl—sharp, piercing, primal howls—setting off an urgent alarm that brought his father running. Tegan remembered nothing more.

A blur of pain, fitful sleep, and distorted fragments of consciousness followed his return home and weeks of recovery.

His father was a constant presence, anchored at his bedside, sleeping on the floor, reading to him from books, infusing the air with the incense of healing herbs, his voice twilling chants like water cascading over rocks in a stream. Intermingled were memories of Elahan laying chamomile compresses over his eyes. Her rough-skinned, bony hands soothed his pain with ointments from bottles warmed in the sun. The earthy smell of the wolf was a constant beneath his window, and the faint smell of cedar smoke, which belonged to the ghostly man, ebbed and flowed. Tegan told no one of his dreams. The ghost, real or imagined, was his friend, his savior.

Since that day the scent of cedar smoke accompanied Tegan in the woods. The footsteps of the silent man remained close, his gait as long and easy and majestic as a cougar.

Awakening from sleep with a heaviness caused by remembered dreams, Tegan heard the soft rustle of animals and then he sensed, rather than heard the approach of the familiar footsteps, the long, quiet gait.

The man entered the stall. He leaned back on his heels and sat crouching, so close Tegan could smell the flavor of his breath. He could also smell his garments—worn deer leather and rabbit and raccoon and the feathers of birds. He pictured him as a mix of Sitting Bull and Chief Joseph of the Nez Perce tribe. The wolf lifted himself from Tegan's body and stretched between them, his tail thumping steadily in the dust.

The man rarely spoke when they were in the woods, and then sparingly, and only to instruct Tegan in their dangerous and secret work, so he was surprised when the man began speaking in a soft, husky voice. "The wolf has served you well."

"Yeah, he has." Tegan reached out and stroked the animal's massive head. "Thank you for giving him to me."

"He is not mine to give. Lelou is here by his own choosing." The man was silent for a moment, and then he continued. "I know you are sad about Nikah. I am also sad."

The boy was not surprised that he knew Nikah was dead. She, too, had a pact of secrecy with the man. How often they met and what they did without Tegan, he did not know, but Nikah had once advised Tegan not to ask. The less he knew, and the less he was involved, the better. One question burned inside him that he wished he had asked her. Tegan often wondered if the man was flesh and blood, or if he existed in a different dimension and moved in and out of the physical world at will.

"There are those in this world who have no qualms about killing people, animals," the man said with an edge to his voice. "They are devils who wear human skin. They must be rooted out and killed, if necessary. You and I will bring Nikah justice. This I promise." He let the weight of his alarming words settle into Tegan's mind like heavy iron anchors. "But first you must tell me what you know about her killer."

Tegan struggled with a tangled nest of feelings, tightly knotted, that he didn't want to unknot. He felt running tremors in his belly. His fear was not only for himself but for Elahan and his father. The wrong decision could put them all in danger. The thought gave him a small, sharp pain in his heart. "I'm not sure what I know. How to put it into words."

"I hear in your voice that you are frightened. There is no shame in that. Life is not safe. Nothing can make it so—nice clothes, a big house, a room full of guns, a mountain of money." The man's stroked the wolf in a long, slow rhythm. "You are afraid, yes, but your heart is still beating. Still fighting. You are a brave boy. You come from a long history of warriors." A long moment of silence stretched between them. "Fear is real, Tegan. But you must not let it control you. When you are ready, we will talk more of this."

Tegan nodded, his throat tightening.

The man lifted the animal's massive front paw and held it close to his face.

"What are you doing?"

"Smelling Lelou's paw. It is like reading a book. A story of the places he's been, his adventures."

Tegan nodded, understanding. He sensed the man was smiling.

The man continued. "In the summer, Lelou smells of grass and weeds and thistles, clay and earth. In the fall, he smells like apples and colored leaves. Do you remember color?"

Tegan turned his thoughts inward. Gold and scarlet and violet shivered in the haze of his memories—the smell of rust, the green of leaves. "Yes, I remember," he whispered. He raised Lelou's forepaw to his nostrils and inhaled deeply. "Now he smells of clean white snow. The green needles of pine trees, and…and the red blood of a rabbit."

"Our last meal," the man said. "Roasted over the fire."

"Sounds good. Sometimes a dead rabbit is left on our porch. Elahan skins it and spends hours making rabbit stew. It is a special feast that we all love. Are you the one who leaves the rabbit?"

"Yes. But that is our secret, yes?"

"Yes." Tegan thought of the many other secrets they shared— the missions—that had to be done with great caution—acts that angered certain men who would not hesitate to take revenge. He pushed those frightening thoughts from his mind and focused on the man before him, this ghostly man that he admired, whose mission had become his mission, whom he obeyed without question. Now Tegan wanted questions answered that had fired his mind for many years. "Where do you live?"

"Nowhere and everywhere."

"What is your name?"

No answer. A deep quiet settled over the stall except for the sound of Lelou's breathing. The barn door creaked open, heavy on its hinges, then closed. The ghost was gone.

The man's words tumbled through Tegan's mind and reverberated through his body with power and force. *You are a brave boy. You will not let fear control you.* The man had spoken those words with confidence, with conviction. Tegan knew in his heart the words were true. He was a warrior, descended from Kalapuya tribes who occupied the fertile Willamette Valley of Oregon on his great-grandmother's side, and the Nez Perce who occupied parts of Idaho, Washington and Oregon on his father's side. His ancestors lived as hunters and gatherers, but they were also known as warriors who fought fiercely to protect their territory. Tegan knew he had inherited the instinct to protect what was rightfully his. He was prepared.

No one could sneak up on him. He could hear and smell them a great distance away. He would fight to the death. Unknown to his father and Elahan, he was armed at all times. Tegan's fingers traced the curved handle of his walking stick, which he had carved into the shape of Lelou's head. The mouth was closed and curved into a smile, the sign of peace. Then his hands slid down to the lower half of the stick, which he twisted. The wooden sheath slid away, revealing the thin blade anchored inside that the ghostly man had given him as a gift for his eighth birthday. He showed him how to keep the blade razor sharp, and in the woods, he taught Tegan to jab it through the air at imaginary villains. Tegan could now spear with perfect accuracy the trunks of saplings, dead center. He shoved the blade back into its sheath and heard it click into place.

He was a warrior. Fear would not control him.

CHAPTER SEVEN

THE MAN LEFT the barn as silently as he had entered. Under the thin layer of new snow, the old snow was thick and crusty, but his movements made no sound. Stealth was second nature, learned from years of observing creatures in the wild. A breeze slipped through the long needles of the lodgepole pines, carrying the scent of unseen birds and animals. He walked backwards using the same set of prints he made entering the clearing, only this time sweeping his marks with a thick bough of cedar, so they disappeared into the incessant white.

He felt a shiver of dread as he glanced toward the cabin, smoke curling from the chimney, lights glowing in the windows. The old medicine woman had learned to live as the white man lived, but he felt stifled when he stepped into the white man's confines. He found most humans intolerable. He had no patience for their emotional complexities, their endless search for elusive happiness, for this cause or that greed. Or their need to collect possessions and house themselves in structures of concrete and wood and glass that had to be locked like vaults in a bank, shutting out the textures and colors and sounds of the natural world.

The man chose a solitary life where nothing was strapped down or permanent and all he owned could be carried on the back of a horse. He had adapted to the wildness, to the habits of weather, the sound of birds, the whisper of plants, the vocabulary of animals. The sky was his ceiling and a constant source of awe and beauty.

He only had to look up to be mesmerized. Like music, the sky was ever changing—one moment an aquamarine sonata dotted with clouds as delicate as Queen Ann's Lace, and the next moment a brooding iron gray symphony that threatened the earth with destruction. His favorite was the night sky when it opened into a vast starlit chasm as clear and sharp as the notes of a woodwind, allowing him a glimpse of infinity.

Now he followed the roar of cascading water to the frozen bank of White Tail Creek that sliced through ice and snow to empty into Nenámooks Lake. There, his sable and white paint, Shantie, stood waiting, his breath tendrils of vapor. His upper body was covered by a thick wool blanket woven by the fingers of the old women a decade ago. The man hoisted himself onto Shantie's strong back and issued a soft grunt. The gelding began to retrace his steps across the creek and into the forest, skirting trees, following an ancient deer trail. The man's thoughts drifted to the beautiful boy taking refuge in the barn from the day's shocking discovery—Nikah, his surrogate mother, murdered.

The man had been troubled by the dangers swirling around Tegan when he slipped into the afternoon darkness of the barn. Overcome with emotion, feeling deep affection, he stood watching him sleep. The boy's chest heaved in and out and his breathing was hurried as though he fought some urgent battle in his dream world.

The man believed he was at fault for putting the boy at risk, for opposing men who knew the ways of the wilderness, as well or better than he. Instead of honoring mother earth, these men plundered her riches for personal gain.

The man was well versed in the calls of birds and animals and understood their meanings, and he expertly mimicked their sounds, but he was rusty in the language of men. Though he had been the boy's companion for years, offering protection, teaching him survival skills, they mostly communicated through touch and smell and intuition, the dialect of the natural world. But in the barn, when the boy awoke, the man found that his words flowed smoothly. Their conversation had softened a callused place in his heart that he had forgotten existed.

In the man's solitary life, deprived of the flesh and warmth of the woman who once had been his wife, bereft of her laughter which he remembered as the purest of sounds, the attachment he had to the old woman and boy were vital. They were his last connection to his own humanness. He would do anything to protect them. Anything.

CHAPTER EIGHT

THE WIRY, TWISTED branches of the live oaks lining the road looked like emaciated arms in the waning light.

"This is it on the right," Granger shouted from behind Sidney on the snowmobile.

She turned into a driveway and parked in front of a well-constructed log house that was surrounded by towering Ponderosa pines. Light flickered in the windows, and smoke curled from the chimney. A detached garage, a sizable shed, and a looming barn were silhouetted against the silver shimmer of Nenámooks Lake.

Alerted by the sound of the snowmobile and their footsteps on the porch, a tall, lanky man with long black hair swung open the door. "Come in," he said solemnly, stepping aside after they removed their snow-crusted boots.

Sidney entered gratefully, the warmth of the fire embracing her like a cloak.

They exchanged introductions, then she and Granger shook out of their heavy parkas and hung them on pegs in the tiled entryway. Sidney surveyed the modestly furnished interior. Small, but comfortable and inviting. She took particular interest in the shelves lining one wall, which displayed beautiful handcrafted baskets, pottery, and intricate woodcarvings of animals.

"I'm so glad to see you." Selena swept in from the dining room and wrapped Sidney in a warm embrace, her cheek flushed against Sidney's numb face. "I was so worried. It's brutally cold out there."

The hug Selena gave Granger was perfunctory but when she pulled away the two locked eyes and held the gaze so long, Sidney thought for an uncomfortable moment they might kiss. Not the time, or place. She cleared her throat.

They both snapped out of some magnetic spell as Tommy said with a sweep of his hand, "Have a seat."

Selena and Granger planted themselves at opposite ends of a couch facing the fireplace. Sidney took one of the two easy chairs facing the couch. Tommy took the other.

An old woman silently entered the room, her body bent into the shape of a question mark, her head craned up and sideways. She nodded to Granger. He nodded back with a respectful smile.

"You must be Elahan. I'm Chief Becker," Sidney said, half rising and extending a hand.

"I know who you are," Elahan said coolly, ignoring Sidney's hand. "You both look frozen. I'll get you something hot to drink."

"Hot sounds great," Sidney said, pulling her hand back. "Caffeine would be a plus."

"Ditto for me," Granger added.

"I'm sure Elahan can rustle up some coffee," Tommy said smoothly, making up for the old woman's chilliness.

Elahan left as quietly as she entered.

Sidney wanted to get right down to business, but she held her patience in check and let Granger direct the flow of conversation. She tried not to fidget while he and Tommy spoke politely about Granger's two excellent quarter horses, which Tommy assured him were housed safely in the barn.

Elahan wheeled in a serving cart holding two mugs of coffee and thick slices of bread smeared with butter and honey. Sidney and Granger helped themselves. Except for the logs crackling in the fireplace, the room was silent for a few moments while the two wolfed down a few bites of the warm bread and sipped the rich coffee. "Thank you, Elahan. This is delicious. I had no idea how hungry I was," Sidney said.

"Yeah, thanks," Granger said, mouth full.

"Cold weather really takes it out of you," Tommy said.

Elahan seated herself in a straight-backed chair in the corner, her face hidden in shadows. Something about her gave Sidney the willies. The old woman's eyes crawled over her skin like icy fingers.

Granger broached the topic of the dead woman. "Can you tell us a little about Nikah?"

Tommy cleared his throat and cast a glance at Elahan, and Sidney thought she read a warning in his gaze.

"We've known Nikah all her life," Tommy said, the light from the fire playing over his pleasant features, brightening his dark eyes. "She was raised just eight houses down. Her parents died in a car accident a couple years back. She lived in the house alone, though she'd been dating Lancer Richards since she was sixteen. Last year, when she turned eighteen, he moved in with her."

"Did she work?"

"Yeah, at the Thunderhead Gift Shop in town. They sell Native American crafts. Made by people here in the village."

"I love that store," Selena said. "I bought some beaded necklaces there."

Granger acknowledged her comment with a curt nod, and continued in his no-nonsense tone. "You said Lancer was abusive?"

"Funny how you think you know someone. We all thought he was a good guy," Tommy said with a look of weariness on his face. Works as a roofer. Hard worker. Takes the winter off. That gave us a chance to see him up close and personal."

"What did you see?"

"His true nature. On the surface, everything looked fine between him and Nikah.

She used to come over a few times a week to help Tegan with his homework. The two had a strong bond. A few weeks ago, she stopped coming. Didn't answer her phone or text messages. Tegan and I went by her place one evening to check on her. It was pitch black. Cold. At first, I didn't see her. But Tegan smelled her. She was sitting on the porch, barefoot, in her nightgown, shivering.

"Seriously?" Granger said.

He nodded. "It was freezing out there, I told her. She said she locked herself out, and Lancer was in the shower. He must have heard us talking because he opened the door, fully dressed, hair dry. Didn't look like he'd been in the shower. Before he could say anything, she said, 'I told them you were in the shower.'"

"Covering for him," Granger said.

"Yep. Lancer was all smiles, oozing charm, like 'Oh, I didn't know you were out here, Nikah.' I could tell she didn't want us to come in, but Lancer opened the door wide and we followed her into the hallway. He stank of booze. That's when I saw the bruises on Nikah's arms, and her eye was swelling up. He had a lump the size of a walnut on his forehead. Looked like they'd had a knockdown, drag-out fight. I was so pissed, I grabbed Lancer by the collar and threw him out the door. "See how you like it," I said. "Don't come back until you sober up."

"You didn't think to call a cop?" Sidney asked brusquely.

Tommy leveled a sober gaze on her but there was intensity behind his eyes. "We do things our own way here, Chief Becker. Most folks around here have a dim view of law enforcement. Too many folks have been treated harshly in the past. Roughed up. Jailed for minor offenses. More so than white people."

A hissing noise came from the corner. Elahan's hands were tightly clasped in her lap.

Recognizing her contempt, Sidney felt her shoulders stiffen, and she said in her own defense, "Not here in Garnerville."

"Not since you took office," Tommy agreed. "So far, you've been fair. You go by the book. Your father did, too. But I can't say that for the last police chief, or cops in other counties."

"I'm sorry you've had bad experiences." Sidney heard emotion creep into her voice, but she couldn't help defending her profession. "Most cops are hardworking civil servants who put their lives on the line every day to protect the public, no matter what their skin color is."

"Sorry, I didn't mean to offend you personally. Or Granger," Tommy said with a distinct conciliatory note in his voice.

She relaxed her posture. "No offense taken."

"So back to Nikah," Ganger said patiently. "The night you kicked Lancer out?"

"Lancer went limping off into the night like a wounded animal. Nikah started crying. I calmed her down, but she wouldn't talk about what happened. Tegan and I sat with her for a while but then she insisted we leave. We did."

"She was protecting Lancer."

"Or herself. She was afraid of him, that was clear." Tommy shook his head. "I had no idea he was a drunk. I found out later he practically lived at the Wild Horse Saloon, the bar up the street. Long story short, the tribal council met and we decided we needed to protect Nikah. Lancer was given his walking papers."

"How did Nikah feel about that?"

"She seemed more frightened than relieved. Maybe she was afraid he'd retaliate."

"Did he try to see her?"

"We didn't see him here again. I stopped by the shop in town a few times to check on her. She told me Lancer was making himself scarce. Whatever that meant." Tommy shrugged. "I got the feeling she wasn't telling the whole story. But she seemed happier.

She started coming over again to see Tegan." Tommy released a deep sigh. "My wife died giving him birth. He's never had a mom. Now he's lost Nikah, too."

"I'm so sorry," Selena said.

Tommy met her sorrowful eyes. "Nikah filled a special need."

"When was the last time you saw Nikah?" Granger asked.

"She was here, what, four nights ago, Nana?"

"Five nights," the old woman rasped.

"She had dinner with us. Then she sat with Tegan for a while." Tommy's voice choked and his eyes glistened with sudden tears. He looked away for a moment, then said softly, "I could hear them laughing from the kitchen."

Sidney asked gently, "Aside from Lancer, is there anyone else who may have wanted to hurt Nikah?"

Tommy gazed, unflinching, into the fire. He shook his head.

Sidney knew he was hiding something. "Elahan, do you know anyone who would want to hurt Nikah?"

The old woman leaned forward in her chair, her face coming into the lamplight, her dark eyes narrowed into slits. "Talk to the mountain man."

"Who would that be, Ma'am?"

"Grisly." Elahan hissed out the name. "Grisly Stokes."

"I never met Grisly Stokes," Sidney said. "You, Granger?"

"No. Never heard of him."

"He keeps to himself." Tommy's face hardened. "Totally self-reliant. A hunter and trapper. Takes tourists out to shoot wildlife. Makes a little money on the side doing taxidermy. Lives off the grid. Back in the woods on the other side of the lake."

"What kind of relationship did he have with Nikah?" Sidney asked.

"Bad," Elahan spat out.

"Bad, how?"

Tommy didn't answer. Sidney looked at him closely. His lips tightened and his expression grew anxious.

"What aren't you telling us, Tommy?" she asked.

"When Nikah came across animals Grisly trapped, she released them." Tommy exhaled a long, slow breath and his voice was low and tense. "Once she found a bald eagle caught in a trap after it dove in for the bait. She notified the raptor center and they came out and rescued it."

Sidney cringed. The inhumane treatment of animals sickened her. She found the business of trapping egregious. Extreme animal abuse made legal.

"You look like you don't approve of her behavior," Tommy said.

Sidney realized she was frowning. "It's trapping I don't approve of. That eagle was lucky. Most animals caught in traps die slow, tortuous deaths."

"I despise trapping, too, Chief Becker," Tommy said. "It's not condoned here in the village."

"Killing a bald eagle comes with fines of up to $250,000 or two years in jail." Granger said. "Did Nikah report him?"

"Couldn't prove the trap was his. The registration number was filed off. But the folks from the center went out to his place and got in his face. Gave him hell."

"That must have angered him," Sidney said.

"It did. About a month ago, Grisly confronted Nikah, and threatened her."

"What did he say?" Sidney said.

Tommy's face darkened. "He said he'd skin her like a deer if he caught her messing with his traps again."

Sidney felt the hair rise on her arms.

"Jesus," Granger said.

"Where was she when he confronted her?" Sidney asked.

"In the parking lot behind the store, after work, at night. She said he scared the holy shit out of her."

"You should have come to us," Sidney said. "We take threats seriously."

"Too late for that now." Tommy's voice was edged with guilt and his shoulders drooped. "Look, don't mention us when you talk to him. The man's unstable. Armed at all times. No telling what he'd do if he thought we ratted him out. If he came across Tegan in the woods..."

"You think he'd hurt your son?"

"I don't want to find out." Tommy sat back with a grim expression, his fingers gripping the armrests.

"We won't mention you. But we need to talk to him," Sidney said. "Soon. We'll need directions to his place."

"Better go in daylight. He has traps rigged up around his cabin."

"Sounds like a real prince," Granger said, sharing an uneasy glance with Sidney. A tragedy was waiting to happen if someone's dog or cat nosed around one of his traps, attracted by the bait—or worse, if a person stumbled upon one. She needed to talk to the game warden to make sure Grisly wasn't going beyond the legal trapping limit.

"Grisly is evil," Elahan whispered.

Sitting in the shadows with her mummified body and grating voice, the old woman spooked Sidney as much as Grisly did. When she was a kid, she remembered rumors circulating about Elahan—that she was a witch who could cast spells on children to make them do her bidding.

As though reading her thoughts, a sudden woodenness came over Elahan. Her face was expressionless except for her eyes, which watched Sidney with unnerving coldness. Then the old lady pushed herself out of her seat and shuffled out of the room, leaning forward on her cane with each step. She heard the faint tapping of her cane and then the sound of a door closing.

Shaking off the residual spooky feeling, Sidney drained her cup and turned to the shelves of handmade crafts lining the back wall. "Who made these? They're beautiful."

Tommy followed her gaze. "We do. To sell at Thunderhead Gifts. Elahan makes the baskets. I do the ceramic pots, and the wood carvings are made by my son."

"Tegan carves wood?" Selena said incredulously. "You let him handle carving tools?"

"He's been carving wood since he was six. He's very careful."

"Why's that surprising, Selena?" Sidney asked, puzzled by her sister's strong reaction.

"Tegan's blind," Selena said. "One slip of a sharp tool…"

Sidney's mouth fell open. "Your blind son made these?"

"These, and dozens of others." Tommy's eyes were intelligent and direct, and Sidney found herself meeting them very easily.

"Sure, he's cut himself a few times, but never bad enough to get stitches. He works under my supervision out in the shop. He loves working with his hands. As you can see, he has amazing talent."

"Yes, he does." Sidney crossed the room to appraise the boy's work. Selena and Granger joined her, exchanging the sculptures, each about eight to ten inches tall, intricately carved.

"You can see the feathers on the eagle," Sidney said. "The fur on the wolf. How does he do it?"

Tommy stood beside them. He lifted a bear and ran his fingers over the finely textured wood. "Tegan sees with his fingers. He has a heightened sense of touch, smell, and hearing. He can sense energy mass and subtle changes in the flow of oxygen moving around him. Tegan is more attuned to his surroundings than the rest of us can ever hope to be. We're too reliant on eyesight, which is very poor compared to animals in the wild. That reliance dulls our other senses."

"The baskets and pottery are beautiful, too," Sidney said.

"Thank you. Part of our heritage. Making everyday objects by hand, taking pride in an individual's unique ability has been a part of every culture everywhere in the world since the dawn of time. Industrialization changed the world. Replacing handmade goods with assembly-line products. Everything from the same mold."

"Cheap and disposable," Selena agreed.

Tommy's smile reached his dark eyes, making them crinkle around the edges. He had shifted into teaching mode. Sidney imagined he was a very inspiring teacher. "My people are trying to keep our culture alive to pass down to future generations. That's why I'll continue to encourage Tegan to express himself through art."

"Tegan's a remarkable boy," Sidney said. "I'd like to speak with him about Nikah."

"It's been a pretty traumatic day for him." Tommy frowned, thinking. "Maybe tomorrow?"

"Tomorrow, then."

The conversation was interrupted by the sound of two vehicles braking to a stop in the driveway, followed by doors slamming and footsteps climbing the porch.

"My two other officers," Sidney announced.

Tommy opened the door to Officers Amanda Cruz and Darnell Wood, bundled against the cold and huffing steam.

"Come in," he said.

Amanda bent to pull off her boots.

"Don't worry about that."

They crowded into the entryway, staying on the square of tiled flooring.

Sidney's entire force was now on the case. While she and Granger patrolled the evening shift, Amanda and Darnell covered the morning-afternoon shift. Though officially working overtime, they both looked alert and professional. Sidney turned to Tommy. "Officer Cruz and I need to process Nikah's house."

"I have a spare key," he said. "She gave it to me in case of an emergency."

"Officer Wood and Granger need to start talking to your neighbors."

Tommy took in Darnell's uniform. "Honestly, Chief, no one's going to talk to a cop showing up at their door after dark. They'll talk to Granger, though. He's well known here." Granger was wearing jeans and a plaid shirt. He and Tommy exchanged a friendly glance. "He makes a point of talking to people when he comes out. Shops at the general store, grabs a beer with me at the saloon. He wears civilian clothes. Not so intimidating."

Sidney had no idea Granger was on such good terms with the villagers. Community relations. Something she needed do more, if she could ever find the time.

"Granger and Officer Wood might want to start at the saloon," Tommy said. "It's Sunday night. They have a rock band that attracts a young crowd. Nikah's friends. I can tag along. My presence might make everyone breathe easier."

"Sounds good," Sidney said. Tommy appeared to be a thoughtful, reasonable man.

"Whatever it takes to find Nikah's killer," he said.

Sidney quickly briefed her two officers on what Tommy had shared about Nikah. "We need to establish a timeline. When was Nikah killed? Who saw her last? When and where? Was someone staying at her house? Has anyone see Lancer or his truck in the village lately?"

The three officers nodded their understanding.

"Let me help," Selena said. "I can go undercover and work with Granger. If it looks like he's on a date, folks will be less defensive. I can be an extra pair of eyes and ears. Help scout out the place."

"Might not be a bad idea, Chief," Granger said.

Sidney thought it over. Her small force would be spread thin investigating this murder. They had to work smart while putting in long hours. Her sister would be an asset. Selena's gentle personality could work in her favor, disarming people. "You're on, Selena. But stay in character. Don't go all Rambo on me."

Selena smiled. "Discreet is the word."

CHAPTER NINE

OUT IN THE GENTLY falling snow, Sidney climbed into Officer Amanda Cruz's department vehicle, a Jeep Laredo, which had seen its better years a decade ago. Amanda was her most experienced officer—a six-year veteran of small-town crime in Auckland before moving to Garnerville two years ago. She was also a top-notch forensic specialist. Processing crime scenes within their own department instead of bringing in a tech from county cut through bureaucratic red tape and gave them access to forensic information in half the time.

Amanda cranked up the heater and condensation fogged the windows. The wipers squeaked into operation. All of Sidney's officers drove old vehicles, the best the town could offer on their small operating budget. Her own Yukon was five years and a hundred and ten-thousand miles old. "How's the Jeep holding up?" Sidney asked as she waited for the defroster to clear the windshield.

"Keeps on keeping on," Amanda said. Her junior officer had dark eyes fringed with thick lashes, an aquiline nose, sensitive mouth, and lustrous hair pulled into a ponytail. Amanda's delicate Latin features belied the grit of her character. "Not great on ice, though. In this shit for weather, I've been sliding around for two weeks. Luckily, everyone else is, too. No high speed chases necessary."

They both chuckled. During Sidney's two-year tenure as chief, her junior officers had rarely engaged in a high-speed chase.

Routine disturbances consisted of traffic violations and petty theft with the occasional domestic, drug bust, and bar fight. Homicide was an anomaly, though Nikah's murder was the second in two months. Worrying, but a far cry from Sidney's former job as a lead detective in Oakland, California, where she worked a dozen homicides at any given time.

The window cleared. Amanda backed out of the driveway and slowly navigated the narrow, icy road.

"Eighth house down," Sidney said.

The Jeep slid a few feet to the left and Amanda got it back on track, peering intently out the windshield. "Never been back here before. How did Two Creeks Village come to be, anyway?"

"Built back in the fifties as lodging for hunters," Sidney said. "Named for the two creeks that empty into the lake from the higher peaks. It went bust in the nineties and sat rotting for a few years, then Tucker Longtooth bought it for nickels on the dollar."

"I've heard of him. Kalapuyan, right?"

"Yep. He wanted to reclaim a portion of the land that belonged to his ancestors, and revive his culture. Kalapuyan tribes once occupied the entire Willamette Valley."

"I read it was paradise back then. Hundreds of little villages. They were remarkable stewards of the land and used the many waterways as trading routes."

"All true. Then the white man's diseases wiped out about ninety percent of them. The rest were herded onto reservations. A lot of their culture vanished."

"What a loss."

"Followed by many broken treaties and false promises from our government."

"A sad stain on our history."

"Anyway, getting back to Longtooth, he attracted indigenous families to the area by offering affordable housing and jobs at the casino. Now, twenty years later, the village is thriving. Properties have been upgraded and they've added a school, cultural center, general store, and saloon. Longtooth is in his eighties now, and still sits on the tribal council." Sidney pointed into the woods. "I think this is it."

Amanda gazed through a thicket of trees on the opposite side of the road from the lake. "Yep. Definitely a house back in there." She parked and grabbed her forensic case from the back. Wading through snow, they followed their flashlight beams up the unplowed driveway to the front of a small wood-planked house. There were no footprints or tire tracks. Drifting snow was the only movement.

"No one's been here in a while," Amanda said, her breath steaming.

Sidney's shoulders tightened as she caught a flicker of light in the front window. She thumbed off her beam. "Cut your beam. Someone's inside."

They watched a ray of light dart across the slated blinds from inside the house, then dart in the other direction.

"A prowler." Amanda's tone was low and tense.

"I'll walk around the house and find the entry point. Wait here in case the suspect bolts out the front. Stay alert."

"Yes, ma'am." Amanda placed her crime kit on the porch and pulled out her service weapon.

Sidney unclipped her holster, pulled out her Glock, and made her way to the rear of the house, her beam pointed at the ground in front of her. Beyond the small circle of light, it was pitch black and the snow muffled the sound of her boots. She found a single set of footprints leading to the back door, which had been jimmied open and stood slightly ajar. The prints looked fresh.

She glanced in the window through a sliver between the blinds and made out the clock above the stove and the outline of a refrigerator. The intruder's beam circled the back of the room, illuminating a dining table and chairs. The flashlight was placed on the surface of the table, casting light onto a hutch, and Sidney made out a shadowy figure with broad shoulders pulling open a drawer and rummaging inside. Here was her chance, while the prowler was distracted.

Sidney inched the door open, praying it wouldn't creak, and moved silently across the kitchen floor until she had the thief in her sights, ten feet away, still bending over the drawer. She thumbed on her light and said sharply, "Hands straight up! Police!"

The suspect, dressed in a black jacket and black knit cap, straightened, gloved hands jutting into the air. Too late, she heard a muffled sound behind her. Someone slammed into her, knocking her off her feet. Her head caught the edge of the table and white light exploded behind her eyes. The next thing she knew she was sprawled on the floor. Beyond the ringing in her head, she heard two pairs of boots fleeing out the door. Sidney sat up slowly, her head spinning. Warm blood trickled down the side of her face.

The light came on and Amanda rushed into the room, shoving her handgun back into its holster. "Christ, are you all right?"

"I think so." She wasn't. Pain reverberated from her temple to the back of her skull. She shook her heard, clearing her thoughts. "Did you see the suspects?"

"Yep. Two guys ran off through the woods. I followed, but before I even hit the trees, I heard a truck engine rev up and peel out. Want me to pursue?"

"No, they could have dodged down any side street by now." Sidney pulled a tissue from her duty belt and wiped the blood off her face.

"Let me take a look at that head wound," Amanda said, squatting beside her.

Sidney winced as Amanda lightly probed the area.

"You took a good one, Chief. One-inch laceration. Not deep. You'll have a nice lump tomorrow. Must hurt like hell."

"Doesn't tickle."

"I'll get a bandage on that." Amanda unclipped her first aid kit from her duty belt, cleaned the wound, and taped a bandage in place. Sidney gritted her teeth, a headache crawling up the side of her head.

"There. That stopped the bleeding." Amanda helped Sidney to her feet. "I'm going to run out and get my crime kit."

Sidney held onto the counter for support until a wave of dizziness passed, cursing herself for not being more conscientious, for allowing the suspects to escape.

Amanda came back in, carrying a bottle of water in one hand and her kit in the other. She pulled some tablets from a pocket and handed them to Sidney with the water. "Pain relievers, Chief."

Sidney thanked her and popped the pills, washing them down with a gulp of water.

Attempting to control her emotions, she summarized in a steady tone, "Two guys. One set of footprints. Where'd that second burglar come from?"

"Good question. Maybe one came earlier and the snow covered his prints."

"And the second joined him within the last half hour. They knew the house would be empty, which means they could be Nikah's killers."

"She may have been murdered here."

They remained standing in the kitchen and made a quick assessment of the small dining and living room area—drawers pulled out, contents spilled across the floor—the kitchen not yet searched.

"I don't think they found what they were looking for," Amanda said.

"No. We interrupted their search. We need to figure out what it was. Could be a key to her murder."

Amanda opened her case, which was equipped with tools for collection and preservation: evidence bags, measuring tape, swabs, plaster of paris. She snapped on vinyl gloves and pulled sterile fabric booties over her feet, then grabbed her digital camera. Everything would be carefully documented before she touched or moved anything.

"While you photograph, I'm going to take a look outside." Sidney stepped off the back porch into the frozen landscape, immediately sinking above her ankles into white powder. The cold air stung her face and white vapor escaped from her mouth. The suspects had been running, leaving no distinctive tread marks from their sliding footprints. With her Maglite beam on high, she followed the tracks to the end of the yard. Ahead, the forest looked dark and foreboding. Impenetrable. Gathering her courage, she entered the black interior and tunneled through massive evergreens covered in white. She felt closed in, the beam splintering around branches. She stopped and listened, scanning the woods. No movement. No sound except the soft roar of water. Feather Creek was somewhere off to her left, rushing down from the mountain to empty into the lake.

She kept moving, negotiating the slippery, uneven ground. The forest finally opened up to the road and ice crackled underfoot where the plow had packed down the snow. The prints of the burglars ended at wide tire tracks made by a truck. The tracks veered onto the road and merged with other tracks. The snow, falling in big loose flakes, had already softened the delineation of the tread marks. Nothing here.

She went back through the trees and circled the house, looking for the second set of boot prints. On the eastern side of the yard, she saw a pattern of shallow indentations that led to the back door; boot prints filled with snow. She followed them back through the woods, ending on the road forty feet north from where the truck had been parked. The prints hugged the road for a hundred feet, crossed over, and became obscured by tire tracks.

This told her the two suspects had indeed arrived separately. The first arrived by foot, suggesting he lived in the village.

After brushing snow off her shoulders, Sidney stepped back into the house and removed her jacket and boots. Ignoring the throbbing in her head, she grabbed a pair of shoe covers from the crime kit and slipped them on, then pulled on vinyl gloves.

She found Amanda dusting for fingerprints in the living room.

Aside from the mess on the floor, the room had a tidy, well-lived-in look. The tan leather couch and lounge chair were worn, the tables and lamps looked like garage sale relics, as did the prints on the wall and the knickknacks lining the fireplace mantle. Clearly, Nikah and Lancer weren't living high on the hog. "What were the burglars looking for that had any value?" Sidney asked. "The big screen TV is still here. Drugs are a possibility. Find anything drug related?"

Amanda was bending over the doorknob of the front door, lifting a fingerprint. "No. The living room looks clean. No drug paraphernalia, no blood, no appearance of a struggle. This crap on the floor came from the bookcase. Just paperbacks and magazines."

"What about a phone?"

"Nope. The second bedroom was used as an office. I saw a laptop and charger in there, but no phone or other small devices."

"I'll go pilfer through the master bedroom. Maybe her phone will turn up," Sidney said.

"Be forewarned. It's a mess. Careful with the sheets. Could have fluids. Hair. The stuff of a lab tech's dreams," Amanda said, a smile in her tone.

Not the stuff of Sidney's dreams. "I'll let you bag those."

"Yippie."

Sidney switched on the glaring overhead light in the master. Mess was an understatement. More like the aftermath of a tornado. An extensive search had been interrupted. The bedcovers were stripped off, mattress askew, clothes from the dresser and closet strewn over the floor.

Three photos in gilt frames on the dresser caught her attention. One showed an attractive gray-haired couple sitting at an outdoor table, holding up wine glasses, grinning at the camera. From the strong family resemblance, Sidney knew they were Nikah's parents. Two people in their prime, enjoying life to the fullest, killed by a drunk driver. Senseless tragedy. The second photo showed Lancer standing on the shore of a lake, shirtless, body bronzed and muscled, holding up a sizable trout. He was a handsome white man with hazel eyes, sandy hair, and a contagious smile. The last photo showed Nikah and Lancer posing at someone's wedding, beaming, eyes sparkling. He wore a gray western-cut suit with a turquoise bolo tie. She looked like an Indian princess in a fringed leather dress with beaded flowers along the bodice. White feathers adorned her long, black hair. Displayed in the privacy of her bedroom, these were obviously cherished photos.

The closet held Nikah's clothes, shoes and handbags. No expensive designer brands. Garments belonging to Lancer were shoved to one side. Several pairs of cowboy boots lined the floor and a few ball caps were stacked on one of the shelves. The couple lived apart, yet Lancer had not removed himself entirely from her life. It appeared Nikah still loved her boyfriend.

Sidney began her search where the burglars left off, looking behind framed prints on the wall, pulling out drawers and searching underneath for taped envelopes. She searched the pockets of every garment, the inside of shoes, the contents of handbags. A few storage boxes on the upper shelf were crammed with old letters, photos, and other mementos from Nikah's short life. Sidney found nothing of consequence.

CHAPTER TEN

CARTING THREE PASSENGERS, Darnell parked the Dodge Ram truck in the ice-slicked lot of Wild Horse Saloon—a wood-shingled building with a long, covered porch and pulsing neon signs in the windows advertising beer. The weathered sign featured the cartoon head of a smiling horse with big teeth and one eye closed in a wink. Selena heard rock music pulsing through the walls as they piled out of the truck. Four men in thick coats huddled at one end of the porch, smoking. Their curious glances turned into arrogant stares when they spotted the police vehicle and Darnell's uniform.

"Let's have a quick word with these guys," Darnell said to Tommy.

"Sure," Tommy said.

"Selena and I will scout out the inside," Granger said.

The music grew piercingly loud when Granger opened the door, but instead of entering, Selena held back. She didn't like the hostile stare on the face of one of the men. Darnell—a clean cut black man with a lean build, two-years on the force, father of two toddlers—had never been placed in a situation where he had to discharge his duty weapon. He was barely out of rookie phase. That gave her cause for concern.

Granger let the door swing shut, also watching the group of men, his brow creasing.

Not one to be intimidated, Darnell shot the men a confident smile. "Evening, guys."

Caught off guard by his friendliness, one man returned a half-smile. Two others kept blank stares. The fourth man, towering and powerfully built, glowered.

"Hey, Fitch," Tommy addressed the big man. "How goes it?"

The big man weaved to and fro, a menacing glare in his dark, hooded eyes. "You love cops so much, Tommy, why don't you go drink in town?"

"This is Officer Wood," Tommy said, a warning in his tone. "He's here because he needs our help."

"Help to throw our asses in jail," Fitch sneered. "This asshole busted me last year. I spent two weeks in a cage."

To his credit, Darnell kept his cool and responded in a cordial tone. "Maybe all cops look the same to you, Fitch, but I remember everyone I've arrested. You're not one of them. Where'd you get busted?"

"In fucking Jackson."

"I'm not with the Jackson Department."

His lips formed a harsh line. "You're still a fucking pig."

"Sir, you've had a lot to drink," Darnell said, his tone shifting from friendly to forceful. "It's time for you to leave. As in, go home."

"You kicking me out?" There was a dangerous note in the big man's tone. He took a step toward Darnell, his huge hands balling into fists. As brawny as a linebacker, he loomed over the young officer by a foot and could no doubt floor him with a single blow. "This is my village, man. It's you who needs to leave."

Selena sucked in a sharp breath, expecting violence to erupt.

"You heard Officer Wood. Time to go," Granger said with steel in his tone, joining Darnell.

"He's a cop, too," one of Fitch's friends said. He was a short, weathered man with a prominent nose and a knit cap pulled down to his eyelids. "You better chill, man."

"Listen to your friend," Darnell said. "Walk away. Right now. Sleep in your own bed tonight."

Fitch sneered, but the added muscle seemed to thwart him. His eyes clouded, as though his brain was struggling to comprehend the situation. A glimmer of realization pierced his soggy brain. He blinked. His fists slowly unclenched and he took a few steps backwards, staggering, grabbing the post to steady his balance.

His buddies, watching with rapt attention, stepped away from him, unwilling to associate with his malignant behavior.

"Fuck you guys," Fitch snarled. He belched, stumbled off the porch and fell flat on his ass, then got shakily to his feet with the grace of a walrus, and lurched across the lot toward the road.

"What's Fitch last name?" Darnell asked, pulling out his notebook and pen.

Two of the men shrugged, faces blank. One had a gaunt face, thick glasses, and an overbite. The other was round-faced and florid. Mismatched bookends, and clueless, Selena thought, like the Bobbsey Twins.

"Drako. Fitch Drako," the short, weathered man said. "He's an okay guy. Army vet." He tapped his temple with an index finger. "PTSD. Hardly ever leaves his house." He tossed his cigarette into a snowdrift. "I'm Little Joe. What did you need help with?"

"We're investigating the death of one of your neighbors," Darnell said.

The three men gathered closer, curiosity raw on their faces.

"Who died?" Little Joe asked.

"Nikah Tamanos."

For several moments the men stood frozen, mouths open, eyes wide.

"We found her body in Whilamut Creek near the bridge a few hours ago."

"Up at the bridge? What the hell?" Little Joe said.

"When was the last time any of you saw her?"

The Bobbsey Twins shrugged, seemingly their fall back response to any question fielded by a cop.

"She was at the school three days ago when I dropped off my grandson," Little Joe said. "She reads..." He shook his head, looking a bit dazed. "She used to read to the first graders on Friday mornings." He gave Darnell a hard look. "Why would she be up at the creek in this fucking weather?"

"That's what we're trying to find out. We're viewing her death as suspicious."

"Suspicious? You mean she was murdered?"

"We believe so," Darnell said. He waited a few moments for the three men to process. "Do you know anyone she was having a problem with?"

The Bobbsey Twins shrugged, their faces revealing zilch.

"No," Little Joe said. "Everyone loved Nikah...except..." His voice trailed off.

"Except who?" Darnell asked.

"That dipshit boyfriend of hers," he said. "Nasty drunk. Temper. He put in a lot of hours here." Little Joe nodded toward the saloon. "Got kicked out a few times. Got kicked out of the village, too, for hitting Nikah."

"When was this?"

Little Joe squinted his eyes, thinking. "Couple months back."

"His name?"

"Lancer Richards. White man. Roofer."

Darnell scribbled notes. "Have you seen him or his truck in the village since he got kicked out?"

The man scratched his jaw. "Can't say that I have."

The skinny half of the Bobbsey Twins was shifting from one foot to the other. He either had to pee or he was dying to divulge information.

"Got something to add?"

Still standing by the door, Selena started to shiver. It was darn cold and getting colder. Seeing that Darnell had things under control, Granger returned to her side. "Let's go in." He placed a hand on the small of her back and opened the door. Immediately, the driving force of rock music assaulted them. A hardworking band—a male drummer, two male guitarists, and a female vocalist—occupied the cramped stage, bodies thrashing. The singer spewed hoarse lyrics while whipping her hair and jumping around in an aerobic frenzy. All four wore tattered jeans and damp T-shirts. Every inch of exposed skin glistened with sweat.

A few tables were occupied by fans bobbing their heads, and on the other side of the room, a bartender worked a counter lined with bodies.

Granger ushered her to empty stools in the middle of the bar. He caught the bartender's eye and held up two fingers followed by a C sign. The barkeep nodded and grinned, obviously recognizing him and his sign language. Several people greeted Granger with waves and smiles along the bar.

"Mr. Popularity," Selena said.

"Natural charm." He smiled and leaned close enough to be heard above the music. "Let's look the part of a couple."

She caught the scent of his musky aftershave. Not too hard an act to play. She nodded, smiling into his blue eyes. He planted a soft kiss on her mouth. Fleeting, but thrilling.

Selena caught her reflection through the bottles on the wall and was surprised by her calm appearance, if a little flushed from Granger's kiss, thanks to Tommy's tea and Granger's presence. Swiveling in her seat, she checked out the place more thoroughly: scarred wooden floor, posters of wild horses on the walls, young patrons dressed in jeans and t-shirts. Millennial night. At twenty-eight and twenty-nine, she and Granger fit right in, barely. Several people shot her furtive glances, making her acutely aware that she and Granger were the only white faces in the room. No chance of blending in with her blonde hair and light green eyes. She focused on the band and the singer's lyrics.

Domination no more!

Speak out!

Fight back.

Take back our land!

Take back our culture!

Domination no more!

Granger enthusiastically nodded his head to the music, or grating noise, in her opinion. He'd always listened to mellow country when they were together: Little Big Town, Lady Antebellum, old Eagles tunes. He was doing a great job of acting, or else he was an avid hard rock fan coming out of the closet.

"Great band," he yelled. "Tomahawks. Play here every Sunday night."

Okay, so he was the later. Good to know these details when in an intimate relationship with a man. Selena realized with a start that she had just imagined Granger as a romantic partner. Witnessing his measured response to a crisis had triggered a shift in her perception. Her lingering attachment to her ex, and her paralyzing fear of failing at love again, had kept her from taking the next step, though she desperately wanted to. Selena took in Granger's handsome profile, his strong body relaxed next to hers, his knee grazing her thigh, and she was flushed with warm affection.

He met her gaze. She made a beckoning motion with her finger. He leaned closer, and she kissed him on the mouth. Gently. He didn't pull away. His tongue parted her lips and their first real kiss got a little steamy. A zing of intense pleasure shot along her nerve endings. When she pulled away, she saw raw emotion on his face and knew hers reflected the same. This wasn't acting.

Someone approached the bar and jostled her shoulder, snapping her back to reality.

Granger cleared his throat and looked away. She refocused her attention, reminding herself that they were here to work. No more distractions.

To Selena's relief, the ear-piercing vocals ended and the band announced they were taking a break. The sudden silence was imbued with the soft murmur of voices and the clink of glasses. The lead singer wiped her face and arms with a towel and descended into the audience and someone handed her a drink.

"Hey Granger," the bartender said, setting down two bottles of Corona, two chilled mugs, and a bowl of mixed nuts. He was twenty-something, clean-shaven, with short, spiky hair and a diamond stud in one ear. Turquoise and silver bands glimmered on both wrists. "Who's your friend?"

"Selena, meet Kato," Granger said.

She and Kato exchanged smiles.

"You're the first date he's ever brought in here," Kato said. "Someone finally whittling you down, big guy?"

Granger winked at Selena.

"What's up?" Kato said. "You on the job? I know you didn't brave these icy back roads for music and beer."

Granger blew out a breath. "Selena and I were out riding this afternoon by the bridge on Whilamut Creek. We found a body."

"A body? Who died?" Kato said loudly, above the din of noise. People sitting close by turned their heads.

"Nikah Tamanos."

There was a collective gasp.

"Nikah's dead?" Kato looked as though he'd been punched in the gut.

"I'm afraid so."

"What happened?" Kato asked when he found his voice.

"Her body was in the creek. Suspicious death."

"Nikah was murdered?" another man asked.

"Yes," Granger said.

"Oh my God! Nikah's been murdered," a young woman screamed, turning to everyone in the bar.

No one moved. Stunned silence. The oxygen had been sucked from the room. People left their seats and closed in around the bar.

"Nikah's dead?" Another woman's shrill voice shattered the silence. "No!"

Selena peered into the crowd. It was the singer in the band, her face distorted with grief, dark eyes brimming with tears

Granger turned in his seat as the crowd cleared a pathway for her. She was around twenty-seven, small-boned, heavily made up, eyes ringed with black liner, mouth painted crimson. Mascara started running down her cheeks. "What happened?"

Granger said gently. "We're just starting our investigation."

"You're sure it's Nikah?"

He nodded. "Tommy identified her."

The woman pressed a hand to her mouth and looked as though she might be sick.

"Sunnovabitch! I don't believe it. Who would kill Nikah?" This from the distressed drummer who also came forward, sporting a Mohican haircut, tinted red. He was a thin, wiry, young man in his late teens.

"I knew something was wrong when she didn't show up here tonight," the singer said in a choking voice. "She didn't answer her phone all weekend."

The drummer wrapped an arm around her and she pressed her tear-stained face into his shoulder.

People peppered Granger with questions, speaking over one another, and it was hard to make sense of anything above the clamor.

"She was in the creek?"

"Someone drowned her?"

"How do you know it was murder?"

Selena silently observed, studying expressions and body language—looking for what, she didn't know. Two Creeks was a small community. These people grew up together and they had a strong connection to Nikah. Everyone looked profoundly grieved by her death. The anger, fear, and need for answers was palpable.

The crowd was so intensely focused on Granger, no one noticed when the door opened, and Darnell and Tommy walked in.

Granger raised a hand for silence and the voices lowered in volume. "Look, we don't know all the details yet. We're trying to piece together the time of her death. If you know of someone who may have wanted to hurt Nikah, or if you've seen any suspicious activity around her house, please talk to us. We want to find her killer as much as you do." Granger nodded toward Darnell and Tommy. "Officer Wood and I will need statements from each one of you."

Heads turned towards Darnell, and Selena felt an icy chill move like a wave over the crowd. One minute everyone was talking, curious, eager to help. The next, their expressions went blank and they drifted back to their tables and seats at the bar. The band climbed back on stage and started packing their equipment.

"What just happened?" Granger said.

She shrugged one shoulder, stumped. "Darnell's uniform?"

Darnell joined the band up on stage and they reluctantly gathered around him.

A couple at one of the tables put on coats and hats.

Granger made a detour to their table. "We need a statement from you."

"We need to leave," the young man said. "My grandma's babysitting. She expects us home."

"Just a few questions," Granger said. "Please take your seats."

CHAPTER ELEVEN

SIDNEY BEGAN RIFLING through articles of clothing on the floor, looking for bloodstains or evidence of a struggle. Nothing. Her eyes fell on the heating vent on the floor, now visible with the last of the garments moved away. She lifted the metal cover and aimed her flashlight into the dark interior. Something reflective caught her eye. Sidney pulled out a tin box and lifted the lid. Adrenalin coursed through her system. *Bonanza!*

Inside were a packet of one hundred dollar bills and a key to a safety deposit box with an attached tag with numbers printed on it. The last item was a silver medallion on a thin leather strap, engraved with an unfamiliar symbol. The design had three interconnected spirals with no open ends, creating one continuous line. The finish was worn and tarnished. The medallion could be decades, or a century old.

Amanda appeared in the doorway, looking alert and enthusiastic. "I'm finished with the front rooms. Thought I'd bag those sheets." Her gaze rested on the box in Sidney's hands. "Find something?"

"A few thousand greenbacks. And a key to a safety deposit box. Hidden in the heating vent."

Amanda whistled. "Youzer! Must be what the thieves were after. Wonder what's in the deposit box. More money? Drugs?"

"That would be my guess. This is the only thing of value I've come across."

"What's that? A medallion?"

"Yes. Have you ever seen anything like it?"

"No."

Sidney made a mental note to have Darnell, an IT expert, get into Nikah's records and find out the state of her finances. She rubbed her eyes and involuntarily touched the bandage on her head. The point of impact still throbbed. She put the wad of bills in an evidence bag and handed the box to Amanda. "Dust this stuff for prints. We need to know who the recipient was. Nikah or Lancer."

"My fingers are feeling nimble tonight."

The bathroom was spotless. Not a hair in sight. In a drawer was one comb, one brush, and minimal makeup. Nikah lived like a nun. The medicine cabinet held a bottle of aspirin, toothpaste, moisturizer, and a glass holding two toothbrushes. Why two? Had someone been a regular houseguest? Lancer? Sidney slipped both toothbrushes into evidence bags.

The kitchen proved to be just be as spotless. Glistening countertops, gleaming sinks. Items in each drawer were separated by dividers, pots and pans were stacked neatly with handles facing in the same direction, and canned and boxed food were lined up uniformly with all labels facing outward. Military precision.

From the tidy broom closet, Sidney found a receipt in a folded grocery bag dated three days ago from the General Store. Friday, 7:48 p.m. Among the items listed were linguini and a jar of tomato basil pasta sauce.

This led Sidney to examine the contents of the fridge, which contained the usual household staples—milk, butter, cheese, eggs, produce—and a plastic container holding leftover pasta in tomato sauce. Inside the dishwasher was one dirty plate, a wine glass, and silverware, which suggested Nikah came home, cooked and ate dinner, and cleaned the kitchen. She was still among the living until 9:00 p.m. That put her time of death between late Friday night and Saturday morning.

Sidney now had her first solid impressions of Nikah's character. She was fastidious, organized, and budget minded. If she was going against the wishes of the village to see Lancer, a man who abused her, she was willful and secretive. Why didn't she stand up to the elders? They had no right to tell her what to do. Then again, it might not be Lancer who was keeping her company.

Sidney joined Amanda in the office, who was leafing through drawers of files and papers. The small room was modestly furnished with a desk, file cabinet, and standing safe; doors and drawers left open. Files were strewn across the floor. A slight bulge under the area rug caught Sidney's eye. She pulled back one corner and discovered a short, cotton nightgown covered in bloodstains. She held it up. "Look at this."

Amanda's mouth set in a hard, grim line. "Nikah met with violence."

"This is probably where she was killed."

As Amanda bagged the nightgown, Sidney studied the wooden floorboards and picked up a faint whiff of pine scented cleaner. "Someone scrubbed this area recently. Let's get some Luminal on this."

Amanda grabbed a bottle from her kit and sprayed an even layer of Luminal over the floorboards. Sidney hit the light switch, plunging the room into darkness. A blue glow about three feet wide emitted from the suspect area, indicating the recent presence of blood. The highlighting effects of Luminal only lasted thirty seconds. Amanda acted fast, taking a long exposure photograph to capture the image.

Sidney hit the switch and light burst back into the room. She heard Amanda's intake of breath. "That's a lot of blood loss."

"Yes, it is. Nikah may have been bludgeoned or stabbed, in addition to being strangled. She was fully dressed when we pulled her out of the creek, but this bloody nightdress suggests she was wearing it at the time of her attack."

"Why did the perp bother to dress her? That's a lot of time and trouble. And why move her to the creek?"

Sidney shrugged one shoulder, stymied. "Murderers aren't rational. They exist in their own delusional world. Play by their own rules." She stood in silence for a long moment, staring at the rug. "This rug looks like it belongs in a bathroom, not an office."

"I agree."

"I think her killer wrapped her in the original rug to carry her out of here."

"Seems likely." Amanda frowned. "If the two burglars were Nikah's killers, why didn't they search the house the night of her murder? Why risk coming back?"

Sidney sighed. "Nothing about murder is simple. This house needs to be processed with a fine-tooth comb. I'll get Stewart over here to help you." Sidney had just sentenced her junior officer to a long night of tedious overtime. "How're you holding up?"

"I'm okay." Amanda smiled. The enthusiasm she had exhibited earlier had diminished, replaced by steely determination. "A mega-dose of caffeine would be helpful."

Sidney respected Amanda's work ethic, which matched her own. "I'll tell Stewart to bring a gallon of coffee."

CHAPTER TWELVE

SELENA POPPED a few roasted nuts in her mouth and washed down the taste of salt and oil with the cold beer. She surveyed the room with a bored expression, slyly observing the remaining patrons. Tommy sat solo at a table near the front door, half obscured by shadow, the light from a neon sign pulsing crimson on his face. After Darnell questioned the band, the female singer excused herself and headed to the back of the bar toward the restroom.

Selena slipped out of her seat and followed her down the darkened hallway through the swinging door. The brightly lit restroom was empty except for the singer, and smelled faintly of disinfectant. The woman's hands gripped the sides of the sink, and her long black hair shielded her face as she quietly sobbed.

Selena stood at the next sink and turned on the water to announce her presence.

The singer stifled a sob, lifted her mascara-stained face, and made an effort to compose herself. She splashed water on her face, pumped a few drops of soap onto her palm, and started washing off her thick makeup.

Selena grabbed a few paper towels and handed them to her. "This will help."

The young woman took the towels, offered Selena a feeble smile, and started wiping the makeup from her eyes.

Biding her time, Selena poked around in her handbag, pulled out a lip-gloss and ran it over her lips, then tugged a brush through her long blonde hair.

The singer scrubbed away the blush, then the lipstick. It was like peeling off a mask. After stripping away the illusion of age the singer looked as fresh-faced as an ingénue. Nikah's age. A fragile vulnerability replaced the hard brassiness of the woman who had dominated the stage.

Selena pulled out a small tube of moisturizer. "This will soothe your skin. That industrial soap is harsh."

"You could strip paint with it. Thanks." Cadence used her index finger to spread the cream over her pretty face. She met Selena's gaze in the mirror with a certain apprehensiveness. "Are you Granger's girlfriend?"

Selena smiled. "We're dating."

"He's a nice guy. Comes in here a lot."

"So I'm finding out. I'm Selena."

"I'm Cadence."

"Perfect name for a singer."

"My parents are musicians." Cadence tossed the used paper towels in the trash bin and turned to face Selena, leaning against the sink. Silver-spider earrings dangled from her ears. "The drummer in the band is my twin brother, Cory."

"I see the resemblance." Both had sensitive faces, finely arched brows, and angular cheekbones. Magenta streaks woven into Cadence's black hair matched the color of her brother's Mohawk. She had a musical voice, unlike the hoarse whiskey vocals she spewed on stage. "How fortunate to grow up with music."

"Understatement. Lived and breathed. We were trained in traditional Native American music. We both play flute, guitar, and drums."

"Very talented."

"We love hard rock. Mom says Cory and I are going through a rebellious stage and we'll eventually come home to our roots."

"You think so?"

"Not anytime soon. We're revolutionaries," Cadence said passionately. "We have a message. We love what we do."

They were both quiet for a moment.

"I'm so sorry about Nikah," Selena said. "Looks like you two were very close."

"She was my best friend. My sister, really." Cadence's voice quivered and she bit her bottom lip. Her eyes were brilliant with tears. "We did everything together."

Feeling a piercing sadness for the young woman, Selena said with feeling, "Terrible to lose someone so close."

Cadence mumbled with a haunted look to her eyes, "I feel so guilty."

"Why is that?"

"We were supposed to get together Friday night. Girl night. I ended up getting a date. I sent a text cancelling on her. She sent a text back saying she was really disappointed. That she really needed to talk to someone." Tears spilled down Cadence's cheeks and she knuckled them away. "I texted back saying I'd call in the morning. I did, but she didn't pick up. I never heard back from her. Maybe if I hadn't bailed…" her voice trailed to a whisper.

"She'd still be alive?"

Cadence nodded.

"Her death is not on you," Selena said softly. "If someone was determined to kill her, they'd find a way."

Cadence's slender shoulders slouched and a tremor passed over them. "Guess that's true."

"She didn't return your call for two days," Selena said. "Was that unusual?"

Cadence wiped her eyes with trembling fingers. "Yes. We texted every day. I always knew where she was. I went by her house yesterday but no one was home. I figured her phone was dead for some reason, or maybe she was with…"

Silence.

"Lancer?" Selena finally offered.

Cadence averted her eyes. "Yeah, maybe. Don't know for sure."

"But she was seeing someone?"

Cadence shrugged.

Selena read determination in the girl's compressed lips that were locking in a secret. She read anxiety, as well. "Do you know anyone who would want to hurt her?"

The girl's face tightened for a moment and a shadow of fear flickered over her face. She abruptly handed back the cream. "I've been in here too long. Gotta go help the band."

Selena gently touched her hand. "I know you want to help find Nikah's killer. If you know something, tell me. I get it, you don't trust cops, but whatever you tell me is confidential. The officers don't need to know where it came from."

Cadence gave her a long, steady look. "It's not the cops I'm worried about."

Selena peered into the young woman's eyes, which had filled with a subtle but detectible agitation. "What is it you're not telling me?"

Cadence glanced nervously toward the door. "I can't talk here. Look, meet me in town tomorrow. Lava Java. 10:00." She straightened her shoulders, put on a brave expression, and strode out the door.

Selena waited a few moments before leaving. When she emerged, Tommy was standing just inside the hallway talking to

Cadence. His hands gripped her upper arms, forcing her to meet his intense gaze.

Selena slinked back into the shadows, chilled by a man holding a woman against her will. The memory of a killer gripping her in the woods bolted from the shadows of her mind. Her heartbeat began to thud in her ears. She fought to settle her mind, to focus on pulling herself back from the brink of a panic attack.

"Leave me alone, Tommy!" The young woman jerked away and hurried back into the bar. Tommy stood stiffly in the doorway, watching her retreat.

After a long moment, Selena stepped from the shadows and sauntered down the hallway.

Tommy's stony expression instantly softened, and he smiled.

The charming, intelligent man she'd met earlier was back. But a darker facet of his character had been revealed, lowering her opinion of him. She forced a smile, walked past him, and took her seat at the bar. Why was Tommy reprimanding Cadence? Perhaps he had been monitoring her—monitoring the entire bar like a principle in a school hallway, keeping folks in line. Perhaps it was Tommy who had sent that icy chill over the crowd, not Darnell. Tommy had been taken into Granger's confidence, and had been allowed to accompany them to the saloon to make folks feel easier. Perhaps he was having the opposite effect.

To Selena's chagrin, Tommy ambled over, took the seat next to her, and signaled to Kato. With a friendly nod, Kato uncapped two perspiring bottles of Corona and slid them across the counter. She had been hoping to engage Kato in conversation, but he quickly moved away and busied himself wiping glasses with a dishtowel.

Selena lifted her bottle and scanned the bar while she sipped. The place had emptied. Granger was standing near the stage talking to the last of the patrons. Darnell was engaged with a couple at their table jotting in his notebook. The band members lumbered off the stage, lugging equipment out of a side door. Cadence disappeared with her brother, each carrying bulky drum cases.

"How are you doing?" Tommy asked.

"Not great. Not one of my best days." She met his eyes. He watched her as he tipped back his bottle and drank. She sensed a strange power emanating from his dark eyes. A chill stippled her skin with gooseflesh. Her intuition was telling her something, a warning, but she couldn't shape it into cohesive thought. To her relief, Darnell and Granger finished up business and joined them at the bar.

Kato slid chilled mugs of beer across the counter. "On the house."

"Thanks, man." Smiling, Darnell gave a little salute, and took a gulp.

Granger also took a gulp. "Man, that tastes good. But I'm on the job. Maybe just one more sip." He lifted his mug, chugged a third of the beer, and pushed the mug away.

"Me, too," Darnell said, and took another gulp.

"Get anything?" Tommy asked.

"Not much," Darnell said, "We know Nikah was alive Friday afternoon. No one saw her after that."

"For such a small community, it's hard to believe no one saw or heard anything," Granger said with a hint of sarcasm.

Selena wanted to share the conversation she'd had with Cadence, but not while Tommy sat listening to every word. "Ready to roll?" she asked.

"Yeah," Granger said. "First, I need to see how the chief is doing at Nikah's place." He pulled out his phone. "I'll make the call outside."

Selena appreciated his caution. Did he view Tommy's presence as a detriment? She cast a furtive glance at the tall, lanky high school teacher. His face was expressionless, just sitting there, hardly moving, fingers relaxed around his beer bottle. Even though there was no discernible change, his presence had expanded, and she felt a tangible energy emanating from him. A power. She feared what was churning behind those dark, mysterious eyes.

Granger walked back into the bar with a troubled expression.

"What's up?" Darnell asked.

"The Chief and I need a ride to her Yukon. We're going to head into town." He looked at Tommy with an inscrutable expression. "Can you catch a ride home with Kato?"

"No problem. He's ready to close up shop."

Granger clasped Tommy's outstretched hand. "Thanks for your help."

"Anytime."

Granger and Selena followed Darnell out into the biting cold. Her fingers brushed against Granger's and he took her hand, squeezed it lightly, and let go, which made her smile a little. They piled into the truck. Selena scrambled into the back behind the steel mesh screen.

Their breath puffed out in the cab and the leather felt icy through Selena's jeans. Darnell revved up the engine and the vents blasted cold air. Her thoughts turned inward and she barely noticed as Darnell pulled out of the empty lot.

CHAPTER THIRTEEN

WATCHING FROM the window, it was well after nine when Sidney saw the headlights of Darnell's truck bounce into Nikah's driveway. She left the house and waded through the soft snow, reaching the truck as Granger climbed from the passenger seat into the rear seat next to Selena.

"What happened to your head, Chief?" Darnell asked as she strapped herself in.

Absentmindedly, Sidney touched the bandage and winced, then she shared an abbreviated version of the nights' events—how she and Amanda intercepted two prowlers, her attack, and subsequent injury. Without a pause, she proceeded to tell them of the tin box and its contents, the grocery receipt, which confirmed Nikah died between late Friday night and Saturday morning, and the discovery of blood in her office, which someone had tried to clean up. "Hard to imagine someone surviving that kind of blood loss."

"Christ," Granger said.

"The prowlers might be the killers," Darnell said.

"They probably wanted that cash," Granger said. "And whatever's in the deposit box."

"I don't think they're the killers," Sidney said. "They would've searched the house the night of the murder. The house needs to be processed thoroughly. Stewart's on his way over to help Amanda." Sidney shifted in her seat and stared out at the drifting snow in the headlights. "How'd your interviews go?"

"No one saw shit," Granger said.

"Why am I not surprised. Fear of cops?" Sidney asked.

"Fear of Tommy," Granger said.

"Tommy?" Sidney turned to view Granger over her shoulder. The shadow from the mesh screen played over his face.

"He's got some kind of hold over these people. Fear or respect. They clammed up when he walked in the door."

"I thought the same thing," Darnell said as he navigated the icy road. "Folks kept glancing over at him, as though gauging his reaction."

"It's a side to Tommy I've never seen," Granger said. "A little creepy."

"Cadence, the singer, said as much when I spoke with her in the restroom," Selena said. "She acted like someone was watching her every move. She didn't want to talk there. She's going to meet me in town tomorrow."

"Sounds like you're the only one who made an inroad tonight," Sidney said. "Maybe tomorrow you'll get some straight answers."

"You want to tag along?"

"No. She trusts you. We don't want to spook her by ganging up on her."

"When I left the restroom, I saw Tommy gripping her arms. He was really angry."

"Don't like the sound of that," Sidney said. "Tommy warrants a closer look. We'll head back out there tomorrow. Talk to folks without Lurch skulking in the shadows."

"What about the skinny dude on the porch, Darnell?" Granger asked. "He was vibrating with eagerness to talk to you."

"He shared something, all right. He said he saw Lancer's truck parked in Nikah's driveway last week. Then he saw her a day later in the general store. She was wearing a scarf, but when she moved it to scratch her throat, he saw a purple bruise on her neck."

"That's scary," Selena said.

"Lancer sounds violent," Sidney said. "Granger and I are heading over to his house to talk to him."

Darnell pulled up next to Sidney's parked Yukon. When she climbed out, she tapped the bag left on the passenger seat. "I know you've put in a long day, Darnell, but I need you to get into Nikah's computer. Look at her financials. Scan through her social media. See if anything crops up."

"I'll get right on it, Chief." Darnell looked and sounded fatigued. Like Amanda, he'd already put in a fourteen-hour day. Sidney felt a twinge of guilt for asking so much from her officers. She demanded nothing less than she asked of herself. A violent killer was on the loose. Until he was caught, she'd drive them hard.

Darnell drove away in a plume of exhaust. Tiny snow crystals sifted down through the branches and the faintly metallic smell of snow was in the air. The Yukon was buried in white and resembled some crouching Arctic beast. Sidney fished out her keys and hit the remote. Granger opened the door on the passenger side and a sheet of snow fell to ground. He helped Selena climb in.

Sidney opened the door on the driver side, waited for the snow to crash around her boots, then climbed inside. The windows were blocked and it felt like entering an ice cave.

"Got a scraper?" Granger asked.

"In the back." She started the engine and cranked up the heater and freezing air blasted the cab. Granger disappeared, the tailgate opened and shut, then he started scraping off the windshield.

"My hero," Sidney said.

"Brrrr," Selena said, her gloved hands pressed between her knees.

"Hang in there. Just takes a minute."

This was the first time Sidney and Selena had been alone all day. Her heart ached when she thought of the trauma Selena experienced. Eleven years her senior, Sidney had been Selena's protector when she was small. As an adult, Selena was taking her own punches and she had shown remarkable resilience. Sidney squeezed her sister's hand. "You had a hell of a day."

"Yes, I did." Softly illuminated by the dashboard lights, Selena's face showed signs of stress, yet the corners of her mouth lifted. "It's also been a good day. I got to play detective. I was part of the A Team."

"You've been a big help. Dad would've been proud."

"Thanks. That means a lot. There's something I forgot to mention. About Tegan."

"What's that?"

"He seemed to know something about Nikah's murder, but he wouldn't tell his dad. I sensed he was frightened."

"Hmmm. He and Nikah were close. He may have seen or heard something."

"Also, be prepared. He hangs out with a huge white wolf."

"You're kidding."

Selena was dead serious. "Not kidding."

"Thanks for letting me know."

"His name's Lelou. He seems friendly enough. Tegan seems to have him under control."

"This case gets stranger by the minute."

"Also, be careful when you go see Grisly Stokes. He sounds scary."

Sidney thought the same thing, but portrayed calmness for her sister's sake. "No worry. Granger and I can handle him."

By the time Granger had all the windows and side mirrors cleaned, the seat warmers and heater were doing their jobs.

Sidney dropped Selena off at home fifteen minutes later. Granger walked her to the front porch, both slipping a little on the walkway. He pulled her close and ducked his head to kiss her. Sidney smiled, grateful her sister was allowing the handsome officer to infiltrate her inner sanctum. After a decade of getting emotionally pummeled by her lying, cheating husband, having a man like Granger fill the void was a blessing wrapped in a big red bow.

CHAPTER FOURTEEN

TEGAN STARTLED awake and bolted into an upright position. He felt a deep chill, but not from the cold. The timber and logs of the cabin groaned and creaked, shifting with the drop in temperature and the wind. He heard the pulse of the antique clock in the living room, keeping time with the rhythmic snores coming from the bedroom of his great-grandmother.

Pushing his covers aside, he wormed his feet into sheepskin boots that were positioned just so by his bed, and grabbed his flannel robe that was draped over the headboard. He tugged the robe over his pajamas, padded down the hallway, and paused at the entrance to the dining room. He felt his father's presence sitting at the table with his back to him. He took a few steps forward and felt the radiant heat of his father's body. And something more. Distress. Tegan reached out to touch his shoulder, then quickly withdrew his hand. His father was hunched over with his face in his hands, quietly weeping. Tegan felt each shudder of his father's body like the tremor of an earthquake. He stood stunned and frightened, camouflaged by stillness.

"Nikah…Nikah," his father softly moaned.

His heart thumping loudly, Tegan retraced his steps and almost collided with Elahan, who stood in the doorway of his bedroom. Her presence was more like smoke than flesh and bone, drifting rather than walking—like the ghostly man. She smelled like the herbs that seasoned tonight's stew—bay leaves, thyme, tarragon, basil.

She stepped aside to let him pass and shut the door behind them. He burrowed under the covers and she sank into the straight-backed chair next to the bed. He sensed concern rather than anger wafting off of her.

"Your father is sad tonight, Tegan," she said in a hushed tone. "He cries when he is alone. He wants to be strong for you, so you know he can protect you from all bad things. Nikah's death has torn holes in our hearts. Grief hangs heavy in our home tonight." She paused and he heard her swallow. "In time, the holes will mend. The pain will get smaller."

"How long does it take to get smaller?"

Elahan sighed. "Weeks. Months. There is no way to measure suffering."

"I hope it's soon. The hole in my heart feels as big as my chest. It hurts really bad. It hurts worse to see dad cry."

"Do not let him know you saw him."

Tegan nodded.

She reached out and pushed his hair back from his forehead, a rare display of affection. He knew the old withered woman loved him with primal fierceness, like a she-wolf or grizzly sow. Etched in his memory was every crease in her face, every sharp angle of her body, and her crooked spine that resembled a tree bent by savage wind. Tears welled in his eyes. He loved her with all of his being, but he feared her more. Elahan walked with one foot in the spirit world. She had powers other humans could not comprehend. When she leveled a piercing stare at him it went through him like an arrow.

Tonight, the tenderness of her touch moved him deeply. He remembered her gnarled fingers rubbing ointment over his burned chest and his back, easing the pain while chanting incantations in her native tongue. Her magic healed him. He often wondered if she bargained with the higher spirits, offering his eyesight as payment for his return to this physical world.

"I know why you cannot sleep," she said. "Your heart is heavy with secrets."

Tegan had confined his secrets to a place in his mind that was shut like a fist that would never open. If his fears were locked away, he could pretend they weren't real.

"I know you're afraid, Tegan. To cast out fear, you must bring it into the light. Let me share your burden."

Tegan sat mum.

"It is more dangerous to do nothing, my boy. That gives your enemy the advantage. Tell me what you know."

Elahan's skeletal hand grasped his with amazing strength. He thought of her as physically frail but her fierce touch evoked the enormous power she carried within. The magic. Tegan felt his hand buckle under the weight of her fierce grip. He began to tremble. The vault cracked open. Memories emerged.

"You are the bravest of all warriors, are you not?" she rasped.

"Yes. I am brave."

"Strong, like Sitting Bull. Like Chief Joseph."

"Strong, like Sitting Bull. Like Chief Joseph," His voice grew stronger.

"Fear will not rule you."

"Fear will not rule me." His chest swelled with a surge of confidence.

"Now tell me what you know."

Tegan felt the secrets forming into words that flowed from his mouth like water in a stream. "When you and Dad were at the tribal meeting yesterday, I went to see Nikah. She invited me to breakfast. When I got there, the front door was open. I went into the living room, calling out her name, but she didn't answer. Then someone slammed into me like a bull. I crashed to the floor and hit my head pretty hard. The person ran outside and took off in a car." The memory made the hair rise on his arms. Tears filled his eyes and his voice grew husky. "I smelled death, Nana. I wanted to run home but I was worried about Nikah. The smell grew stronger when I entered her office. She died in that room."

Elahan's fingers pressed painfully into his palm. "Go on," she said.

"A dark force held me there, like strong hands on my shoulders. I fought back with all my strength, and I finally broke free. I ran home and hid in the barn." He swallowed, licked his dry lips. "Lelou was there. He always seems to know when I need him. I stayed in the corner of the stall until I heard you and dad come home." Tegan wiped his eyes with shaky fingers, humiliated that he cried in front of Elahan.

"Tears cleanse the soul like rain cleans the forest," she said softly. "You have earned the right. You faced fear. Fear tried to own you, but you fought back." Elahan sank next to Tegan on the bed. He leaned into her and she looped one arm around his shoulder. Her other hand stroked his head, brushing the hair from his warm face. Her touch had the effect of mesmerizing him. Slowly, his shoulders relaxed and he seemed to float in a misty world that existed between sleep and wakefulness.

"There is something else you are hiding," she said in a voice that sounded far away. "Tell me."

He spoke freely, as though in a dream. "Last week when Lelou and I were down by the creek, I sensed we were being followed. I didn't hear anyone but I could smell a presence. The sweat of a man, and also the blood of dead animals, and a stink I didn't recognize. This man meant to hurt us. Lelou stood in front of me and growled a vicious growl. The scent of the man slowly disappeared." Tegan paused, and he took a deep breath. "Last night, the same scent was outside my bedroom window. I believe this man carries death with him."

"Why have you not told me this?" The sharp alarm in Elahan's voice woke him from a trance-like state. Suddenly alert, his nerves tingling, he pulled away. He said in his own defense, "I recited prayers to push the evil away."

Her voice was gently reprimanding. "You are no longer a child, Tegan. To become a man, you must think and act like a warrior."

"What would a warrior do?" he asked, his voice wavering.

"A warrior does not sit and wait for his enemy to come and destroy him. A warrior acts. Attacks first. A warrior becomes stronger by banding with other warriors."

"Are you a warrior?"

"Yes. A great warrior. We will work together. We will make a plan." Tegan felt her body stiffen as she reflected in silence. "Our enemy has come to our door. It is dangerous for us to stay here. We must leave the village and lure this evil man into the wilderness. We must learn his purpose, and kill him, if need be."

Her words went through Tegan like an electric shock. He had never heard a person speak openly of killing another person. The thought was alien and terrifying. Elahan's words echoed those of the ghostly man.

There are devils who wear human skin. They must be rooted out and killed, if necessary. You and I will bring Nikah justice. This I promise.

Tegan was thankful Elahan had not drilled him for more secrets. He would sooner slash his wrists than deliberately betray his shadowy companion. If Elahan knew of what he and the ghostly man did in the woods, that their actions may have brought this evil to their door, her wrath would know no bounds.

"Evil and Goodness live on this earth side by side," the old woman said. "You must learn to be strong to keep evil away."

"How do I become strong?"

"I will teach you."

Elahan's fingers found the tender, throbbing knot where Tegan's skull had crashed to the floor. He winced. Murmuring a poem he didn't understand, Elahan tapped lightly on the lump with two fingers, then she pressed harder. The pain intensified. Tegan sucked air between his teeth, then tightly clenched his jaw. His eyes watered and overflowed. The pain reached a crescendo, like a hot knife piercing his skull, but he did not cry out. Slowly, the agony ebbed, and Elahan's healing magic breathed a shimmering energy into his entire being. Every fiber of his nervous system leapt awake. He felt a sense of heightened strength and confidence that he had not known before. A power. The medicine woman was an invincible force. Together, they would succeed in bringing the evil man to his knees.

The two sat in silence for several minutes as the wave of energy surged through his system and slowly ebbed away. His mind and body relaxed into a soft state of peacefulness.

Elahan's quiet voice floated in the silence. "I know the man who is your special friend came to you in the barn tonight."

Her words jolted him. How did she know about the ghostly man? Tegan wasn't sure the man was even real. "How did you know?"

"I've had a bad feeling in my bones for many days. I felt the presence of evil drawing near. I summoned him."

What?

"We spoke. It was his wish to speak with you."

Tegan's heart raced. He bolted upright. "What is he? A spirit guide?"

"He is a man. As real as your father."

Tegan was nearly bursting with impatience. "Who is he?"

"His name is Moolock."

The Chinook word for elk. A good name for a man who is strong, who blends with nature, who smells of the woods, who doesn't trust humans. Tegan swallowed, waiting for more.

"Tonight, we agreed it was time for you to learn Moolock's story. The dark spirit of death has been unleashed. That changes everything. Moolock can no longer be invisible. He must act. And we will act with him."

"What do you mean?"

"He will take us on a journey. To protect you. And to hunt."

A chill prickled Tegan's scalp. *Hunt what?*

"What I tell you must never be repeated. Do you understand?" she said.

"Yes," Tegan whispered, absorbing the seriousness of the conversation.

"If Moolock learns you spoke of this to anyone, even your father, you will never see him again."

Tegan's throat tightened as he conjured the gentle, easy presence of the man who had been his companion in the woods these last three years. With Nikah gone, if he were to lose the ghostly man as well, the loss would be too great. The void would swallow Tegan. He might never find his way back to his untroubled life here in the village. "I promise, Nana. I will go to my grave with this secret."

"Let's us not speak of death tonight, my boy," she said with a touch of humor. "We do not want to attract that prophecy."

He smiled, nodding his agreement. "Tell me, Nana. Who is Moolock?"

She heaved out a long, deep breath from her bony chest. "Moolock is your great uncle. He is my son."

Long moments passed as Tegan digested the weight of her words, and another long moment passed before he found his voice. "Your son? How can that be? You are so old."

Elahan laughed, a rare and lovely sound. "My boy, I have not always been as gray and wrinkled as a sagebrush lizard. Once I was young and fresh and pretty. Like Nikah. My hair was as black as the raven. I was a strong girl. I could cook and sew and work like a mule. I could flirt with men. Many were taken with me. Many came to my father and asked to have me as a bride. I chose Black Bear Chetwoot. He was a farmer, a good hunter, a good provider. He was handsome and bold and funny. I was a foolish girl. I think I married him because he made me laugh."

Tegan smiled, trying to imagine Elahan as young and fresh and pretty. He had only known her as dry and wrinkled, her bony frame thrust forward, as though being pulled to the earth like a dead tree. Now she spoke with a lyrical quality to her voice. It was like listening to a melody, a fairy tale. He hung on every word, putting them to memory.

"As you know, Black Bear and I had one son, Chac Chac," Elahan said. "He is your grandfather. My dear husband died of cancer when Chac was a small boy, and for many years after, I felt his absence keenly. Because I wanted Chac to have a man, a teacher in his life, I married Vane Whitebone. He taught high school on the reservation in Lost River Valley. It was too soon to marry. I did not choose well. Those were barren years. No children came forth." Her voice shadowed with sadness. "Vane and I divorced. We had no love for each other. I vowed never to marry again."

She paused for a moment and sighed deeply. "Many years later, when I was forty-two, a handsome man came into my life. He reminded me of my first love, Black Bear, only he was stronger in character, and more powerful." Elahan's voice took on a dreamy quality, as wistful as a young woman's, and Tegan felt she was breathing in the memories, reliving them. "This man was my truest love. What young people today call a soulmate. We had many happy days, and many, many happy nights." She was silent for a full minute and Tegan felt she had wandered away from the room, away from the cabin, and traveled into her past. Then her soft voice filled the quiet again. She had returned. "Soon my stomach grew large with child. I was surprised. It was a time of great joy.

Moolock was born when I was forty-three. A gift from the spirit world."

This was a story that Tegan had never heard before. It was strangely beautiful to listen to Elahan speak of youth and romance and love. Somewhere in that mummified body, the heart of a young woman pulsed. "Why didn't Dad talk about Moolock?"

"Your father and Moolock were born the same year." The elation in her voice disappeared. "He was a baby when Moolock was a baby. Chac did not approve of our relationship. He thought it was sinful that we created a child. He never allowed Moolock and Tommy to meet. The handsome man and I never married."

"Why didn't you marry him, Nana?"

She was silent for a long moment and her sadness weighed heavily on his spirit.

"I will share a painful secret because tonight you shared painful secrets," Elahan said. "A secret that no one knows except Moolock."

"I promise not to tell," he said eagerly.

"Moolock's father already had a wife."

The confession took Tegan's breath away. He could not find words to express his shock. His face must have told it all, for Elahan's breathing also stopped for a moment.

"This is why I never told you," she said in a tone filled with remorse. "Why I never told Tommy. People are quick to judge."

The silence that lengthened between them was heavy and awkward. Tegan reached out and covered her hand with his. "I won't judge you, Nana."

Elahan cradled his hand between her own and he was comforted by her touch. "The handsome man did not love his wife. They no longer lived together but she would not let him go."

"What happened to him, and to Moolock?" he asked.

"Ah, that is a long story. The handsome man and I lived together for many months. It was the happiest time of my life.

Then he was called to war. Vietnam. He was killed. His remains were returned to his family, to his wife." Elahan's voice choked and she took a few moments to compose herself. "I wanted to raise Moolock. I didn't care what others thought. But the handsome man's parents were rich and powerful. They used their money to take Moolock from me. They lived far away. They would not let me see him." Her voice choked again and trailed away to a whisper. "That sadness still fills my heart."

Tears escaped down Tegan's cheeks. "I'm sorry you hurt so much, Nana."

She softly cleared her throat and stroked his hand. "You are a special boy, Tegan. You feel things deeply. You have my power. Moolock's power. But you are young. You don't know how to use it. That can be a danger to you and to others. It is like carrying a loaded gun with no safety."

"Teach me, Nana," he said passionately.

"Yes, my boy. In time."

Tegan's head was full of questions. "How did Moolock come back into your life? Who is Moolock's father?"

"It is late, Tegan. You must rest. Store your energy. You will need it. Moolock will teach you. He will tell you everything."

CHAPTER FIFTEEN

GRANGER AND SIDNEY stood on the porch of the single-story, ranch-style house for a full minute, laying on the doorbell, then the knocker, waiting for the sound of interior footsteps to approach the door.

Nothing.

Lancer's truck, parked in the driveway, was covered with an inch of snow. He'd been home for at least an hour.

"Either he's avoiding us," Sidney said. "Or he can't get to the door."

"Could be passed out drunk."

"Sounds like a medical emergency," she said dryly, and tried the door handle. It gave. She pushed the door open and she and Granger beamed their lights into the living room. The room had been ransacked.

"Holy shit," Granger said.

"We're going in," she said quietly. "Stay alert."

They unholstered their Glocks and entered, gun hands resting on top of their flashlight hands, following their beams through the living room, skirting objects on the floor.

"Help...help..." a hoarse voice cried out. They followed the sound down a hallway to a bedroom. Their beams illuminated a man sitting in the center of the room, hands and legs bound to a chair.

"Is anyone else in the house?" Sidney asked.

"No. They just left out the window."

In a heartbeat Granger was over the sill and lowering himself to the ground. Sidney watched him disappear down an alley between the two houses. She holstered her gun, switched on a lamp, turned to the man, and gasped. Part of his scalp had been sliced along the hairline and the wound was bleeding freely. Blood dripped down his face and spattered his white polo shirt. One eye was swollen shut and his bottom lip was split.

Unnerved, Sidney grabbed a folded hand towel lying on the bed and pressed it against the man's head. He moaned and tried to jerk away.

"Hold still. I need to stem the bleeding."

He winced, but didn't move. "How bad is it?"

"Not too bad. Two-inch laceration. Are you hurt anywhere else?"

"No."

"Sir, are you Lancer Richards?" Sidney asked.

"Yes."

With her free hand, Sidney hit her lapel mic and radioed dispatch. In a town as small as Garnerville, the ER was often empty. She wanted to make sure a doctor would be waiting. "Hey Jesse. Contact the ER. We're bringing someone in who needs stitches."

"Copy that."

A noise from the front of the house sent her hand back to the hilt of her Glock, but then she heard Granger call out, "It's me." He appeared in the doorway, eyes widening as he took in the bleeding man and the ransacked room.

"See anything?" Sidney asked.

"Two men. They got away in a dark pickup." His eyes met Sidney's and a silent communication passed between them— probably the same men from the village.

"Could you fucking untie me?" Lancer said, straining against his ties.

"Bear with me a second, Lancer. We need to document this for our report. Granger, take a few pictures."

Granger took a couple shots with his phone, and then got to work on the knots.

Once freed, Lancer rubbed his wrists and stretched his legs, flexing his feet.

"I'll get something to wash off the blood." Granger left the room and returned holding a washcloth in a pan of water.

"Let me do it." Lancer wrung out the cloth, covered his face and pulled it down with both hands, repeated, leaving just a few specs of red in the folds of his neck. Despite his swollen eye, Sidney recognized him from the photos in Nikah's bedroom. Sandy hair, blue eyes, even, white teeth.

Granger attended to Lancer's wound while Sidney held the towel to his forehead to catch escaping blood. "Who were those men?" she asked.

"No clue." Lancer's fingers gripped the armrests. He was struggling to keep a handle on his rage. "They wore ski masks. They were dressed in black from head to toe. Wore gloves."

"Were they young, old?"

"I'd say in their twenties, or thirties." While Lancer gritted his teeth, Granger applied a bandage and wrapped gauze tightly around his head.

"One was about my height, six-two. Athletic build. The other was around five-ten, husky."

Very observant. Sidney fished out her phone. "Lancer, do you mind if I record our conversation?"

He shrugged. "Go ahead."

She pressed the record icon, and asked, "What were the men looking for?"

"Hell if I know." Lancer clenched and unclenched his fingers, working the circulation back into them. "They kept asking me about a key, and some fucking medallion. I didn't know what they were talking about."

Sidney understood exactly what they wanted. The contents of the tin box. "Did they say what the key was for?"

"A safety deposit box. I don't even have one."

"Did they say what was in the box?"

"No."

"What was the medallion all about?"

"Don't know. I asked, and the fucker hit me. Called me a liar. Said I knew exactly what it was."

"How long were they here?"

He squinted and stared at the floor, thinking. "I got home around nine. Ate a sandwich, took a shower. They surprised me when I came out in the hall. One had a gun. A .38, I think. They tied me up in here. That must have been around nine-thirty."

Sidney glanced at her watch. "It's ten. A half-hour sound right?"

"Yeah. I lost track of time." He heaved out a breath. "The tall guy kept hitting me. Yelling for me to answer. But I couldn't tell him what I didn't know. The shorter guy started tearing the place apart. The tall guy pulled out a freaking hunting knife and held it to my temple. He sounded desperate, like he would do anything to get me to talk. He said he was going to scalp me if I didn't tell him. Every time I said I didn't know, he cut me." Lancer grimaced, and said between clenched teeth, "Hurt like hell. Still does."

Sidney believed he was telling the truth. Not too many folks can stand up to torture.

"Freaking Indians," Lancer hissed.

"You think they were Indians?"

"They were going to scalp me." He touched his bandage, winced. "What do you think?"

"Did they say anything that led you to believe that?"

"No. I couldn't see much of their faces, just around their mouths and eyes. They had brown skin and brown eyes. I saw a lock of black hair hanging out of the short one's mask in the back."

"Can you tell us anything else that might help us identify them?" Sidney asked. "Anything unusual?"

He thought for a moment. "Not really."

"Did either use the bathroom?"

"The tall guy kept me pretty distracted, but I think I heard the toilet flush."

"I'll go take a look." Sidney made her way down the hall to the bathroom. Unlike the rest of the house, it had not been searched and looked tidy. Nothing on the counters. She looked in the toilet. No bodily waste, so no DNA. The waste can was empty. Then she spotted a crumpled tissue on the floor between the can and the wall. Someone had missed the can. Sidney lifted the tissue with her ballpoint pen, and walked back into the room. "Did you drop this tissue on the bathroom floor?"

"No. I just use toilet paper."

"Maybe we'll get some DNA." Sidney pulled out an evidence bag, deposited the
tissue, and sealed it.

"Thank God you showed up when you did. They would have killed me." Lancer's eyes sharpened on hers. "Why are you here, anyway?"

"We'll get to that in a minute," Sidney said. "First, I need you to answer a few questions."

"Shoot."

"Are you involved in illegal activities?"

"No," he said emphatically. "You can ask anyone. I don't touch dope."

"What about Nikah?"

"Hell no. She's as clean as they come. Barely even touches alcohol." He looked sheepish for a moment, swallowed. "I drink too much. I'm trying to quit. I promised Nikah."

"They kick you out of Two Creeks for drinking, Lancer? For hitting Nikah?"

He inhaled deeply. Clenched his jaw. She saw anger spark in his eyes.

"You beat your girlfriend?"

His fists clenched and unclenched. "Okay. I hit her once. One time, dammit! And yeah, I drink. So do a lot of guys up there. But none of them got kicked out of their homes."

"Did Nikah stand up for you?"

"No. She should have. But they're her fucking people. She does whatever they say." He glowered. "Shows where her loyalty lies."

"They kicked you out. She didn't stand up for you. That must have made you mad."

"Hell yeah, it made me mad!"

"You were at Nikah's last week. Were you two seeing each other again?"

"No."

"Nikah had a bruise on her neck the day after you were seen at her house. Did you hurt her?"

"What? No! I just went to pick up some clothes. She wasn't even there. She was at work. What do you mean, a bruise? Did she say I hurt her?"

Sidney and Granger exchanged glances. Lancer was either a good liar, or he genuinely didn't know Nikah was dead. She needed to find out which. She let a long silence stretch between them. Generally, suspects were uncomfortable with silence and started filling in the blanks.

Lancer fidgeted, shifted in his seat. "What's going on here? Did Nikah send you?"

"No. Nikah didn't send us."

"Then *they* sent you…"

"Who's that, Lancer?"

"The tribal council. They'll do anything to get me locked up. They want to make me the fall guy. I'm not going to let that happen!" Lancer's face flushed bright red and the cords in his neck stood out like rope.

"Fall guy for what, Lancer?"

"Ask them!" He peered up at her through his one good eye, piercing blue. "Talk to Nikah. She'll tell you. She promised me she'd move out of there. Get away from the Village tyrants. "After a long pause, he continued. "We agreed to get back together when I'm six weeks sober. It's been three. We'll rent out her house. She'll move in here with me."

"Can you tell me where you were Friday night?"

"Friday night?" He thought for a moment. "I was here. Watching TV."

"Can anyone vouch for you?"

He looked from her face to the recorder, and back again, as though realizing how serious the situation was. "What do I need an alibi for?"

There was no way to soften the hammer blow she was about to deliver. Sidney drew in a deep breath, and said gently, "I'm sorry to tell you this, Lancer, but Nikah is dead."

Stunned silence.

"What? I don't believe you! What freaking game are you playing?"

"It's no game. Nikah's dead. That's why we're here tonight."

His face was expressionless. "What happened?"

"She was murdered."

Lancer shook his head and looked like a man trying to come out of a trance, and grasping threads of reality. His eyes locked on Sidney's. "Was she strangled?"

Sidney waited a moment too long to answer. "Why would you ask that?"

"Oh my God. She was strangled, wasn't she?" Lancer leapt from the chair and started pacing the floor in an agitated manner. "I knew this would happen. They wouldn't listen. It's their fault she's dead." Lancer suddenly looked faint. A sound that was part scream, part sob tore from his throat. He slumped back in the chair, leaned over with his head in his hands, and wept. His chest heaved, and sounds she barely recognized as human escaped from his mouth.

Granger and Sidney watched in silence. Granger's expression of abject misery mirrored her feelings exactly. Witnessing a person's raw grief was the most gut-wrenching part of the job.

Lancer eventually lifted his tear-stained face, wiped his nose with the back of his sleeve, and said hoarsely, "Was she raped?"

"I can't answer that until we get lab results. She was found in Whilamut Creek by the old bridge."

A sort of wild terror leapt into his eyes. "Jesus. Someone put her in that icy water?"

"I'm afraid so." A moment passed while she let that register. "Do you know why anyone would do that?"

"Purification. Water sustains life. It's sacred. It has spiritual meaning." He stared intently at the floor, thinking, and added in a shaky voice, "He strangles women. Now he's killed Nikah."

"Who killed Nikah?"

"The Stalker."

Granger's eyes widened.

The hair stood up on Sidney's arms. "Does this stalker have a name?"

Lancer shook his head. His hands were shaking.

"Okay. Take a breath. Granger, get him some water."

Granger left the room and returned with a glass.

Lancer drank half of it. Head bowed, he stared at the floor, gripping the armrests as though they were lifelines.

"You okay?"

He lifted his head, nodded.

"Can you tell me about this stalker?"

Lancer gulped in a breath. "It started about six months ago. A trespasser was roaming through the village at night. Some of our neighbors started finding tracks going through their properties, always coming up from White Tail Creek. At first, the elders didn't take it seriously. Then things started going missing from barns and sheds. Power-tools, things that could be sold." Lancer paused to catch his breath. "More tracks were found, under bedroom windows, like he was spying on folks."

"The Stalker started peeping?" Granger asked, a deep frown creasing his brow.

"Yeah. He was watching women who live alone, and teenage girls." Lancer cleared his throat again. "Men started taking turns patrolling the village at night. Everyone was pretty shaken up. Then, no tracks for a while. We figured we chased him out." He cleared his throat. "About two months ago, Badger Woods and his wife said their dog started barking at two in the morning. When he looked out the window, he saw a figure darting through the trees down by the creek. Next day, they learned a thief had broken into their neighbor's house. He'd stolen jewelry while they slept. The Stalker had been in their bedroom! Over the last few weeks, there were two more house thefts. Jewelry and small valuables were stolen while people slept in their beds."

A sense of growing unease tightened Sidney's stomach and she saw Granger's posture had stiffened. "Let me get this straight, Lancer. People in Two Creeks saw tracks from an unidentified trespasser for weeks, followed by an outbreak of thefts in barns and sheds. No one did anything. The thief got braver. He started entering homes and stealing things while people slept."

He nodded.

Alarm bells were sounding, but Sidney waited patiently while Lancer took another drink of water. Then he dropped a bombshell. "A month ago, a woman was attacked."

Sidney couldn't hide the shock in her tone. "Raped?"

"Yeah. At home, in her own bed. Rumors had it that he strangled her for kicks."

"Who was the victim?" Sidney asked.

Lancer shifted in his seat, pulled an ankle over his knee, played with his shoelace. "I don't know. The elders closed ranks. They put out a warning to the community that a rapist was on the loose but they kept the details private."

Sidney tried to keep judgment out of her voice. "Why didn't they notify us?"

"The victim didn't want to report it. This kind of thing, a sex crime, is humiliating to a woman. And to the whole village. Like we can't protect our own. Nikah told me she wouldn't report it if it happened to her. Everyone knows it's the victim who's put on trial in court. And minorities never win, do they?" Lancer gave her and Granger an accusing stare, as though they were the enemy. "The village preferred to handle it themselves. Their way."

That had a sinister ring to it. "What do you mean, their way?"

"You'll have to ask them," he said.

The tactics these untrained villagers might employ distressed Sidney deeply. When civilians chose to take the law into their own hands, it didn't end well. Innocent people got hurt. "So, Lancer, what was done to make the village safe?"

"Everyone kept their guns close at hand. Armed and ready. More men patrolled the neighborhood at night, working in shifts. Including me. Didn't do much good. We continued to find prints creeping from house to house. Two weeks ago, there was another rape attempt. The woman chased him away. There were rumors flying around that she'd been punched and strangled."

His next words surprised her.

"That's when the elders came down on me."

"Why is that?"

"The woman gave them a partial description. It was dark, but she was certain he was a white guy. Approximate height, same build, and shoe size as me. Now everyone thinks I'm the Stalker." Lancer stared straight ahead, blinking, breathing hard. "There's not a scrap of proof, but that's the real reason I got kicked out." His gaze shifted to Granger. "Hell, Officer, you could be the Stalker. You're about my height, same build. But no, the villagers decided it had to be me. Since then, I've been getting threatening text messages. A guy in the village told me if another woman got hurt, I was a dead man."

"Who specifically said that?"

"Doesn't matter who," he said angrily. "It's a collective threat."

"Humor me."

"Name's Fitch."

"Fitch Drako," Granger said. "Met him tonight at the saloon, Chief. Big guy. A drunk. Itching to crack someone's head open. Preferably a cop."

Granger and Sidney shared a glance of mutual outrage. Violent men were running loose, raping, killing, threatening people's lives, and law enforcement had been left in the dark.

"Make a note to talk to this Fitch character," Sidney said, and turned back to Lancer. "These threats didn't keep you from going back to the village last week. Did you spend the night with Nikah?"

"No. I told you. I just stopped by to pick up some clothes. Nikah and I haven't seen each other since I moved out. She didn't believe for a second that I was the Stalker. But she insisted I quit drinking before she'd see me again." Tears welled in his eyes. "I wanted her back. I've been going to AA meetings every night. Lot of good it's doing me now."

"Staying sober will do you a lot of good," Sidney said. "That's what Nikah wanted. Do it for her."

He held her gaze, and nodded.

Her dispatcher crackled over the radio. "Yeah Jesse?"

"Dr. Caulfield is at the ER waiting for you."

"Tell him we'll be there in five." She looked at Lancer and said gently, "Want to change your shirt? Grab a jacket?"

Lancer looked shaken as he glanced down at the bloodstained shirt he was wearing. He grabbed a plaid flannel shirt from the pile of clothes on the floor and changed into it.

Sidney asked, "You're a roofer, right?"

He nodded.

"Since you're off for the winter, it would be a good idea to leave town for a while. Give us time to find this stalker and the thugs who beat you. Your life appears to be in danger, and I don't have the manpower to protect you."

"I have a winter job," Lancer said. "Plowing snow. I intend to show up for work tomorrow."

"I'd listen to the chief," Granger added. "Take a breather. It wasn't hard for these two jokers to get into your house tonight. They might come back. Plus, you got folks riled up at Two Creeks. You don't have an alibi for the night Nikah was killed, and you have a history of drunkenness and abuse."

Lancer winced. He leveled a heated gaze on Granger. "No one's chasing me out of my home a second time."

Sidney sighed. Over her seventeen-year career, she'd witnessed too many seemingly intelligent people who put their lives at risk over misplaced pride, and pay a heavy price. "Okay, Lancer. Give it some serious thought. You've been warned. Let's go."

CHAPTER SIXTEEN

IT WAS AFTER 1:00 a.m. by the time Sidney wolfed down a peanut butter and jam sandwich and remembered to set the state-of-the-art alarm system, installed after Selena's attack. In the event the alarm was triggered, the security company would contact the Garnerville police department, vis-à-vis her dispatcher, Jesse, who would in turn contact Sidney, thus completing a loop that would start and end at her address. An ironic smile touched her lips. If she had to be dragged out of bed to investigate a break-in, at least she could do it in her nightgown.

Sidney's muscles were tight with fatigue while her mind was a beehive of activity. She fantasized about driving to David's house, stealing into his bedroom and melting into his warm embrace. Deep, stirring kisses and extraordinary sex was always the most effective sleep remedy. Instead, she climbed the stairs to her room, stripped off her uniform, and fell heavily into bed. She knew she would lay awake for some time, processing every detail of the day's grim events.

***

Sidney woke damp with sweat, heart pounding her rib cage. It took a while for the effects of a nightmare to loosen its hold, for her to realize she was home, safe in bed. The dream felt so real. She had been stumbling in a white, frozen world along a creek gripped in ice, her bare feet sinking into ankle-deep snow. Dressed in a thin nightdress, the cold assaulted her like ten thousand needles stinging her flesh. Then her limbs went numb, her knees buckled, and she collapsed. Heavy, menacing steps gained ground behind her. Panting breaths grew louder. A scream welled and lodged in her throat as a figure loomed over her, gloved hands reaching down... Heart racing, Sidney fumbled for her phone on the nightstand and she mumbled to Siri, "Call David Kane."

David answered in five heartbeats, his voice hoarse with sleep, "Sidney, are you okay?"

"Yes," she said, struggling to compose herself. "I had a horrible nightmare. It seemed so real. I still have goosebumps." She swallowed, wetting her dry throat. "Sorry for waking you. I just wanted to hear your voice."

"I'm glad you called, and that you thought of me when you needed a hero. Not as good as having you here in my bed, though." His deep voice filled her with a sense of calm, and longing. She imagined being pressed against his warm body, the soft hair on his chest tickling her flesh.

"Rough day, huh?"

"Pretty awful." She didn't tell him that when she closed her eyes the face of a dead woman stared up at her through ice. "But talking to you is helping."

"Want me to come over?" His voice sounded deliciously warm. "I could help you even more."

"There's nothing I'd like more. But I have to say no." Sidney stifled a yawn and glanced at the clock. Her eyes burned from lack of sleep and she needed to be at work in three hours. "Need some shut eye. I won't see much of it the next few days."

"No afternoon visit today, huh?"

"No. Sorry."

"I'll miss you." His voice changed minutely, and she heard his disappointment. She felt the same.

"Miss you, too," she said softly.

"Maybe later tonight? I can swing by for a bit. I don't mind if you just use me for my body."

"Hmmm," she smiled, thinking about his many talents. "Sounds enticing."

"Call me anytime. I'll pop right up. I mean, right over."

"You devil," she said, thinking about his sublime virility. "I'll call if I get finished with work at a reasonable hour. I..." Sidney hesitated, catching herself. She almost said *I love you*. Careful. She and David had only been dating six weeks. Too soon to say those three thorny words. They implied something not yet established between them. Commitment. Something she was ready for. But was David? The thought that their relationship was just a convenience to him frightened her. She remembered the downward spiral she endured after she and Gable went their separate ways. Two long years of celibacy, and a melancholy that haunted her, especially when she was alone in the dark. "I...I hope you have a wonderful day," she stammered. Groan. Lame.

"Goodnight, beautiful," he murmured.

"Goodnight, David."

CHAPTER SEVENTEEN

AT 8:00 A.M., worn faces with puffy eyes stared back at Sidney from around the table in the conference room. Her entire staff was present, coffee mugs and pastries positioned within reach, laptops open. Winnie, the nerve center of the station and administrator extraordinaire, looked wide awake and alert, dressed fashionably in a purple turtleneck and big hoop earrings. She sat next to Selena, who had inadvertently become a valuable part of the investigation. Sidney gave her the official title of investigative consultant, which made her chest puff out a little at breakfast this morning.

Sidney and Winnie arrived early to start a crime board, which now held an array of photos, including Nikah's frozen corpse and Lancer Richards, bloodied, and tied to a chair.

Standing at the head of the table, Sidney glanced up from her notes and opened the briefing. "This will be a short meeting. We have a lot to do, and not much to go on. We're investigating two separate cases. We have two sexual assault victims, and a murdered woman, Nikah Tamanos, pulled out of Whilamut Creek yesterday. A burglar/rapist, coined the Stalker, is terrorizing Two Creeks Village. Two violent burglars ransacked Nikah's home, and later, brutally beat Lancer. They were in search of these items, which I found stashed in a heating vent in Nikah's bedroom." Sidney pointed to a photo of the tin box and its contents. "Getting into the safe deposit box this morning may shed light on where this money came from, and who these thugs are."

Sidney paused to sip coffee from her mug, then filled in the details of the Stalker's trail of crimes. "The Stalker is smart, and brazen. He enters homes while folks are sleeping, and he's eluded detection for six months. We need to find out if any of these crimes are related." Sidney paused to reflect on the photos, stroking her chin and turning possible angles over in her head.

Amanda filled in the silence. "Maybe Nikah's death is a separate incidence. A date gone horribly wrong. The extra toothbrush in her bathroom suggests she'd been seeing someone."

"And we know it wasn't Lancer," Sidney said.

"My guess, Nikah's murder was committed by the Stalker," Granger said. "He's been spying on the villagers for months. He's a rapist. A woman alone in a secluded house would definitely have caught his attention."

Darnell weighed in. "The fact that his second rape attempt failed may have altered his M.O."

"That's possible. The Stalker's need for violent stimulation may be escalating," Sidney said. "He's gone from trespassing, to burglary, to rape. Murder may be the next logical step."

"Her death could be a hate crime," Winnie piped up. As a woman of mixed race, she was highly sensitive to the rash of racially motivated crimes erupting across the country.

"Let's hope not," Sidney said, taking another swig of coffee. She then related Lancer's excommunication, and the threats of vigilantism by the Two Creeks villagers. "These crimes could trigger a race war. I don't believe Lancer's the Stalker, but he fits the description of the man who is. We're looking for a Caucasian male, about six–two, with a lean, muscular build. That puts Lancer right in the bullseye."

"And a lot of other white guys, too," Winnie said, nodding toward Granger with a mischievous sparkle to her eye. She smiled and everyone laughed at the absurdity of it, including Granger.

"We're at the starting point," Sidney said, casting her glance around the table. "Until we get lab and autopsy reports, we're working blind. Keep scratching in the dirt until something tangible crops up." She nodded at her forensic specialist. "How'd it go last night, Amanda?"

"Long night. Could have used a lot more coffee," she quipped. "Stewart and I went through every room, thoroughly. Everything we collected went to the lab." Her brow furrowed and her tone held disappointment. "Unfortunately, the prints on the tin box were smudged, except for two partials. I couldn't get a clear match from the database."

"Darnell, find anything on Nikah's laptop?" Sidney asked.

"Not much." He sat forward in his seat. "Nothing popped out as suspicious. Her declared income matches her salary. Modest but regular deposits went into her savings every month. She was sensible about living on a budget." He sighed. "No clue where she got that wad of cash."

Sidney noted his frustration and wondered if he'd gotten any sleep. She knew Darnell could get a case under his skin like an itch, as she did, and was unable to leave it alone.

"As far as social media," Darnell continued, "Lancer has no active accounts. His emails and texting were limited to work, a few friends, and Nikah. Nikah dabbled a little on Facebook and Twitter, but pretty mundane stuff. Downright boring, actually."

"Hmmm. No leads there." Sidney went to the sideboard and refilled her mug. She stirred in two sugars and a half-inch of cream. "Well, let's all get to work. Granger and I are heading over to the tribal council meeting. Darnell and Amanda, you two canvas Nikah's neighbors. Selena, keep me posted on your meeting with Cadence. Winnie, get me a warrant from Judge Rosenstadt to open

Nikah's safe deposit box. Then prepare a press release, and notify the mayor we have another murder on our hands. Bare facts only."

"Gotcha. Lean and mean." Winnie scribbled notes on her legal pad.

"Stay alert. We got some dangerous folks running around out there half-cocked."

CHAPTER EIGHTEEN

THOUGH THE ROAD that followed the gentle curve of Nenámooks Lake was freshly plowed, Sidney felt patches of ice under her tires, and drove cautiously. Wind-driven clouds raced across the sky, dragging shadows across the forest below. Snow transformed the landscape, burying everything familiar under rolling mounds of white.

As Sidney passed Nikah's house, Granger pointed out the yellow crime scene tape that Amanda had strung across the driveway. The bright sun and blue sky lifted the ominous pallor that had hung over the house last night, and portrayed a neighborhood of peaceful country charm. Across the road, she caught a glimpse of the sparkling lake between the trees. A wholesome family community—until night fell. Then it turned into a place of terror, where a dangerous predator lurked in the shadows, waiting to strike.

Another mile slid under the tires before Sidney turned into the unplowed parking lot of the Tribal Cultural Center. Three SUVs were parked in the front of a two-story wood-planked building with lots of windows and eaves hung with glistening icicles.

A Toyota Tundra pickup pulled in behind her and parked next to the Yukon. A bundled man exited at the same time as she and Granger. The wind whishing through the trees cut right through them and their breath steamed in the cold morning air.

The man was dressed in a thick jacket, collar turned up, hands gloved in leather, with the muffs of his hat pulled over his ears. He flipped the bill up from his face and motioned for them to follow him through the double glass doors. Standing just inside the entrance, embraced by the comforting warmth, they stamped their feet to shake the snow off their boots.

The man pulled off his hat and Sidney saw him clearly. Though he appeared to be around eighty, his face had not grown soft with age. His creased skin stretched over strong cheekbones, a high forehead, and a prominent chin. White braids fell in front of his shoulders and his bulbous nose was red from cold. "Name's Tucker Longtooth," he said, offering a sad smile. He pulled off his gloves and extended his free hand.

So this was the visionary who bought Two Creeks Village two decades ago and developed it into a haven for Kalapuyan families. He had a kind face and a noble bearing.

"I'm Chief Becker," she said. "This is Officer Wyatt."

He turned to Granger and his eyebrows arched in recognition. "Hello, Granger."

"Morning, Tucker."

"Sorry to see you under such sad circumstances," the old man said.

"Me, too."

Sidney hid her surprise as they all shook hands. Granger's chummy familiarity with the villagers was becoming increasingly evident.

An attractive woman, mid-forties, came into the hallway from a doorway across the lobby, dressed a forest green sweater and skinny jeans tucked into mid-calf boots. Her shiny black hair hung straight down her back and she wore light makeup and a grim expression. "Good morning Tucker. Morning, Officers. We're meeting in here. I'm Jenna Menowa."

She didn't crack a smile as they shook hands and Sidney detected a current of hostility residing just below the surface. An icy welcoming committee.

Their boots sounded hollow as they followed Jenna over a polished cement floor into a large auditorium. Stacks of folded tables and chairs, and a podium and video screen occupied a large section of one wall. Across the room, winter sun poured through the large windows, highlighting photos and posters of colorful ceremonies and celebrations. Sidney was fascinated by the dancers in full native regalia of vibrant fabrics, dramatic plumage, and brightly colored beads—looking part human, part exotic animal.

A long table with six folding chairs had been set up near the podium where two men and a woman with a pronounced stoop to her back stood talking. Sidney recognized Elahan and Tommy Chetwoot immediately. Both wore stern expressions and looked clearly put out by this impromptu meeting. Then she realized they were mirroring her own expression, which reflected irritation bordering on anger. This was not going to be a happy occasion for anyone, but allowing her anger to drive her actions would not solve any problems. Hopefully, diplomacy would.

She extended her hand to Tommy, and said in a pleasant but professional tone, "Thank you for setting up this meeting."

"You're welcome." He looked at her with a little too much intensity and gave her hand a slightly too-hard squeeze.

The other man, in his mid-twenties, was dressed in jeans, a white button-down shirt, and a navy blazer. Tall and lean with short-cropped black hair and expressive brown eyes, he possessed the casual sophistication of a young entrepreneur you might meet at a hip tech company. Introduced as River Menowa, he bestowed her with a charming smile while holding her hand a few beats longer than necessary.

Smooth. Sure of himself with women. "You have the same last name as Jenna," she remarked.

"My mom. I'm visiting from California."

"Land of sunshine. The snow must be a shock."

He chuckled. "Haven't been warm since I got here. Been fighting a nasty cold." As if to accentuate his point, he pulled out a handkerchief and blew his nose.

"What business are you in, River?"

He stuffed the handkerchief back in his pocket. "Software development. Small company. Not public yet."

"You sit on the tribal council long distance?"

He shoved his hands in his pockets and rocked on the balls of his feet. "I'm not on the council. Just here to support Mom."

Jenna shot Sidney a disapproving look from across the table.

Elahan had seated herself next to Jenna, making a handshake unnecessary. Still, Sidney nodded to her.

Elahan nodded back, her witchy quality subdued this morning. She wore a long black dress adorned with strings of beads. Her wild white hair had been restrained in braids that wrapped around her head like a crown. In the light of day, her face appeared as creased as parched earth, her eyes as black and glassy as obsidian. Her gnarled brown hands rested on a leather satchel embellished with intricate beadwork in a floral pattern.

"Please have a seat, Officers." Tucker sat at the head of the table and gestured for Sidney to sit next to him. She shook out of her heavy coat and hung it on the back of her chair. Granger did the same, taking the last vacant seat next to Elahan.

A bottle of water had been placed at each setting. Sidney unscrewed the top and took a cool sip while studying the group over the bottle.

"We understand why you're here, Chief Becker," Tucker stated in a grave tone. "The news of Nikah's death sent a shock wave through our village. We're a very close-knit community. It hit several of us here at this table especially hard. Nikah was like a granddaughter to me." He paused, looked down at his tightly clasped hands, and blinked several times. Then he raised his gaze to hers, his dark eyes moist, and cleared his throat. "We are grieving deeply this morning. But you asked for this emergency meeting with the council. We are respecting your wishes. What is it you want from us?"

All eyes fixed on Sidney, and she felt the heat of resentment pouring from the two women.

"First, let me extend our deepest sympathies. We're sorry to intrude on your grief. However, we are investigating a murder. A vicious killer is roaming free. Time is of the essence." She paused, letting the gravity of her words sink in. "It came to our attention last night that in addition to Nikah's murder, your community has been plagued by other serious crimes, ranging from trespassing, to peeping, to home break-ins, to sexual assaults on two women."

Surprised expressions appeared around the table. "How do you know this?" Tommy asked.

"In the course of an investigation, many things come to light. Things people want to keep hidden. I find it alarming that these crimes have gone unreported to law enforcement, and have increased in severity." *And borders on criminal neglect.* "If we had been called in earlier, the perpetrator might have been caught, and some of these crimes might have been prevented."

"Really, Chief Becker?" Jenna said, her hostility out in the open. "It's easy to make sweeping assumptions after the fact. So typical. Our people have always been low on the white man's priority list, if we don't fall off completely, unless you want to harass us for crimes we didn't commit. Then you operate at lightning speed."

Sidney took a few moments to organize her thoughts before she responded. *Diplomacy.* "We're not here to root up past grievances committed against your people, Jenna. For whatever you may have suffered, I sympathize. I really do. But past injustices should not reflect upon my department. We treat people fairly. I know I've been negligent in coming out to Two Creeks and getting to know you as neighbors. For that, I apologize. What I hope to establish going forward is cooperation and mutual trust. Let's focus on doing what is necessary to make your community safe again."

"Christ, you sound like a politician," Jenna hissed.

Sidney's anger rose swiftly and sharply. A rebuttal blossomed on her tongue. She sucked in a deep breath, released it, and chose to ignore Jenna's remark. She was not here to win debate points. "Bottom line, your village is being held hostage by violent offenders. We need your help to track them down and put them behind bars."

"What do you mean by multiple offenders, Chief Becker?" Tucker's brow furrowed and he leaned forward in his seat. "We thought one man committed all of these crimes."

"When we arrived at Nikah's last night, we discovered two men ransacking her house. They got away."

Eyes widened in surprise around the table. Shock flashed on Tucker's face, followed quickly by sharp concern. "So, the Stalker has a partner?"

"The burglary may be a separate incident. After we left Nikah's we went to question Lancer. We interrupted a burglary in progress at his house as well. We believe by the same two men. These were not crimes of stealth and premeditation, which seems to be the Stalker's M.O. These burglars were sloppy and seemed to be in a hurry. Lancer was tied to a chair and had been beaten severely."

There were audible gasps around the table and troubled expressions. Even the two women had transitioned from indignation to unease.

"Do you have any idea who these burglars are?" Tucker asked.

"We're examining evidence that might shed light on their identities."

"What were they looking for?" Tommy asked with a bewildered expression.

"We have the items in our possession." Sidney fished out her phone and brought up a photo of the medallion. "Here's one of them. Do you know what this is?" She passed the phone around the table and everyone took a look. Their shrugs and baffled expressions told her it wasn't a common Indian artifact.

"It could be Native American," Tommy said. "But from a tribe in a different part of the country."

Disappointed, Sidney put away her phone. "Another concern. Lancer told us he'd been asked to leave the village because you think he's the Stalker."

A guarded look was exchanged between Tommy and Jenna.

"One of the victims ID'd a man who fit his description," Tommy said.

"That's it? That's all you got?" Sidney asked. "It was dark. The victim was no doubt in shock, which could have skewed her perception." Sidney kept her tone neutral but firm. "If these women had gotten rape kits, we might have collected fluids, fiber, hair, that could positively ID the Stalker. As it stands, we have nothing. No DNA. Unless the women kept something from their attacks…clothing, underwear, sheets..."

Tucker frowned. "I don't know. Perhaps..."

Jenna's lip curled with contempt. "Lancer may very well be the Stalker. You can't prove he isn't. It's always the outsider who betrays us. Lancer had no right to tell you of our personal issues here."

Sidney forced her voice to remain calm. "Informing law enforcement of criminal activity is not a betrayal. It's an obligation. Let me be very clear, Jenna. Crimes committed in this village are not your personal business. They fall under our jurisdiction."

"We can take care of ourselves. We don't need outsiders prying into our lives. Stomping on our rights. Passing judgment on us."

"How's that been working for you?" Granger asked with an edge of anger. "Two women have been assaulted. Nikah was murdered. Houses have been burglarized. How many more have to be victimized before you admit you can't protect them?"

"Don't patronize us," Jenna said.

Tommy jumped in, his voice heated. "What makes you think you can do a better job of protecting us than we're doing ourselves? You operate with a four-man crew. You're already spread thin, two cops working each shift, dealing with the whole of Garnerville. What are you going to do, ignore other emergencies and spend each night patrolling our village? We're already doing that. We have patrols of eight men, on foot and in vehicles, patrolling streets and yards every night. Many of us are experienced hunters, experienced trackers. We know the layout of the forest and our own properties." His voice rang with frustration. "And yet this stalker keeps slipping through our dragnet. Playing cat and mouse. Taunting us. He thinks he's smarter than we are."

"He always seems to be one step ahead of us," Tucker said. "Like he knows firsthand what we're doing."

"Like he lives here. And is privy to your strategies," Sidney said.

"Yeah," Tommy said. "Lancer fits the description and he was the only white guy living here."

"I understand your concern, Tommy, and your frustration. But I don't believe Lancer is your man."

"Because of your accusation, he's getting threats," Granger said, his eyes flashing. "Some big bruiser by the name of Fitch Drako said he'd kill him. If Lancer's harmed in any way, that will be on you. You need to tell your people to back off."

"I'll talk to Fitch," Tucker said emphatically.

"I appreciate the lengths you're taking to root this guy out," Sidney said in a calmer tone. "But your efforts haven't produced results. It's time to let us do our job."

"What could you do that we haven't?" Tucker asked.

"We could have gotten a canine unit out here. Now, with this fresh snow, his scent is covered. We had forensic specialists in Nikah's house all night. They might find fingerprints and other evidence that could ID her killer. We have national databases of sex offenders, fingerprint and DNA matches. If the Stalker is in the system, we'll find him."

"Criminals slip up," Granger added. "They make mistakes. We can catch this guy if we work together."

Sidney cast a glance around the table and saw that Jenna looked unconvinced. Elahan sat with her arms crossed, expression inscrutable. Her restless eyes had watched Sidney the entire meeting. She watched every movement, every lift of a hand. Her eyes moved but her head was still. It was unnerving.

River had been silent, avoiding her gaze. His hands were tightly intertwined, turning the tips white. He sat with his jaw clenched, and would no doubt side with the council. Sidney tried hard not to hold their prejudices against them. No telling what kinds of traumatic experiences these people encountered at the hands of law enforcement in the past.

For an uncomfortable length of time, no one spoke.

Finally, Tucker filled in the silence, speaking with quiet dignity. "Please try to understand our position, Chief Becker. We are a self-reliant people. We've had to be, just to survive. Here at Two Creeks, we are self-governing, committed to preserving all things Kalapuyan. Here in the center, we celebrate our culture, our language. We pass our heritage on to our children." He ran a large-knuckled hand over his face, and she recognized the weariness of grief in his eyes. "We're a democracy. The members of this tribal council were elected by the people of this village. We've been entrusted to manage the affairs of this community with fairness and honesty. We listen when our people speak. The majority of villagers agree that we should deal with our problems internally."

"I understand what you're saying, Tucker. And I respect your commitment to your village. This council is well equipped to handle day-to-day concerns, but Two Creeks is not a federally recognized sovereign nation. You don't have the same rights as a reservation. You don't have a legitimate police force that can deal with violent crimes. I repeat, Two Creeks falls under our jurisdiction." Sidney felt the tension mount around the table, which made her stomach tighten. "As such, we'll continue to go forward with our investigations, which means we'll be coming into the village as often as needed to talk to you and your neighbors. It would be wise to tell them to work with us. If we discover that anyone is deliberately obstructing our investigation by withholding evidence, we'll have to arrest them." She leveled a hard gaze on Tommy, a warning in her glance.

He blinked, and stared back as though realizing the seriousness of the circumstances.

No such realization dawned on Jenna. Anger still colored her cheeks. In a harsh tone, she spouted something in a native language. Elahan responded, then Tommy jumped in and the indecipherable conversation continued for a full minute, unabated.

"Want to share some of that in English?" Granger asked politely.

Jenna glared at him. "I said all we need now is for the press to catch wind of this. They'll descend upon us like hornets and harass us. Print filthy lies."

"Finding the men who committed these crimes is our main concern," Sidney said. "Not your discomfort with the press. We'll release a statement today. All the residents of Garnerville deserve to know that a murderer and rapist are at large, so they can take precautions. We'll be setting up a hot line so people can call in leads." Sidney took a slug of water, trying to hide her irritation. She did not enjoy bullying and threatening these people, or widening the divide they already felt with the rest of the community—but she would, if necessary. "Now, I would like the names of the two women who were assaulted, and the names of the couples who were burglarized while they slept."

"They don't want to come forward," Jenna said.

"They don't have a choice. They're witnesses in a murder investigation. We can talk to them here, or we can escort them to the station and talk in the interrogation room."

Jenna shot darts of venom at Sidney. "I'll talk to them first. Warn them the Gestapo is coming." Her sharp words echoed in the cavernous room.

Sidney chewed the insides of her cheeks to keep her anger in check.

Fortunately, Tucker spoke first. "That's enough, Jenna. How about extending a little courtesy to Chief Becker?" The old man leveled a stern gaze at the younger woman, scolding her in a fatherly tone. "The chief is our guest. She's only doing her job, and doing it well from what I can see. Nikah's death needs to be avenged. By whatever means necessary." His gaze swept the table, resting momentarily on each member's face. "Everyone, and I mean everyone, will cooperate with these officers. Give them whatever help they need. Is that clear?"

Jenna brooded, but she nodded.

"Clear as rain," Tommy said, looking somewhat chastened.

Tucker directed his attention to Sidney. "If anyone here tries to stonewall you, Chief Becker, let me know. I'll set them straight."

"We appreciate that," Sidney said, relief shuddering through her. Tucker, the elder statesman of the village, was backing up her department. She wasn't sure what Tucker meant when he said Nikah's death needed to be avenged by whatever means necessary, but she didn't like the sound of it. The sooner her department apprehended these assailants, the better.

"Jenna, get Chief Becker the contact info she needs," Tucker said, and added with a weary sigh, "I must excuse myself. I have other business to attend to. This meeting is adjourned. Thank you for coming, Chief Becker, Granger."

"Thank you for meeting with us." Sidney made a show of placing several business cards on the table.

Tucker took a card, shoved it into the breast pocket of his flannel shirt, and pushed himself away from the table. Chairs scraped backwards as the other members followed suit, each picking up a card.

Tucker shrugged into his jacket and pulled on his hat, then he helped Elahan into her long black quilted coat. There was tenderness and respect in the way he met her gaze and offered his arm. Her expression softened and a smile touched her lips. A silent, intimate communication passed between them. They linked arms and walked out together.

"Follow me into the office," Jenna said coldly. "I'll give you what you want."

"Granger, would you mind?" Sidney said.

"Sure thing, Chief."

"Pass the contact info for the burglary victims to Amanda and Darnell," Sidney added. "Those interviews are a priority. Tell them to get descriptions of everything stolen, and then get the list to Winnie. We'll see if anything turns up at pawnshops. Tell them to work as partners today. As long as a killer is targeting this village, none of us operates solo."

"What about the two women?"

"I'll interview them myself." In Oakland, Sidney had been trained to work with sexual assault victims. Deeply traumatized people needed to be treated with empathy and sensitivity. "I'll meet you in the lobby in five."

Granger caught up with Jenna and River, who excluded him by speaking in their native language. Their rudeness lowered Sidney's estimation of the young man considerably. Like mother, like son.

Tommy was folding the table and chairs and stacking them against the wall. Sidney waited. He glanced her way.

"Can I have a word?" Sidney asked.

"Of course." He leaned a folded chair against the wall and approached her.

"Sometime today, I'd like to talk to Tegan, if he's up to it."

"Hmmm." His brow creased. "Tegan was very moody when he left for school this morning. Not sure he'll talk to you. He'll be home at 2:30. If you want to swing by at that time, we can play it by ear."

"We'll make that work. Thanks." She paused for a moment, then asked, "Why were you scolding Cadence last night after she spoke to Selena in the bathroom?"

"Selena witnessed that, huh?" He huffed out a breath. "I was warning Cadence to keep quiet about the sexual assaults. We don't want it to get into the press. We don't want reporters casting a stigma on the men in the village. There's already a perception in this country that Native American men are drunks. Uneducated. Abusers. That's not how it is here. We're decent citizens." Tommy swallowed. "It was wrong of me. I'll apologize to her."

"Do that. Encouraging folks to obstruct our investigation is a crime."

"It won't happen again. Look, I apologize for being such a hard-ass. I think living in isolation here in the village makes it easy for some of us to make assumptions about the outside world. Especially Jenna. She had a rough life before she moved here last year. She married a white man after River left for college. He brutalized her. The white cops took his side most of the time. He never saw a day of jail time. Jenna had to escape while he was passed out drunk, with nothing but the clothes on her back."

"I'm very sorry to hear that," Sidney said, feeling a stab of pity for the woman. "That certainly explains her attitude."

"Her anger is a cover for fear. She hardly ever leaves the village. She's terrified she'll run into him."

"Where does he live?"

"Small town south of here. Sweetwater."

"That's not far." She thought for a moment. "Could he be the Stalker?"

"No. If he was, Jenna would be dead."

A chill touched Sidney's spine. She was reminded of Selena's best friend and business partner, Ann Howard, who's drunkard of a husband beat her for years. He would have killed her, if she and her son had not killed him first. Sidney pulled a pen and notebook from her pocket and handed it to Tommy. "His name and address please."

"You are thorough, Chief Becker. I'll give you that." Tommy scribbled across the page and handed the notebook back to her.

"One last thing. Tell me about Grisly Stokes."

"Grisly?" His faced pinched with dislike. "What do you want to know?"

"What does he look like?"

"Tall, lean build, ugly as sin."

"He's white?"

"Yeah, he's white as you can get. A white nationalist. A survivalist. Mistrusts the government, the law. Hates minorities, especially Indians. Doesn't like sharing these woods with us."

"Does he know these back woods as well as you do?"

"Yeah. Maybe better."

"He ever come to the village?"

"Yeah. He brings his hunting clients to the saloon on occasion. They sit there and drink and stare at us. Like we're a freak show."

Creepy. "Granger and I are going to talk to him. Thanks for your time." She turned to leave.

"Chief Becker," he said quietly.

She faced him.

"Grisly is dangerous. Be careful."

Sidney smiled, touched that he was showing concern. "Careful is my middle name."

His brown eyes softened and held hers for a moment. "If I can help in any way, let me know. I mean that sincerely."

"Appreciate it." They shared a guarded smile, then Sidney walked out to the lobby looking for Granger. She wondered if Tommy's change of heart signaled a bit of trust was growing between them. She suspected he was a smooth manipulator, a chameleon. Her trust would be hard won, as she was sure his would be.

CHAPTER NINETEEN

DRESSED IN YOGA clothes under her down jacket, Selena drove down Main Street and pulled to a stop at the only traffic light in town. She would have to rush back to her yoga studio to teach a class in forty-five minutes.

Historical downtown, with its beautiful brick and stonework buildings, looked peaceful in the morning light. Despite the ice and snow, townsfolk were milling on the sidewalks holding take-out cups of coffee, chatting, strolling in and out of shops. Stores were displaying festive winter decorations with snowflakes stenciled on windows and evergreen wreaths on doors. Life was proceeding as usual with everyone oblivious to Nikah's murder. After the press release went out to the local papers, an undercurrent of fear would creep through the county. Everyone had barely gotten back to normal since the arrest of the serial killer last month.

Through the frosted window of the newly opened Art Studio, which had previously been Moyer's Tack and Feed for fifty years, Selena saw a circle of students standing in front of easels facing the instructor, David Kane, who was Sidney's new lover. Selena was thrilled for her sister. No one here measured up to the handsome detective she left behind in California. When David, a widower, moved to town from San Francisco, sparks flew between them from the start.

It astonished Selena to see how fast her sleepy town was changing, no longer ardently blue collar with farmers and ranchers making up the majority. Boutiques and trendy cafes were replacing dusty antique stores and greasy spoons. Urbanites wanting a slower lifestyle were moving in from the cities.

The light changed to green and Selena stepped on the gas, craving a hazelnut latte. She parked in a slot and strolled into Lava Java, which was almost empty after the morning rush.

Cadence was already parked at a quiet table in the back corner with her hands wrapped around a cup of coffee. She wore a grave expression but she gave Selena a friendly wave.

Selena ordered a latte and two chocolate croissants, wove around a few tables, and handed Cadence one of the pastries.

"Hmm. Still warm. I love these," Cadence said with a sweet smile.

"Me too. My hips, not so much."

Cadence pulled her warm pastry apart to reveal the gooey chocolate interior. She took a bite, chewed, and washed it down with coffee. Her fingers barely poked out of the sleeves of her oversized red sweater, giving her an almost waif-like appearance. It astonished Selena that this was the same screeching singer that dominated the stage at the saloon last night.

"How are you doing?" Selena asked, chewing on her croissant.

"Not good. I cried most of the night. I can't believe Nikah's gone. That someone killed her. It's really scary. Like, who's next?"

Selena lost her taste for her pastry and lowered it to her plate. "I'm so sorry for what you're going through."

Cadence presented her with a perceptive stare. "You've been through this, too, haven't you? Losing someone close."

Selena nodded. "Two babies in three years. Miscarriages."

"That's rough." Cadence was quiet for a long moment. "Does it get easier?"

"Yes," Selena said softly, thinking of the upstairs nursery with the closed door that she never opened. After losing Alyssa six months into her second pregnancy, the grief was so thick she could barely breathe. There was a vacuum into which everything tumbled. A great, gaping black hole. Now, eighteen months later, the loss didn't dominate every waking hour—until something jolted a memory—the peal of a child's laughter carried on the wind...

"That's why I wanted to talk to you," Cadence said. "I knew you'd understand."

"You know something about Nikah's murder?"

"Maybe." Cadence took a deep breath and blurted her words as though needing desperately to get them out. "We've had a stalker in the village for several months. I think he's the killer."

"The police know out about the Stalker, Cadence. They found out last night."

Her eyes widened. "They know?"

"Yes, but just the bare facts. They're up at your village right now, questioning people. If you have something to add, you need to tell me."

Cadence stared into her coffee, her fingers fidgeting with her napkin.

"Do you know the women who were attacked?" Selena asked.

"Yes," she said quietly, meeting her gaze. "One is a close friend. The same age as Nikah."

"The other?"

"She wants to stay anonymous."

Selena thought she saw a flicker of terror in the young singer's eyes. "Do you want to tell me about your close friend?"

Cadence's gaze fastened on Selena and seemed to draw courage from her sympathetic expression. "It happened about a month ago. My friend lives with her parents but they were gone for the weekend. Something woke her around 3:00 in the morning. When she opened her eyes, she saw a man standing in the doorway of her bedroom. He was shadowy, but she could make out some details from the nightlight in the hall. He wore gloves and a long shirt. He was naked below his shirt. He had a knife in one hand.

The man blinded her with his flashlight and said he'd kill her if she made a sound."

A chill raced along Selena's spine. "Terrifying."

The color drained from Cadence's face. Her lips started trembling.

"Are you okay?"

She nodded. "Give me a moment."

It dawned on Selena that Cadence was speaking of her own experience. The embarrassment and shame of such a personal violation had to be abhorrent and frightening. Talking about it in the third person somehow made it easier.

"The man tied her hands behind her back and..." She paused, groping for the right words.

"And forced himself on her," Selena finished for her.

Cadence nodded. "He strangled her to the point where she almost passed out. When he finished, he told her again that if she made a sound, he'd kill her."

Selena said nothing, just listened. She was almost overwhelmed with pity for the young woman. Her own terror resurfaced for a nauseating moment as she remembered her encounter in the woods with a killer.

"The man started rummaging through her drawers and closet," Cadence continued. "She heard him in the other rooms doing the same. After a long time, there was just silence in the house. My friend managed to free herself, grab her phone, and call her mom. Her folks were two hours away at the coast, but they called Tucker and he came over right away with his wife. They untied my friend and took her to their house. She was in shock. They had to tell her what to do as though she were a child. They had her take a hot bath and scrub herself. They did a healing treatment, burned sage, and chanted to drive away evil spirits. When her parents arrived, they all spoke in another room in hushed tones. It was decided that the whole village needed to know a woman got raped, but they instructed my friend not to tell anyone she was the victim. It would come to no good."

"No one thought to call the police?"

Cadence's shoulders dropped a fraction of an inch under her baggy sweater. "We don't ever call the cops. For anything. Discrimination against Native Americans is the dirty secret no one talks about. Women in particular. We experience sexual assault more than any other ethnic group in the country. Ninety percent of the offenders are white. We rarely get justice in court."

Her head dropped until her ebony hair fell in a curtain over her face. After a long moment, she met Selena's gaze. "I can't help but wonder what would've happened if they reported the rape to the police. Maybe Nikah would still be alive."

"We don't know what would've happened," Selena said. "We don't even know if her killer is the Stalker. Try not to torture yourself with those kinds of thoughts. Let the officers do their job. I trust them. If anyone can bring justice to Nikah, and your friend, it's Chief Becker."

Cadence shuddered. "I pray that's true."

"Is there anything your friend remembers about the Stalker's appearance?"

"He was tall, with an athletic build. And he had a peculiar smell." She wrinkled her nose. "Like some kind of chemical, or building material. Kind of like what road work in the hot sun smells like."

"What about his voice?"

"He disguised it. He kept it low and hoarse."

"This is very helpful, Cadence. Can I share it with Chief Becker?"

"Yes." She stared out the window at the people treading carefully on the sidewalk. A couple walked by laughing. A mother holding the hand of a child ducked into a gift shop. "Look at them.

So carefree. So content. That used to be me. Now we all live in fear at the village."

Selena searched for words to reassure her, and hoped she wasn't delivering false hope.

"Things will return to normal. This man will be caught."

"I wish I shared your confidence." Cadence met Selena's eyes. "You probably know what people in the village are saying? That Lancer is the Stalker."

"Yes, I heard."

"I felt so sorry for him and Nikah. They heard all the gossip. They saw how people looked at them. They felt really isolated. Then came the final blow. The tribal council asked Lancer to move out of the village."

"That must have been difficult."

"Yeah, it was hard for Nikah. Her friends and neighbors thought her boyfriend was a pervert. It hurt her to see him go, but she also believed it was for the best. Lancer needed to get his drinking under control."

"He was abusive."

"That's the rumor going around. But it's not true. I would've known. Nikah would've told me. Yes, he did hit her once. But she hit him first. On the forehead with a frying pan. I think he struck out in self-defense. Lancer was a sloppy drunk, not a mean drunk."

"His car was seen at her house a while back. The next day, someone ran into her at the General Store and saw a bruise on her neck. Do you know how she got it?"

"No." She looked troubled. "But it wasn't Lancer."

"How can you be so sure?"

"I know him. Lancer is a gentle person. He and Nikah were like family. I've hugged him many times over the years. I know what his body feels like. I know how he smells. He isn't the Stalker."

Inadvertently, Cadence had given herself away. Unless she had firsthand experience of what the Stalker felt like, smelled like, how could she know he wasn't Lancer?

At once, Cadence sat back and realized her mistake. Her hand flew to her mouth and her face flamed red. "Shit."

"It's okay, Cadence," Selena said softly. "I won't repeat what you told me, except to Chief Becker. She'll inform her three officers. I know them. They'll respect your privacy."

"Thank you." Her body caved in a little and she looked weak with relief. "I'm so glad the police are coming to help. This whole situation has gone from bad to worse."

"You are a credible witness for Lancer's innocence. Why did the other woman say it was him?"

"She didn't. She described him the same way I did. She thought his eyes might be a light color, but she's wasn't sure. The certainty that he's white started with someone in the tribal council."

Surprised, Selena puzzled over this. "Who?"

She shrugged. "You'll have to ask them."

Selena sipped her coffee, thinking. "One more question, Cadence. It's possible Nikah was seeing someone. Do you have any idea who that might be?"

"You mean romantically?"

"Yes."

"Funny you should ask that. She'd been acting secretive lately. That may be what she wanted to talk to me about the night she died. I may know who it is." Her brow creased and fear flickered across her face. "But I can't say."

"It's important that the police talk to him. He may have information that could help find her killer. No one will know his name came from you."

She hesitated, and then said in a low voice, as though confessing a sin, "Tommy Chetwoot."

"Tommy?" Selena raised her brows. "What makes you think that?"

"She was dodgy when I brought him up. Always changing the subject. Driving by her house, sometimes I'd see him coming or going. Or she'd mentioned he was stopping by to pick something up, or drop something off, or to have a cup of coffee. Pretty cozy, if you ask me."

"Hmmm. He's at least twenty years older."

"Yeah, but he's really good-looking. And smart. And he has money."

"Money? He's a high school teacher and herbalist. Not exactly an oil executive."

"He chooses to live humble. His family is loaded."

"Elahan has money?"

"Yes. Through her son, Chac. Casino money. He's part owner. Look, please don't mention that this information came from me. They have a lot of power in the village. They can make my life difficult."

"It never came from you," Selena assured her.

Cadence drained her cup and her beautiful dark eyes met Selena's. "I want to thank you for listening, and not judging me. I'm glad I remained anonymous. There are rumors going around the village. Finger-pointing. It seems everyone's blaming the victims. Some say the victims must have enticed the Stalker in some way."

"That's cruel, and ignorant. It's not your fault you were attacked. The man who did this is a violent criminal. A sociopath." Selena toned down her indignation and gently squeezed the young woman's hand. "You're an innocent victim. You have nothing to be ashamed of."

Tears welled in Cadence's eyes. "I feel dirty. I can't get the smell of him out of my head. I can't forget what he did. I wonder if he's out there, watching me."

Selena was afraid for her. Cadence had a legitimate fear. The Stalker obviously had been watching her. How else would he have known she was home alone the night she was attacked? "I think you should take precautions. Keep someone with you at all times until this man is caught."

Cadence chewed her lip and looked frightened. She nodded.

"I also recommend you talk to someone about what happened to you. A professional. I have the name of a grief counselor. I'm in her group. She's really helped me."

"I don't know..."

Selena pulled a card from her purse and placed it on the table. "Come once and see how you like it. You don't have to say anything. Just observe." Selena gave her a warm smile. "I'll be there. You can sit with me."

Cadence shoved the card into her purse, put on a brave face, and yanked on her parka. "I better get going. I'm late for work."

CHAPTER TWENTY

A WOLF'S HIGH-PITCHED howls of distress reached Moolock through the quiet of the snowy morning from a quarter-mile away. He pressed his heels into the gelding's side and Shantie instinctively headed toward the yelps at a quick gait. As they neared the location, shrouded by evergreens, he heard unnatural, frenzied thrashing in the brush. A sharp tinge of anger tightened his chest. He slipped off Shantie's back, grabbed his bolt cutters and catch pole and steeled himself for what he might see as he advanced through the snow. In the past, he'd found many trapped animals too late. The pitiable creatures died slow deaths, suffering from dehydration, blood loss, hypothermia, starvation. Some became so desperate to escape they broke teeth trying to chew or twist off their own limbs.

To prevent the wolf from panicking further, Moolock murmured in canine language, offering the consoling sounds a mother made to her pups. The thrashing and frantic yipping stopped abruptly. Moolock separated the boughs of two pine trees and stepped quietly into the small clearing. A young male wolf stood panting, exhausted, watching his every move with large amber eyes. His head was lowered, ears straight up, one hind leg stretched straight out behind him, caught in the jaws of the trap. No blood stained the snow, but excessive crisscrossing paw prints indicated the animal had been trying to free itself for some hours. The wolf was magnificent, with the soft, thick coat prized by the fur industry. His fur was light gray, the outer hairs tipped with black. The backs of his ears were red, his muzzle gold, and his throat and belly white. For a moment Moolock imagined his hide through the eyes of the trapper who had buried the cruel device, fashioned into a coat covering a rich man's body.

As he approached, Moolock's quiet movements and soft tones subdued the wolf. With a motion so fast it was a blur, Moolock lowered the loop at the end of his pole over the animal's head, tightened it around its neck and pressed its head to the ground while reaching down and releasing the springs on the trap. He then eased the loop from its neck. The animal locked eyes with his for a long moment and Moolock had the sensation of staring into its soul, into the heart of God. The creature leapt to its feet and bounded off into the brush with an exuberant flurry of snow.

For a moment Moolock shared its exhilaration, then his eyes focused on the trap and anger flooded his system. As he suspected, the registration numbers had been filed off, as were most of the traps he found these days. Wolves were protected in Oregon. But that didn't stop a few heartless bastards from slaughtering them, and other animals, with impunity, hidden from the eyes of the law in the vast reaches of the backcountry. Moolock had covered seven square miles by horseback in the last two days, confiscating a dozen illegal traps and releasing two coyotes and a red fox. He destroyed four body snares, designed to kill an animal by strangulation or by crushing its vital organs.

Moolock snapped through the chain with his bolt cutter and carried the trap back to Shantie, where he added it to the other confiscated traps in his canvas pack. Some inexplicable warning murmured in a distant region of his mind before his ears picked up the snick of metal on metal, the unmistakable sound of a clip snapping into the magazine of a rifle. Moolock dove for the ground as high velocity rounds tore holes into the trunks of nearby trees. The air inside the clearing filled with smoke and bits of pulverized wood. The sound was deafening. Shantie shrieked and took off at a gallop.

When caught in a firefight in Afghanistan, Moolock was often scared shitless, but military training was ingrained and he performed his duty relying on muscle memory, as he did now. Lying flat in the snow, he pulled his Sig Sauer P320 handgun from its leg holster and aimed in the direction of the shots. Through the veil of snow and swirling debris, he focused on a copse of cedars thirty feet away. He fired, emptying his magazine. Pieces of branches exploded into the air.

Moolock clipped in another magazine and waited until the wisps of smoke cleared and the last piece of debris drifted to the ground. Nothing moved. He lay immobile, every muscle tense, gripping his weapon until the pounding of his heart and the tingling in his hands subsided. The shooter had fled, was injured, or dead.

Moolock sprang to his feet. In a crouch, he ducked behind the cover of trees and made a roundabout path to the place where the shooter had been rooted. From there he cast his gaze to the spot where he and Shantie had stood. Clear shot. Moolock had been lucky. Fast action saved his life. He took the near-death warning to heart. This trapper, who was engaging in illegal activities, was tired of Moolock interfering in his business. Now he wanted him dead.

With tension thrumming through his system, Moolock followed the trapper's boot prints into the woods and immediately spotted a small red stain in the snow. Then the prints spread farther apart. The man was running, dripping blood. He'd caught one of Moolock's bullets. Not enough blood loss to be life threatening, but certainly bad enough to need immediate attention. The boot prints led to the tracks of a horse, which had been mounted and spurred into a quick gait. After another quarter mile the tracks disappeared into White Tail Creek.

Moolock retraced his steps back to the clearing, thinking about the coldblooded trapper who had no qualms about killing. He had seen this trapper's boot prints in the forest many times before, but only once had they crossed paths in real time. Several months back in the dry heat of summer, this man had silently watched him teach Nikah and Tegan how to dismantle a trap and release a raccoon. They found the trapper's prints shortly thereafter. The man had fled on this same horse. His presence had raised an alarm. Moolock warned Nikah never to go out into the backcountry alone. She agreed. But two weeks ago, she confessed she had been going out on her own all along, dismantling traps and releasing animals. A trapper tracked her down and she barely got away in her car. The man later surprised her in a dark parking lot in town and viciously threatened her. Moolock saw she was frightened, though she tried to hide it. He was frightened for her. Nikah was strong-willed, and he knew that regardless of his stern warnings, she would continue to do what she passionately believed in.

Now Nikah was dead. Slaughtered, like these animals. A chill touched his spine. Was this trapper her killer? Moolock wasn't worried for himself, but for Tegan. The boy was in imminent danger. Distracted by his dark emotions, Moolock had missed the warning signs and allowed this man to creep up on him, watch him, hold his life in his hands.

The emotion that welled inside Moolock surprised him. It wasn't bitterness or guilt. It wasn't even sorrow. It was anger, and it coursed through him like venom. Not since Afghanistan had he felt emotions so intense. Memories of soldiers blown to pieces by IEDs flickered in his mind. With effort, he shut them down.

Moolock could not put off what needed to be done. This man had to be rooted out, and killed, if necessary. He whistled and Shantie sauntered back into the clearing.

CHAPTER TWENTY-ONE

SELENA WENT OUT to her Jeep and called her sister. "Where are you?"

"We just got out of a meeting with the Tribal Council. I'm waiting for Granger. What's up?"

"I just had coffee with Cadence."

"How'd it go?"

"Ready for a bomb? She was the first rape victim."

"Holy Hell," Sidney said. "Hold on, I'm going out to my car so we can talk in private."

Selena heard her sister crunching through snow, then a car door slammed and Sidney got back on the line. "Brief me. Speak slowly. I'm recording this. Go ahead."

Selena recited their entire conversation as close to verbatim as she could remember, then added, "Tommy Chetwoot is a piece of work."

"Yeah, he is. Full of surprises and glaring omissions."

"It may have been a harmless friendship," Selena said, "But if he was interested in Nikah, that would have given him good reason to contrive a story about Lancer to get him out of the village."

"True. Now we learn the Stalker may not even be white."

"Tommy may be the council member who directed everyone to look in that direction. Pointing the finger at Lancer."

"Possible. But there's another council member too, a woman, who may have started that rumor. She's very hostile toward white people. White men in particular."

Selena chewed this over, unwilling to release Tommy from her train of thoughts. "Tommy could be Nikah's killer. Maybe she rejected him. Maybe she was going back to her boyfriend. Dad used to say turn over every rock."

"He did." Sidney chuckled. "You're good, Selena. Lancer did say they were getting back together. I'll dig around a little more. See if Tommy had romantic intentions. See if he has an alibi for the night Nikah was murdered. Jealousy is a powerful motive."

Selena glanced at the sky. Light snow was feathering the windshield. "Well, I'm signing off. Got some serious business to attend to."

"Yoga class?"

"Yep. My students will be lining up, eager to get a calming dose of mindfulness. After yesterday, I need it, too. Big time."

"I hear you. Send some my way."

"Namaste, Sis."

With another chuckle, Sidney disconnected.

CHAPTER TWENTY-TWO

GRANGER TREKKED OUT of the Cultural Center and hopped into the Yukon, his notebook gripped in one hand. "Got the info, Chief."

"Get it to Amanda, pronto," Sidney said.

Granger got on his cell phone. Radio traffic could be listened to by scanner. Sensitive information was always relayed by phone.

While Granger spoke to Amanda on speaker, Sidney pulled out of the lot and followed the curve of the lake, leaving the village behind.

"Make a list of every item that was stolen," Granger said, "Then get the list to Winnie and tell her to send it to all the local pawn shops."

"Listen," Sidney added. "The Stalker may not be white. And he has a peculiar smell. A chemical, or building material."

"Yech. That opens up a whole new suspect list."

When they disconnected, Sidney said to Granger, "Selena gave me the name of one of the rape victims. Cadence. Who's the other?"

He flipped a page on his notebook. "Tammy Muehler. Forty-five. Husband was out of town. That's all Jenna would give me."

"Hmmm. A woman home alone. Same as Cadence. How did the Stalker know those details?"

"He must hang out where people congregate and talk. The saloon, the general store, the cultural center." He cleared his throat. "Gotta be someone who blends in. I doubt Grisly blends in."

"A tall, white man? He'd stand out like a mongrel at a poodle show. Tommy said he drinks at the saloon sometimes."

"That's more feasible. He could've seen Cadence perform. Maybe she sparked his interest."

"People shoot off their mouths when they drink. He may have overheard something about her being home alone. Run a background on him."

Granger's fingers got busy tapping the keyboard.

Sidney focused on the road. The sky had turned cast iron gray and light snow was falling. She turned the wipers on low and they squeaked across the windshield. The forest was denser on the east side of the lake and the land rose in elevation, blocking the view of Two Creeks Village on the opposite shore. The snow was deeper and unplowed driveways were few and far between. Mostly summer cabins out here.

"Grisly's got a record," Granger said. "Drunk and disorderly. A domestic four years ago. Charges were dropped. Sexual assault three years ago. No conviction. Since then, he's been clean. A couple traffic violations." He glanced up from the computer and met her gaze. "History of violence against women. But nothing stuck."

"There's always more going on than what crops up in a courtroom. We need to get in his face about the domestic and the assault."

A couple more miles of forest flew by with no sign of human habitation. Grisly's domain was isolated, far from the amenities of civilization. She slowed to a crawl when she caught sight of a newly plowed driveway. The name Stokes and his address were crudely painted on a mailbox. She made a hard left onto the narrow driveway and followed it around a bend, the tires skidding on ice.

The driveway opened to a clearing. A good-sized barn stood on the left and a sturdy log cabin was off to the right, roofs covered by thick mantles of snow.

She and Granger exited the cab and advanced toward the cabin. The wind blew frost from the trees, making her eyes tear a little.

Pow-WHOP.

A sharp crack exploded, followed by a guttural boom that rolled over the terrain. A bullet shot from a high-powered rifle struck a tree fifteen yards away, making a blunt and solid airborne grunt.

The shooter had aimed to miss. Still, Sidney's heart beat like a war drum. Granger's sharp intake of breath was followed by an angry curse. Her eyes darted toward the origin of the shot. A man was silhouetted in the entrance of the barn.

"You're trespassing," his deep voice bellowed. "What do you want?" The rifle was now pointed at the ground.

Sidney saw that the police emblem on her vehicle door was frosted over. Huddled in their thick jackets and hats with earflaps, she and Granger didn't look like cops. "I'm Police Chief Becker," she yelled back. "This is Officer Wyatt. You Grisly Stokes?"

"Yeah."

"We need to ask you some questions."

"Got a warrant?"

"Do we need one?" Sidney asked. "You doing something illegal on the premises?"

In answer, Stokes spat on the ground, leaned his rifle against the doorframe, and approached through the softly falling snow. He was decked out in a matching camouflage jacket and pants and thick-soled hunting boots. He was tall with limp blond hair and pale eyes deeply set in a bony face. A beak-like nose protruded from a scruffy beard and his cheeks were flushed beet red from the cold. A real charmer.

Stokes stopped about five feet away and stared long and hard at Granger. His cold, unblinking gaze turned to Sidney, moving from the top of her head to her feet—a tactic she was familiar with from years of encounters with hardened criminals who tried, and failed, to intimidate her. Unfazed, Sidney stared back with the kind of scrutiny that made criminals feel uncomfortable.

Grisly blinked first. "So, what do you want?"

"There's been a murder in Two Creeks Village," she said. "We're questioning everyone in the vicinity. See if anyone noticed anything."

"What night was she murdered?"

"How'd you know it was a woman?" Granger asked. "How'd you know it happened at night?"

He shoved his hands deep into his jacket pockets. "Just a hunch."

"Psychic," Granger said with sarcasm.

"Any more psychic hunches you care to share?" she asked, looking for any nuance in his expression.

His face remained immobile, no hint of emotion. "Probably a domestic. Those wigwams are known to beat the crap out of their women."

"How do you know this?" Sidney asked. "You spend a lot of time over there?"

"Just stop in for a beer now and then. Closest bar around." His gaze traveled from her to Granger and back again. "So, who's dead?"

"Nikah Tamanos."

His face changed. A flicker of recognition quickly morphed into a mask of stone. "Don't know her."

"We heard you do," Granger said. "You had a beef with her."

"Don't know what you're talking about."

Their breath puffed out like smoke signals. Flakes were gathering on their hats and shoulders, and turning Stokes's beard to white. Granger yanked on his fur-lined gloves. Sidney noticed the biting cold numbing her own fingers, but her gloves were in the Yukon. She slid her hands into her pockets. "What do you do for a living, Grisly?"

He shrugged. "Take folks out to hunt. Some trapping. Taxidermy."

"We heard Nikah released a couple of your trapped animals. That right?"

"A couple? Bloody hell. She made it her mission to screw me. She not only released my animals, she destroyed my traps. I found five or six traps a month that had been messed with."

"How'd you know it was her?"

"I came across one of my snares that had just been set off. I tracked her, and caught up to her as she reached her car, parked on a fire road. I gave her hell. She locked herself in her car and took off. Never said a word. No apology. Nothing. Just that look…"

"What look?"

"A look that said fuck off."

"That must have made you mad," Granger said, his face reddening with cold.

"Hell yeah, it made me mad."

"You threaten her?"

Stokes sawed his jaw back and forth. Looked away.

"You threaten to skin her like a deer, Grisly?" Sidney asked.

He swallowed, gulped in a deep breath and puffed out a cloud of vapor. "I said that just to scare her. I didn't mean nothing by it. I lost my temper. Who wouldn't? She was messing with my livelihood." He paused, said emphatically, "I didn't kill her."

"Where were you Friday night?" Sidney asked, feeling the cold penetrate her pants.

"Here. All night."

"Can you prove that?"

He shrugged. "No. I live alone."

"Your wife…?"

"She ran off a couple years back." His tone was expressionless but something cold moved in his eyes.

"We might want to talk to her."

"Good luck. She disappeared."

Sidney and Granger exchanged a glance. That sounded ominous. "What's her name?"

Stokes's expression went through several transformations. "Dolores. Dolores Stokes."

"You mind if we take a quick look at your operation?"

"Yeah. I mind." He shot Sidney a long, chilling look. "It ain't none of your business."

"I'm investigating a murder. You threatened the victim," Sidney said forcefully. "You make me come back with a warrant, we're gonna tear your house and barn apart."

"You fucking people just can't leave me alone, can you?" His jaw clenched tight and she saw he was struggling to compose himself. After a long moment he said in a calmer voice. "All my licenses are up to date. I'm totally legit."

"Then you won't mind us taking a look around. What's in the barn?"

"Shit." The tendons in his neck strained as he turned in the opposite direction and began walking to the structure.

They followed.

Stokes opened a squeaky door and the stench of decay hit her like a smack in the face. Inside the dark cavernous space, the smell was almost overwhelming. There were antlers and pelts and animal heads everywhere—on the floor, hanging on the walls, strewn over the rails of empty stalls. She recognized bear, coyote, elk, fox, stag, and smaller animals—raccoon, woodchuck, even squirrel and rabbit. Looked like a lifetime of trophies. A slaughterhouse.

Sickened, Sidney felt a tightening at the back of her neck. Could this much slaughter be legal? She pulled out her phone and snapped a few pictures, then turned to Grisly. "Want to walk me through the tanning process, starting with a dead animal?"

"It's all natural. Organic." He exhaled a tense breath and shoved his hands into his pockets. "First, I peel off the animal's skin to make a pelt."

"A pelt is the animal's skin with the fur still attached?" she asked.

"Correct. Then I dress it. To stabilize it."

"To keep it from rotting," Granger explained with a sour expression.

"What chemicals do you use?" Sidney asked.

"Formaldehyde and chromium."

She whistled. "Toxic."

"I wear a mask."

"Anything else?"

He shrugged, a hard, unflinching look in his eyes. "Can't tell you off the top of my head. The chemicals come pre-mixed."

"Let me help him out, Chief." Granger got on his phone, typed in something, then he scrolled through a website. "Got it right here." He frowned at the screen, and read: "The process of tanning, dying, and shearing relies heavily on chemicals that include aluminum, ammonia, chlorine, chlorobenzene, copper, ethylene glycol, lead, methanol, naphthalene, sulfuric acid, toluene and zinc." He looked up from his screen. "Which are all listed as carcinogens. Toxic to humans."

"So much for natural and organic," Sidney said with a shiver of revulsion. "Too bad all these toxins aren't listed on the label of each garment. People might think twice about what they're hanging on their bodies."

"Look, this is all legal. Don't like it, take it up with your congressman."

The double doors in the back were opened to the outside and a flurry of movement caught Sidney's eye. She and Granger crossed the barn and stepped outside, craving clean air. Under an overhang, a deer and a fox hung upside down. She couldn't take her eyes off the amount of blood, steaming, pooling under the carcasses. Blood sprayed out across the snow, as red as wine. A darker shade of red stained the wall, which looked like it was regularly hosed off, but the blood had permanently saturated the wood. Half buried in the stained snow was a bobcat, ice forming in its shaggy fur. Crows were hovering over it, stealing an occasional peck at its corpse.

"Christ." Granger's face reflected Sidney's disgust.

Stokes advanced toward the crows, waving and cursing. He grabbed the bobcat by a hind leg and pulled it under the overhang, bumping into the hanging fox. He pushed it out of the way and smeared blood over his hand. He crouched to clean his fingers in the snow.

Sidney's gut churned. Why this inhumane treatment was legal, she could not conceive. Why people needed to adorn themselves in fur at the expense of an animal's life, she could not conceive. She took a few more pictures. "I've seen enough," she said, disgusted. "Let's get out of here."

She and Granger cut a path back through the barn and out into the clearing, gulping fresh air, with Stokes trailing behind. Their bodies formed a triangle, and Sidney inhaled his pungent odor of sweat and tanning chemicals. She backed off a step. She found the man vile and repugnant. "That's a lot of dead animals," she said scornfully.

He scowled. "All legal. Some go way back. Years. Others belong to my customers. I condition their pelts. Mount their heads. All legal. You can check."

"I plan on it."

Stokes's scowl deepened. "The game warden stops by here every few weeks. Name's Mead. Harper Mead."

Granger scribbled in his notepad.

"Now if you're done, leave. As you can see, I have work to do."

"Just a few more questions," Sidney said. "You mentioned abuse takes place at the village. Abuse against women is something you know a lot about. We've seen your record. You beat your wife, Grisly. That why Dolores left?"

The question caught him by surprise. He flinched. "She...she dropped the charges."

"How long were you married?"

"Three years."

Granger scribbled.

"She got family here?"

"Sister in town."

"Name?"

"Eliza Mitchell."

"Address?"

"Elm Street." His eyes narrowed almost into slits. "Look, don't believe a thing that bitch tells you. She never liked me."

I wonder why, Sidney thought. "Tell us about the woman you sexually assaulted."

"Didn't assault nobody. I was never convicted."

"Her name?" Granger held his pen poised over his pad.

"What are you digging up all this old shit for? I've had no arrests for years. This is harassment."

"Her name?" Granger repeated, more forcefully.

"Fuck. Tammy Muehler."

A chill made Sidney's scalp prickle. Her eyes widened and locked on Granger's. Tammy Muehler was the Stalker's second victim. "She's Native American."

"You think I don't know that?"

"You seem to have a problem with the people at Two Creeks. Why is that?"

He shrugged. "They ain't my people. If they left me alone, I'd leave them alone."

"What do you mean by that? You retaliating for your traps being messed with?"

"No. I don't have nothing to do with those people. Just drive through. Stop in at the General Store and saloon, is all."

"How'd you and Tammy hook up?"

"Look, is this really necessary? It happened years ago."

"Humor me."

Frowning deeply, he kicked at a chunk of ice with his boot. "Hell. I stopped by the saloon one night. Just wanted to unwind. Grab a couple cold ones, and be on my way. This woman, Tammy Muehler, slithered over and sat next to me at the bar. Started sucking down whiskey like there was no tomorrow. I ignored her. She was a sloppy, loudmouthed drunk, singing with the band, laughing too loud, sliding off her fucking stool. I paid my tab and got up to leave and she asked for a ride home. I didn't want nothing to do with her. I don't hang with wigwams. Then I thought, hell, why not? I'll do my fucking civic duty. Make sure she gets home safe. When I got to her place, she could barely get outta the truck. I had to half drag her to the door." He wiped his mouth with the back of his hand, compressed his lips, and studied his boots for a moment.

Probably considering how to present the rest of his story in a noble light, Sidney thought.

Stokes looked up with a fixed expression of indignation and continued. "Later, the cops showed up at my place and arrested me. She said I raped her."

"Did you, Grisly? Did you take advantage of an inebriated woman?"

"Hell no. I dumped her off and left. I swear. A football team could have come over and raped her. She was too drunk to know the difference."

"Only she wasn't, was she? She had enough wherewithal to call the cops the minute you left."

"She's a lying bitch," he said with such vehemence, spittle flew, and his shrill voice sliced like an ax blade through the quiet of the clearing. It was a long moment before he spoke again, his anger tamped down. "Okay. We had sex. But she came on to me. She wanted it. I just did her a favor. Long story short, the charges were dropped. That was that."

Sidney's shoulders tensed. Anger simmered in her gut. She had no doubt Grisly raped Tammy. She would have liked nothing better than to cuff him and take him in, let him rot in a cell, but she had no proof. No confession. She needed to dig up the old report, scour it, see if a rape kit had been conducted, see if any small thing had been missed. In many instances, it was some minute detail that broke a case. Her phone vibrated against her thigh, interrupting her concentration. It was Winnie. Sidney walked a few feet away and answered quietly, "Hey, what's up?"

"The warrant for the safety deposit box is here in my hot little hands," Winnie said. "Waiting for you."

Sidney felt a little thrill of anticipation. Hopefully that deposit box would hold some answers. "Great. We're heading back soon." Sidney disconnected, and turned to Grisly. "We're not done here. Don't even think about leaving town. We'll have more questions for you."

With a look that explicitly radiated hatred, he turned his back and started trekking to the barn.

Only too happy to separate from his foul company, Sidney nodded toward the Yukon. "Let's roll."

CHAPTER TWENTY-THREE

SIDNEY AND GRANGER strapped themselves into their seats. She pulled out of Grisly's driveway, her fingers stinging with cold on the steering wheel.

"Man, what a freaking' sleaze ball," Granger said. "He makes me want to take a shower."

"Yep. One pretty nasty character."

"Don't know how he can stand his own body odor. And that barn. I was trying not to gag."

She wrinkled her nose, remembering. "A hell hole. Grisly's a predator in every sense of the word."

"When it comes to the Stalker, he fits the bill. He's an experienced hunter who knows these woods. He doesn't have an alibi for the night Nikah was killed. He's tall and lean. He has a history with two of the victims."

"He clearly hates women." Her hands tightened on the wheel. "I have no doubt he raped Tammy. It's not a stretch to imagine he'd go back and do it again."

"Making her pay for calling him out. A lot of pieces fitting together."

"We have nothing that warrants an arrest. Maybe Tammy can give us something. Contact her. Ask when we can talk to her."

Granger dialed. After respectfully identifying himself, he asked Tammy if they could swing by. A long pause. "Tammy? You there?" Another pause. "Great. Thanks." He disconnected.

"She works in town at the Thunderhead Gift Shop. Told us to drop by any time, though she wasn't happy about it."

"Can't blame her. Not an easy thing to talk about." Sidney glanced at him. "Winnie's got the warrant for the safety deposit box. The gift store's a couple blocks down from the bank. We'll hit both when we get back to town."

"Can't wait to see what's in that box," he said with a note of excitement.

"You and me both." The squeak of the wipers directed Sidney's attention back to the outside world. The snow had let up and patches of blue sky broke through the haze of clouds. As they approached the outskirts of Two Creeks Village, her stomach rumbled loudly, broadcasting her need for food.

"You on a starvation diet, Chief?"

"Not intentionally." When entrenched in a case, Sidney often pushed through the entire day without eating. Not healthy. "You hungry?"

"You gotta ask?"

"You have a black hole where your stomach should be," she chuckled. "Is there any place in the village to eat?"

"They make sandwiches at the general store."

"Ham and Swiss sounds pretty good right now."

"I'm craving roast beef with horseradish and chili sauce on rye. Badger, the owner, slow-roasts the beef on his outdoor grill. It's super tender."

She grinned. "Call ahead. Have two of those babies ready to go."

"Yes, ma'am." Granger returned her grin and got on the phone.

***

The general store looked like it was straight out of an old western film: a red, wood-planked structure with a gable roof and a long, sloping porch that creaked when they crossed it. Bells jingled on the door as they entered and

Sidney felt like she was stepping back in time. On the right was an old-fashioned deli area with an antique counter and a rounded glass case showcasing sandwiches, salads, and desserts. Behind the counter, shelves displayed Native American crafts and antique farm kitchen accessories. Shelves laden with goods ran the length of the scarred floorboards and refrigerated units took up the back wall. A young man waited at the counter and an older couple sat at one of the worn wooden tables. All heads turned as they shuffled in.

"Hey Granger," the seated man said, friendly.

"Hey Pokie."

The smell of rich coffee permeated the air and drew Sidney's attention to the counter. She got in line behind the young man while Granger exchanged pleasantries with the couple, then he joined her.

Behind the counter, a heavyset man with a single black braid down his back glanced over his shoulder from an espresso machine and shot them a smile. He had a square, pleasant face with blunt features and sparkling dark eyes. "Hey Granger. Be right with you." The machine stopped hissing. He placed a cup crowned with steamed milk on the counter, took the young man's money, and turned to Sidney and Granger.

Granger introduced him as Badger Woods.

"Pleasure to meet you, Chief Becker."

"Hey Badger," she said. "Nice shop."

"Thanks. Got your sandwiches ready. Just need to wrap 'em up."

The friendliness of the villagers encouraged Sidney to seize the moment. By now everyone in the village knew they were conducting investigations. Maybe these folks could be coaxed into talking. "On second thought, Badger, we'll eat here. Give me a mocha latte, too. Large." The desserts made Sidney's mouth water. "And box up a piece of that chocolate ganache cake."

"You got it."

Granger ordered a no-frills coffee, black.

"Have a seat," Badger said. "I'll bring your order over."

The young man, in his early twenties, dressed in faded jeans and a plaid lumberjack shirt, hovered nearby, holding his cup until they seated themselves at a table, then he ambled over. She and Granger looked up at him. Long hair, glossy and deep black, hung loose over his shoulders and his thin face was still and solemn. His chocolate-colored eyes locked onto Sidney's with an intensity she found both disturbing and curious.

"Something I can do for you?" she asked.

"I need to tell you something."

Granger kicked out their extra chair with his foot. "Have a seat."

The man sank into the chair and carefully placed his cup on the table. A tortured look crossed his face. He cleared his throat but said nothing.

"What's your name?" Sidney asked. Small talk generally loosened a person's tongue.

"Canim. Canim Silvermoon."

"You live here?"

He nodded. "Born and raised."

"You work? Go to school?"

"I help my dad at the shop. Silvermoon Welding."

"I know your dad," Granger said. "Max. Good man."

Canim's face relaxed and he gave a hint of smile.

"You look about Nikah's age," Sidney said gently, venturing into the delicate subject of her death.

"I've known her all my life. We were friends and classmates." He swallowed and continued in a low, conspiratorial tone. "I saw something you might need to know."

"What's that?" Sidney's senses were tuned on high.

"A BMW was parked at her house Friday night."

Sidney felt an adrenalin spike. "What time was this?"

"Nine-thirty. I was coming back from the saloon. Walked by her house." He released a long breath. "It's not the only time it was parked there. I saw it once before. Early in the morning when I was leaving for work."

"You know who it belongs to?"

He shook his head. "Doesn't belong to anyone in the village."

"You know the make, model, color?"

"Black, 320i, fairly new. Maybe a couple years old."

Granger whipped out his notebook and scribbled.

They were interrupted as Badger placed their sandwiches and drinks on the table. Though the food looked and smelled incredible, they ignored their lunches, and the sudden silence at the table communicated their need for privacy. Badger walked away.

"Did you see the license plate?" Sidney continued.

"No, it was too far away. Mostly hidden by trees. The only reason I saw it, I sometimes cut through a corner of Nikah's property to get home. A shortcut. I live with my parents just down the road from her house."

"Anything else you can tell us?" Sidney asked. "Did you see the owner? Anyone coming or going from her house?"

"No. Never."

"Can I get your contact info, in case I need to reach you again?"

"Sure." He fished his wallet from his rear pocket, pulled out a card and jotted down a number on the back, then handed it to her. "That's our business number and my cell phone number."

Sidney slipped the card into her breast pocket for safekeeping. "You've been very helpful, Canim. We appreciate you coming forward."

"I want Nikah's killer caught. She was a beautiful person. She didn't..." he choked, and gulped in a deep breath. "She didn't deserve to die. I gotta get to work." Canim pushed himself up from his chair, nodded with moist eyes, and left the store.

"Wow," Sidney said. "That's a bombshell."

Granger took a big bite out of his sandwich and said out of the corner of his mouth, "Sounds like Nikah did have a lover."

"Yeah, if it was a man who owned that car. Whoever it was, her visitor was probably the last person to see her alive." Sidney picked up her sandwich and was about to take a bite when Badger came back to the table to drop off her cake in a take-out box. "You see anyone driving a black BMW around here, Badger?" she asked.

"Can't say that I have. That's a little rich and impractical for this area."

"BMW, you say?" The female voice came from the table next to them. Sidney turned to the elderly couple, focusing on the woman whose gray braids fell out of a fuzzy, multi-colored knit cap. She was sixtyish, carrying at least a hundred pounds of extra weight, and her well-padded face melted into a sizable double chin.

"Yes, ma'am," Sidney said. "Black. A newer model."

"I'm Shasta. This is my husband, Pokie."

The couple looked like bookends. Pokie was equally padded and had matching gray braids that fell from a fuzzy knit cap, only his was navy blue. They both wore black turtleneck sweaters and jeans. She wondered if their underwear matched.

Shasta's hazel eyes sparkled with curiosity and she leaned forward in her seat. "This have to do with Nikah?"

"Yes, ma'am."

"Jenna Menowa's son drives a BMW."

Sidney glanced at Granger, who was busy packing his mouth with food. His eyes widened.

"River Menowa," Sidney thought out loud, picturing the handsome young entrepreneur with the dazzling smile and confident manner. A ladies' man. It was completely feasible that if Nikah was going to take a lover, it would be River. If so, it was puzzling that at the tribal meeting he showed no indication of knowing Nikah, nor did he display a hint of grief. The young man was either a skilled actor, a sociopath, or he wasn't the owner of the BMW.

"River's BMW is a dark color," Shasta was saying. "Not sure if it's black. He doesn't live here. Comes to visit every so often." She nodded at her husband. "Sam and I helped him out the other day."

"That fancy car of his got stuck in the snow," Pokie said, wiping pastry crumbs off his rounded belly. "He was trying to put on chains. Didn't know what the heck he was doing. I put them on for him."

"He's a nice enough young fella," Shasta said. "A bit full of himself. He tried to pay Pokie."

"Whipped out a hundred-dollar bill from his wallet. There were plenty more in there, too." Pokie snorted. "Didn't seem to understand that in this village, neighbors help neighbors. I didn't do it to get paid."

"You ever see him with anyone from the village besides his mom?"

They glanced at each other, thinking. Shasta said, "Well, he came to the winter celebration at the Cultural Center a couple weeks back. He stands out, he does, in his nice city clothes and city talk and that rich man's look. Seems more white than Indian."

"I saw him there, too," Badger weighed in. "When the ceremony was over, several young ladies were fluttering around him like butterflies."

"He attracts the girls, he does," Shasta said.

"Do you remember who the girls were?"

"Sure," Badger said. "Cadence, Shea, and Nikah."

Bingo.

"Did he leave with any of them?"

"All of them. They were headed over to the saloon."

"Ever see them together again?"

They shook their heads.

Granger stopped chewing for a moment, one cheek packed as full as a chipmunk's. "He ever come in here, Badger?"

"Yeah. A few times. Picked up coffee and pastries in the morning. A bottle of wine and steaks one night."

A romantic dinner for two? "Which night?" Sidney asked.

"Hmmm. I can tell you in a minute." He went behind the counter and tapped some keys on his laptop. "I don't carry much wine. He bought the Pinot Noir Wednesday night at 7:00 p.m."

Granger scribbled, then looked up and thanked him.

"Any of you familiar with Grisly Stokes?" Sidney asked.

She heard a sharp intake of breath from Pokie. Shasta pursed her lips as though she'd just bitten down on a lemon, and Badger's face tightened with animosity. She'd hit a nerve. All three started talking at once, their tones ranging from irritation to fury.

"Okay, one at a time. Badger, you first."

Badger stood with his hands on his hips. "He comes in about once a week. Mostly to buy beer. He's…" Badger paused, his eyes scanning the ceiling while he groped for words. "There's no nice way to put this. He's a prick."

"Understatement," Pokie said.

"Go on, Badger," Sidney persuaded.

"No manners. He walks in here like he's god or something. Never says please or thank you. Never smiles or makes small talk, but he stares down his nose at us, like we smell or something."

"He's the one that smells," Pokie said.

"Stinks, he does," Shasta added. She visibly shivered. "He always has dead animals in the back of his truck. Blood dripping off the tailgate, smeared on his clothes. He's a walking butcher. Everyone hates him."

"We hunt to put food on the table," Badger said. "We use every scrap of an animal. Grisly hunts for sport. To put a new trophy on his wall."

"Did he have a beef with Nikah?" Granger asked. "Apparently, she messed with his traps."

Pokie snorted a humorless laugh. "She wasn't the only one. Just about everyone here messed with his traps, whenever we found one. A few trappers out there are poaching, big time. Filing off registration numbers. We know he's one of them. He's got too many animals to be legal. Too many traps."

Sidney felt the hostility wafting off the villagers.

"Have any of you seen Grisly wandering around the village at night?" She asked.

Dead silence. None of them would meet her eye.

"Look, we know about the break-ins," she said. "We know two women have been attacked. If you want to help us find the Stalker, tell us what you know."

Badger cleared his throat. "The problem is, none of us has any proof it's Grisly. Some people think it's Lancer. We take turns patrolling the neighborhood but he slips in and out like mist. Raping women wasn't enough. Now he killed Nikah."

Shasta nodded, fear raw on her face.

"You sound convinced the Stalker committed all these crimes," Granger said, wiping his mouth with a napkin.

"We never had much crime here before," Pokie said.

"What do you think, Chief Becker?" Badger asked. "You think there's more than one sicko running around here?"

"We're investigating all possibilities," she said evenly.

Badger wiped his hands on his apron and nodded at Sidney's food. "Well, we better let you eat, Chief. You haven't touched a thing."

"Thanks for your help." She lifted her sandwich and took a bite. The tender beef practically melted in her mouth. She sipped her latte. After completing her meal and draining her cup, Sidney had one last question to ask. "What can you tell me about Fitch Drako?"

"Fitch?" Badger raised his brows. "Not much. Hardly ever see him. Comes in for groceries every now and then. Very quiet. But polite."

"He keeps to himself," Pokie added. "He's a vet. Been back from Iraq a few years. Lives alone. Can't hold down a job." He tapped his forehead. "Demons. PTSD."

"He drinks a lot?"

Pokie shrugged. "Never seen him drunk. Comes to the saloon on a rare occasion. I think he hunts for his food. Seen him skinning a deer behind his garage once when I was walking down by White Tail Creek. Runs right behind his house."

"So, he's not a troublemaker?"

"No. Keeps a low profile."

"Last night at the saloon he was plastered, and revved up," Granger said. "He was itching to take someone's head off. Preferably a cop."

"I've never seen him like that," Pokie said, scratching the back of his neck. "Just like Badger says. He's quiet and polite. Must've been an off night."

Filing that info away, Sidney and Granger got up to leave, putting on their jackets, hats, and gloves. She smiled at Badger and the older couple. "Thanks. Appreciate your time."

"Come back and see us again," Badger said.

"You can count on it."

CHAPTER TWENTY-FOUR

SIDNEY PRESENTED the warrant to the manager of First Bank of Garnerville, Dudley Schneider, a balding man in his fifties with stooped shoulders and a bookish manner. He was quick to accommodate them. He identified a John Kruger as the owner of the contents of the box, who resided at Nikah's address. Clearly an alias. Most likely Lancer, using a phony ID. The box had been rented a week ago and had not been accessed since.

Schneider led them through a locked metal door into a windowless room stacked with deposit boxes. Sidney's stomach fluttered with anticipation as she pulled vinyl gloves from her duty belt and snapped them on. Schneider located box 064 and inserted his key as Sidney inserted hers. The lock clicked. She pulled out the long, thin metal box and placed it on a table in the middle of the room. Schneider promptly left.

Sidney lifted the lid. Her profound disappointment was echoed by Granger's exasperated sigh.

"Damn," he breathed.

"Damn," she repeated.

The box was empty except for an antique silver key about four inches long with a smoky patina and an intricate, decorative handle. Upon closer look, Sidney realized it was embellished with the same symbol as the medallion found in the tin box. The two were a pair—same material, same beautiful craftsmanship—but like the medallion, it presented no clue, no answer to the mystery of Nikah's death. "What the hell does this open?"

"Million-dollar question."

Sidney slipped the key into an evidence bag. Granger unfolded a larger bag and she slipped in the box, then sealed and labeled both.

Dudley Schneider's eyebrows arched when they appeared back in the lobby with the bagged box.

"This is evidence," she said before he could protest. "We'll return it as soon as the lab releases it."

"Next stop, Tammy Muehler."

***

They stashed the box in the back of the Yukon, drove two blocks down Main Street, and parked in front of Thunderhead Gifts. As they entered the shop, Sidney inhaled the earthy scent of sage incense and recalled her many pleasant visits here, selecting unique treasures as gifts for friends. An impressive variety of Native American crafts were tastefully displayed on shelves and walls. She immediately recognized Tommy's pottery, Elahan's baskets, and the exquisite wood sculptures carved by Tegan. Sidney imagined Nikah working here, stocking the shelves and catering to patrons, along with the woman who now stood behind the counter waiting on a customer. Sidney and Granger busied themselves looking at merchandise until the customer left, then Tammy locked the door, turned the OPEN sign around, and faced them.

She didn't look like the drunk, loudmouthed woman Grisly had characterized. Just the opposite, in fact. Tammy was petite, with a slender figure, a sheath of glossy black hair, a delicate face with large dark eyes, and a full, sensuous mouth. Tammy's persona could be described as demure. She wore skinny jeans and a white tunic with intricate beadwork stitched along the collar and cuffs.

"There's a break room in the back," Tammy said in a soft, lilting voice. She gestured for them to follow her through a curtained doorway, down a hallway, into a small room equipped with a kitchen and an oak table and chairs.

"Have a seat. Can I get you coffee?" she asked. "Perrier?"

Sidney was still jacked up on caffeine from Badger's latte. She and Granger both opted for Perrier. When they were settled with their chilled bottles, Tammy sat quietly with a tense expression.

Sidney cleared her throat and initiated the difficult conversation. "Tammy, we need to talk to you about some unpleasant topics. As you know, we're investigating Nikah's murder."

She nodded. "Yes, word has gotten around. You're questioning everyone in the village."

"We aren't questioning so much as hoping folks will share information."

"I see," she said, her tone wary. "I don't really have any information about Nikah. We were more acquaintances than friends."

"We're also investigating crimes committed by the Stalker."

Her face paled. She tilted her head and coughed into her shoulder, said hoarsely, "Sorry. Aren't they one and the same?"

"Two burglars ransacked Nikah's house last night. We have reason to believe this was a separate incident from the crimes committed by the Stalker.

"Great. One maniac running around isn't enough. Now we have three." Her hand tightened on her bottle and she gave Sidney a direct stare. "Jenna told you Cadence and I were the women attacked."

"Yes. We've already spoken with Cadence."

"Poor Cadence." Her eyes shadowed. "She's too young to cope with this kind of horror. She still lives with her parents. A very sheltered life." She heaved out a ragged breath. "It's been hell for me, too."

"We understand this is an intensely painful and private matter," Sidney said gently. "Are you willing to talk to us?"

Tammy stared at her Perrier bottle in silence.

"It could help us catch him," Sidney said. "Put him in a cage where he belongs. Keep him from doing this to anyone else."

"The experience was terrifying." Tammy's eyes widened so that the whites were showing, then her face crumbled and her eyes filled with tears. She pushed back her chair and stood in front of the sink, staring out the window at the rear parking lot. Trees laden with snow ringed the lot and several parked cars braved the cold, frosted in white. A shudder passed across her shoulders. She crossed her arms, hands cupping her elbows, and spoke so softly Sidney had to strain to hear.

"It happened two weeks ago. My husband was out of town for the weekend on business. I didn't like being left alone, but I felt safe enough. I had a loaded gun under his pillow." She swallowed.

"Take your time," Sidney said.

Tammy drew in a long breath, blew it out. "Something woke me in the middle of the night. Before I was even fully conscious, a bright light blasted into my eyes. I felt the mattress sink on my husband's side and a man's voice whispered, "Don't say a word, or you're dead. Turn over."

Silence.

Tammy licked her dry lips, continued. "I was lying on my side, facing him. I knew if I turned over, he'd tie my hands behind my back, like he did to Cadence, and I wouldn't stand a chance. 'Okay,' I said to him, while reaching under the pillow. I grabbed the gun and aimed it at the flashlight. He shrieked, turned off the flashlight, and took off running. I heard him crash into the wall in the hallway. Moments later the front door slammed shut. I locked myself in the bathroom and called Tucker. He and a few other men had been out patrolling. They arrived within minutes and searched the house. Searched the outside of the house. They didn't find anything. Just footprints coming up from the creek." She turned and leaned back against the sink, her arms still crossed, fingers gripping her elbows, and faced them. "It all happened so fast. Just a couple minutes."

"Terrifying," Sidney said. "You were very brave."

Tammy was trembling. Her anxiety had become visible. "I was in survival mode. I acted on instinct."

Sidney pushed on, her tone soft and gentle. "Is there anything you remember about him? His voice, a mannerism?"

Tammy narrowed her eyes as though in deep concentration. "No."

"We were told you saw him. That he had light-colored eyes."

"That may have been a false memory, I realized later. When he turned off the light, I saw a face for a fleeting moment. Later, I imagined he was..." her voice trailed off.

"Grisly Stokes?"

"Yes."

"Could it have been Grisly?"

"I don't know. He never got close enough for me to feel his body, or smell him. Grisly has a smell you never forget."

"Yeah, we noticed."

"You talked to him?"

"Yep. This morning."

She looked at Sidney and Granger with appreciation. "You two have been busy. You've probably learned more overnight than the whole village did in six months." She scowled and her voice took on a tinge of anger. "Too bad you weren't on the job when Grisly raped me three years ago. Those asshole cops never investigated. They took his word over mine. One of the reasons no one here has faith in law enforcement."

"I'm sorry you were treated that way," Sidney said sincerely. "I hope my department can restore your trust. For the record, I believe you. I believe Grisly assaulted you."

She released a weary sigh. "Thank you."

"Can you tell me what happened that night at the saloon?"

She chewed her bottom lip for a moment, lost in thought. "It happened three years ago, but I remember it vividly. I was going through a rough patch with Shiloh, my husband. We were separated. He was staying with a friend. I was pretty depressed. A couple of my girlfriends thought going to the saloon and listening to music would cheer me up. Normally, I don't drink, but I did that night. Too much. Trying to drown my sorrows, I guess. I'm ashamed to say I acted badly. Obnoxious, to everyone. My girlfriends tried to get me to go home, but I made a scene and they left without me. I sat at the bar next to Grisly. I'd never talked to him before, but I'd seen him around the village. He had a bad reputation and most everyone just ignored him. He asked if he could buy me a drink. If I hadn't been so drunk already, I would never have accepted. After I downed that one, and another, he suggested driving me home. I was out of it. I said okay. I just wanted to pass out in bed.

When we got to my house, I couldn't even unlock the door. He took my key and got me inside. Then he sat me on the couch. I thanked him, expecting him to leave." Tammy's voice vibrated with emotion and her face wrenched with pure hatred. "Instead, he raped me. I fought and screamed, but he held me down, put his hand over my mouth. It was like a vise. When he was done, he called me a filthy whore. And left."

Her fingers trembled as she reached for her Perrier and took a long sip. "I called the cops immediately. They were horrible. Kept asking me how much I had to drink, and was I sure it was Grisly, and was I sure I hadn't consented to sex. Drunk as I was, it was still humiliating. They said they'd go talk to him. They ended up arresting him, but it was just a formality. The next day a cop came back and took another statement. He said it was just my word against his, so they'd probably have to let him go. They released him that day. That was that."

Tammy's fury was palpable. Sidney's gut rumbled with emotion. Granger sat with his jaw tightly clenched, eyes radiating anger. It was clear the insensitivity of their fellow officers offended him as much as it did her, though they both knew law enforcement wasn't solely to blame. It was society as a whole. The systemic lack of empathy in which rape victims were regarded, and disbelieved, was widespread and appalling. Sidney drew in a deep breath and controlled her tone. "Did you have a rape kit?"

Tammy shook her head. "I didn't know at the time I needed one. I had a lot of bruising. No one ever saw it but me. The second the cops left, I showered. I couldn't wait to get his smell off me."

Sidney hid her disappointment. The officers should have driven her to the ER, made sure she got examined. Tammy had fought back. Grisly, too, should have been examined for bruises and scratches. Without evidence of a forced assault, there was nothing on which to build a case. "I'll review your report when I get back to the station, Tammy, but I don't want to give you false hope. It doesn't look good. We're going to look into other possible crimes Grisly committed. If I can get him into my interrogation room, I'll try to squeeze a rape confession out of him."

"Thank you, Chief Becker, for treating me with dignity," Tammy said. "Just being heard, and being taken seriously, means more than you can imagine."

Sidney stood and Tammy came into her arms. Her figure felt slight and the top of her head didn't quite reach Sidney's shoulder. For a long moment, Sidney held her as she would a child, offering comfort before releasing her.

CHAPTER TWENTY-FIVE

ANOTHER STORM had rolled in out of the northern October sky from Canada and soft snow had fallen while they spoke with Tammy. The Yukon was coated in white. Back in the driver's seat, Sidney hit the steering wheel hard, cursing Grisly and the inadequate justice system that continually failed women.

Granger sat listening. "I hear you, Chief. I feel the same way."

"Tammy's story is all too common." Sidney met his eyes. "I saw it over and over in Oakland. Woman not believed. Sex offenders going free. A woman is raped every two minutes in this country, Granger. That number is doubled among Native Americans. Only a small number of complaints ever make it to court, and only about half of those get convictions. Victims get no closure and are left dealing with trauma for the rest of their lives."

"While their attackers walk, free to find another victim," Granger said. "We're going to get this guy, Chief. And the bastard that killed Nikah. We'll make them pay."

Granger's emotions were running high, as were hers. Still, she knew better than to make predictions that might not materialize. Despite their best efforts, they might not wrap up the Stalker case anytime soon. They were dealing with a highly functioning perp who had eluded skilled trackers for six months. No DNA or other evidence had been collected. Back in Oakland, with even a dozen investigators on her team, some felons were never apprehended.

Cases went cold. She hoped her two cases wouldn't fall into that category.

In the meantime, there was nothing to do but keep plugging away at every lead. "Let's go talk to this game warden," she said. "What's his name?"

"Harper Mead."

"Let's see if he's been giving Grisly too much leeway."

***

A lone truck emblazoned with the official department logo was parked in front of the Fish and Game office. It was a one-room cabin off the highway on the outskirts of town. Boughs heavy with snow leaned against the frame and smoke curled from a chimney pipe that was almost buried on the roof.

Harper Mead was holed up inside sitting behind a counter that took up half the floor space. A pellet stove radiated heat in one corner. His eyebrows arched as they walked in and he quickly switched up his computer screen, but not before Sidney saw he'd been playing solitaire.

Gray-haired, stocky, with a bland face that had been burned and weathered by the sun, Meade looked like he was fast approaching his career expiration date. He wore a uniform much like their own, though his duty belt with his radio and gun were slung over a chair. Meade pushed his bifocals up on his forehead and stood with his hands resting on the counter. He smiled at Sidney in a rather stiff grimace. "Afternoon, Chief Becker. What brings you out this way?"

Her jacket covered her nametag, but she wasn't surprised that he knew who she was. Her photo was routinely published in the paper. "Afternoon. You Harper Meade?"

"Yes, ma'am."

"We'd like some info on Grisly Stokes."

"Grisly?" His expression soured and he ran a blue-veined hand across his chin. His voice dropped an octave and became nuanced with suspicion. "What kind of info?"

"Seems he has an undue number of dead animals in his barn. You been out there recently?"

"Not for a while. Never a pleasant experience. Let me look him up." He pushed his glasses to the end of his nose and his fingers got busy on the keyboard. He scanned the screen for a moment before looking up. "He's legal. No citations."

"Who inspected Grisly last, and when?"

"That would've been me." His eyes narrowed as he read the screen. He coughed, and then gazed at her with an unreadable expression. "July fifteenth."

"Are you kidding me?" Granger said. "Five months ago?"

"We're understaffed." Flushing deeply from his neck to the tips of his oversized ears, he responded weakly, "I'm one of two game wardens for all of Linley County. That's thousands of acres of forested land. Dozens of hunters, trappers, and fishermen to keep track of. You know how many outsiders come through here every month?"

Sidney took a deep breath to subdue a sudden rush of anger and pulled out her phone. She found the photos of Grisly's barn and handed the cell to Meade. "This what his barn looked like when you were there last?"

With a blast of cold air, the door opened and a man shuffled in barricaded in a bulky jacket with the hood over his head. His legs were encrusted in snow past his ankles. He pushed back his hood to reveal a youthful, ruddy face, his head sheathed in a knit cap pulled down to his eyes. He yanked off his gloves, held out his hands to the heat of stove and worked his stiff fingers open and shut. He said with friendly familiarity, "Hey, Chief."

"Hello," she said, not recognizing him.

"It's me, Sander Vance." He pulled off his cap and a halo of unruly red hair tumbled around his ears. "I look different when I'm not in my summer uniform."

Now she recognized him. She had encountered Sander routinely over the years on country roads and lakeshores, doing his job, examining licenses and the bounty of hunters and fishermen in the backcountry. "Of course," she said, not wanting to be steered off course from her conversation with Meade.

Meade was scanning through each photo on her phone. "I know this looks bad, but Grisly's always been legal. A lot of these animals were killed by his clients."

"Are you aware that one or more trappers are poaching? Filing the registrations off of their traps? The villagers at Two Creeks have found quite a few. They believe Grisly's one of them."

Meade's eyes shifted to the left, then returned after a long pause. He shrugged one shoulder, said in a robotic tone, "Don't know anything about that."

Meade was a terrible liar. He knew something, and was looking the other way. Why? Was he taking bribes? Being threatened? Or was he just lazy as hell?

"Do you ever talk to the folks at Two Creeks?"

"Hmmm. Been a while."

"Maybe five months ago," Sander said.

"How about you tear yourself away from your solitaire game, Harper," Sidney said, her voice strained. "Get yourself out of this warm, comfy cabin, and head over to Grisly's barn. How about you make sure he has a license for every dead animal on his property. And while you're at it, examine every one of his traps."

For a moment, a long moment, Meade stood expressionless and utterly still. Then his face tightened with indignation. "You have no authority here, Chief Becker. We're state employees, working for the Department of Fish and Game. We don't answer to you."

"No, you don't. But Bob Houston, the Oregon Director of Fish and Game, is a personal friend of mine. A very good friend. If you want to be a game warden long enough to see your pension, don't make me put in a call to him."

Meade blanched. He licked his lips, and said, "You see the weather out there? It's dangerous to be on the road."

"Drive slow," Sidney said.

"Time's a wasting. You better get started," Granger said, looking like he wanted to grab Meade by the collar and yank him over the counter.

Meade took his sweet time piling on his winter gear. He tightened his mouth and shot darts of hostility at them, limping suddenly and wincing as he doddered out the door.

Sander had removed and hung his coat over the back of a chair in front of the stove. He was tall and gangly with a pleasant, freckled face and alert blue eyes. In the strained tension remaining in the room, he replaced Meade behind the counter, moved to a sideboard and poured coffee into a mug. "It's deadly cold out there," he said in a guarded tone, his posture stiff as he stirred sugar and powdered cream into his coffee.

"Yeah, we noticed," Sidney said in a controlled tone, sorry she had lost her cool in front of Sander. The stress of the last two days was building up, looking for any small release. "How about you, Sander? You find any illegal traps?"

"No. Never."

"You ever get out to the village?"

He shook his head. "That's Harper's responsibility."

"Have you been out to Grisly's place?"

"Nope. Like I said, that whole area around Nenámooks Lake is Harper's area."

"Take a look at these photos. Tell me what you think."

Sander drew close and scanned her photos, then released a long, ragged breath. "Looks disgusting, and highly suspicious." He frowned and continued in a heartfelt tone, "If it's all the same to you, Chief, I'd rather not be drawn into this blowup with Harper. He's a decent guy. Been on the job for thirty years. Just three months from retirement. He's not well. Bad heart. Bad knees. He's just hanging in there long enough to get his pension."

"I appreciate your loyalty, Sander, but Harper isn't doing his job. Wrongdoers are going unpunished. Animals are being slaughtered. Your loyalty should be to your job. Protecting the environment."

"It's not as bad as you think, Chief. I've been doing a lot of his field work." Sander swallowed and his Adam's apple traveled the full length of his long neck. "Just haven't gotten out to Grisly's yet."

Sidney admired the young man's principles, which influenced her decision to go easy on Meade. After all, he had put in thirty years of service, and truth be told, he didn't look at all healthy. She wasn't going to stand between him and his pension. "If you care about Harper, why don't you get out there and help him with Grisly? Make sure he doesn't cut corners. We'd like to bring Grisly in for questioning."

"Sure. Will do." He looked down at his cup for a moment and then his gaze met hers. "There's something you should know."

"What's that?"

"Grisly came in here a few days ago. He said he spotted a big white wolf in the backcountry near Nenámooks Lake. He wanted Harper to give him a license to hunt it."

A chill prickled Sidney's scalp. Selena had told her that Tegan hung out with a huge white wolf—an animal that caused no one any harm and provided a blind boy with companionship and comfort. Now Grisly, a sick predator to his core, wanted the wolf's carcass as a trophy. "What did Harper tell him?"

"He said absolutely not. Wolves are protected in Oregon. I thought Grisly's claim was outlandish. Oregon has grey wolves.

No white wolf has ever been spotted in these parts before." He shook his head. "I found it disturbing how excited he was at the prospect of killing that animal. He creeped me out. One scary dude."

"Couldn't agree with you more. All the more reason why you need to get out there to provide backup for Harper."

That jolted Sander into motion. They left the cabin together and climbed into their respective vehicles. Sander peeled out in record time, holding his radio mic up to his mouth.

"Hey, Chief, are you really on good terms with Bob Houston?"

One corner of her mouth tilted upwards. "I met him once, for about a minute."

Granger chuckled. "Thought as much."

Sidney pulled out of the lot and glanced at her watch. Almost 2:30 p.m. Tegan would be getting home from school and she was anxious to speak with him. She also felt an urgent need to tell Tommy that the white wolf might be in danger. The need to get Grisly behind bars loomed large in her mind.

CHAPTER TWENTY-SIX

TEGAN WASN'T REALLY surprised when the head of their small school appeared in his classroom, approached his desk, and whispered to him to follow her. Out in the hallway, Tegan immediately smelled the sweet, spicy smell of Elahan. Cinnamon. Cloves. A hint of ginger. She had been baking apple bread when he left for school this morning. "Hi Nana," he said.

"Kloshe sun," she answered, greeting him in Chinook.

"I'll leave him with you," the woman said, and then her footsteps hurried down the hall to her office.

"I have everything ready, my boy," Elahan said quietly. "Grab your jacket. Come with me."

He found his outer garments among the many coats hanging from pegs in the musty hallway and hurriedly put them on. Elahan had advised him that morning to dress warmly, and when he stepped out the back door into the stunning cold he was thankful he had worn his warmest jacket, mittens, snow boots, hat, and long johns under his trousers. Flakes landed softly on his face and caught in his eyelashes as they crunched across the frozen meadow into the forest. The metallic smell of snow blended with the scent of pine and juniper as they zigzagged around the prickly boughs of trees. The distant sound of water grew louder as they approached White Tail Creek. Whimpering with pleasure, Lelou leapt and danced around him, snow flying, his tail swiping Tegan's legs.

Tegan found the wolf's massive head and stroked the fur around his ears. "Hey boy, hey, hey. We're going on an adventure."

Tegan followed the jingle of bits and the rich scent of horses and found Gracie idling next to Granger's gelding, Taba, on the path that ran parallel to the roaring creek. They were saddled and packed and covered with buffalo hides for warmth.

"Where are we going, Nana?"

"Shhh. You must be quiet. Voices carry. We'll talk when we get out of the village."

Tegan heard Elahan mount Taba and take the lead. He followed suit, putting a foot in the stirrup, hoisting himself upon Gracie's back, and wrapping a hide around his shoulders.

CHAPTER TWENTY-SEVEN

IT WAS STILL SNOWING when Sidney pulled into the Chetwoot driveway. The cabin door jerked open before they knocked and Tommy appeared, clearly agitated, wearing a panicked expression. "Tegan's gone." He furiously spewed words in his native language before reverting back to English. "What was she thinking? In this freezing weather!"

"Slow down, Tommy," Sidney said. "Take a breath. Can we come in?"

He stepped aside and the three faced each other in the living room. He was dressed in teacher garb—khaki pants and a button-down blue shirt, his black hair tied at the nape of his neck.

"Who took Tegan?" Sidney asked.

"Elahan." He paced in a small circle, one hand pressed to his forehead, as though warding off a migraine. "She left a note." He snatched a sheet of notebook paper from the coffee table and handed it to her, groaning all the while that Elahan must be losing her mind.

Sidney drowned him out and read the old woman's small, gnarled handwriting.

Tommy, it is not safe for us here. Do not come after us. We must do what needs to be done. Elahan

"Why does she think it's not safe? And what's this about doing what needs to be done?"

"I don't know." The muscles tightened on his face, sharpening his features. "Must have something to do with Nikah's killer."

An ominous warning fluttered in Sidney's stomach. "Is she thinking of going after someone?"

Tommy appeared even more distraught, his breathing picking up momentum. "God, I hope not."

"Does she know who killed Nikah?"

"I think Tegan knows," he said with a crack in his voice that left his face unguarded. His fear was visible.

"That's why she thinks it isn't safe," Sidney said, an alarm blaring in her head. "The killer may think Tegan knows something. Elahan's afraid the boy's in danger."

"What does he know?" Tommy asked, clearly shaken. "Why didn't they talk to me?"

Sidney caught Granger's angry expression. Her officer stood still for a moment and visibly collected himself before voicing what she had been thinking. "Why didn't Elahan come to us? We could have kept Tegan safe. Gone after the perp."

"She doesn't trust the police," he said with a hard, unflinching look in his eyes. "I never thought she'd take off like this without alerting me."

Sidney asked, "Are they in a vehicle?"

"They're on horseback! Can you believe it? In this weather?" Tommy focused on Granger. "I'm sorry, but they took one of your horses."

Granger paled and opened his mouth, but Sidney spoke first, "When did you find this note?"

"Twenty minutes ago. When I got home from teaching my class."

"How long have they been gone?"

"Judging from how much snow filled the prints leading from the barn, I'd guess a couple hours."

"Which way are the tracks headed?" Granger asked.

"Away from the village. Following a trail back into the woods to the northwest."

"Was the wolf with them?" Sidney asked.

"Yes."

"Where do you think they went?" she asked.

"No clue. There's nothing out there but trees and snow."

"They must have a destination in mind," Sidney said. "Think, Tommy. Any vacation cabins back in there? Ski sheds?"

"I don't know. Probably." He paced again. "I can't think straight."

"What provisions did they take?"

"Cold weather gear. Some heavy animal furs. I checked the gun cabinet. They took a rifle and a handgun. She would've packed a good supply of food."

"Sounds sensible enough," Granger said. "I can't imagine Elahan putting Tegan in danger."

Tommy blew out his breath, shook his head as if to clear it. "Not intentionally."

"Does she know survival skills?" Granger asked.

"Better than most. Those heavy furs would keep them warm in Siberia." His posture stiffened. "But that's not the point, is it?"

Shooting Granger a wary look, Sidney agreed. "We need to find them." If Elahan's mission was to interact with a killer, a blind boy and an old woman were no match for someone who might be young and fit, and possibly an experienced woodsman. The threat of violence, of someone getting injured, or killed, pressed heavily upon her. They were losing precious time, while snow was filling the horse prints left behind. "I'll call search and rescue. In the meantime, you should get a group of villagers together. You said you have good trackers here."

Tommy put up his hand. "Already done. Shadow and Coyote Burne are getting ready as we speak. They'll be here shortly. I'm going with them."

"Taking snowmobiles?" Granger asked.

"No. The forest is too dense. They're bringing horses."

"Look, don't let your guard down out there," Sidney said. "There's a dangerous killer running loose. You also need to watch out for that wolf. Grisly tried to get a license to shoot him."

"Seriously?" Tommy's lips went white with rage. "That fucking psycho. If he hurts that wolf, or a hair on my family's head, we'll kill him. We'll be well-armed."

Great. Angry men tearing through the forest ready to shoot at anything. Sidney could see any number of things going wrong with that scenario. Law enforcement should be managing these men.

"I'll go with them, Chief," Granger offered, as though reading her thoughts. "My other horse is still in the barn."

Sidney mulled this over. Granger was levelheaded. As a Marine, he had combat and leadership experience. He knew how to keep his subordinates safe. He grew up in these hills and understood the terrain. On the other hand, she knew he was pushing himself hard. Neither she nor any of her officers had gotten much sleep, and the day had already been demanding. "Sure you're up to it?"

He gave her a convincing grin that brightened his neon blues. "Compared to being in the trenches in Afghanistan, this is a cinch."

Sidney felt like hugging him. Granger was a good man. A good cop. Tough. She nodded her consent. "Go with them. Take the satellite phone. Stay in touch. I want regular reports."

"Will do."

Tommy's gaze swept over Granger's uniform. "You need some appropriate clothing. Let's pile on some cold weather gear. Follow me out back to the mud room."

The two men left the room and Sidney migrated to the fireplace where a fire had been reduced to crackling red embers.

While warming her back she called Captain Jack Harrison at the Sheriff's department.

"What's up, Chief?" Harrison said, skipping a greeting and getting straight to business. A call from Sidney meant an emergency. When you're in the job of saving lives and property, every second counts.

"We got an old Indian woman and a boy on horseback out in the back country. They've been gone about two hours."

"Deliberate, or lost?"

"Deliberate. They have food and warm clothing. We have reason to believe they're out hunting a dead woman's killer. We need to find them before all hell breaks loose."

"A boy and an old women going after a killer?" He whistled. "A dangerous game. You talking about Elahan Chetwoot?"

"Yes. And her great grandson."

"Sounds like I could be putting my men into the middle of a shootout."

"If we find them fast enough, we could avoid violence."

"Where's she headed?"

"Northwest. Away from the village."

"Nothing but horses can get back in there."

"A search party is leaving from the village shortly. Granger is going with them."

"They'll make better progress than we could. By the time we got horses saddled and trailered out there, it'd be past nightfall. It's snowing. We wouldn't be able to see shit." He kept his voice within the range of reasonable tones, but she sensed an underlying tension. "We'd be riding blind, looking for a needle in a haystack." She heard him sigh. "I've had several encounters with Elahan over the years. That old woman is tough as nails. And wily. She could outwit a fox, and she can certainly outwit a search party. If she doesn't want to be found, they won't find her."

Sidney said nothing, digesting his words.

"The storm's passing tonight," he continued. "Tomorrow we'll have clear skies and good visibility. We can get a plane out. We'll see more from the air than we could on the ground. If Elahan doesn't return home tonight, we'll head out at daybreak."

"Sounds sensible, Jack."

"Keep me posted."

"Sure thing. Talk in the morning." She disconnected, anxious for the search party from the village to get moving.

The sound of boots hitting the front porch drew her attention to the window. Three saddled quarter horses stood in the driveway, two with rifles in scabbards. She opened the door to the Burne twins who had the hoods of their parkas pulled over their heads. They were surprisingly young, maybe late teens, with burnished skin, and curiously light brown eyes. They had a sense of urgency about them and refused to come in. The taller of the two hurriedly introduced himself as Coyote, and his sister as Shadow. "Where's Tommy? We need to cut out."

"We're here." Granger and Tommy trudged around the corner of the cabin, bundled in snow gear, Granger leading a saddled chestnut bay. He and Tommy both carried rifles. As the four mounted, their posture and expressions communicated a unified sense of purpose.

"Be safe," she called out.

Granger shot her a little salute.

The sky had darkened and Sidney's uneasiness intensified. She didn't feel completely confident that the Burne twins had the experience to find their way through the wilderness. All familiar landmarks had vanished under shifting dunes of white. She hoped they'd prove her wrong. The plodding hoofs, jingling bits, and murmur of voices faded as they headed out into the snow-muffled afternoon.

***

The search party threaded its way through a maze of trees, their bodies thickly dusted with snow. Granger shifted in his saddle, feeling an urgency to close the gap between themselves and the old woman and boy. They moved cautiously, allowing the animals to feel their way over uneven ground. Low hanging clouds and mist blocked the view of the lake, his main point of reference. He pulled his compass from a pocket and hung it from his saddle horn. They steadily veered northeast with the twins in the lead and Tommy pulling up the rear.

They came to a spur of woodland spilling down the slopes of Beartooth Peak, a bare granite pinnacle jutting high above the tree line. The single file horse tracks they followed moved steadily forward while the paw prints of the wolf zigzagged, as though he was scouting, sniffing out danger. The tracks led to Beartooth Creek, a fast-moving ribbon of water outlined in silver against the blackened woods. As soon as they hit the creek trail, he heard a groan from Coyote, echoed by Shadow. Coyote dismounted and crouched over something on the ground.

"What is it?" Tommy called out, his voice edgy. He and Granger nudged their horses closer and gazed at the disruption in the virgin snow. Coyote was brushing the lighter flakes from deeper, frozen tracks with his gloved hand.

"Fuck," Tommy said.

Dread tightened Granger's gut. The shod horse tracks of another rider had come up to the trail from the creek and were following the two riders and the wolf.

"Recognize those tracks?" Granger asked.

"I recognize the shoes. The farrier is Kevin Chutes. White man. Puts an identifying diamond mark on each shoe. No one at the village uses him..." his voice faded as he caught Tommy's intense stare.

"But you know someone who does."

"Yeah." Coyote's jaw tightened. "Grisly Stokes. He has a big, gray Morgan."

Granger's adrenalin jumped. "So, you think this is Grisly?"

Coyote's eyes flashed with animosity. "Possible."

"How far ahead is he?" Tommy asked. Despite the cold, sweat had broken out on his upper lip.

"At least an hour. See how far apart the prints are?" Coyote said. "This rider is moving at a good ambling gait."

"We need to catch him," Tommy said.

"Can't go too much faster," Coyote said. "Could be dangerous for the horses. Might be ruts, gopher holes under this snow. Could cripple a horse in a second."

"Let's match his stride," Granger suggested.

In answer, Coyote mounted smoothly, pressed his heels into the sides of his black spotted appaloosa, and got back in lead position matching the ambling gait.

CHAPTER TWENTY-EIGHT

MOOLOCK HAD ARRIVED at the agreed meeting place and had everything ready well in advance. He and Shantie were coated in white when he spotted the wolf and the two horses emerging out of the misty creek like phantoms, seeming to glide over the snowdrifts like canoes on a lake. Dusk was settling, adding a shade of charcoal gray to the colorless landscape. He needed to get them to warm shelter right away. He moved out of the cover of towering trees and lifted a hand in greeting. "Kloshe sun."

Elahan did the same. "Kloshe sun."

They wasted no more time on small talk. Taba and Gracie fell into line behind Shantie. Moolock led them back through the shadowy woods, his Maglite carving a pathway until he reached the sheared face of a granite cliff that loomed overhead like a monolith. He dismounted and helped the old woman and boy. Wrapped in buffalo hides covered in snow, with only their eyes visible above their scarves, they looked like prehistoric creatures, half human, half beast.

With some effort, Moolock slid a makeshift door that leaned heavily against the rock cliff to one side. A jagged, vertical crevice in the granite was revealed, large enough for a horse to shimmy through. He had built the wooden frame during the summer and recently covered it with evergreen boughs to blend in with the surroundings. Brandishing a flashlight, Elahan and Taba entered first, followed by the boy and Gracie, then the wolf. Moolock slapped Shantie on her flank and she entered last.

Instead of following, Moolock grabbed a snow shovel and a wide broom made of cedar boughs and ventured back down the trail to the creek. Walking backwards, he remolded the snow, wiping away horse tracks, and brushing the surface until it appeared smooth. Effectively, the three had just vanished without a trace. He positioned the heavy door back in place, squeezed through, and let it slam against the wall.

CHAPTER TWENTY-NINE

SIDNEY HAD JUST gotten into the Yukon when static crackled over the radio followed by the urgent voice of her dispatcher. "Hey, Chief."

"Yeah, Jesse?"

"There's a big structural fire on the east side of Nenámooks Lake. A game warden by the name of Sander Vance called it in. Property owned by Grisly Stokes. Fire department's just arrived. The address is…"

"I know where it is," she cut in.

"Looks like there's a casualty."

Her breath stopped. "Who?"

"Don't have that info, ma'am."

"I'm ten minutes away. Tell Amanda and Darnell to meet me out there. Contact Dr. Linthrope and Stewart Wong. They'll need to remove the body."

"Will do."

Heart racing, Sidney disconnected, switched on the lights and siren and peeled out. Just when she thought things couldn't get any worse in her community, they had. Far worse. Who was dead? What was burning?

After a harried drive, she arrived to find the driveway blocked by an ambulance and fire trucks from both Garnerville and Jackson. It had stopped snowing but dusk darkened the sky with a murky gloom. Sidney parked on the shoulder and hiked up the ice-rutted driveway. Rounding the bend, she spotted a dozen animated firemen silhouetted against an inferno of leaping flames and dense black smoke. Grisly's entire barn was engulfed. Fed by an abundance of fuel, the fire writhed, roared, snapped, and hissed, and leapt several stories high. Hurtling missiles of debris shot from the roof, which was starting to cave in on itself. Clearly, nothing inside would survive. All evidence of Grisly's wrongdoing would be incinerated. Melting snow and water from the hoses created icy sludge that spread in all directions, making walking tricky.

She scanned the landscape of organized chaos and spotted EMTs working over a prone body on a gurney. She approached with dread, shocked to see the unconscious patient was Harper Meade, hooked up to oxygen and an IV. Sander Vance stood watching the techs, his face ashen and pinched with worry. The deep creases on his forehead softened when he saw her. Looking like a man clearly out of his depth, he raised his voice above the roar of fire and surging water. "Chief Becker. Thank God you're here."

"What happened to Harper?" Sidney asked, snapping into her professional persona.

"Grisly shot him."

Holy Shit. "How bad is it?"

"Bad."

"Where's Grisly?"

Sander cocked his head toward the barn. "In there."

Sidney's fingers tingled as though receiving an electric shock. Stunned for a moment, she collected her thoughts. A man shot. Another dead. On her watch. On top of her rape and murder cases. All hell was breaking loose. "What happened? Bare facts. I'll get a full report later."

"I got here just after Harper," Sander said, speaking slowly and methodically, as though in shock. "The barn was already burning. Flames were shooting out of the open loft. Harper was behind his truck, exchanging gunfire with Grisly, who was shooting from the barn. Harper got hit in the abdomen. I drove straight up to the barn, crouched behind the truck door and unloaded my Glock. Grisly fell backwards. Before I could get to him, the support beams of the loft gave way and a mass of burning rubble blocked the door. I called for help, and did what I could to help Harper. Everyone arrived within minutes. Got right to work."

"You okay?"

He nodded, roughly wiping his eyes with a gloved hand. "Sorry. I hope Harper makes it."

"Me, too." Sidney said, shaken that it was her directive that sent Meade into this dangerous situation. She scanned the clearing, visualizing what had taken place—the old game warden with health issues, slow on reflexes, going up against a professional hunter. For a moment, a wave of guilt threatened to upend her. Sidney suppressed her emotions and forced her focus back on the job. "Did Harper say anything? How the fire started? How the shootout started?"

Sander sniffed, replied hoarsely, "He said Grisly was pouring fuel from a gas can around the barn when he arrived. Harper told him to stop. Grisly ignored him. Harper pulled out his duty weapon. They exchanged fire." Sander shook his head and looked at the blazing barn, eyes haunted. "Harper never had to fire his gun before. First time for me, too. I killed a man tonight."

"You did what you had to do." Sidney swallowed past the lump in her throat, thinking of the many times she'd been forced to fire her weapon over the years, and the three men who died as a result. "Sometimes we have to make hard decisions. Act on instinct. Goes with the job."

He nodded.

"I'm sorry, Sander, but I'm going to have to take your service weapon." They both knew it had to be held as evidence and taken to the State Forensic Lab. "When things calm down, I'd like you to walk me through everything in detail."

"Yes, ma'am." He unclipped his holster and handed over his Glock pistol as the EMTs rushed past them with the gurney.

"If it's all right with you, Chief," Sander said, "I'd like to catch a ride to the hospital with the EMTs. My truck's blocked in. I want to stay with Harper."

"Of course." Impulsively, she reached out and put her hand on his arm. "Keep me posted."

With a sad smile, he nodded and hurried off.

Sidney hiked down to her vehicle and deposited the gun in her service bag. She made a call to Judge Rosenstadt, explained the circumstances, and secured a warrant. Next she called Winnie and instructed her to recruit one of their auxiliary officers to pick it up and deliver it. Pronto.

Sidney watched the firemen wrestle their hoses until Darnell and Amanda came plodding up the driveway, faces etched in shock. As they approached, the reflection of the fire brightened their faces and danced in their eyes. Darnell held two takeout coffee cups. Amanda gripped the handle of her forensic kit.

"What the hell?" Darnell said. "Looks like a bomb went off."

"What a mess. Jesse said there was a casualty." Amanda shifted her forensic case to her other hand, her dark eyes studying the clearing, looking for a body. "What happened?"

Sidney gave them the abbreviated version.

"Jesus. Grisly's dead?" Amanda asked. "Is Meade gonna make it?"

"Don't know. He didn't look good."

"Who started the blaze?" Darnell asked.

"Grisly. Trying to destroy evidence, no doubt." Sidney nodded at the two cups Darnell was holding. "Are those for show, or is that hot coffee?"

"Hot coffee, Chief." Darnell's serious expression lightened, and he passed her a cup. "Your favorite. Mocha latte."

"Bless you, my child." Sidney sipped the rich coffee blended with chocolate.

"They have an amazing deli at the General Store," he said with a smile.

"So I discovered." Simple things meant a lot in stressful times. His smile widened, lifting her spirit a little.

"Killer roast beef sandwich, too," Amanda said. "I saved you half." She pulled a foil-wrapped packet from her pocket.

"My saviors. I'm starved." Sidney unwrapped the sandwich and spoke in between bites. "Brief me on your interviews today."

"We hit the village pretty hard," Darnell said. "Most folks are convinced a white man is the Stalker."

"Right," Sidney said. "One of the assault victims thought she saw his eyes."

"Some villagers point the finger at Lancer, some at Grisly," Amanda said. "There's no evidence to support either theory."

"Grisly raped a woman named Tammy three years ago. The cops didn't properly investigate the case. That got a lot of people up in arms, hating cops," Darnell said.

"Gives the rest of us a bad name." She met Sidney's eyes without flinching. "The villagers appreciated that we're taking our job seriously. Maybe we'll build some trust."

"Learn anything about Grisly's history?"

"Only that he was a real asshole," Amanda said. Her generous mouth tightened into a thin line. "Been living here for a decade. No one knows where he came from. He regularly hit the saloon and General Store, but made no friends. Seems he had an attitude problem. He took up with a woman a few years back, but she never came into the village. Word is he wouldn't let her leave the property unless he accompanied her. Then she disappeared." Her eyes narrowed for a moment. "Highly suspicious."

Darnell chimed back in. "Everyone's convinced he was poaching, and apparently had a black-market supply channel for moving illegal fur and meat."

"He's viewed as a pariah," Amanda added.

"Whatever elicit business he had going on, it just went up in smoke," Sidney said. "What else you got?"

"Descriptions and images of items stolen by the Stalker," Darnell said. "They've been forwarded to Winnie. She's notifying pawn shops."

"Good work. Both of you." She finished the sandwich, crumpled the cup, and shoved it into her pocket. "Anything related to Nikah's death?"

"One interesting note," Amanda said. "She was seen at the saloon with a guy named River Menowa. Comes here to visit his mother. Sounds like they were pretty cozy."

"Cozy, how?"

"Dancing cheek to cheek. Laughing. Flirting."

"Did you talk to him or his mother?"

"We were headed over there when we got the call to come here."

Sidney took a deep breath and squared her shoulders. "There's a lot to do. We need to process this crime scene. Amanda, you and I are going to search Grisly's cabin. Darnell, scout around the property. Stay alert. Grisly placed traps around the periphery. We don't want you to lose a foot. Look for anything linking Grisly to Nikah's murder and the sexual assaults."

"Yes, ma'am." Amanda saluted.

"Ready and able." Darnell pulled the flaps of his hat down over his ears.

Sidney smiled to herself, proud of her subordinates and their upbeat attitude.

A loud explosion jerked their attention to the barn. Something highly flammable sent a new wave of flames shooting through the roof. Burning debris lit up the sky and embers drifted down on the clearing like rain. Still, the firemen were making progress. The flames on one side of the barn had been doused and thick black smoke that smelled of chemicals belched out like the breath of a dragon.

Sidney looked steadily at the log cabin, as if by sheer will she could intuit the motives of the violent man who had lived there. The cabin looked as though it had sprouted out of the earth rather than having been built by human hands. The roof was covered in thick snow and icicles descended from the eaves like blades. Sidney and Amanda climbed the porch and paused at the door to snap on vinyl gloves. "You ready?" Sidney asked, bracing herself for more animal trophies and Grisly's indelible stench.

"Yeah. I'm holding my breath."

CHAPTER THIRTY

FOLLOWING HIS BEAM of light, Moolock navigated the narrow tunnel for a hundred yards, where it opened to a large cavern from which four other tunnels shot off through the mountain. The mouth of the cave was hidden from the outside world by Skookumchuck Falls, a small creek that tumbled from the roof of the mountain to the basin below. Normally a misty, delicate curtain of water, the falls had frozen into a sheet of ice that resembled fluted glass.

The secret cave was an ideal place in which to take refuge when it was too wet or cold to sleep outdoors. During the summer months, Moolock had stacked enough wood in one of the tunnels to keep himself warm and dry all winter. In another tunnel, he had stockpiled hay and feed for Shantie.

Oil lamps flickered along the corrugated walls and Moolock had left a fire burning in the pit, creating a warm nest in the center of the chamber. The old woman and boy had stripped off their outer garments and laid the bear hides near the flames to dry. Tegan had unpacked the horses at the far end of the cave and placed their provisions near the fire, and he was now brushing the animals as they grazed on piles of fragrant hay. Elahan had heaped more logs on the fire pit and the flames leapt tall and bright. The billowing smoke escaped through a crevice in the ceiling. Moolock turned up the wick on an oil lamp, so it enlarged the diameter of light around her.

Crouched near the fire, the old woman distributed food from several containers onto plates—roasted chicken, corn pudding, bean casserole, and apple bread. Though the food was cold, his stomach rumbled with hunger and anticipation. Elahan was an alchemist, using seasonings and herbs to elevate common ingredients into mouthwatering meals. Lelou sat at her side, soaking in the warmth, eyes alert, waiting to be fed.

Observing the homey scene, Moolock realized how foreign it was to be an integral part of a family. He was unaccustomed to feeling accepted and needed. Since his discharge from the Army five years ago he had never shared his personal space with anyone. He felt most comfortable being mobile, moving his camp routinely, staying anonymous. Most folks would view him as a miscreant, a throwback to the Stone Age—camping out or living in a cave in a rough, primitive manner. No plumbing. No heat. No washing machine. No TV. No computer. No phone.

A potent mix of emotions, long buried, rose to the surface. Moolock's eyes moistened as the piercing longing for home and family caught him unprepared. After his wife's death, he built up a thick reserve and had come to believe he was immune to this kind of neediness. Blinking back tears, Moolock removed his parka and looped it over the back of one of the three camp chairs he had arranged by the fire. His long hair tumbled around his shoulders and he tied it back with a strip of rawhide. He stood with his back to the fire watching his two guests with a keen, almost anthropological interest.

Tegan put away the grooming brush and explored the dimensions of the cavern, sweeping his walking staff in front of him, gauging the texture of the floor. He touched the walls, the curtain of ice at the cave's opening, and the wooden crates that held Moolock's few belongings. The boy picked up a buckskin shirt adorned with fringe, pressed it to his face, and smiled. "This smells like you in the summer, Moolock. Bunchgrass, sunshine, and earth." He held up a micro fleece pullover sweater with a quarter zipper at the neck. "Now you're wearing white man's ready-made clothes."

"Warmer," Moolock said. "I prefer the ways of our people, but I'm a practical man." Today he wore snow pants, thermal long johns, and a thick wool sweater. Strangely, the boy touching his personal possessions did not feel intrusive, but more a gesture of tender intimacy. Tegan had a desire to connect with his uncle on a deeper level. Moolock's mouth curled up with pleasure.

"He likes you," Elahan said, sharing his smile.

Moolock met her gaze—this old woman, his mother, who was steadily bringing him back into the realm of men. A great wave of tenderness swelled his heart. They shared the acute pain of Moolock being ripped from her life as an infant. They shared the joy of being reunited after decades of separation. The blood bond between them was stronger than any force on earth.

Tegan's hand deftly stroked a long handmade bow, and then a shorter one, and then his fingers carefully examined two buckskin quivers full of arrows adorned with beads and feathers. "These are beautifully made," he said. "Is the wood juniper?"

"Yes."

"Why is one bow shorter than the other?"

"The shorter one gives me greater accuracy and mobility when I'm shooting from the back of a horse."

"Are the strings sinew?"

"Yucca."

"Plant?" Tegan looked surprised.

"Well-made plant fiber string is better than animal fibers. It holds the most weight, resists stretching, and it remains strong in damp conditions."

Tegan pulled an arrow from the quiver and examined it carefully. "Are your arrowheads flint?"

"Obsidian. Volcanic glass. Sharper than a surgeon's scalpel."

Tegan nodded, his face reflective, then he asked eagerly, "Will you teach me to make a bow and arrows? And how to use them?"

"Yes. When the weather warms." Though the boy was blind, Moolock did not think his request unreasonable. Tegan's ability to use sharp tools to carve intricate animals, to use the hidden blade in his staff as a weapon, to hit a target with accuracy, was astonishing. Like the old woman, Tegan had special powers. He could sense the shape and distance of objects in his immediate sphere, and he had the gift of prophecy, sensing the mood of destiny before it unfolded. Moolock, too, had powers, but not as profound as Tegan's. Or Elahan's. The magician.

"Come eat, my boys," Elahan rasped.

Tegan's staff skimmed the floor and identified the chair. Tegan sank into it. The wolf lifted himself from the floor and put his massive head in the boy's lap, his tail thumping the floor.

Elahan threw a large bone covered with meat and fat outside the circle. With a growl of delight, Lelou pounced on it and began gnawing. Tegan thoroughly cleaned his hands with a sterile wipe. Elahan placed a plate on his lap and pressed a fork in his hand. Tegan used his left hand to feel the food on his plate and guide it onto his fork. He ate hungrily.

Elahan and Moolock took the other two seats and also ate in earnest, the blazing fire keeping the deep chill at bay. No one spoke until hunger was abated, and then Tegan broke the silence. "This cave is really cool. Is this where you live?"

The reluctance Moolock normally felt about divulging details of his personal life evaporated. Here, his life was laid bare, his few possessions on display, his isolation exposed. His soul felt the need to connect deeply with this boy. "I live here when it's cold and wet. In the warmer months, I sleep outdoors. There's comfort in watching the drifting landscape of stars overhead, the moving clouds. It reminds me there is a power greater than ourselves in control of the universe." Moolock scraped his plate and chewed his last bite of apple bread. He held out his plate. "Elahan, may I have more of everything, please?"

"Why do you call her Elahan?" Tegan asked. "She's your mom."

Moolock contemplated the question before answering. "You're right. It's just something I need to practice. I'm not used to it. We were separated for most of my life. I called my adoptive mother "mom."

"Where were you?"

Moolock cleared his throat. This was a lot of conversation, a lot of introspection, and his brain was freezing, resisting.

"He went to New England to live with his father's family," Elahan said, lubricating a new channel of communication. "They had money. Power. He was raised in the white man's world. A rich man's life."

"White man? Your father was white?" Tegan could not keep the stark surprise from his voice.

Moolock was still tongue-tied, trying to untangle memories that were booby-trapped with painful emotions. He had trained himself not to think about the past. Not to feel.

"Yes, his father was white," Elahan said. "His name was Forest Wainwright the Third. He was a doctor who came to the clinic at the Lost River Reservation twice a week. I worked as his office girl. That was a long, long time ago." She squinted into the fire, thinking. "Forty-three years."

"I never pictured you with a white man, Nana."

"I never did, either. But Forest was a special man. He didn't judge people by skin color. He treated everyone the same. With kindness and dignity. Forest loved the simple ways of our culture, the ways of our people, living close to nature."

"And he loved you." Tegan smiled.

"Yes." Elahan smiled back. She leaned over and placed another log on the fire. A constellation of embers flew into the air and she brushed a few from her boots. "Forest and I had many happy months together. Then he went to Vietnam. They needed doctors. I was heavy with child." She turned to Moolock and her voice trailed off to a whisper. "Your father never came home. He never met his beautiful son."

Silence. Neither of them brought up the next chapter of the story, the part where Moolock was stolen from Elahan by rich strangers and a biased court system.

"What was your life like in New England?" Tegan asked.

Moolock forced himself to pick up the threads of the story his mother left dangling. "I was raised by my father's parents, Tegan. It's true. They had money. A staggering amount of money." He spoke in a slow monotone, organizing his thoughts, loosening his tongue. "And yes, I lived a life of privilege. Everything was given to me. Cars. Clothes. Trips around the world. The best schools. The best education. As expected, I became a doctor, like my father and grandfather before me. I worked in New Haven for many years and made a lot of money, as was expected. But I always felt something crucial was missing from my life. I'd gone through a bad marriage and divorce. I felt hollow inside." Moolock stared into the fire, listening to the pop and hiss of flames licking the wood.

"Tell me more," Tegan said impatiently.

Moolock sighed, reluctant to drum up more memories, but he forced himself to continue. The boy had a right to know. "I learned about the shortage of trauma care available to soldiers injured in combat in the Mideast. I admired my father for making the sacrifice to go into a war zone to help others. I thought it was my turn to help. Long story short, I joined the army. I ended up serving as a trauma surgeon for four years on a forward operating base out in the middle of nowhere in Afghanistan. My team took care of soldiers with life-threatening injuries. We saved countless lives." He swallowed, and his voice grew softer. "I met my second wife there. Emery. She, too, was a trauma doctor. Emery was gifted. Beautiful. Brave. We worked side by side. We lived in a tent, worked in a tent, ate in the cafeteria with hundreds of soldiers, in a tent." Moolock smiled. "Guess that's where I learned to live simply. Yet, I was happy. Fulfilled." He paused a few beats as his thoughts traveled back in time. He recalled the scent of the desert, the earsplitting sound of bombs, the acrid smell of explosives, the agonizing cries of wounded men.

"The working conditions were dangerous," Moolock said. "Almost every day we had incoming rocket attacks and indirect fire. We'd hear the siren and have to get down because the rockets had been loaded with shrapnel. Taking care of patients under those conditions, putting on our Kevlar and blocking out what was going on around us, was difficult. In the end, Kevlar couldn't save us. A rocket exploded right outside our surgery tent." Moolock's voice hardened. "Everyone died. Horribly. The other doctors, the nurses, the patients. Emery. Only I survived. I sustained a traumatic brain injury that put me in a coma for weeks. When I woke, and found out what happened, I died inside. My spirit, my will to live, shriveled up like a plant that gets no water. No sunlight. Part of me wanted to be with Emery."

Moolock gritted his teeth and forced the memories of his painful recovery, the mind-numbing grief, back into the shadows. After a few long moments, he was able to speak again. "I was in rehab for months, recovering from the brain injury. I had to relearn how to talk without slurring, how to think straight. Going back to work was out of the question. I was damaged. Emotionally. Physically. I couldn't function in the busy world anymore. What I needed was simplicity. Quiet."

"Is that why you came here?"

He nodded. "Miraculously, I found Elahan...Mother...by going through my grandfather's old records. When I called her and identified myself, she didn't say anything for a very long time. I thought she didn't want to meet me, but then I heard her sobbing. It broke my heart. We spoke several times over a period of weeks, and I eventually explained my situation—that I was suffering from a TBI, and taking enough prescription drugs to numb a horse. She took charge, which is what I desperately needed. She commanded me to come to Oregon. I did. Like an arrow launched at a target, I was irrevocably drawn here. That was five years ago. Mother helped me to live on my own, to replace the drugs with natural remedies. I couldn't be around people. Anyone. Only her. I couldn't be in a house. Too stationary. Structures felt like targets waiting for a bomb. Irrational, I know. But I'm not an entirely rational man anymore." He gestured to his living arrangements. "As you can see."

"Over time Mother taught me native ways. She helped me heal. In short, she saved my life." Moolock heaved out a deep breath, feeling drained, and bruised by the battering of remembered grief. He stood and walked to the wall of frozen water, closed his eyes, and tried to empty his mind of wildly ricocheting thoughts.

A tap on his shoulder made Moolock open his eyes. Tegan's face was tilted up to his, his dark eyes brimming with tears. "I'm glad you came home to us."

Moolock wrapped his arms around the boy's slender frame and hugged him fiercely.

"Can I touch your face?" Tegan asked. "I want to know what you look like."

In answer, Moolock squatted and sat back on his heels.

The boy read his face with his sensitive fingertips as though studying Braille. "You have a strong nose, strong cheekbones, a broad forehead, light color eyes."

"They're hazel," Moolock said, soothed by the boy's gentle touch, his gentle voice. Moolock's anxiety lost its sharpest edges.

Tegan fingered his hair. "Your hair is sable. Like a fawn."

"You are correct."

"You're handsome."

Moolock smiled.

"What's your white man's name?"

"Forest Wainwright the Fourth," Moolock said. "I'm afraid my grandparents weren't too imaginative."

"I like Forest. Full of trees. But I like Moolock better."

"Me, too. It's the name my birth mother gave me." He caught Elahan's beatific expression, the adoring light burning in her eyes. His gaze fixed on hers and he placed his hand on his chest. "The name I feel in my heart."

"So, Moolock," Tegan said. "What's the plan? How long do we stay in this cave?"

"Not long," he said, brushing Tegan's hair back from his eyes. "I'm leaving in the morning. I won't be back until it's safe for you to return home."

"You're going out there to kill a man." Tegan's voice vibrated with emotion. "Take me with you. I can help you."

"That's not an option," Moolock said. "Please don't try to follow me. Don't leave your nana here alone. Can you promise me that?"

The boy's expression was crestfallen. He nodded.

"It's late," Moolock said. "Time to get some rest."

"First we must pray to our sacred spirit," Elahan said. "We must ask for your protection and guidance. Come sit."

The three sat cross-legged in the flickering firelight and Elahan began chanting in her native tongue, low and soft, with a surprising lilting sweetness to her voice. Then Tegan joined in, his voice clear and strong and sure. Their voices rose and fell—at times deeply melancholy, at times soaring and exuberant like birds bursting into the sky. Moolock had never participated in ceremonial chanting and had not used his voice in song for years, but he felt an irresistible urge to join them. He hummed along, softly and tentatively, then he awkwardly repeated the simple lyrics. He lost track of time and after a long while the chanting became instinctual, and he felt his spirit freeing itself from the encumbrances of the physical world. The harmony of voices—rhapsodic and evocative—carried Moolock's spirit to a place of lightness, wellbeing, and eternal knowledge. He came to understand and accept that his fate tomorrow was already destined.

He would do everything in his power to eradicate the malicious threat facing his loved ones. The man he would encounter was cunning, ruthless, and as ghost-like in the wild as Moolock. Whether Moolock would survive the day, he did not know, but the powerful magic of spirit would be with him. He would fight his enemy to the death, if need be.

CHAPTER THIRTY-ONE

SIDNEY PUSHED OPEN the door and she and Amanda entered Grisly's private domain. Sidney could not have been more surprised. Though Grisly lived off the grid with no electricity, and his barn looked like the devil went on a killing spree, his cabin was clean and organized. Kerosene lamps hissed from three corners of the room, casting flickering light across the sparsely furnished interior. A fire crackled in a wood stove in one corner, emitting welcoming warmth. The rustic kitchen counter held a large, shallow sink with a pump handle. The shelves above the oil stove were filled with orderly stacks of dishes, pots and pans, and foodstuff. A small, square table and two upright wooden chairs, an old but serviceable couch, and a desk that held a laptop computer and printer took up the living room. Between the wood stove and the door was a floor to ceiling bookshelf crammed with books. A rustic ladder led to a loft bedroom, tucked beneath the rear half of the roof's steep pitch.

"Looks like Mr. Clean just torpedoed through this place," Sidney said. Even the plank walls looked sanded and finished.

"Cleaner than my place."

"You have a two-year old. You get a free pass."

"Thanks, I'll remember that the next time I step on a squeaky toy in the middle of the night. Get a load of all these books," Amanda said, reading titles. "Tony Hillerman. Jack London.

Everything Louis L'Amour ever wrote. I'd have guessed he was illiterate."

"Me, too. But have they been read?"

Amanda leafed through the pages of a couple paperbacks and found the pages worn and dog-eared. "Yep. Several times."

"Different world in here from the barn," Sidney said. "No dead animals. No pelts. No smell. How'd he keep that stench from coming in?"

"Good question. Must've showered in the barn, or rolled around in the snow like a polar bear."

"Saves water," Sidney chuckled. She studied a handful of framed photos on one of the shelves. Most depicted Grisly with hunting buddies posing with their kill. One surprised her, taken about a decade ago. Clean shaven, hair neatly trimmed, dressed in khakis and a polo shirt, Grisly stood in front of a small but respectable suburban home on a sunny day. One arm was wrapped around the waist of an attractive woman and the other around a six or seven-year old boy. All three grinned at the camera, squinting against the sun. An average American family. Comfortable. Happy. Sidney removed the photo from its frame and read an inscription on the back, scrawled in a feminine hand.

Stokes family—Jessica, Grisly, and Justin. Jackson, 2008.

"Looks like he once had a normal life in Jackson," Sidney said. "What happened to his wife and son? How'd he end up living in the woods like Liver-eating Johnson?"

"Who's Liver-eating Johnson?"

Sidney met Amanda's widened eyes. "He was a trapper who lived in the 1800s. His wife, from the Flathead Indian tribe, was killed by a Crow hunting party. Johnson took out his revenge by killing and scalping more than 300 Crow Indians, and eating their livers."

"Seriously?"

"Seriously."

"Yech. Makes Hannibal Lector look like a choir boy."

Sidney replaced the photo in the frame. "Grisly the violent rapist with the torture chamber barn sure doesn't jibe with this photo. Or this cabin. It's too clean, too normal."

Amanda shrugged. "I don't get it either. Maybe he's in witness protection and had to leave his respectable life."

"Maybe he has dual personalities," Sidney quipped. "One a respectable citizen, the other a hostile redneck."

"Or this is a twin brother, and Grisly's the evil twin."

A knock at the door announced the arrival of the reserve officer with the warrant.

Sidney thanked him profusely for coming out in these weather conditions.

Now they could legally search the premises. "Well, let's get to work. Not much here. Shouldn't take us too long. Hopefully, we'll find some answers."

She and Amanda worked in companionable silence for twenty minutes, sifting through household items in drawers and cabinets. Grisly's gun cabinet was unlocked and a rifle appeared to be missing, corroborating Sander's version of the shootout.

While Amanda sorted through folders in Grisly's desk drawers, Sidney climbed to the loft, which was occupied by a double bed and an old cedar chest. Inside the chest she sorted through folded clothes and old shoes, and discovered a photo album. Sitting on the bed, she leafed through a chronology of Grisly's life, which included photos of his wedding, the birth of his son, and holiday celebrations. In one shot, Grisly posed in front of a van with a business name and logo painted on it: Stokes Plumbing. A folded newspaper clipping was tucked into the last page. Sidney unfolded the worn and yellowed page. The headline made her breath catch.

Woman and Child Found Dead in Jackson Home

A 29-year-old woman and a juvenile were found shot to death in an apparent murder-suicide. Investigators believe the woman shot the child before shooting herself.

The woman's husband discovered the bodies when he arrived home from work.

Sidney scanned through the rest of the article, which stated the husband had a history of domestic abuse. The police had responded to calls by Jessica Stokes on several occasions. In addition to serving a short stint in jail, her husband, Grisly Stokes, had completed an anger management course.

Sidney refolded the article, closed the album and sat quietly. She didn't hear Amanda come up the stairs and was startled when she heard her voice.

"Sorry, Chief."

"No worries."

"Nothing downstairs. You find something?"

"Yeah. The reason Grisly did an about face. He came home from work and found the bodies of his wife and son in a murder-suicide."

"That's horrifying," Amanda said, eyes wide. "A woman killing herself is bad enough, but taking the life of a child..." She shuddered. "Unthinkable."

"Something a person never recovers from. He'd been abusing her. Must have pushed her to the brink."

"She took an abused woman's ultimate revenge," Amanda said. "That would make any man run for the hills and hide out."

"Didn't cure his penchant for violence, though."

They heard the cabin door open downstairs and Darnell called out, "Chief?"

"Up here," Amanda called back.

"We're coming down."

"Follow me outside," Darnell said. "You've got to see what I found."

Deeply curious, Sidney and Amanda pulled out their Maglites and followed Darnell out into the frigid night air, their breath steaming. They rounded the house and their beams illuminated two pathways neatly carved through the snow. One led to an outhouse, the other to a small barn. Sidney saw that Darnell's earlier boot prints had taken a side trip off the paved path, through the trees, and back again. Before she could comment, he took off in the same direction, stamping new holes in the snow.

She shone the light on his retreating back. "Where're you going?"

"You'll see. Follow me."

About thirty feet in, Darnell halted in front of a metal trap door that he had wrenched open and thrown back against the frozen earth. He directed his flashlight beam into the hole, revealing a sturdy wooden ladder and the corner of an earthen room.

"How the hell did you find this?" Sidney asked, impressed by Darnell's investigative skills.

"I saw a pattern of very faint footsteps leading toward it. Then there was a noticeable depression in the snow the size of this door. I scraped away the snow, and discovered this. Careful coming down. Brace yourself. You aren't going to like it."

"Thanks for the warning." They descended into the underground dwelling. Feet planted firmly on the earthen floor, they turned and cast their beams across the room from corner to corner. Though prepared, Sidney's stomach twisted. The cavern, about twenty feet square, held stacks of animal pelts in rows on the floor, some shoulder high. Sidney recognized bobcat, beaver, fox, otter, coyote, rabbit, and others. For a long moment, no one spoke. Finally, Sidney found her voice. "Here's proof of Grisly's illegal trapping and hunting business. Looks like it's been going on for years."

Anger rippled across Amanda's delicate features. "You don't have to be an animal rights extremist to know this kind of killing is just plain wrong. Letting an animal suffer in a trap, then clubbing it to death to make a few bucks on a pelt, is sick." She fingered the top pelt on a stack of beaver furs. "It takes thirteen of these to make one knee-length coat. Thirteen animals! Tortured for a single coat. No one needs to wear fur."

"Here in Oregon, seven-hundred trappers reported killing 23,000 animals last season," Darnell said. "Does that seem right to you?"

"No, Darnell. It doesn't," Sidney said. "And a lot more go unreported. Like these. Unfortunately, the fur trade is booming. Millions of animals are trapped every year and their pelts are sold to designers."

"Hunters and trappers would drive animals to extinction, if they could," Amanda said hotly.

"Unfortunately, that's happened too many times," Sidney said. "Countless species have been wiped off the face of the earth. Wolves, trumpeter swans, and Humboldt martens are just a handful of animals hunted to extinction here in Oregon. Swans and wolves are being reintroduced. But there are fewer than two hundred martens left, and it's still legal to trap them."

"If they don't get protection, they'll disappear this year, or next," Darnell said.

"Poor creatures," Amanda said sadly.

Sidney sighed and shifted her attention to the matter at hand. "We'll have to get a game warden out here to do an inventory of these pelts. We need to find out who was partnering with Grisly and where he's been unloading this stuff. You'll have to get into his computer, Darnell. See if you can dig up anything."

"Will do. I found something else, too, Chief."

Back outside, Darnell slammed the trap door shut and led them along the other path to the small barn tucked away under ponderosa pines. They viewed a small corral dotted with fresh manure and the hoof patterns of a shod horse.

"Grisly owns a horse," Sidney said, surprised. "Is it in the barn?"

"No. Someone took it out for a ride. I followed the tracks into the woods. They lead to White Tail Creek, going west. I'd say the rider left a couple hours ago."

"We know the rider isn't Grisly. He's dead." Sidney rubbed her tired eyes, thinking. "So, who's this mystery rider? This creek runs near Two Creeks Village, doesn't it?"

"Runs right through it, Chief," Amanda said. "The Stalker used it as a route to sneak up on houses. A few times they found his prints, and horse tracks, leading to and from the creek, but when they tried to follow, the tracks disappeared into the water."

"Hmmm. Sure casts more guilt on Grisly. He could have ridden his horse over, done his grim deeds, and made a clean getaway. We need a good tracker out here."

"Maybe Tucker Longtooth knows someone," Amanda said.

"Give him a call."

The beam of a flashlight splintering between the trees caught their attention.

"Looks like someone's searching for us. Let's head back."

One of the firemen from Jackson met them. "Fire's out, Chief Becker. The M.E. is here looking for you."

Sidney thanked him and they walked into the clearing together. Amanda got on the phone to Tucker.

The firemen were cleaning up and retracting their hoses and a few were milling inside the hollowed-out structure of the barn with flashlights, searching for Grisly's remains.

"Tucker is sending someone over by the name of Magic, Chief," Amanda said. "I'll wait for him down below."

"Good. When he arrives, you two are done here for the night. The fire inspectors will take over. Get your reports done. Darnell, get into Grisly's laptop. We'll meet at the station at nine o'clock sharp."

Sidney joined Dr. Linthrope and Stewart Wong who stood watching at a large opening where the entrance of the barn used to be. Half of the roof had caved in but parts of the four walls still clung to the towering skeletal structure. Burnt lumber and charred objects were strewn across the floor as though tossed by a hurricane.

Working with axes, the firemen uncovered Grisly's body within minutes and signaled to them. They trekked through rubble and sludge to reach the charred human figure lying on its back. The scene struck a chord in her memory. It had a grim familiarity to other burnt corpses she'd witnessed in the past, all victims of homicide. White bone gleamed through blackened flesh. Empty eye sockets stared. The teeth were bared in a lipless grin. All clothing was incinerated. The remaining tissue that hadn't burned was essentially mummified. His rifle lay beside him, the stock burned half way through.

Stewart bagged the rifle, and then got to work snapping shots from every angle, his flash producing bursts of light in the darkened dwelling. Wearing vinyl gloves, Dr. Linthrope crouched over the body and identified a bullet hole in the chest, then turned the corpse onto one side. His light beam searched the charred back, but no exit wound was visible. "The bullet must still be in there," he said. He brushed some debris off both feet. The remains of a boot had melted into the right foot, but the left foot was bare, burned down to the bones. "Hmmm. Why is he only wearing one boot?"

"The other melted?" Sidney asked.

He shook his head and pushed his glasses higher on his nose. "Subjected to the same external conditions, both feet should be a match."

For several minutes the Captain and his men carefully sifted through the debris surrounding the corpse until they recovered the other burned boot, several feet from the body.

"The investigators will do a more thorough search tomorrow to recover the rounds fired from the wardens guns," the captain said. "We'll get them to the lab."

"Good. Nothing more to be done here." Dr. Linthrope stood, and with a nod, gave the men approval to seal the remains in a body bag, load it onto a gurney, and cart it to his van.

Pulling off his vinyl gloves and replacing them with bulky, fur-lined mittens, the doctor walked with Sidney behind the gurney. "This is a first, Sidney. Two murders in three days. Reminds me why I left my job in the city." Linthrope's tone was gentle. He gazed at Sidney through wire-rimmed glasses with paternal fondness. They had come to deeply respect one another over her two-year tenure. Despite the evening's grisly call to duty, the doctor's quiet but efficient manner instilled confidence and trust. At seventy-one, he showed no hint of slowing down. His intellect was still scalpel-sharp, but his eminent retirement loomed on the horizon.

"I hear you," she said. "My hope for a quiet job in the country writing parking tickets didn't pan out. With all the new development and strangers moving to town, this could someday be the new normal."

"Let's hope not." He turned to her and noticed her deep frown. "What's niggling you?"

An uneasy feeling had worked its way into her consciousness and refused to be ignored, like the resonance of a tuning fork. "It may be nothing, but why was Grisly only wearing one boot?"

"Could be a simple explanation. Though I can't think of one at the moment."

"Grisly wouldn't be dumping gas out in the snow with only one boot on. He immediately engaged in a shootout with Harper.

Why would he stop to take off a boot?" She chewed her bottom lip, thinking. "I've been in homicide too long. My instincts are telling me something ain't right."

"I trust your instincts." He was silent for a moment. "You want an autopsy, don't you?"

"Sorry, Doc, but yeah, I do."

"I'll do both postmortems tomorrow, starting with Grisly bright and early. Nikah Tamanos right after."

"Thanks, Doc." Sidney smiled her appreciation. It was a lot to ask of him.

"Could have some interesting results for you."

"I hope so. We need a break."

Sidney said her goodbye and they parted ways. She climbed into her SUV and watched the men load the body into the van. When the van pulled out, Darnell's truck, parked directly behind, became visible. The motor was running and Amanda and Darnell were sitting inside, keeping warm. Headlight beams flooded the road and a truck hitched to a horse trailer slowed and pulled in behind them. Magic had arrived. Bundled like an Eskimo, he got out and hiked to the back of the trailer. Amanda met him as he hustled out a quarter horse, saddled and ready to go.

Good. Her junior officer had things under control. Sidney didn't envy anyone being out in this weather tonight, which made her think of Granger. A long three hours had passed since he'd left with the small search party from the village. She checked her phone and sure enough, a text had come in twenty minutes earlier.

We lost the trail. Can't find a thing out here. We'll probably be heading back.

Sidney expelled her breath in a long, soundless sigh. The old woman and boy were still out there in the frozen wilderness. A lot of folks, including herself, would not sleep well tonight. She texted back: *Keep me posted.*

A sudden wave of exhaustion overtook Sidney. A mountain of paper work waited at the station, but she didn't have the mental capacity to face it tonight. She revved up the engine, cranked up the heater, and pulled onto the road. Halfway to town, her phone buzzed. It was David.

"Hi, David," she said softly, trying to transition from a hardened cop with vaulted emotions to the soft, resilient, utterly feminine woman she became in David's presence.

"How are you doing?"

"It's been a very long day." Voice infused with fatigue. No energy to flirt. "I'm going to hit the sack like a bag of cement."

"Had dinner?"

"Too tired to eat, unless it's through an IV."

"Running on fumes, huh? Not good. You need to keep that gorgeous body of yours well nourished. Tell you what. I'm going to stop by with my famous melt-in-your-mouth lasagna. Still warm from the oven. I'm going to feed it to you like a baby, and then I'm going to massage you to sleep. No self-interest. No hidden agenda. Tonight, it's all about you. Deal?"

Tenderness for David warmed her. Sidney was an ace at keeping her state of mind invisible to others, but not to David. He disarmed her. He intuited what she felt when she didn't know how to express it herself.

"You there?" he asked.

"Yes." She cleared her throat, suddenly wanting to feel his strong arms holding her close. "I'm a mess. My hair and clothes smell like smoke."

"Smoke?" An edge of concern crept into his voice. "What happened?"

"Huge barn fire."

"Everything okay?"

"No. But under control for the moment."

Silence. David didn't press her. He finally said, "Come home safe."

"I will. See you in twenty minutes."

CHAPTER THIRTY-TWO

SIDNEY ENTERED the house quietly through the laundry room that also served as a mudroom. Normally a welcoming committee of four cats assailed her, clinging like Velcro and mewing loudly. But tonight she was greeted by a row of thick coats hanging on pegs and an assortment of winter boots hugging the wall. She removed her heavy outerwear and boots, hung up her duty belt, and deposited her gun in the safe. The dining room was softly lit with candles, the table set for two. David was in the kitchen, humming over the counter with his back to her. Selena, no doubt, had retreated upstairs with the four fur balls to give them privacy.

David was dressed in faded jeans, a forest green flannel shirt, and wool socks. She took a moment to admire his broad shoulders and narrow hips and imagine the smooth, lean muscles rippling beneath his clothing. "Smells good," she said, entering.

He turned and smiled in the relaxed, easy fashion that always had a calming effect on her. "Hey. The weary Amazon warrior returns. Hungry?"

"Starving."

David was two inches taller than Sidney's own six feet. He pulled her close, his cheek against hers. He was warm, almost flushed. She knew this man intimately—every contour, every bone, every line radiating from his eyes. She knew him in bed. She loved his intelligence, his humor, his lack of ego, the ease she felt in his company.

His hands wandered along her spine, pressing out the tension. "You're tight. Tough day, huh."

She nodded, not wanting to think about anything except how good David felt. He lowered his head and kissed her. Slow. Sweet. Sexy. His lips felt soft, his chest hard against hers. The horror of the last two days, for the moment, evaporated.

"I missed you to the point of distraction," he said softly. "I couldn't wait to hold you close."

His words thrilled her.

"Let's get you fed." He pecked the tip of her nose, gently pulled away, and gestured to the dining room. "Sit."

She did. He brought in two plates laden with green salad and squares of lasagna, then poured her favorite Barolo into their wine glasses. He sat close, his knee touching hers beneath the table.

Sidney dove in, eating a third of the lasagna before coming up for air and sipping the delicious wine. This was comfort food at its best.

David ate slowly, watching her with amusement.

She paused long enough to form two sentences. "Sorry, I'm eating like a bear. I'm starved, and addicted to your cooking."

He smiled. "Makes me feel appreciated."

"I'm addicted to you." She leaned over and planted a warm kiss on his mouth. "What did you do without me today?"

"Went to work."

David meant that figuratively. As a business, the Art Studio probably just broke even, but making a profit wasn't David's purpose. The purpose was to create a place for artists to congregate and share their passion, and for David to teach, which he thrived on.

"I taught a couple of classes. And I started a new painting. A portrait."

"What motivated you to do that?" she asked, surprised. David never painted the human form. He was a gifted landscape artist, and his work commanded impressive prices from choice galleries and well-heeled patrons. His use of bright colors and the effects of light reflected his love for Impressionism.

He shrugged one shoulder. "Wanted to try something new. Get out of my comfort zone."

"Whose portrait?"

"Yours."

She stopped eating and blushed with pleasure. "Really? What am I doing in the portrait? Not wearing a uniform, I hope."

He chuckled. "Actually, you're nude."

"What?"

"I'm painting you from memory," he said with a wicked grin. "I have very good memories."

"I don't want people to see me naked, David."

"Don't worry. It's for my eyes only. I'll hang it in the bedroom."

"What if Dillon walks in? He'll know we're doing the hanky-panky."

"Hanky-panky? So that's what we're doing." He laughed. "Wasn't sure how to label our relationship."

Sidney waited, hoping he'd expand on the subject. She desperately wanted to know if they were in an exclusive relationship, or just friends with bennies. She felt uncomfortable bringing up the topic herself. If this was just a casual fling to David, she wasn't prepared for that kind of massive letdown tonight. But David didn't pursue the topic. He gently brushed a strand of hair from her eyes. "Don't worry. Dillon won't recognize you. You're looking away, and your face is in shadow."

"In that case, you have my blessing. When's the unveiling?"

"I'll let you know." He sipped his wine and watched her for a moment over the rim of his glass, his brown eyes soft and mesmerizing. "Want to talk about your day?"

"Not really."

"Maybe it would help."

She blew out a breath. "Where to start?" It was hard to believe that it was only yesterday afternoon that she had gotten the call about Nikah's death while snuggling in bed with David. A mountain of crime had materialized since then. "Seems the whole county is going nuts. Two people killed, one seriously shot, animals poached, and a series of burglaries and sexual assaults at Two Creeks Village." She sighed. "In addition, an old Indian woman, her great grandson, and a huge white wolf are out in the wilderness somewhere and a murderer may be following them."

David's eyes grew wider as she spoke and he whistled under his breath. "Holy hell. That's enough crime for a year. You couldn't make this stuff up."

"No, you couldn't."

"How are you holding up?"

"I'm not sure that I am." She felt her shoulders tense as the burden of her responsibilities weighed down on her again. "Somehow, all of these crimes are interconnected. If I can fit a few pieces together, the rest of the puzzle may fall into place. A lot revolves around the murder of a young Native American woman and a medallion and key to a safety deposit box that I found in her home."

"What was in the deposit box?"

"A decorative key with the same design as the medallion."

David eyes brightened. As an art historian who studied symbology, his interest was piqued. "Do you have photos?"

"I do. Maybe you'll recognize the symbol." She fished out her phone and scanned through her images, then passed him the phone.

David's eyebrows arched. "Of course. The Triskelion." His gaze lifted to hers. "This ancient symbol is known as the "Spiral of Life." He followed the circular curves of the symbol with an index finger. "These three spirals are interconnected with no open ends, creating one continuous line. As you can see, each spiral turns in the same direction. They represent balance, harmony and continual motion. The flow of life. The earth's cycles and seasons."

"Where does it originate?"

"That's the interesting thing. It's been found on different continents in different hemispheres. The most famous is Newgrange, in Ireland, a large circular mound with an inner stone passageway and chambers. It was built during the Neolithic period, making it older than Stonehenge and the Egyptian pyramids. This symbol is carved in the rock at the main entrance. Triskelions have also been found on artifacts in Columbia dating back to 300 to 1000 AD."

"On the other end of the planet."

"Correct." David narrowed his eyes, closely studying one photo, then the other. "The craftsmanship of these two items is similar. I'd say made by the same artist. They appear to be very old, and may be quite valuable."

"Someone else obviously thinks so. That's what spurred the break-ins and the beating of a man," Sidney said. "Possibly even her murder."

"I could send these photos out to my contact, Sid. Antiquities experts. See if anything clicks."

"Would you?"

"For you, doll, anything," he said with a Bogart accent.

Sidney smiled, pushed her plate aside, and drained her glass. "Thanks for bringing me dinner, David. It revived me. I believe I found the energy to shower. Want to stick around for a bit?"

"Sure." His eyes twinkled. "I'll clean the kitchen."

"Nothing sexier than a man in an apron holding a sponge."

He grinned. "I bet you say that to all the guys."

"Meet me upstairs in ten minutes," she said. "First door on the right."

His grin widened.

***

The hot water drilling her tired muscles felt rejuvenating, soothing away the stress of the day. Sidney stepped into the steaming bathroom, toweled dry, and slipped into her terry cloth robe. She brushed her teeth and moisturized, combed her damp hair, and padded into the hallway. The house was dark and quiet. No light shone under the door of her sister's room at the other end of the hall, but dim light illuminated the doorway of her own bedroom.

With an exquisite anticipation humming in her veins, Sidney entered and shut the door behind her. David was seated at her desk, thumbing through a book of native birds under the soft light of a knock-off Tiffany lamp. He looked too big for the small room she grew up in, which hadn't changed since her high school days— same queen size bed, a small desk equipped with her laptop and printer, and a bookcase sagging under the weight of dozens of mystery novels. This was the first time she'd invited a man into her room since her senior year, and a silly shyness suddenly overtook her, as if her mother might suddenly march in and send David home with a few sharp words.

She shook off the feeling and closed the space between them. He turned to her without getting up and smiled. "I can picture you in here as a child, Sidney, and as a teenager, growing into the beautiful woman you are today." David stood and pulled her close. His gentle kisses deepened. His warm hands slipped inside her robe and caressed the contours of her hips and buttocks. Sidney breathed in his familiar smell of soap and sandalwood aftershave. He touched her nipples with the tips of his thumbs and felt the weight of her breasts in his palms. Sidney's body made the shift towards him, to his body, and she felt his erection with an intense and sudden longing.

"Lay down," he said huskily.

Sidney let the robe slip from her shoulders and fall to the floor, then she laid back and watched him undress, revealing his smooth skin and muscled limbs, his beautiful erection a declaration of desire for her. The smallest hint of a smile played around his lips as he lowered himself to the bed, confident in his masculinity, in his unique abilities. He kissed her slowly, unhurried, his hands finding her sensitive areas, allowing her feelings of pleasure to expand and grow. She surrendered to an ache that deepened in intensity, a piercing need that had no name but craved expression and ultimately, blissful release.

***

Sometime during the night Sidney woke to find the room pitched in black. She reached across the bed but David was gone. The smell of their lovemaking lingered on the sheets. Remembering, her lips curved into a smile.

The phone buzzed, breaking the hypnotic spell. The clock read 11:15 p.m. Her fingers fumbled for her phone on the nightstand. It was Granger.

"Hey," she said sleepily.

"Sorry to wake you, Chief. You said to give you an update."

Her brain sharpened as her thoughts shifted to police work. "You're back."

"Wish that were the case. I'm using the satellite phone." He sounded exhausted, his voice strained. "I'm still out in the backcountry. We're staying on the trail as long as the old woman and boy are out here. Tommy's convinced they can survive the cold, but something else bothers me more. Another rider was following them, about an hour behind."

Sidney's stomach tightened. "You think he caught up to them?"

"Doubt it. I underestimated Elahan. That old woman is shrewd. She drove their horses in and out of Beartooth Creek a few times. That's why we lost her. In the dark we couldn't find her last exit point. The tracks of the other rider disappeared in the water, too. A guy from the village named Magic intercepted us. He'd been following the tracks all the way from Grisly's property. Said you sent him."

"Yeah, we did. I guess Magic told you Grisly's dead."

"Yep. Can't believe it. Sounds like all hell broke loose. If Grisly's dead, who's riding his horse?"

"Good question. Whoever it is, I doubt his intention is friendly."

"My thoughts, too."

Sidney didn't reply. Her long exhalation expressed her deep frustration.

"The twins headed home. Magic brought some down bags and a tent," Granger continued. "We're setting up camp. Tommy, Magic, and I are aiming to get a good start at dawn."

"Stay warm."

"Three guys in a small tent? Should be like a sauna."

"You get hold of Captain Harrison?

"Yep. They'll have the chopper out scouting the terrain first light."

"Good. They might have better luck than people on the ground. Be safe out there."

CHAPTER THIRTY-THREE

MOOLOCK'S SLEEP was haunted by nightmares. He woke to find himself thrashing in his sleeping bag on the thin rubber mat that protected his body from the icy floor. His ears still rang from the wailing siren at the base, followed by the ear-splitting shrieks of exploding rockets, and the tortured wails of wounded men. He opened his eyes. The dream vaporized. But his heart raced for several seconds while his memory played merciless tricks.

The hazy light of dawn filtered into the cavern through the frozen waterfall, illuminating the figure of the boy huddled in his sleeping bag just feet away. Elahan crouched near the pit stoking the fire into popping, dancing flames. The steaming coffee pot sat on the grill, and the aroma from something sizzling in the cast iron pan made his stomach clench with hunger. The wolf lay on the other side of the pit, gnawing hungrily on a gristly bone.

Hearing him rustle as he slipped out of the bag, Elahan turned and put her finger to her lips. "Shhh."

"It's okay. I'm awake," Tegan said sleepily.

"Then come eat."

Moolock and Tegan pulled sweaters and pants over their long johns, yanked on socks and snow boots, and joined her. Moolock poured coffee from the pot into a tin cup. Elahan heaped large portions of eggs, potatoes, and bacon onto plates and they settled into the camp chairs and ate heartily. They made small talk and Moolock's mind sharpened from the strong, black coffee.

"Thank you, Mother. That was delicious," Moolock said with forced cheerfulness. He nodded toward the frozen waterfall where the soft morning light had turned golden. "Looks like sunshine out there. That means good visibility. I'll go pack a few things and then I'll be heading out."

Tegan fingered a soft deerskin pouch that hung from his neck on a string of rawhide. His medicine bag contained sacred items that held supernatural powers—sage and sweetgrass from the plant world, a tuft of Lelou's fur from the animal world, a crystal from the mineral world that Elahan had placed in his palm when she healed him from his burns, and most powerful of all, from the world of man, a lock of Elahan's hair. The boy started to pull the pouch over his head. "Take this with you, Moolock. For protection."

"No," Elahan said sharply. "What your bag contains is sacred, and good medicine for you alone."

At her tone, Tegan dropped his hand as though burned.

The boy's selfless gesture touched Moolock deeply. Tegan had been willing to part with his most prized possession to keep him safe. A wave of tenderness swelled in his chest and he placed his large hand over the boy's small hand. He said gently, "Your nana is right, Tegan. The magic in your bag is your magic. I have my own." He reached beneath his shirt and produced his own pouch, made of parfleche and painted with natural dyes. "Mother gave me this on the day we were reunited. Over time, I've added a few things—seeds, fur, roots, feathers. The magic has served me well. Kept me safe in the woods all these years."

"I have something for you both, to add to your medicine bags." Elahan reached inside the collar of her black flannel dress and pulled out her own pouch which hung low to her breast. Made of sturdy fabric, it was decorated with small, glistening beads. She loosened the strings and plucked out three polished turquoise stones. The stones, placed on her lap, fit together like puzzle pieces.

"I have carried this stone next to my heart for sixty-five years. It was given to me by the medicine man of my village on my wedding day when I was eighteen years old. It holds very potent magic. Two days ago, I broke it into four equal pieces. Tommy has one piece in his bag. I will keep one, and the other two are for you. Four pieces to unite the four people in our family. Together we are strong. When we are apart, the magic of this stone will hold us together. When we face danger, the stone will draw strength from the rest of us. The magic of this stone will increase your hunting and fighting skills. It will allow you to heal yourselves and your allies. It will hinder your enemy, and it will even alter the weather to do so."

"Thank you, Nana," Tegan said with feeling, holding his stone in his closed fist and whispering a prayer. Then, with great reverence, he placed the turquoise in his pouch and tightened the strings.

Moolock's throat was thick. "Thank you, Mother." He rubbed the beautiful polished stone between his fingers, and imagined the power of Elahan's magic rushing into his skin, into his spirit. He said a silent prayer asking for guidance and protection, then placed the treasured stone in his pouch.

In military fashion, with a straight spine and a soldierly stride, Moolock began to prepare for his mission. He packed provisions, haltered Gracie, and secured a few of the heavy buffalo hides to her back. He saddled Taba, shoved his rifle into the scabbard and strapped his holstered pistol to his thigh. All the while he felt the presence of the wolf, the boy, and his mother standing nearby, watching attentively.

"Why are you haltering Gracie?" Tegan asked. "You're taking two horses?"

"Yes," Moolock said. "I must also take Lelou. A man is following the tracks of these two horses and the wolf. I'll need them to lead him far away from this cave." He pulled his leather hat lined with rabbit fur over his head and turned to Elahan, taking a moment to memorize her face. "Goodbye, Mother."

"Goodbye, my son." Her eyes were old and knowing, and the sharp edges of her cheekbones pressed against paper-thin skin.

Don't burden her, Moolock thought with a pang that hit straight under the breastbone. Don't let her see your doubts. His mission was to extinguish a dangerous threat to himself and his loved ones. Though he was ex-military, he was not an infantryman. He was a doctor. Trained to save lives. Not take them. He would defend himself if he was under attack, but he didn't know if he was capable of outright murder.

Moolock tenderly kissed his mother's withered cheek and an odd protectiveness tightened his chest. "If I don't return by morning, promise me you'll head back to the village."

"You will return," Elahan said fiercely. Something happened to her face then. Her features ironed into perfect stillness, and it was as though something moved at the bottom of a deep lake, sending a surge to the surface. He felt a thrumming current like electricity transfer from her body to his. Moolock stood as still as his mother. Time stood still. Then he released a long, slow breath, awestruck and speechless, and managed to nod.

"I'll walk out with you," Tegan said, grabbing Gracie's reins and turning in the direction of the tunnel they used last night.

"I'm leaving from a different tunnel today," Moolock said. "Come, Lelou." The wolf fell into step behind him. The Maglite beam lighted the way through a narrow passage in the back of the cavern. The hooves of the horses stamped the stone floor behind him. This tunnel was longer. To the boy it must seem to traverse the entire mountain. At last stunning daylight appeared. They emerged on a thin slip of shoreline hidden from the opposite bank of Beartooth Creek by evergreen trees. The bright sun reflecting off the water was glaring. Moolock reached into his pocket for his shades and scanned the sky through the lenses—deep blue, with cumulous clouds lined along the distant horizon like schooners, scudding westward.

Tegan handed over the reins and stood at Moolock's side, vacant eyes staring at nothing. "I hear fast-moving water."

"Beartooth Creek comes right up to this cliff. I'll travel back through the creek and come out below the point where you exited last night. Then I'll go due east."

"I smell a storm coming in, Moolock. A big storm."

"Yes. It's on the horizon. Moving west."

Tegan's fingers curled and flexed, curled and flexed at his side. Close to tears, he let out a single sob and hid his face in the folds of Moolock's sheepskin coat. "I wish you would take me with you. I hear things you don't. Feel things. Smell things. Together, our power is doubled."

Moolock rubbed the boy's back, feeling his bony frame through his sweater. "You heard your nana," he said gently. "The magic of the four stones will protect me. I'll return this evening."

Tegan untangled his fists from the coat and tilted his face upwards, presenting Moolock with a brave but wobbly smile. Then he flung his arms around the neck of the wolf. Lelou slurped the boy's face several times before Tegan tore himself away and darted into the tunnel.

Moolock's eyes were hot and burning when he placed his boot in the stirrup and hoisted himself into the saddle. He directed both horses into the water.

CHAPTER THIRTY-FOUR

THE BUZZ OF Sidney's phone woke her from a dead sleep at 8:00 a.m. Bleary-eyed, she glanced at the ID. It was Dr. Linthrope. She pulled herself into a seated position. "Hello, Doc."

"Sorry to wake you, Chief. I know sleep is a valuable commodity these days."

"Actually, I owe you. I slept through my alarm. I have a meeting at the station in an hour. Don't tell me you've already done Grisly's autopsy."

There was a long pause. "You better get down here right away."

"I'll be there shortly." Spurred by the note of urgency in his voice, Sidney threw the covers aside, stormed into the bathroom and indulged in a two-minute shower, and dressed in a clean uniform. She flew down the stairs, through the living and dining rooms into the kitchen, headed straight for the coffee pot. "Good morning."

Sitting at the table in her chenille bathrobe, a cat curled on her lap, Selena looked up from the paper with raised eyebrows. The other three cats were stretched across the carpet, drowsing in sunbeams pouring through the window. "You off to the races?"

"Running late. Anything in there about Nikah?" Sidney filled a travel mug nearly to the brim.

Selena pushed off the tabby and padded into the kitchen. "Yes. A small article, front page. Just the bare facts, from Winnie's press release. A woman was found dead in a frozen creek. Period. Doesn't identify her. Doesn't hint at murder."

"Good. For now."

"Let me make you a smoothie."

"No time." Sidney secretly hated Selena's smoothies. No one should be drinking pulverized kale and spinach and hemp, and the other weird stuff Selena put in the blender. She usually poured Selena's smoothies down the drain when she got to the office. After adding milk and sugar to the travel mug, she screwed the lid on tight.

A cabinet opened and closed behind her, then Selena stuffed a protein bar into Sidney's breast pocket. "This will keep you going until lunch."

"Thanks." A protein bar she could tolerate. Sidney detoured around her sister, hurried into the laundry room, and grabbed her duty belt.

"So, what's going on with the case? Any suspects?"

"Not yet." Sidney buckled the bulky duty belt around her hips and turned to the combination lock on the safe.

"What about last night? Don't I get any details about David?"

Sidney met her sister's curious gaze, and grinned. "A little slice of heaven." She opened the safe and made sure the magazine of her Glock semi-automatic contained a full load before holstering the weapon.

"So, what's going on between you two? You've been mum for weeks."

"No ring, no wedding proposal, no commitment, if that's what you mean. But the sex and food are great. No expectations." She swallowed. "We've only been dating six weeks."

"You've been doing a lot more than dating, Sidney," Selena said. "I'm jealous. I haven't had sex in a year."

Sidney met her sister's somber gaze. "Maybe it's time you did. Granger's clearly smitten. You can't hold a good man off for long."

A delicate blush colored Selena's cheeks and her countenance softened. "Yes, I know."

"He's a special man."

"Soon," Selena said softly, as though sharing a secret, then she changed the topic. "What about the murder case? I'm a consultant. I should be privy to what's going on."

"A consultant doesn't have unlimited access, Selena." Sidney assessed her sister for a moment. "I'll give you an update this evening. I promise. Right now, I need to get to the morgue. Then a meeting at the station." Sidney yanked her police jacket off the peg and wrestled her arms though the sleeves.

"Will Granger be there?"

"No. He's out in the field, which reminds me…" Sidney paused to check her text messages. Sure enough, one was from Granger posted at 7:00 a.m. She read out loud, "We're heading out, Chief. S&R is already in the air."

A touch of alarm appeared on her sister's face. "Heading out where? Why is Search and Rescue involved?"

"We're looking for someone." Sidney kept the details mum. She didn't need to alarm her sister further. Outside the window the weather was clear and bright, as Captain Harrison had predicted, and snow glistened like diamonds in the early morning light.

"Is it dangerous? Should I be worried about Granger?" Selena asked.

"No," she said, which was half true. "He's with expert trackers." Before her sister could ask another question, Sidney gave her a quick hug and hurried out the door.

***

Sidney crossed the lobby of the small community hospital to the elevator and descended to the basement. The sound of her footsteps was amplified in the sterile tiled hallway as she passed the open door of the forensic lab. Inside, she spotted Stewart Wong at his workstation, his head bowed over a microscope. An astringent chemical odor reached her nostrils as she pushed through one of the double doors at the end of the hall and entered the morgue. The spotless room was equipped with cold storage compartments, a cleanup area, and a stainless-steel slab in the middle of the room, currently occupied by the charred corpse of Grisly Stokes. She sucked in a breath as she confronted the ghastly remains in the unforgiving bright light. The facial skin had been burned back to the scull and his teeth were bared in a hideous grin. His opened chest cavity looked like the hull of a ship, stripped of internal organs.

Wearing a clear plastic mask, a lab coat, and gloves, Dr. Linthrope was weighing a liver on a scale. She approached and inadvertently wrinkled her nose as she caught the smell of the corpse. She would never get use to the smell of death.

"Good morning," the doctor said brightly, displaying his normal good cheer. He stripped off his gloves and mask and pushed his wire-rimmed glasses higher on his nose. Beneath his cumulous of white hair, his hazel eyes sparkled with enthusiasm. "Ready for some interesting news?"

"What'cha got?" she said, itching with curiosity. The doctor's enthusiasm was contagious. Clearly, he had unearthed something of consequence.

"Cause of death is a 9mm gunshot wound to the chest, which matches the service weapon of Sander Vance. No surprise there. Ready for the bombshell?"

"Yep. Lay it on me."

"This isn't Grisly Stokes."

His words hit home like a sharp thwack to the head. "What?"

"Dental records show the proud owner of these choppers is Lancer Richards."

"Lancer?" Sidney stood stunned, trying to digest the full implication of his words.

"You okay?"

She shook her head and thought out loud. "How can that be? What was Lancer doing in Grisly's barn? Why was he trying to burn it down? Makes no sense."

The doctor's eyes narrowed. "You knew him?"

Her eyes met his steady gaze. "Granger and I found him beaten and tied to a chair at his house two nights ago. We warned him he was in danger. Told him to leave town. He wouldn't listen. I never thought he'd be killed by a game warden."

All cheer disappeared from Linthrope's face. "It's not your fault he's dead, Chief. Circumstances were beyond your control."

The emotion she'd kept buried overnight surfaced in a sickening rush. Her words came out etched in guilt. "I sent the two wardens over there last night to investigate Grisly. One was critically shot, and the other was forced to kill a man. Clearly, they were out of their depth."

"The game wardens are not the nice guys you think they are," he said soberly.

"What do you mean?"

"Better follow me to the lab."

Reeling, Sidney followed him down the hall. Stewart lifted his head from his microscope as they entered. Linthrope motioned for her to take a seat at a small table in the corner. "Got those reports, Stewart?"

"Right here." Dressed in a white lab coat over grey slacks and loafers, Stewart picked up a file, pulled out a chair, and joined them.

Sidney removed her jacket and hung it on the back of her seat, then leaned forward, eager for useful information.

Stewart ceremoniously opened the file, lifted the top sheet of paper, and cleared his throat. "First, Lancer Richards's toxicology report. No drugs or medication, but his blood alcohol level was .12 percent."

"Wow. That's high."

"Stinking drunk is the unofficial term."

"He relapsed," Sidney said, reflecting. "Nikah's death drove him back to drink. Most people would not have been functional, yet he managed to drive over to Grisly's in the ice and snow, set a barn on fire, and engage in a gun fight."

"Irrational behavior, for sure."

"What else you got?"

"These reports are in chronological order, Chief, corresponding to the dates the forensic samples were submitted to the lab. Starting with the night we processed the residence of Nikah Tamanos. Nothing conclusive identifies the two intruders who broke into her house. The blood found on the floor in the guest room is a match to Nikah. Fingerprints found throughout the house belonged to both Nikah and her boyfriend, Lancer."

Sidney felt the dull thud of disappointment. So far, nothing useful. "Anything else?"

Stewart pushed his glasses higher on his nose and nodded with a sly smile. "We also identified prints found in the bedroom. A match to River Menowa."

"River?" Sidney's adrenalin spiked. "I met him at the tribal meeting yesterday. Where in the bedroom?"

"The nightstand. The headboard."

Finally, a substantiated lead. "Just as I suspected, he *was* having an affair with Nikah."

"Presumably. We couldn't identify the DNA on the extra toothbrush in her bathroom or the fluids on her sheets, but it's safe to assume they'll match River Menowa. We'll need a DNA swab from him to confirm."

"We'll get one today. We can now place River in Nikah's house. That makes him a strong suspect." She remembered River's smooth charm and his lack of emotion regarding Nikah, even though he'd been sleeping with her. One cold bastard. "He's an ace at hiding his feelings. What else is he hiding?"

Stewart raised his head and met her gaze, his eyes gleaming behind his glasses. "We're just getting warmed up here, Chief. We also matched prints on the top bill of the money packet in the tin box. Guess who they belong to?"

With every nerve standing at attention, Sidney's patience ran out. "This isn't Jeopardy, Stewart. Give me the name."

"Sander Vance. We also found his prints, along with Lancer's, on the decorative medallion and key."

Sidney sat speechless.

"That's not all. There's one more piece of evidence linking Sander to Nikah and Lancer. The DNA on the crumpled tissue you found in Lancer's bathroom the night of the break-in…"

"Matches Sander Vance," Sidney finished for him.

"No. Harper Meade."

Sidney sat pressed back in her chair as surprise rippled through her. "The two game wardens are the home invaders? Holy hell! They've been working together all along."

Dr. Linthrope smiled. "Told you they're not choir boys."

Sidney rose to her feet and started pacing, her thoughts swirling like debris in a windstorm. "They broke into Nikah's house. Then broke into Lancer's house and viciously beat him. Beneath that boy next-door façade, Sander has a vicious streak. He'd started scalping Lancer. Who knows if he would have completed the job."

Shock showed on the faces of the men.

"You would have noticed the bruises and stitches, Doc," Sidney said, "If he wasn't burnt to a crisp."

"Holy moly," Stewart said, eyes wide. "Maybe he killed Nikah."

"I'd put my money on him over River," Sidney said. "Lancer must have been partnering with the wardens. Exchanging a lot of cash."

"If they were partners, why were they beating him?" Stewart asked.

"They really wanted that tin box he'd hidden," Sidney said. "Aside from that wad of bills, that medallion and key may be very valuable. Sander's prints are on them. Maybe Lancer stole them from him."

"Goes to motive," Stewart said.

"But why did Lancer pretend he didn't know them?" Linthrope asked. "He took a vicious beating, yet protected them."

"Probably to keep himself from being implicated," Sidney said. "Stands to reason. The wardens had to be working with Grisly. Probably taking bribes to look the other way."

"Was Lancer working with the poachers, too?" Stewart asked.

She shrugged. "Possibly. Maybe he burned down the barn to destroy evidence."

"What about the shootout?" The doctor asked, scratching the back of his neck.

"Bad blood. He crossed them. They probably learned we confiscated the box, which erased Lancer's leverage. I'm wondering now if his death was deliberate."

"My thoughts exactly," Linthrope said.

"Maybe they were getting revenge, or trying to keep him quiet," Stewart said.

"In any case, Sander knew the corpse in the barn was Lancer, yet he led us to believe it was Grisly."

The doctor's brow furrowed. "Nasty characters."

Sidney blew out a breath and shook her head. "Grisly's still alive. He must be the rider following the old woman and the boy."

The two men looked at her with questioning expressions, clueless to the other drama playing out in the backcountry.

She quickly filled them in on Elahan's exodus from the village with the boy and the wolf.

"Holy moly," Stewart repeated.

"Harper's in the hospital, but I'm going to bring Sander in for questioning. You two did great work." Sidney smiled her appreciation, grateful to have a first-class forensic team in a town as small as Garnerville. Her smile was warmly returned.

Sidney glanced at her watch. Nine a.m. Her two officers would be waiting at the station. "I gotta run. Keep me posted on Nikah's postmortem." Sidney left the building, her mind buzzing like an irritated beehive. Back in her vehicle, she radioed dispatch.

Jesse answered promptly. "Yeah, Chief?"

"Get hold of Captain Harrison, Jesse. Tell them we've identified the rider following Elahan as Grisly Stokes. Advise them to exercise caution. He's dangerous. Use the phone, not your radio." Game wardens had radios that monitor local LE frequencies. Putting this info over the air would let Sander know they were on to him.

"Copy that, Chief."

Sidney disconnected and tried calling Granger. No answer. She left a text with the same info.

CHAPTER THIRTY-FIVE

WASTING NO TIME getting to the station, Sidney entered through the back door, bypassing the lobby and her office, and entered the small conference room. Darnell sat hunched over a laptop, gazing intently at the screen. Amanda stood over him, peering down with an equally intense stare. They glanced up as she strode in. Darnell looked bleary-eyed and his face was shadowed with morning stubble.

"What alley cat dragged you in here this morning?" Sidney asked him.

"Darnell was up most of the night, Chief," Amanda said. "Looking through thousands of photos."

Feeding into the no nonsense mood of the room, Sidney asked briskly, "What'cha got?"

"I'm inside Grisly's computer," Darnell said, his dark eyes flashing. "This is one of his most visited sites. It's exclusive. Members only. I'm sure he thought its security was rigidly enforced."

"But not from an expert hacker?"

He grinned. "Take a look."

Sidney sank into a chair and Darnell turned the screen toward her. On a site called *Game Exchange*, with *Hunter & Trapper News* as the subhead, Darnell scrolled through an endless newsfeed of photos depicting hunters and trappers posing with their kills. "This is a site where hunters can show their wares and auction them off to the highest bidder. Darnell pointed to a photo with his pen. "Check this out, Chief."

Sidney peered more closely. Two men, shown from the chest down, were holding up the carcass of a large gray wolf between them. Strewn on the ground at their feet were multiple carcasses of beavers, bobcats, and coyotes. The caption underneath read: *A good week's work. Bids for wolf pelt start at $900.*

"Sunnovabitch," Sidney said, fury constricting her chest. "Poachers. Did you get a hit on the contact info?

"No. This was taken a year ago. The contact number is obsolete. Probably a burner phone. But they did leave identifiers. First, the guy on the left. Take a close look at this." He zoomed in on the man's hand and Sidney noticed a jagged, one-inch scar near his wrist bone, shaped like a "Z."

"Okay. I see a very recognizable scar."

Next, Darnell zoomed in on the boots of the same man where the blade of a knife was half buried in the ground. The handle, hand carved from some kind of animal bone, was masterfully engraved with a skull and crossbones in front of a waving banner. "This is a one-of-a-kind, custom-made knife."

"Okay."

"Now look at the guy on the right." Darnell zoomed in on a pocket of the orange safety vest the hunter wore, which was partially ripped at the seam. The pocket was stained by several drops, and a larger smear of blood.

Darnell switched to a different screen depicting various photos of men hunting and fishing. "This is another popular hunting site." He pointed to a crouched man panfrying a rainbow trout over a campfire. Two men milled in the background, facing the river.

"Is that Sander Vance cooking?" Sidney asked, squinting.

"Yep. Sure is. Look at this, Chief." Darnell brought up a photo that was a closeup shot of the man's hand gripping the handle of the pan. Lying on a cutting board on the edge of the pit, beside chopped garlic and an onion, was the same custom knife.

Sidney frowned. "That's incriminating. But the knife could belong to one of those other men."

"Maybe. But this scar is Sander's." Darnell zoomed in on the man's hand. The jagged scar near his wrist was unmistakable.

"Holy shit."

"Sander was poaching," Amanda said hotly. "Advertizing. Making a profit."

"Killing a wolf is a federal offense," Darnell said. "Punishable by up to $100,000 fine and a year in jail.

"He's racking up enough offenses to put him in the slammer for years," Sidney said.

"We're just getting started here, Chief," Darnell said. He scrolled through a few more pictures of Sander's campsite and froze on the two men. "See the man in the orange vest facing the river?"

"The vest has the bloodstain on it, right?"

"Yep." Darnell scrolled down, and brought up another photo of the man, facing the campsite.

The hair rose on Sidney's arms. It was Grisly Stokes. "You just put Grisly and Sander together as partners in crime!"

The young officer beamed and turned back to the computer screen. "Here's one last surprise for you, Chief. Taken two years ago." Darnell went to yet another site, scrolled through more photos, and pointed out two men decked in camo gear. Each held a fan of hundred dollar bills and looked as giddy as lottery winners. The photo was fuzzy, but the men were still recognizable as Lancer and Grisly. They were in a distribution warehouse where thousands of hides of every shape and size were piled on shelves and tables. "From this warehouse," Darnell said, "The furs are sold at auction to clothes designers all over the world, but primarily in Russia,

China, and South Korea. Draping oneself in fur has become prestigious among the newly rich."

"We now have evidence that Grisly and Lancer knew each other well, and apparently hunted together," Sidney said. "But was Lancer poaching with him? That's the question we need to answer. Most of the pelts in that warehouse came from legitimate sources."

"But the fur industry is largely unregulated, Chief," Amanda said. "Making it easy for poachers like Grisly to offload their bounty."

"With no accountability," Darnell added.

"Impressive work, Darnell," Sidney said, clapping him on the back. "How in holy hell did you root out this stuff?"

He shrugged one shoulder. Modest.

"Steely determination and long hours," Amanda said with an admiring gaze.

"I really want to bust these bastards," Darnel said. "Grisly got his due. Now we have proof that Sander and Lancer worked with him." He shot her a smile, fatigue etched on his face, but his smile faded when he saw Sidney's tightened jaw. She gestured with one hand. "Take a seat, Amanda. I need to update you two on the postmortem results." Sidney expediently walked them through the autopsy and lab reports. The expressions of the officers shifted from surprise to dismay.

"So Grisly is alive, and Lancer is dead," Amanda said, shaking her head. "And it's possible the wardens deliberately killed him. This case gets stranger by the day."

"And it's Grisly who's out there tracking Elahan and Tegan," Darnell said. "And the wolf."

"Yep. After seeing what a gray wolf brings in, I can imagine what a rare white wolf of that size would garner. Hopefully, Grisly will be brought in without anyone getting hurt. In the meantime, we have more than enough probable cause to get an arrest warrant for Sander. Amanda, see if he'll come in voluntarily. Play it cool.

As far as he knows, we just want to go over the details of Grisly's death. He doesn't know we did an autopsy." Sidney knew it was best to have a junior officer contact him. A request directly from the police chief might arouse his suspicion.

"So, he thinks we just swallowed his story. Why would he pretend it was Grisly he killed?"

"He wants us to think he didn't know Grisly. Couldn't tell him from Mr. Magoo.

Distance himself from the poaching business."

"I won't trust him until he's cuffed," Amanda said. "Unconscious would be better."

Sidney felt a burn in her stomach. Her officers were wary of Sander with good reason. The warden was cunning and malicious, and a great actor. He hid his true character behind his badge and a display of loyalty to his job. She had been blind-sided. "Call him. If he doesn't respond, we'll go pick him up." Sidney turned her attention to the mountain of paperwork waiting to be processed. "I'll be in my office."

Sidney sank into the swivel chair behind her desk and tried to organize her thoughts. Her department was too understaffed to deal with these kinds of complicated cases. She and her officers were being forced to pull their attention away from their daily patrols and everyday problems. Their visible presence on the streets discouraged crime and gave citizens peace of mind. Fortunately, nothing of consequence had erupted in their two-day absence.

She called Judge Rosenstadt, requesting an arrest warrant and a search warrant. Then she buzzed Winnie and instructed her to pick them up. Sidney disconnected and her phone buzzed immediately. It was David. "Hey, David."

"Good morning, Sunshine." His cheerful voice momentarily transported her to the world beyond the station where folks went to jobs every day that didn't put their lives at risk.

"Sleep well?" he asked.

Despite the stress, she felt a flutter of excitement in her stomach. "Like a baby. Thanks to you. You have a way..." her voice drifted softly away.

"So do you, babe," he murmured. "So do you." A moment of silence brought warm memories to the surface.

"So, what's up?" she said in her professional tone, breaking the spell.

David's tone also returned to normal, edged with a touch of excitement. "I got a response from one of my contacts. He knew exactly where that key and medallion came from. They were stolen from the estate of a collector in Sweetwater two years ago. Vincent Schuman. They're valued at over a hundred-thousand dollars."

Sidney whistled. "That's some serious motive for murder."

"Yes, it is."

"Thank you, David," Sidney said. "You've been very helpful."

"Gotta go, huh?"

"Yep."

"You free tonight?"

"Maybe. I'll call you later."

A fleeting moment of intimacy hung between them before Sidney disconnected. She turned her attention to her paperwork until Amanda entered her office a half hour later with the warrants in hand.

"Did you reach Sander?" Sidney asked.

"Nope. Darnell got the approximate position of his phone's GPS. He's at home, off Anderson Quarry road. It's in our jurisdiction."

"Let me call the Sheriff. See if we can get some backup."

The call to the County Sheriff didn't pan out. Sidney exhaled her frustration and looked up at Amanda. "The SWAT team is engaged on the other side of the Cascades. We're on our own. We need to bring Sander in ASAP."

"We'll do what we have to do, Chief," she said solemnly. "Gear up. We leave in ten minutes."

CHAPTER THIRTY-SIX

BULKED UP in their body armor and winter gear, the two officers stood silently in the hallway outside Sidney's office. Sidney sized them up. Though neither had ever been placed in a work situation where they had to fire a weapon, both officers practiced at the range routinely and were crack shots. Sidney knew how they operated in a crisis situation. She trusted their instincts. And she trusted they would react appropriately to whatever lay ahead. She sensed their adrenalin pumping, as was hers. "You good?"

They responded simultaneously, "Yes, ma'am."

"When we get to Sander's place, stay alert," she said emphatically. "Stick to training. Copy?"

"Copy," Darnell said.

Amanda nodded.

"Let's roll."

The three rode in Sidney's vehicle, Amanda in the passenger seat and Darnell in the cage. The highway out of town tunneled through a towering forest stripped of color by ice and snow. Overhead, the clouds had congealed into a dark, brooding mass, forecasting another snowstorm. The clear skies Captain Harrison had predicted didn't last long. The storm would force down the chopper and hamper search efforts on the ground. Through the pillars of trees to the east, the vapor rising off the lake gave the morning an ominous, morose quality, reflecting Sidney's mood exactly.

Heavy white flakes started to fall. Inside the warm cab her two officers sat in silence, listening to the rhythmic path of the wipers crossing the windshield. Sidney caught Darnell's expression in the mirror, gaze fixed out the window, jaw clenching and unclenching. She felt a surge of fierce protectiveness for her two officers, who followed her directives without question, trusting her judgment, ready to put their lives at risk. She would take a bullet for either of them before betraying their trust.

"This is it," Amanda said. "Turn left."

Sidney slowed, almost missing the turn. As she bore onto the poorly plowed road, the wheels spun, seeking traction. She slipped into a low gear and the vehicle proceeded to bump along the ice-rutted road.

"The quarry's been closed for a decade," Darnell muttered. "Nothing left but piles of rocks and mutilated land. Who the hell lives out here?"

"Trolls and toothless rednecks," Amanda answered. "And Sander."

Behind the veil of snow, a ramshackle two-story farmhouse jutted up from the frozen landscape, growing in size as they approached. Gray smoke rose from the chimney, curling into the cold morning air.

"Looks like the house in *Psycho*," Darnell said. "Norman Bates is home, dressed as his dead mother."

"Thanks for the uplifting image," Amanda said.

Sidney rounded the drive to the front of the house and saw white exhaust billowing from the back of a truck parked in the driveway. Both doors were open, and Sander was midway between the vehicle and the porch, a bulky traveling bag gripped in each hand, his breath smoking. He stiffened as his gaze met hers. He dropped both satchels, rushed up the steps to the porch, and disappeared inside the house.

A prickling sensation dropped into Sidney's gut like a stone. "He's on the run. We just caught him. Shit. He's going to make us go in after him." The same unease overtook her that she used to feel in Oakland when entering a building where a suspect was holed up. She knew something bad was about to go down, but didn't know what form it would take, or how bad it would be. She didn't know what to be afraid of but knew enough to be afraid. Muscle memory kicked in. Sidney took command. "Amanda, we're going in through the front door. Darnell, watch the back. Don't be a target. Move fast."

Out in the brisk cold, Darnell darted out of sight. Sidney and Amanda crossed the tattered ice, moved rapidly up the stairs, and positioned themselves on either side of the front door. Sidney quickly scanned the living room through the paned window. It appeared to be empty. She tried the door. Unlocked. She pushed it open with enough force to slam it against the interior wall.

"Sander, come out," she yelled. "We just want to talk."

Long moments passed. Nothing. The only sound came from logs crackling in the fireplace.

Feeling her adrenaline humming, Sidney nodded. Pistols held in a two-hand grip, they made a slow orbit through the room, scanning it in slices, missing nothing. "Clear," Sidney said.

They did the same in the dining room and kitchen. "Clear."

Through the window, she saw Darnell stationed on the porch, his head doing a left to right swivel and lifting to the second story, duty weapon held in shooting position. Sidney inched to the hallway and panned the opening without exposing her body. A stairway led upstairs. Two narrow flights. No cover. Basically, a close-range shooting gallery. They would be sitting ducks if Sander was waiting at the top, armed. Her heart picked up speed.

Amanda's mouth tightened. She nodded.

Crouched, crablike, backs close to the wall, they climbed steadily, guns aimed at the upper level. They slipped fast around the newel post and made it to the top landing without incident. The hallway was just as dangerous. A funnel. Sander could come out with an automatic weapon and mow them down in a heartbeat. Four doorways needed to be cleared one at a time. Crossing a threshold, they could be hosed from the inside.

Slowly and methodically they advanced down the hall as one unit, Sidney's muzzle pointed to the right, Amanda behind her left shoulder covering the length of the hall. Heart knocking like a parade drum, she threw open the first door and entered the room. Stripped bare. No furniture. Closet empty. "Clear."

Amanda entered the bathroom on the left while Sidney covered the hall. "Clear." She stepped back into the hallway, beads of sweat on her upper lip, and fell behind Sidney. There were two doors remaining, opposite each other. Sander was behind one of them. Sidney stopped and listened, then advanced, staying close to the wall. Arms extended. Both hands on the pistol.

She opened the door on the right, entered briskly, gun arm going from left to right. No movement. This was Sander's bedroom. Unmade bed, clothes draped over an armchair, a dresser with open drawers, garments hanging out. The closet was half empty, hangers scattered on the floor. He had packed hastily. "Clear."

Turning to the last door on the left, they stood on either side.

"Sander, come out peacefully. Let's talk. We don't want to hurt you."

Nothing.

Sweat dampened Sidney's back. She reached for the handle, pushed open the door, entered quickly with Amanda at her side. Empty. The closet door was closed. Standing to one side, she threw it open with her left hand, gun in her right to take him down if he lunged. But he wasn't in the closet.

She met her officer's astonished eyes.

"How'd we miss him?" Amanda asked, voice low, cautious.

"Let's go back," Sidney said, anxious about Darnell alone on the porch.

They were midway down the hallway with Sidney in the lead when she heard a faint rustling from above. She turned as Sander dropped from a ceiling opening and grabbed Amanda from behind with violent force. Her gun flew five feet and fired when it hit the floor. The round smashed into a wall and the ear-piercing explosion reverberated through the small space as though in an echo chamber.

Ears ringing, Sidney assessed the situation in the blink of an eye. Sander held Amanda tightly against his chest with his left arm while his right hand pressed a hunting knife to her throat. A thin line of blood trickled down her neck into her jacket collar. Sidney's gaze swept to Sander's face.

Gone was the boy-next-door countenance. His features were hard and pronounced, as though the skin had been stretched tightly over the bones. A hideous grin was fixed to his face as he stared into the muzzle of her semi-automatic pistol. Then Sander hid his face behind Amanda's head, so only one eye peered out. Sidney glanced at her partner, noting the sudden paleness of her skin, eyes opened wide. Amanda mouthed, "Shoot him."

Impossible. Too small a target.

"Lower your gun," Sander said in a low, measured voice that chilled her blood. "I'll slice her neck clean through."

"Put down the knife, Sander," Sidney said quietly, determined to keep her face straight while the nerves fired underneath. "This will not end well for you. I don't want to hurt you, but I will. You're a second away from a bullet to the brain."

She caught a quick blaze from his eye like that of an animal in a trap. A desperate man was a dangerous man.

"Drop the knife," she said in a firm, soothing tone, like a mother speaking to a naughty child. "Think about your future. You've only racked up a few misdemeanors," she lied, not letting on that she knew about the antiquities theft, the poaching, the break-ins. "No big deal. You have a good record as a game warden. That'll help you in court. But kill a cop and you don't stand a chance. It's a lethal injection any way you look at it. Make the right choice, Sander. Lower the knife."

No one moved. They stood frozen in time as though in a photograph. Sidney held her breath, her spine so rigid it felt hewn in oak. Something inside her chest compressed tighter. She didn't want to blow this man's brains out, but she would in an instant if the chance arose. The ceiling seemed to slip lower, the walls constricted, her hand grew clammy on the gun.

Sander's face appeared for a second then dodged back behind Amanda. Something minute had shifted in his expression—a slackness around his mouth, a dullness to the eyes. She felt fear pumping off of him.

"Okay, okay." Sander dropped the knife to the ground and slowly extended his arms above his head.

Amanda's face seemed to crumple a little and then it hardened. Fury ignited in her eyes. She twisted away from Sander and kicked the knife away from him. She stepped behind him and said with steel in her voice, "On your knees. Hands on top of your head."

Sander obeyed.

Trying to control her heaving stomach, Sidney kept the pistol trained on him while Amanda yanked one of his hands back, cocked his wrist and cuffed it, then brought the other hand down and cuffed it. Sidney admired her junior officer's self-discipline. The urge to pummel Sander must have been overwhelming.

Clenching her jaw, Amanda picked up her weapon from the floor and carefully holstered it. "Look at his knife, Chief."

It was the custom-made knife from the photos on Grisly's laptop—a strong piece of evidence linking Sander to poaching. Sidney bagged the knife, then radioed Darnell.

"Yeah, Chief."

"We have him."

Amanda shoved Sander in the small of his back. "Move, asshole."

They ushered him downstairs and Sidney took a good look at him in the filtered light coming through the windows. Morning beard, hair a tangle of red curls falling over his forehead. Jeans and sweatshirt wrinkled. Looked as though he wasted no time on grooming in his hurry to escape.

While Darnell kept Sander under guard, Sidney pulled out her first aid kit and attended to Amanda's throat. "Just a flesh wound," she said with a sigh of relief. She cleaned the wound with a cotton swab and applied a bandage. "You did great up there. Certified badass. Steel nerves."

"I can say the same for you, Chief." Amanda cast Sander an icy glare. "If I'd been the one holding the gun, the fucker would be dead."

"Fuck you!" Sander said, spit flying. "I wish I'd sliced you deeper."

"The sooner you're locked in a cage, the better," Amanda snapped.

Sander cast Sidney a furtive glance to measure her reaction.

Wanting nothing more than to give Sander a verbal lashing, she buried her animosity beneath a neutral expression. Sander's full cooperation was needed when she questioned him. To achieve that, she had to come across as fair, and sympathetic.

Sander's lip curled up in a sneer. "What am I being charged with? You had no right to arrest me."

"Let's lower the temperature, Sander," Sidney said calmly. "If you aren't guilty of anything, why were you packed up and leaving town in such a hurry? Why did you attack my officer?"

"You broke into my house without a warrant. I was defending myself."

"That's how you want to play this?" Darnell said. "We're the bad guys?

Sander struggled to restrain himself, but anger vibrated off him. "Anything you confiscated is not admissible in court."

Of course, he was referring to the stolen jewelry and money. Nice try. "Actually, Sander, I have a search warrant and an arrest warrant. You never gave us the chance to give them to you." She produced the two warrants and held them up to him. "You can read these at the station."

Sander licked his lips, suddenly nervous.

"Take him out to the truck," Sidney said. "Keep the heater running."

Amanda and Darnell patted Sander down and escorted him out into the snowstorm to the Yukon. When they rejoined Sidney, Darnell was carrying Sander's bags, coated in snow, and Amanda handed her the keys from his truck.

The two officers set to work searching the house. It wouldn't take long. Sander lived like a transient—minimal furnishings and the barest stockpile of household supplies. Sidney turned her attention to his bags. The first held nothing of interest: a shaving kit, a pair of running shoes, rumpled clothing. The second bag produced his laptop computer and two faux leather briefcases. Inside the first case Sidney hit pay dirt: rows of neatly stacked packets of hundred dollar bills. The other case was locked. Sidney looked through Sander's key ring. One key looked like a match. She inserted it, heard the lock click, and lifted the lid. "Wow. Come look at this."

Amanda went down on her haunches, brows raised, and Darnell squinted at the assortment of jewelry sealed in plastic bags: rings, lockets, watches, bracelets. Even to Sidney's untrained eye, the pieces appeared to be very valuable. "Recognize anything?"

Amanda's eyes widened. "Holy hell."

"Some of this stuff was stolen from the village!" Darnell said.

A smile formed on Sidney's lips.

"Sander is the fucking Stalker!" Amanda said. "We got him!"

"Jesus. Sander? Who would've thought?" Darnel said. "The villagers were right. The Stalker is a white guy."

"They'll be ecstatic," Amanda said.

Sidney sobered. "We worked hard. We put in the hours. Here's the payoff. A violent perv is off the street."

"He robbed people," Darnell said. "Attacked women. Poached animals. Killed Lancer. Is there anything this guy didn't do? He must've killed Nikah, too."

"Possible. We can't prove it yet. He can claim self-defense for Lancer, and Nikah was already dead when we caught him ransacking her house. We need hard evidence to get him for murder." Sidney glanced at her watch. "Nikah's autopsy should be wrapping up right about now. Hopefully, the doc will have something we can use. I'll head over there when we get back to town." She jerked her chin toward the door. "Let's roll. Book Sander and get him in the grill room. Let him stew until I return. Maybe it'll soften his attitude."

Outside, the wind was moaning under the eaves and the snow was blowing sideways. Icy pellets whipped Sidney's jacket and stung her face. They stored Sander's baggage in the back of the Yukon and climbed into the cab, brushing off snow and ignoring their prisoner, who sat hunched in the cage next to Darnell, gaze fixed out the window.

Sidney revved up the engine. The wipers squeaked against the windshield. The vehicle rattled over the road. The air was warm, but it failed to alleviate Sidney's deeper chill. Her thoughts drifted to the drama unfolding in the wilderness. An old woman, a boy, and a white wolf were out in this shit storm with a sociopath tailing them. No word of progress from Granger.

Not wanting to dampen the victory of apprehending the Stalker, she kept her troubling thoughts to herself.

CHAPTER THIRTY-SEVEN

LYING ON A RIDGE halfway up Beartooth Peak, peering through high-powered binoculars, Moolock could see the land spread out below him for a hundred miles. Forest dominated the valleys, swelled into the hills, and was carved into parcels by arteries of rivers and creeks. Far off in the distance, in miniature, Lake Kalapuya glittered like a sapphire, surrounded by the snow-laden rooftops of Garnerville. Beartooth Creek slithered through the frozen landscape like a turquoise snake in its relentless journey to the Cascades.

He located the clearing where he exited from the creek with the two horses. From there he rode along the water for several miles, then detoured through the woods to a dilapidated cabin that had once been a refuge for cross-country skiers. Below and just to the east, Moolock could see the cabin and the surrounding meadow clearly. He saw the tracks of the two horses and the wolf that he led into the barn, and the two sets of boot prints and paw prints that led from the barn to the cabin. It had been easy to fake another set of footprints with an extra pair of boots he brought, pressing them into the snow as he marched to the house. Two previously shuttered windows were now open to the daylight and smoke curled from the chimney of the wood stove, giving the cabin an inhabited look.

He left the cabin from the rear door wearing snowshoes, brushing away prints with a few sweeps of cedar branches.

Moolock removed the snowshoes and climbed several hundred feet of steep terrain to crawl out on this granite shelf that jutted into open air. Up here, the wind was shrill and icy, but he welcomed the discomfort. It kept him alert. Next to him, the wolf lay as still as the Sphinx, his fur blowing in the current, his ears at full attention as though sensing the danger ahead.

The stillness of the morning was disturbed by the distant sound of a helicopter, angling across the sky above Two Creeks Village, slowly spiraling outwards. Search and Rescue, he presumed. He prayed the chopper wouldn't travel this far west. The rider would be spooked, and would retreat, and all of Moolock's well-laid plans would be wasted.

Twenty minutes crawled by.

Nature seemed to be scheming in Moolock's favor. Islands of cumulous clouds were congealing into one dark, brooding mass, moving northwest across the sky like a continent. The snowstorm Tegan had predicted would force the chopper out of the sky. He touched the small bulk of the medicine bag through his jacket and silently expressed his gratitude for the power of the stones. Elahan's potent magic was altering the weather system, as she said it would, supporting Moolock's efforts.

Now for his plan to be effective, the rider had to make an appearance on the creek trail before the snowstorm swept in and hid him from view. The clouds moved across the sky with extraordinary speed, edging past the town, the village, blocking the sun, casting the land into white oblivion. The sound of the chopper vanished.

Moolock's gut tightened as the clouds traveled closer.

Another twenty minutes passed.

Then thirty.

No rider appeared.

The roiling mass of clouds sailed steadily westward and fingers of fog reached Beartooth Creek. Within minutes the entire trail would be obscured. Soft flakes, preceding the full brunt of the storm, drifted in Moolock's direction, catching on his coat and Lelou's fur.

He released an anguished cry and reluctantly lowered the binoculars. His shoulders were tight and his entire body was stiff with cold. He had no choice but to peel himself away from the ridge and retreat down the mountain before the mist made his descent icy and treacherous.

Lelou sprang to his feet, his intense gaze focused below, his low growl jolting Moolock's attention back to the creek. He lifted the binoculars and scanned the trail and wondered if his eyes were betraying him. He'd been focused on the white landscape for so long he was now imagining things. Moving on the edge of the fog were apparitions, ghosts. But one ghost materialized as a man riding a horse, moving along the trail at an ambling gait.

Moolock adjusted the settings of his lenses and focused closely on the rider. Wearing a dark trench coat, a raccoon hat, and a thick scarf that hid his features, he sat straight and tall in the saddle. Like a soldier out in the field scouting for an enemy, he slowly swiveled his head from left to right, and then he veered off the trail into the woods in the direction of the cabin. Moolock was certain this was the man who had tried to kill him in the woods only days before.

With Lelou in the lead, Moolock cautiously trekked down the mountain and through the woods to a rise at the rear of the cabin. From here he had a view of the barn, three sides of the cabin, and a good portion of the meadow. The ground was shrouded in drifting mist that gave the structures the appearance of floating. Snow was falling in thick, heavy flakes.

A subtle movement drew his attention to the south side of the barn. A flicker. Moolock lifted his binoculars and made out a barely discernable outline of a man blending with the shadows. The man opened the barn door a crack, peered into the interior, then disappeared inside, but not before Moolock caught the glint of the pistol in his right hand. Moolock viewed the scene with an exquisite hyper focus. Everything seemed to move in slow motion. Lelou nudged him hard, and the fabric of reality snapped back to normal.

It was time to enter the cabin, and wait.

CHAPTER THIRTY-EIGHT

NIKAH'S NUDE BODY had replaced Lancer's burnt corpse on the metal slab when Sidney arrived back at the morgue. It was grimly ironic that both murders took place on the same weekend, and that the lovers were sharing the same autopsy slab this morning.

Doctor Linthrope was washing his hands at the sink while Stewart sewed the post-mortem incisions with thick twine using standard baseball-style stitching. The two arms of the "Y" ran from each shoulder joint and met at mid-chest with the stem running down to her pubic region. The colorless body, remarkably preserved due to the freezing temperature of the creek, was now an empty shell, drained of blood, stripped of larynx, organs, and brain. Staring at her corpse, Sidney shuddered. So young. She found it hard to imagine Nikah as the vibrant woman described by Tommy and other villagers.

"Busy day, eh Stewart?" she said sullenly.

"Yep." He glanced up, and returned to his work, focused.

Hearing her voice, Dr. Linthrope dried his hands, turned and smiled, his bushy gray brows lifting in greeting. "Chief Becker. You're back." He snapped on a pair of vinyl gloves and joined her at the slab. Stewart finished his stitching and stepped aside, revealing a full view of the body and the telltale signs of trauma.

"Jesus, it looks like she was tortured," Sidney said, noting red indentations around her throat and wrists, and a baseball size bruise on her thigh.

"At first glance, you would think so, but that's not the case," Dr. Linthrope said. "If you look closely, you'll see there are several less pronounced ligature markings in addition to the prominent ones."

Stewart held up one of Nikah's hands.

Sidney gave the wrist a careful inspection, then leaned over and studied the woman's throat. The doctor was right. Layers of barely visible marks circled Nikah's wrists and throat, in addition to the ones inflicted most recently that were noticeably red.

"My guess," Linthrope said. "She engaged routinely in rough sex and bondage."

"A gasper," Stewart mocked, using the colloquial term for erotic asphyxiation.

The doctor shot him a glance.

Stewart instantly wiped the smirk off his face.

"Deliberate choking to restrict oxygen to the brain for sexual arousal," the doctor said.

"Erotic asphyxiation," Sidney said with a touch of surprise. It didn't fit the wholesome profile of Nikah she'd fabricated.

"That would explain the pattern of marks going back a few weeks."

"So, her death was caused by accidental strangling," Sidney said. "Things got out of hand. Her partner didn't realize until too late that she wasn't breathing."

"Erotic asphyxiation is certainly life threatening, but it wasn't the cause of death." Linthrope lifted Nikah's head and turned it to one side, revealing a two-inch gash behind the left ear. "Blunt force trauma. The skull was fractured. She probably died instantly."

Sidney's mouth went dry as she stared down at the livid gash in the white flesh. "Someone really let her have it."

He nodded, lips tightening, the senselessness of Nikah's death momentarily leaving him speechless. It was rare for Linthrope to let his emotions cloud his normal reserve. As professionals, they learned to compartmentalize, store the darker side of their business in a vaulted place. Not always successfully.

"That explains all the blood," Sidney said, blinking at the memory of the wide pool of blood the Luminal detected in Nikah's office. "What caused the wound?"

His brow creased. "Hard to say. A sharp pointed instrument of some kind. This bruise on her thigh most likely occurred when she fell."

"Time of death?"

"Best estimate is between eleven p.m. and four a.m. Friday night."

"Toxicology?"

"She had a high dose of Ambien and alcohol in her system."

"Ouch. Not a good combination."

"Not at all. It would dramatically increase the potential for sleepwalking, sleep-eating, even sleep-driving. Other symptoms are dizziness, loss of coordination, impaired cognition and judgment."

Sidney processed the information and summarized what she'd learned so far. "So, Nikah was having rough sex with the same partner for a period of weeks, which indicates they cared for each other at some level. Sometime Friday night after having sex, most likely impaired, she sustained a blow to the head by a sharp instrument. She was dressed in her nightgown, but her killer took the time to dress her, clean up the blood, and cart her body out to the creek." Sidney paused, ruminating. "That speaks to a very conflicted individual. On the one hand, he bludgeoned her. On the other hand, he took the time to dress her. Not only in jeans and a sweater, but boots and a jacket. He didn't just dump her naked body in the backcountry somewhere. He put her in the creek where he knew she'd be found."

"Exactly."

"Why did he move the body at all?" Stewart asked, raising his brows.

"Good question," Sidney said. "It makes me wonder if the killer was Native American. Water is sacred. The origin of life. Purifying. Maybe her killer thought the creek would wash away her sins, and his."

The doctor's perspective was more pragmatic. "Or he wanted to wash away DNA evidence."

"And there's that." She met his steady gaze. "Did you find anything to ID the killer? Any fluids?"

"Yes, indeed. She'd been sexually active prior to her death. We found traces of semen in the vaginal canal. The sample was sent to the lab."

"We know she'd been seeing River Menowa," Sidney said. "We need to get his DNA swab to the lab ASAP." Though Sidney suspected Nikah's lover was Native American, she wasn't ready to dismiss Sander as a suspect. The Stalker was a sadistic offender who took pleasure in choking his victims. The sexual violence Nikah engaged in would appeal to his nature. Sidney felt overwhelmed, thinking of logistics. So much to do, and her small staff was already overworked. She looked at her watch. "Thanks for getting these autopsies done so quickly."

Both men nodded, and smiled.

Sidney left the morgue and paused in the lobby to call Amanda. She instructed her to bring River Menowa in for questioning.

"Copy that," Amanda said. "I'm on my way."

Outside, the snow had ceased and the sky had taken on a deep metallic sheen. Grey clouds brushed the trees that surrounded the mist-shrouded lake. She climbed into her vehicle, headed down Main Street, and pulled to a stop at the town's traffic light. A handful of townsfolk braved the cold, shoulders hunched against the wind, steps hurried and purposeful on the sidewalks. Against the gray pallor of day, lights glowed from the Art Studio, warm and beckoning. Sidney caught a glimpse of David at the front of his class, dressed in jeans and a ski sweater. Memories of last night's love fest sent a shiver racing through her. She indulged in a moment of wistful yearning, the sense of pleasure postponed, but within grasp. Then her foot hit the gas and she half skidded across the icy intersection.

CHAPTER THIRTY-NINE

SIDNEY USED her key card to enter the rear door of the station and encountered Darnell in the hallway, coming to meet her.

He flashed a smile, teeth white against dark skin. "Sander is sulking in the grill room. I have coffee and a ham and Swiss sandwich waiting for you."

She grinned. "How'd you know I'd be starving?"

He tapped his temple. "Cop intuition."

"Detective material." She followed him into the audio control room, no bigger than a broom closet, and studied Sander through the one-way mirror while devouring lunch.

The game warden sat slumped in his chair, legs outstretched beneath the scarred metal table. There was an unnatural stiffness to his body, and the fingers of his cuffed hands nervously drummed the table. She sensed he was coiled with tension, ready to go on a rampage, dissolve into sobs, or retreat like a turtle into some dark, hidden place. She had witnessed every kind of emotion coming from men in Sander's position—men who knew their crime spree had come to an end and they were facing serious jail time.

Darnell handed her Sander's file and she leafed through the photos he'd printed out, impressed by his thoroughness. Again, the diligent young officer had gone the extra mile, pulling some of Sander's personal background information off social media. Sidney washed down the last of the ham and Swiss with coffee while reading through it. "Good job, Darnell."

Aside from red-rimmed eyes, Darnell looked alert. "Just doing my duty," he said, light-hearted, thumbing a few buttons. "Audio and video are ready to go."

She nodded toward Sander. "We're gonna go slow and easy. Take notes."

"Sugar approach. Got it." Darnell pulled a notepad and pen from his breast pocket and followed her into the windowless room that had a polished concrete floor and dull white cinderblock walls. They scraped back metal chairs and seated themselves. Sidney sat across from her prisoner under the glare of fluorescent lights.

Sander sat up straighter in his chair, his cuffed hands tightly clasped on the table.

"Would you like some coffee?" she asked gently. "A soft drink?"

"Nah. I'm good."

"I'm sorry we had to bring you in under these circumstances," she said, giving him a sympathetic look.

He blinked, his expression wary. Not what he expected.

Sidney had a reputation for being tough as nails out in the field when the occasion called for it, but this was different. She needed to dissuade Sander from asking for a lawyer, which would shut down the interview immediately.

"We've known each other a long time," Sidney continued. "I've run across you patrolling lakes, rivers, woods. Doing your job. Doing it well. You grew up around here, right?"

"Born and raised, just outside of Jackson." His voice was hesitant. Cautious.

"You come from an outdoor family?"

"Hunted and fished my entire life. With my dad and brothers."

"Went to Jackson High?"

"Yes, ma'am."

"Big in sports, from what I remember." So the notes said.

"Baseball, basketball, you name it." His shoulders relaxed a fraction of an inch.

"Your team made the State championship," Darnell said, and smiled.

"That we did." A twitch of a smile. "Team effort."

"We need to ask you a few questions, Sander." Sidney continued to use honey in her tone. Friendly. "This conversation is being taped."

His pale blue eyes darted across the ceiling and located the video camera. A deep furrow appeared between his brows.

"Is your name Sander Vance?"

"Yes."

"You're employed by the state of Oregon as a game warden in Linley County?"

"Yes."

"How many years?"

"Six."

She kept her eyes lowered to his file for a long pause, then looked up. "You have a sterling record."

"Yes, ma'am. I love my job."

She sighed. "You know how this works, Sander. You have the right to remain silent. Anything you say can and will be used against you in a court of law. You have the right to speak to an attorney, and to have an attorney present during any questioning."

Sander nodded.

"Just to be clear, I'm on your side. We're both in law enforcement. We know how the stresses of the job can build up. We've all been tempted to push the envelope, step into the gray area on the fringes of the law." She smiled. "Work with me. I'll see if I can keep your charges to a minimum."

"Yes, ma'am."

"Tell me what you know about Grisly Stokes."

Sander shrugged. "Nothing. Only what I told you last night."

"What about Lancer Richards?"

"Don't know him."

Sidney gave him her piercing stare.

He looked away.

"If you want to help yourself, Sander, you need to talk to me. Tell me the truth."

He shrugged. Clenched his jaw. He needed convincing.

Sidney opened the file folder and laid the two photos on the table of Sander cooking fish over the campfire. "Is this you, Sander?"

"Pretty obvious," he said.

Sidney tapped the close up photo with the tip of her pin. "This is the same knife we confiscated from you today. Correct?"

"Yeah."

"Could you hold out your hands please?"

He did, cuffs clinking.

Sidney tapped the jagged scar on his wrist. "Unique scar." She then laid down the photo of the two hunters with the carcasses of the wolf and other animals, pointing first to the knife, then to the scar.

Sander's face drained of color as he tied it all together.

"Want to try again? Who is this man with you in the picture?" Sidney was testing him to see if he was going to be straight with her.

Sweat broke out on his upper lip. "You probably already know. It's Grisly."

"So you and Grisly know each other well. You're partners."

A vein swelled on his forehead. "Don't know what you mean. I don't have any partners." He jerked his chin toward the photo. "That was a one-time deal."

"I don't think it was." To emphasize her point, Sidney laid down a photo of the hidden cache of furs behind Grisly's cabin.

Sander swallowed hard, his Adam's apple riding up and down his neck. "I don't know anything about that."

"Oh, I think you do. I think you know a lot of things." Sidney slid a photo of Lancer's charred corpse under his eyes. "Like the identity of this body."

Sander winced, pushed it away with a jerk of his hand.

"The autopsy shot holes in your story about killing Grisly last night. You knew it was Lancer. The three of you were in business together."

He kept his gaze focused on the table.

"Work with me here, Sander. As you can see, we've already put most of the pieces together. Help me fill in a few blanks. I'll let the judge know you cooperated. I'll ask him to be lenient. If you don't help me, Grisly will. They'll cut him a deal, and you'll get the stiffer sentence."

He blew out a ragged breath, nodded.

"The stolen goods we found in your bag identifies you as the man who's been terrorizing Two Creeks Village. Burglarizing. Assaulting women. You're the Stalker."

Sander's face flushed crimson from his collar to her hairline. "I'm not the Stalker. Everyone knows it was Lancer."

"Convenient to blame a dead man," Sidney said. "We also know you and Harper broke into Nikah's house, and Lancer's house."

"Don't know what you're talking about," he said, with a nervous quiver to his tone.

"We have proof," she bluffed. The only proof they had was a wadded-up tissue used by Harper and discarded in the bathroom. Sander was guilty by association. "You had a pretty big gripe against Lancer. Gave him a pretty good beating. Even started scalping him. Maybe you were angry enough to intentionally kill him."

"As far as the beating, he asked for it," Sander said passionately. "But I didn't mean to kill him."

Sidney felt a tremor of elation. He had just confessed to the home invasions and beating Lancer.

Realizing his mistake, Sander clenched his jaw so tightly Sidney thought it might crack. This was the moment where he implicitly understood that he was going down. He lifted his cuffed hands and wiped the sweat off his face with a sleeve.

"Face facts, Sander," Sidney said gently. "No lawyer is going to exonerate you of all of these charges. You're gonna do time. How much depends on your willingness to talk to us."

"I didn't mean to kill anyone! I didn't rape anyone!"

"Just an innocent bystander?" Darnell interjected coldly. "Watching your pals do the dirty work?"

"That's not what I meant."

"What did you mean?" Darnell asked.

Sidney shot Darnell a warning glance, and said gently. "Let's begin with last night, Sander. Walk us through it."

Sander nodded, licked his dry lips. "When I got to Grisly's place, Lancer was already on the scene, armed with a rifle. He was drunk. Raving mad. We tried to calm him down, but he kept screaming that Grisly killed Nikah, and he wasn't going to let him get away with it."

Darnell was scribbling away.

Sander continued, his voice animated, "Lancer was so pissed that Grisly wasn't there, he grabbed a gas can and started throwing gas on the barn. He lit it before we could stop him. Then he headed toward the cabin to burn that down, too. We warned him to stop but he wouldn't listen. Harper fired at his feet. Lancer thought we were trying to kill him. He fired back. Shot Harper. Shot at me, too, and missed. I had to defend myself." Sander rubbed his hands over his eyes, and suddenly looked haggard and about five years older.

"I never shot anyone before. He forced my hand. I had to shoot him, or he would have killed Harper and me."

"What happened next?"

"I called 911 to get help for Harper. Lancer's body was out in the middle of the clearing, so I dragged him into the barn."

"By his feet? You pulled off a boot?"

"Yeah." Sander huffed out a tortured breath and slowly met Sidney's eyes. "You know the rest. We didn't mean to kill him. I swear. You can ask Harper."

"We will. Why did you tell me it was Grisly?"

"I wasn't thinking. It all happened so fast. I was trying to distance myself. Pretend I didn't know Lancer or Grisly. I didn't want to be associated with the poaching business. But you found the pictures." His shoulders slouched. "You can see I'm not innocent."

Darnell met her eyes with a small glimmer of triumph. Another confession. Poaching. He continued scribbling.

"Why did Lancer think Grisly killed Nikah?" Sidney asked.

Sander shook his head. "That's a long story."

"We got time. We aren't going anywhere."

Sander retreated into silence. He fidgeted, slumped in his chair, crossed and uncrossed his legs. Anxiety peeled off of him in waves.

"Talk to me, Sander. Help yourself."

His jaw sawed back and forth. A drop of sweat rolled down the side of his face. Finally, he said, "I can give you the identity of the Stalker, but first I want a guarantee of a deal."

"You have my word. I'll talk to the judge personally. Let him know you cooperated fully." She paused for effect.

A look of suspicion crept over his face.

"You can trust Chief Becker," Darnell said earnestly. "She keeps her word."

Sander slouched lower in his chair and picked at a cuticle on his thumb, face sweating.

They waited. A minute ticked by. Sidney wanted to shake him. Darnell's shoulders lifted and tightened. Sidney finally broke the silence. "You're gonna have to trust me, Sander. This is your last chance. Tell us why Lancer thought Grisly killed Nikah."

Sander looked up from his hands, having paled so that his freckles appeared brighter than before. He met her gaze, and blurted, "Because he attacked other Indian women."

"How do you know this?"

"One night when he was drunk, he bragged about it. Said he raped a woman he met in the saloon a few years back. He also admitted to raping a singer from the village. Grisly talked about those women like they were trash, like they were second class citizens."

Sidney sat speechless. The information he revealed was privileged. Only the rapist and a few people on the Tribal Council knew the identity of the rape victims. "How do we know you aren't the rapist?"

"Because Grisly showed us pictures. They're on his phone."

"Pictures of what?"

"The women he raped. One had her hands tied behind her back."

Sidney met Darnell's eyes, exchanging their revulsion for Sander and Grisly in a glance. Wrestling to control her temper, she asked, "So you knew Grisly raped women, but you did nothing about it?"

Sander's eyebrows arched, and he nervously wet his lips. "What was I supposed to do? We're partners. He's a good friend. More like a brother. Would you turn in your own brother?" He redirected his focus to his hands, tightly clasped, and said feebly, "He said he wouldn't do it again."

Sidney studied Sander with narrowed eyes. Even though she had devoted a career to getting depraved offenders off the street, she could still be sickened by their coldblooded lack of conscience, their lack of empathy for their victims. Sander was as guilty as Grisly. His compliance allowed Grisly to remain free to attack again. He failed to sexually assault Tammy Mueller a second time, but the emotional wounds he inflicted would traumatize her for the rest of her life. Despite Sidney's best effort to keep her feelings under control, her voice toughened. "So, what you're telling us, Sander, is that Grisly is the Stalker?"

"Yes...and no."

"What do you mean? Which is it?"

He glanced up at the camera and then leveled a direct stare at Sidney, challenging her to back off. She held his gaze. Sweat gleamed on his face. "I mean the Stalker isn't just one person. All three of us were in on it together. We all broke into those homes. Me, Grisly, and Lancer."

Adrenalin charged Sidney's system. She could feel her pulse beating in her temples. "Keep talking. Explain."

He cleared his throat. "We'd been doing pretty well with our trapping business until about six months ago. Then it suddenly went bust. Our fur trader told us he couldn't take that many pelts anymore. His distributor was getting suspicious. He told us to sit on our inventory for a few months. So that money source just dried up. Grisly and I could wait it out. We were just stockpiling our money anyway. Saving it to start a legitimate business together. We were both tired of the animal trade. The loss of income hit Lancer the hardest. His roofing job didn't bring in much and he was going through his stash fast, gambling, doing drugs, drinking."

"Did Nikah know?"

"Only about the drinking. Nothing else."

"Go on."

Sander shifted uncomfortably in his seat. "One night we were out drinking in town and Lancer told us he'd been doing some neighborhood thefts to bring in some extra money. Easy stuff. Stealing tools and shit from barns and sheds. He said he wanted to start robbing houses. He knew which villagers were well off, flashing expensive jewelry and electronics. He knew who had dogs, who didn't. The villagers were so naïve, they didn't even lock their doors."

Sander closed his eyes for a moment, thinking, and when they reopened, he appeared to be resigned, at last, to complete cooperation. "It sounded like easy pickings. So I thought, what the hell, I'd give it a try. The three of us started taking turns, maybe a couple times a month. One of us went into a house, one kept watch. Lancer was right. It was easy." Sander scratched his chin. "For a while, anyway. Then folks got riled up. Men started patrolling the neighborhood. I had a close call one night and had to hightail it down to the creek. I ran a half-mile through the water before they stopped following me with dogs. Scared the hell out of me. After that, I backed out of the whole deal. I had a job. I didn't need the money that bad. But honestly, for Grisly, it was a thrill. A game. Outwitting the villagers and invading their personal space got him off. He did all the break-ins while Lancer worked out the logistics. As part of the search party, Lancer knew exactly where the patrol was. He texted Grisly and kept him informed."

"Nice racket," Sidney said with sarcasm.

Oblivious to her derision, Sander agreed. "Yeah, it was. He and Grisly raked in some nice loot. Jewelry, laptops, money, drugs, guns. You name it. Some stuff people wouldn't even report. Then everything changed."

"What changed?"

Sander stared at his hands, brow deeply furrowed. "That's when the singer got raped, and she claimed a white guy did it. Right away, people started accusing Lancer. Lancer was royally pissed. He confronted Grisly. Grisly just laughed, and said, "So what? The bitch was asking for it."" Sander shook his head. "Grisly has no respect for women. Especially Native American women. He thought because he was white, he could do whatever he wanted, without consequences. But not this time."

"What happened?"

"Lancer slugged him. Hard. Blackened his eye. Told Grisly he was done. He was finished with their partnership, completely. By that time though, it was too late. The villagers ran Lancer out of there a couple weeks later."

Darnell's dark eyes sparked with rage. "So Lancer also knew who the rapist was, but instead of reporting it, he took the rap. Leaving Grisly to assault again?"

Sander's face flushed crimson.

"So Lancer quit working the village at that point?" Sidney said.

He nodded. "Any thefts after that, Lancer wasn't involved. But he went bat shit crazy. He lost his home, his neighbors hated him, his girlfriend kicked him out. He blamed Grisly. Grisly sold the guns and electronics on the black market. Easy to move. Lancer accused him of cheating, not giving him his fair cut. Grisly just told him he was full of shit. Grisly and I stored the loot in that hidden cellar with the furs. We were just sitting on it. But Lancer wanted to cash out some of the jewelry. We said no. We needed to wait for the heat to cool down and then we'd move it in another city." Sander spoke in a low, controlled voice, but there was no disguising the anger simmering below the surface. "Last week, Lancer cut the padlock off the cellar. Stole our two cases."

"The money and jewelry."

"Yeah."

Sidney nodded sagely, as if sympathizing with his plight. "Must've made you mad,"

"Damn straight." The pulse pounded in his neck.

"That's why you broke into Nikah's place, and Lancer's," Sidney said in an understanding tone, encouraging him. "Looking for those cases."

Sander nodded, his face as menacing as a thunderhead just before a storm breaks. "I can understand his beef with Grisly, but he stole from me, too. We'd been friends since grade school. But he changed. Since moving out of Two Creeks, he acted like those villagers were his people, not us." Sander's voice vibrated and a strain of violence boiled over, tightening the muscles on his face. His fists clenched and pulled at the cuffs on his wrists. "He wouldn't tell me where the cases were. I despised him for that. He needed to be taught a hard lesson about loyalty."

"So you beat him."

"I had to. I admit I may have hit him harder than I should have. But he wouldn't talk. Stubborn as hell. Harper tore his place apart but couldn't find the cases."

"So you started slicing his scalp open?"

"He fucking made me do it!" Sander's voice rose with every word. "He finally talked. We got the two cases back. They were under the floorboards in the laundry room."

Sidney gave him a minute to get control of himself. She checked her texts and saw that Amanda had River Menowa waiting in the lobby. She turned back to Sander. "Just a few more questions, Sander. How did Harper play into all this?"

"He's not involved in anything. I told him Lancer stole some stuff from me. Harper never asked what it was, just said he'd help me get it back. All he did was help me search the two houses. I swear. Please don't press charges against him. I got him into enough trouble. Because of me he's lying in a hospital bed fighting for his life."

Though she sympathized with Harper, as an accomplice to burglary and assault, he was far from innocent. Not to mention he slammed into her at Nikah's house. The head injury she sustained could have been far worse. A judge and jury would determine his guilt, not her. "So you got your two cases back," Sidney said. "But a couple of things were missing."

Sander gave her an appraising look. "The medallion and key. Those two pieces are worth more than everything else put together. I made the mistake of telling Lancer about them."

"Where did they come from?"

"The home of a villager. A woman who lives alone. It was easy to clean her out. We got a laptop, an unregistered gun, some diamond jewelry, and the medallion and key."

"You know her name?"

"Jenna Menowa."

"Jenna?" Sidney repeated, suddenly comprehending the outrage the woman directed at Lancer at the tribal meeting. Jenna believed Lancer was the Stalker. The Stalker broke into her house and stole possessions valued at over a hundred grand. Anyone would see red. Originally, the medallion and key were stolen from a collector in Sweetwater two years ago, the same time Jenna moved from Sweetwater to Two Creeks. Was she the first thief? Sidney made a mental note to bring it up when she questioned River.

Sidney marveled at the interconnectedness of these crimes. Sander had implicated himself and his two friends in a serious string of offenses—burglary, poaching, rape. She needed to squeeze a little more information out of him while the pan was still hot and greased. "Tell me Sander, who murdered Nikah?"

His eyes widened in surprise. "Don't know anything about that."

"You were in her house two nights after her murder."

"We didn't know she was dead. We scouted the house and saw she wasn't home. I just wanted to get my stuff back. We would never have hurt her."

"Did you see any signs of a disturbance?"

"No."

"What about your friend Grisly? Did he attack her?"

"I don't know. You'll have to ask him."

"Where is he?"

Sander shrugged. One knee started bobbing. "Haven't got a clue."

"You can stop covering for Grisly. We're going to get those photos he has on his phone. We have enough on him to put him away for decades. Don't muddy your good standing with me by withholding evidence. Where is he?"

"Out hunting."

"You're trying my patience."

"This won't come back to me, will it? He'd kill me."

"No," Darnell said. "He'll be in a cage. He'll never hurt anyone again."

"Hunting what?" Sidney said, although she already knew the answer.

"That fucking white wolf."

"Only the wolf?"

"What else would he be hunting?" Sander's pale blue eyes lost focus. He glanced away, looking spent from spilling his guts.

Sidney regarded him in silence for a few moments searching for a trace of deceit. Convinced he had confessed all he knew, she glanced at her watch, then lifted her gaze to the camera. "The interview with Sander Vance was completed at 2:45 p.m."

"Okay, Sander, that's it. Thank you."

Darnell was already rising to his feet. "I'll get him into a cell."

"Then retrieve those photos from Grisly's phone." They had to be on Grisly's computer as well, floating in the digital cloud.

CHAPTER FORTY

GRANGER HAD BEEN out in the wild with Tommy and Magic since the crack of dawn. Fatigue tightened his shoulders and his mind was struggling to stay alert. He had spent a miserable night in a cramped tent with two grown men, all three stuffed into their sleeping bags like burritos. If he moved the wrong way, his knees poked Tommy, or Magic's bony knees poked him. Between Magic's snores that rumbled through the tent like a plane engine, and Tommy's incessant, tormented tossing, Granger got little sleep.

Magic, fifty-five, thin and wiry, with a weather-worn face and long braids, rose energetic and ready to go. Granger and Tommy rose blurry-eyed, and obediently swallowed the bitter coffee Magic brewed on a small propane stove. They gnawed jerky for breakfast while riding along the creek trail in the stunning cold.

The morning started out sunny with excellent visibility. The breath of man and horse mingled, steaming in the early morning air. They continued to follow the tracks of the unknown rider who persisted in trailing the elusive old woman. The pattern of tracks disappeared and reappeared, usually a few hundred feet downstream on the opposite bank. Granger couldn't help but admire Elahan's wiliness.

After a couple of hours in the saddle, clouds and fog began to roll in and light flakes drifted in their direction. The chopper had swooped overhead several times but finally called it quits and headed back to town.

Rounding a bend, they came upon the abandoned campsite of the lone rider, and dismounted.

"He spent the night here in a tent." Magic said, studying the snow flattened in the shape of a square. His eyes brightened after he poked a stick into a few manure piles left behind by the rider's horse. His mouth turned up in a smile. "It appears he slept in and got a late start. These horse pies aren't completely frozen. He didn't leave more than thirty minutes ago."

Adrenaline humming, Granger walked the perimeter and discovered something a few feet away nearly buried in snow. An Old Crow bourbon whiskey bottle, empty. "Here's why he slept in. He must have been in a stupor this morning. Nursing the mother of all hangovers."

"He's riding slow," Tommy said. "Probably hurts to move fast."

"Let's go," Magic said. "If we hustle, we can catch up to him pretty quick."

Granger felt a twinge of hope. If they didn't find Elahan, they would at least grab this stalker and eliminate the immediate danger. They mounted their horses and hit the trail at a good clip. The sky darkened and the wind gusted, biting their cheeks. Naked branches of trees clacked together and fat snowflakes swirled from a heavy sky. Granger hunched his shoulders, brought his collar up to his ears, and tugged his scarf over his face.

They hadn't gone a mile when a warning alarm blared in his head and the men stopped in their tracks. A saddled, gray Morgan stood off the trail, partly hidden in the trees.

Pow-WHOP.

A sharp crack exploded, followed by a guttural boom that rolled over the terrain. The three men scattered, each dismounting in the woods and taking cover. Tommy and Magic grabbed their rifles. Granger pulled out his Glock pistol.

Pow-WHOP.

Through the gauzy curtain of snow, a haze of gun smoke appeared above a felled tree thirty yards away and was instantly carried sideways by the wind.

Using sign language, Granger signaled for the men to give him cover. They did. Rounds exploded. Granger saw the snow and earth rip up in front of the dead tree as the two men sprayed the area with bullets. The air thickened with gun smoke. The shooter stayed pinned down, unable to get off a shot. Granger sprinted from tree to tree, circling behind, and dodged behind a ponderosa pine where he had a clear view of the shooter. Crouched low, dressed in camo, gripping his rifle, the man crouched low. It was Grisly. Most likely stinking, shit-faced drunk to make such a stupid move—firing upon three men, putting himself in a weak position that could easily get him killed, adding an attempted murder charge to his already impressive criminal record.

Granger had a clear shot. "Put the gun down, Grisly!"

Grisly whipped around and fired. Rounds tore into the trunk of the ponderosa and sprayed Granger's face with sharp bits of bark. The shots rang in Granger's ears. His pulse raced. "Put the gun down. Or you're gonna die out here. You don't stand a chance. We've got you surrounded."

Grisly fired more rounds. Chips of bark exploded like wayward missiles from the trunks of surrounding trees. Then another deafening silence. His magazine was spent. Granger stepped out from behind the tree and watched his two partners rush Grisly from the side. Magic slammed Granger's head with the butt of a rifle and he fell backwards in the snow. Tommy kicked the weapon aside and the two men pulled him to his feet. He stood stunned and wobbling but he wasn't seriously injured, thanks to the cushioning of his Elmer Fudd hat. Granger exhaled, releasing the tension he'd been holding.

Tommy got right in Grisly's face, speaking in his native tongue, squeezing the trapper's throat in a tight grip, breathing hard, emitting bursts of vapor.

"Chill, Tommy," Granger said, as he approached.

Tommy tossed him a look of rage, but dropped his hand.

"Why the hell are you out here terrorizing an old woman and a boy?" Granger asked.

"I don't give a shit about the old witch and the kid," Grisly said, slurring his words. "It ain't me they have to worry about. I just want that fucking wolf."

"Where you're going, you'll never kill another animal," Tommy hissed.

Grisly's bloodshot eyes met his and held a hard, cold stare, challenging him.

"Who do they have to worry about, Grisly, if it isn't you?" Granger asked, his voice controlled, though his nerves were firing underneath. "Is someone else out here hunting them?"

Grisly smirked. The smell of alcohol ghosted off of him. "Yeah. But you won't find 'im. He's like a coyote. Smart. Quiet."

"Who is he?"

"Don't know. He's been following me. Stays out of sight in the woods. I only caught a glimpse of him a couple times."

"What does he look like?"

"Dressed in black. Raccoon hat. Rides a black quarter horse."

"When did you see him last?"

"I heard him splashing through the creek at dawn," Grisly said, weaving.

The three men were silent, digesting the news. Was Grisly telling the truth? Or had he been hallucinating in the throes of drink? Or was he jerking them around?

Tommy looked gut-punched. Magic's cheek twitched. Obviously, they believed him.

The snow dusted the four men and their horses white.

"No use looking for his tracks," Grisly said. "They'll be covered by now. In this storm, there's only one place he could be headed."

"Where's that?" Granger asked with a twinge of hope.

"An old, abandoned cabin a couple miles from here. I've holed there before in shit weather like this."

Granger had no choice but to take him at his word. "Tie his hands, Tommy. Let's get him on his horse. He's going to take us to that cabin."

CHAPTER FORTY-ONE

DARNELL ESCORTED River Menowa into the grill room. Tall and handsome, River could have been a model for winter wear in his expensive Canada Goose parka and Duckfeet Arhus boots. Under his jacket, he wore designer jeans and a blue button-down business shirt. He removed the parka and threw it over the back of his chair and took his seat. Sidney and Darnell sat in their usual places, quietly accessing the young man who was so adept at hiding secrets behind a charming façade.

River looked around, taking in the stark room. "I like what you've done with the place," he said. "No frills school of design."

Sidney smiled, and said pleasantly, "Fits the budget. Thanks for coming in. We just have a few questions for you."

"Of course." His expressive brown eyes met hers. "I'm not sure why I'm here. I don't know how I can help your investigations. As you know, I rarely visit Two Creeks."

"True, but you were there the last few days. During the time Nikah Tamanos was killed."

His brow furrowed. "Sounds ominous. Am I a suspect?"

Sidney was waiting for the moment she could recite his Miranda rights, which she would carefully couch in a reassuring tone. Without that precondition, River could confess to being the shooter on the grassy knoll, or to killing Jimmy Hoffa, and she wouldn't be able to use it as evidence. If she Mirandized him too soon, he could spook and lawyer up. If she waited too long, important details might slip out that wouldn't be admissible in court. "These are just routine questions, River. We're interviewing many villagers. You never know what random bit of information might help us out."

He shrugged. "Sure. Fire away." Smooth. Sure of himself.

Wanting to keep him at ease, she kept her voice light and friendly. "First, let's establish your whereabouts so we can get that out of the way. Where were you late Friday night?"

"At my mom's house," he said a little too quickly, as though he had prepared for the question.

Darnell started scribbling. River looked at him nervously. Darnell lay down the pen.

"Did you know Nikah Tamanos?"

"Yes. We were friends."

"Dating?"

He blinked. "Why do you ask?"

"Other villagers mentioned seeing you together."

His demeanor changed instantly. Muscles tightened around his mouth and his eyes narrowed while he thought of the appropriate reply.

Sidney filled in the answer for him, speaking gently. "We know you were lovers, River. Your fingerprints were found on her headboard and nightstand. Someone saw your BMW parked in her driveway the night she died."

River wasn't under arrest, but just being in an interrogation room was intimidating. On top of that, having evidence thrown at you that implicated you in a murder hit like a sucker punch. Her intent was to disarm him. It worked. Even though River gave off the aura of cool, she could sense his nervous tension. "We know Nikah had sex the night she died. DNA was found on the bed sheets. Do you mind if we take a DNA swab so we can rule you out as a suspect?"

He licked his lips. "Yes, I mind."

"I don't think you understand how this works, River," she continued in a soothing tone. "Giving a DNA sample isn't a choice. Look, I'm going to be straight with you. We have enough evidence to arrest you for murder one. I can have a compulsion order from a judge over here in ten minutes." She paused to let that steep for a few seconds. "If your DNA is a match, that means you were the last person to see Nikah alive, which makes you my primary suspect. I could arrest you right now, but I'd like to give you a chance to present your side of the story."

River sat quietly. Looking for an out.

They always wanted an out.

His self-control remained intact and his face revealed no emotion. "Okay. You can have a DNA swab. It'll be a match to me. We had sex. That doesn't mean I killed her."

It was time.

"River, you have a chance to help us out here. To help yourself. To help the villagers understand what happened. Are you willing to do that?"

He nodded, his face shadowing with emotion.

Sidney recited his Miranda rights.

River eyed her, listening.

"You don't have to talk to us. You understand that, right?"

"Yes."

His stiff posture relaxed and Sidney knew her gentle tone had soothed him. She nodded to Darnell. He took his cue. He left the room and a moment later returned with a water pitcher and some paper cups. She poured a cup for all three of them. River drank his immediately. She refilled it.

She slid a photo of the key and medallion across the table. "Recognize these?"

His face blanched.

Sidney tapped the photo. "We know these two items were originally stolen from a collector in Sweetwater named Vincent

Schuman. Your mother lived in Sweetwater at the time they were stolen. The Stalker then stole these items from your mother's house in the village. Your mother believed Lancer was the Stalker. Lancer's girlfriend ended up dead. You were sleeping with her. Are you keeping up with me? I don't believe in coincidences, River. Somehow all of this fits together." Sidney's tone sounded curious, not threatening. A friend talking to a friend. "Maybe you can shed some light on it for me."

There was silence in the room. River shifted uneasily in his chair. His dark-eyed stare became bold and defiant. "Mom didn't steal that stuff. They belong to her. Heirlooms from her side of the family going back generations. Mom's married name is Schuman. She was married to Vince. If anything, he stole from her. He knew Mom took them, but he reported them stolen. He collected the insurance."

Sidney didn't know when she learned to be alert to male anger, but she was an ace. She sensed River was striving to control his temper. When he spoke, his voice was even, but she could hear its strangled wrath.

"That bastard beat the holy crap out of Mom on a regular basis. She got away from him barely alive, with only a few possessions, including these." He tapped the photo. "Mom didn't report Vince's fraud because he would find out where she was. We're both convinced he'll kill her if he gets half a chance."

Sidney listened, slowly digesting the information. "I understand your concern, River. We'll look into your claims, discreetly. If these items belong to your mom, they'll be returned."

"Thank you."

"How long had you been seeing Nikah?"

"Just a couple months. I've known her since Mom moved to Two Creeks. But she had a boyfriend. We only hooked up after Lancer split the scene."

"What happened the night she died?"

River went quiet, arms crossed, possibly buying time to fabricate his story. "We didn't have a date. With us, it was spur of the moment. She called me around nine and asked me to come over."

"Is that how it normally was for you? Casual?"

"Yes. I let her run the show. She was in a vulnerable place. Lancer was being accused of being the Stalker, and he'd been asked to leave the village."

"How'd that make her feel?"

"Messed up. Super depressed. She didn't believe Lancer was the Stalker, but she felt a lot of shame for bringing an outsider, a drunk, into the village. She heard the gossip, saw how people looked at her. They wanted to say something comforting, but they couldn't. They believed he did it." He sighed. "I got that she still loved him. But he was a drunk and she wanted him out of her life. As a friend, I lent a sympathetic ear. We had sex without obligations."

"So, what happened the night she died?"

He went quiet again, staring at the door as if imagining being on the other side of it. He drained his cup of water, wiped his mouth. "When I got to her place, I saw that she had emptied an entire bottle of wine. She was pretty ripped. I thought about leaving, but she said she was down in the dumps and really needed a friend." A new quality came into his voice. His measured tone gave way to tenderness, but tenderness haunted by a tinge of sorrow. "Against my better judgment, I stayed. She drank more wine. We ended up in bed."

"You cared about her."

His brown eyes softened. "Very much."

Was the rough sex Nikah's idea, or his? Sidney decided to leave the details of their sexual preference private.

"What happened next?"

"We didn't get to sleep until around two. Nikah had been having problems with insomnia. She'd just gotten a prescription for Ambien and she popped a couple to help her sleep. They knocked her out. I woke up early, around five. Nikah was dead to the world. I decided to take the opportunity to have a look around, see if I could find my mom's stuff. About fifteen minutes later, Nikah found me searching her office. She was swaying and holding on to the door frame for support."

Bright spots of color now burned in River's cheeks. "I'd found the key to Nikah's safe in a drawer and had it open, going through her private stuff. She asked me what the hell I was doing. I told her I was looking for the heirlooms Lancer stole from my mom. That he was the Stalker." River swallowed, shook his head with a look of wonder. "Nikah turned into a mad woman. She started screaming incoherently that Lancer wasn't a criminal. Slurring her words. She grabbed a pair of scissors from the desk and came at me like a wild animal. I raised my arms to defend myself. She slashed me."

The hair rose on Sidney's arms as she imagined the violence of Nikah's attack. She was attuned to every nuance of expression, every tone in River's voice.

"I've relived what happened next over and over." His eyes closed and he struggled to keep his voice steady. "I wish I had acted differently, but it was instinctual to defend myself. I shoved her away. She tripped and hit her head on the corner of the desk. Then her head hit the floor, hard." He shuddered. "It was horrible. Violent. Blood streamed out of her hair and spread across the rug. It happened fast. In an instant." Anguish distorted his features and he covered his face with his hands.

Sidney and Darnell exchanged a glance. River had just confessed to murder. "It's okay. Take your time," she said gently.

Tremors passed through River's shoulders. Finally, he pulled a handkerchief from the pocket of his parka, wiped his moist eyes, and said hoarsely, "I tried to revive her, but she wasn't breathing. No pulse. She was dead."

His tears made his eyes harder to read, but Sidney believed he was telling the truth. Nikah's erratic behavior was consistent with symptoms induced by Ambien and alcohol. And Doctor Linthrope surmised that the blows to Nikah's head killed her instantly. "May I see the wound?"

Without answering, River unbuttoned and pushed up the left sleeve of his shirt. He peeled back a gauze bandage and revealed a red gash about three inches long that had been crudely stitched. "Mom sewed it up for me."

"What did you do next?" Sidney asked, getting him back on track.

"I didn't know what to do. I was in shock. In hindsight, I know I should have called you, but instead I called Mom. That was a mistake." The words lodged in his throat as though struggling to come out. "She came over right away and took control. After thinking everything through, she said we had to move Nikah out of the house and remove every trace that I'd been there. She was convinced if we called the cops, I'd be accused of murder." Creases of frustration notched his forehead. "Sorry, but Mom has a blind spot where law enforcement is concerned. The legal system never took her side when she reported Vince's abuse. His high-priced lawyers got him off every time with a slap on the wrist."

"I'm sorry to hear that," Sidney said in an even tone, though her temper was flaring over Jenna's wrong-headed interference. "That won't be the case here. You'll be treated fairly. Please, go on with your story."

River released a deep breath. "We followed the custom of our people. We washed Nikah's body and dressed her in clean clothes. To aid her in the afterlife, we did a cleansing ceremony and sang a funeral song. Mom told me to go. She'd clean up. We wrapped Nikah in the rug, and I laid her on the back seat of my car. I didn't think twice about taking her to the creek. She loved that spot by the bridge. She told me it was the one place where she always felt at peace. Where she felt close to the spirit world. I slipped her into the water, and it felt right. Cleansing. Releasing her back from where she came."

The room was quiet for a few moments while Sidney assessed River. His story was convincing. He had no priors, not even a traffic ticket. But he was a smart businessman with a dozen employees. He knew right from wrong. By his own admission, he knew he should have called law enforcement instead of his mother. Jenna's misguided advice put him at risk of a murder conviction. Sidney's sympathy went only so far, and it had reached its limit. "We'll need to get those scissors to the lab."

"They're on Nikah's desk." River's eyes shadowed. "Mom wiped off the blood."

Of course she did.

Darnell raised his brows. "Just curious. Why'd you leave the sheets on the bed? You must have known we'd process them."

"Mom never got the chance to clean Nikah's room. I knew the sheets would tell a story. That we were lovers. But I didn't think you could place me at her house the night she died."

"Why didn't your mom get the chance to clean her room?"

"Someone came into the house. She panicked and ran out."

"Who came in?"

"Tommy's son. Tegan. But of course, he's blind. Mom wasn't worried that he'd identify her."

"Tegan was in Nikah's house?" Sidney asked, alarmed.

"Yes. But the blood was cleaned up by then. There was nothing for him to see."

Maybe not with his eyes. But if Tegan got a sense that Nikah had been killed, and he believed he had just intercepted her killer, that would have been a terrifying experience. Tegan might have thought the killer would come after him, which could explain why he and Elahan fled the village.

She turned back to River. "I don't believe you're a murderer, River. But even if you killed Nikah justifiably, it's still a homicide. We'll have to investigate it thoroughly. Dr. Linthrope will have to determine if Nikah's head wound is consistent with hitting the desk. He'll need to find trace evidence of your blood on Nikah's scissors."

River seemed relieved, as though a great burden had been lifted from his chest.

"But you should have listened to your instincts and used better judgment. If you had called us to the scene, this would all be resolved by now. But you chose to conceal a homicide, alter and destroy evidence, remove a body without release from the proper authorities, and you illegally left it on public land."

River's eyes locked on Sidney's. "So, I guess you're going to arrest me?"

"Yes."

He nervously licked his lips. "What about my mom?"

"We're going to have to hold her accountable, too. You'll both be taken into custody, but fortunately, not for murder."

River looked worried. "If this gets into the paper, Mom's cover will be blown. Her life will be in danger. Vince will be sure to see it. He'll find a way to kill her."

Sidney sighed. They should have thought of that before breaking the law. "We can't keep this under wraps, River. A local woman died. Everyone will want to know what happened."

"What's next?" River asked.

"If you can't afford a lawyer, we'll get a public defender assigned to you. There'll be a hearing for probable cause in the morning. Your lawyer can post bail and you'll both be released."

Sidney turned to Darnell. "Book him. Tell Amanda to get out to Two Creeks to bring Jenna in."

"Let's go, River." The two left the room.

Sidney took a moment to collect her thoughts. It had been an emotionally-charged day, between her visits to the morgue and her two interrogations. River and Sander were in custody, but Grisly was still out there, following Elahan and the boy. She scrolled through her messages. One was from Granger.

We have Grisly. But there's another suspect out here. We're going after him.

What the hell? Another suspect? Sidney wrote back:

Alert me the second you have him in custody. Be careful!

CHAPTER FORTY-TWO

A LIVING ROOM, a kitchen, and a small bedroom made up the interior of the creaky, musty cabin. Standing on the rotting floorboards in the doorway of the kitchen, Moolock was satisfied with the appearance of the living room. It had been stripped of furnishings years ago, but now a single propane lantern hissed and sputtered in one corner. Barely illuminated on the far side of the room were two figures seated in front of the wood stove that he had fashioned out of buffalo hides.

Moolock turned on the iPod he'd brought and placed it in the shadows. The room filled with the chorus of two voices passionately chanting in a native tongue. He turned up the volume just loud enough to be heard from outside the cabin. The lone rider would be more daring if he believed Tegan and Elahan were engrossed in this diversion, and not focused on a man lurking outside who had malicious intentions.

Lelou suddenly growled and stared intently at the front door. Moolock, too, heard something. A small sound. A sound that penetrated the timbers of the house.

The wolf trembled in his stance.

Moolock unholstered his pistol, grabbed the wolf's collar, and stepped back into the darkness of the kitchen. He felt the familiar heaviness in his chest, the pounding of blood in his temples when the warning siren wailed in Afghanistan. He was in that zone that anticipates an intense blast of danger.

The door handle turned slowly. Then the door opened wide enough to allow a big man to quietly slip into the room and shut it behind him.

Moolock assessed him in the blink of an eye. A half-foot taller than himself. A powerful build under a long, black coat. Features hidden by a raccoon hat and knit scarf. A mountain of a man.

The intruder lifted his pistol toward the dummies, and growled, "Shut the fuck up. Hands above your heads."

A tense moment of complete stillness followed.

With a bloodcurdling growl, Lelou jerked out of Moolock's grasp and attacked, hitting the man from the side and knocking him to his knees. His weapon fired. An explosive pop was followed by a sharp metallic crack as the round hit the stove. Then the man jerked his gun towards Lelou.

Unable to get a clear shot past the wolf, Moolock rammed his body into the man's arm. The pistol fired again. Moolock felt a burning sensation in his upper right arm. His own gun hit the floor.

Lelou's jaws clenched down on the intruder's wrist, but the man had the strength of a bull. With a piercing cry, he threw Moolock aside and wrenched his arm free of Lelou's teeth. He struck the animal sharply on the skull with the hilt of his pistol and the wolf collapsed, blood streaming over his face. The man sprang to his feet and swung his weapon toward Moolock.

Lying on his back, Moolock had no time to go for his weapon, which lay two feet away. He slammed his foot into the man's knee and heard an agonizing shriek. Moolock grabbed his Sig Sauer. He and the man shot simultaneously. Moolock felt a hot piercing pain in his side and saw a bullet hole appear below the man's left cheek. He swayed like an oak tree in a fierce wind, and then crashed to the floor, shaking the walls.

Moolock lay stunned, gunshots ringing in his ears. His hands shook. He was having trouble concentrating, and knew he was in the throes of shock, but he did his best to assess the situation. He had taken two bullets and felt a warm wetness over both wounds. The large man sprawled across the floor with a bullet in his brain was most likely dead. The wolf's breathing was ragged. Before he could help Lelou, Moolock had to attend to his own wounds, or he'd lose consciousness and bleed out.

Moolock always carried first aide essentials on his person, including a tourniquet and pressure dressings. He removed three Israeli bandages from an inner coat pocket and tore off the packaging. Gritting his teeth, ignoring the burning pain that intensified with every small move, he removed his upper body clothing and examined the wounds. He sighed his relief. The arm wound was a through-and-through. No arteries or bones affected. The second bullet grazed his torso just beneath the ribs, leaving a furrow in which deeper layers of skin and tissue had been removed. He treated the upper arm first, hissing through his teeth as he placed the sterile sides of the absorption pads against both the entry and exit wound, then he wrapped the limb tightly. He did the same to the other wound, winding the bandage around his waist as best he could with an injured arm.

Next, he examined the wolf. Lelou lay on his side, panting, legs twitching, chest heaving. Moolock used his T-shirt to wipe away some of the blood. The animal had taken a good blow. The laceration was deep and needed stitches, but it wasn't life threatening. Moolock wrapped the third compression bandage around the wolf's head to stem the bleeding. Now they both were in need of urgent medical attention.

Moolock felt weak, woozy. Grunting with pain, he wrestled into his clothes, stepped over the legs of the big man and swung open the door to a blast of cold air. His legs felt heavy and shaky, but he needed to make it to the barn. He needed to ride out in search of help. A wave of dizziness overtook him on the porch. Tongue dry, thoughts sluggish. Feeling himself lurching forward, he grabbed hold of the snow-covered handrail to steady himself.

He made it to the bottom of the steps before falling headlong into the snow and then the world faded to black.

CHAPTER FORTY-THREE

THE SNOWFALL had ceased and the clouds were clearing, revealing patches of blue sky. In its wake, a flawless blanket of white covered grass and shrub, boulder and tree. If not for following the creek, Granger and his men would not have known where the trail lay. All traces of horse tracks made by Elahan's horses and Grisly's ghost rider had been erased. Their hope of finding the cabin, which might be sheltering the old women and boy, rested on the shoulders of the devious and inebriated trapper. Propped on his horse with his hands tied to the saddle horn, Grisly led the way, head bobbing drunkenly with the motion of his horse. As if by radar, he veered away from the creek and led them directly into the snow-covered forest.

Once he got his bearings, Granger saw a logic to the way the path cut a berth through the trees, and realized they were probably following an old elk trail.

"How far?" Tommy asked Grisly impatiently.

Grisly shrugged.

"How far, asshole?" Tommy asked again.

"Fuck you."

Granger interceded, his voice holding a threat. "Lose the attitude, Grisly, and maybe I won't throw you in the tank with a bunch of puking, pissing drunks when we get back."

Grisly's eyes flattened and his tone sounded strained. "The cabin's about a mile up the trail."

"Let's get a move on."

They rode at a faster clip and got to the edge of a wide clearing within fifteen minutes. The first thing Granger saw was a big, black quarter horse tethered inside the cover of trees. Then he saw a ramshackle cabin and barn in the middle of the meadow. Smoke puffed from the chimney and a dull light flickered in the windows.

"That's his horse," Grisly said. "The guy tailing me."

A hard knot of dread tightened in Granger's gut. The rider had parked his horse out here so he could sneak up on the house. He hoped to hell they wouldn't find the old woman and boy injured or dead inside.

"Elahan and Tegan may be in there," Tommy said with a touch of panic, the worry in his eyes bordering on agony. He pulled his rifle from its scabbard.

Magic did the same.

"Hold on," Granger said. "He could pick you off like fish in a barrel." He lifted his binoculars and scanned the area around the house. "Holy shit. Someone's lying in the snow. A man. We need to act. Magic, Tommy, ride around to the back of the cabin to the left. Stay in the cover of the woods. I'm going to the right. Get up close to the house. Work your way around to the guy on the ground." He grabbed Grisly's reins. "You're coming with me."

The men rode through the trees to the back of the house without incident and dismounted, except for Grisly. "Keep your mouth shut," Granger warned him, tying Grisly's horse to a porch rail, then he quietly crept up to the rear door. Magic and Tommy disappeared around the corner of the house.

Pistol in hand, Granger opened the door and cast his flashlight beam into the dark kitchen. Nothing moved but dust motes. Eerily, the sound of chanting came from the next room. He crossed the floor to the living room, blood thumping cold and slow in his ears. A man lay on the floor, his face in a pool of blood. Next to him, lay Lelou, his head bandaged. Two immobile figures sat in front of the wood stove. What the hell? He waved his light over them and saw the figures were just mounds of buffalo hides. He crouched over the man on the floor, located his carotid artery, and after a few seconds detected a weak pulse.

The door banged open and Magic and Tommy carried the other man inside. "We looked through the window," Tommy said, panting. "Saw the room was clear."

"He alive?" Granger asked.

"Yeah," Tommy said, and nodded to the man on the floor. "What about him?"

"He's in bad shape. And Lelou's hurt."

"Any sign of Elahan and Tegan?" Tommy asked, his expression hard and anxious.

"Sorry, no."

The man moaned as they lowered him to the floor. Granger ran out to his horse and grabbed his first aid kit and satellite phone and rushed back. The chanting had ceased.

Tommy was bent over Lelou, stroking him and mumbling quietly. The animal whimpered back.

Granger handed his satellite phone to Magic. "You need to use this outside. Call for AirEvac. These men need to get to the ER, ASAP."

Another moan drew Granger to the white man carried in from outside. He had long brown hair and rugged features. He was trembling and his face was ashen. Granger quickly assessed his vital signs and located the man's two wounds, each bound by a pressure bandage that probably saved his life. The man's lids fluttered open and dazed hazel eyes stared up at him.

"You're okay," Granger said, studying him closely, impressed by his medical skill. "Looks like you took care of yourself."

The man asked weakly, "The other guy?"

"Barely alive," Granger said.

"Go treat him," the man said, his voice a hair above a whisper.

Granger immediately recognized the other man as the oversized Indian who had been spoiling for a fight at the Wild Horse Saloon. A vet with PTSD.

"Fitch Drako," Tommy said, surprised.

"Up to no good," Granger said. A bubble of anger rose inside him when he thought of the man's intention, but he pushed it down. Drako's skin was cold and sweaty, his pulse weak but rapid, his pupils dilated. Granger didn't hold out much hope for him, but he concentrated on stemming the blood flow and applying a pressure bandage to his head. When he finished, he packed up his kit and examined the entire room, piecing together what had taken place. The buffalo mounds had been designed to look like Elahan and Tegan. The chanting convinced Drako they were inside the cabin and distracted. The white man was lying in wait. The blood stains near the door showed signs of a struggle and multiple gunshots.

"Airlift will be here within twenty minutes," Magic announced, coming back in.

Granger nodded, and heard the injured white man calling Tommy by name.

Tommy crouched over him. "How do you know my name?"

"Not important." The man coughed and cleared his throat. "Elahan and Tegan are safe."

"Where are they?" Tommy asked, his voice raw with emotion.

"In the cave beneath Skookumchuck Falls."

Tommy's eyes moistened. "Jesus. They're alive."

"Use the tunnel east of the creek. It's hidden by branches."

"I know exactly where that is."

"They're safe," the man repeated. "Take them home."

Tommy fingered the pouch hanging from the man's neck and said with a note of amazement. "This looks like Elahan's work. Did she make this for you?"

The man nodded. "It has the power of the stones. It brought you to me."

Tommy blinked. "Who the hell are you?"

"My name is Moolock."

"Moolock, you have my deepest gratitude." Tommy gently took the man's hand. They held each other's gaze for a long moment, and Granger saw something indefinable flicker in Moolock's eyes.

"The horses are in the barn." Moolock closed his eyes, his mouth went slack, and he appeared to drift off.

"What's with the pouch?" Granger asked.

In reply, Tommy stood and pulled out his own pouch from under his shirt. It looked almost identical to Moolock's.

"What's a white man doing with a medicine bag?" Granger asked.

"I don't know. Elahan only makes these for family." He and Granger shared a look that was a combination of wonder and puzzlement.

"Moolock has some kind of strong connection to you," Granger said. "The wolf came here with him, and probably got hurt protecting him. Moolock treated him. Judging from the way this room is set up, I'd say Moolock went to great lengths to lure Drako here. Probably to save your family. He put his life on the line. Drako shot him twice."

Tommy cast Drako a hard glance, his face tight with fury. "Why the hell was he following Elahan and Tegan?"

"Good question," Granger said. "Go get your family. Take them home. We're good here. I'll look out for the wolf."

"Thank you," Tommy said with feeling, placing his hand on Granger's shoulder. "I'll let you know when we get home." The door shut behind him.

Granger exhaled a breath he didn't realize he'd been holding. The knot of anxiety eased inside him and it felt like the pressure of the world had been lifted. The old woman and boy were safe. Moolock, whoever he was, and the wolf, would recover. Grisly was facing serious jail time and Fitch might not survive the day. Two dangerous characters had been taken out of circulation.

CHAPTER FORTY-FOUR

AFTER THE TWO HORSES splashed across White Tail Creek, Tommy wove through the forest until he located the tunnel at the bottom of the sheered granite cliff. Finding it took some time. Moolock had done an excellent job of camouflaging the opening with a rough wooden frame covered in cedar boughs. Tommy tethered the horses, muscled the makeshift door to one side, and entered the tunnel. Anxious to reunite with his family, he quickened his gait as he followed his beam of light through the narrow passageway. His entrance into the cavern came with a shock and a vicious rush of adrenaline.

Tegan stood at an angle, facing Tommy with a bow and arrow pointed directly at him, the string stretched taut. Elahan stood armed with a rifle, one eye squinting behind the scope, her gnarled finger on the trigger.

"It's Tommy." Sighing her relief, Elahan lowered the rifle.

Tegan let out a harsh sob, so loud it startled Tommy. The boy placed the bow on the ground and nearly flew across the floor to wrap his arms around his father. His breath came out in hitching gasps.

"Thank God you're both okay," Tommy choked, eyes brimming.

The trying ordeal of riding a horse through the wilderness in freezing cold had taken a toll on Elahan. Her face looked drawn, her body appeared even more shrunken and frail. Tommy's own muscles ached and his joints were stiff. He could only imagine how she felt.

In a rare display of affection, Elahan joined them, her spidery arms embracing them in a fervent hug. Fierce affection for his family tightened Tommy's chest and left him breathless.

Elahan pulled away, fear darkening her eyes. "Why are you here, Tommy? Where is Moolock?"

"Where's Lelou?" Tegan cried.

"They're both injured, but they're going to be okay," he said. "Let's sit down. I'll tell you everything."

They migrated to the camp chairs where a blazing fire roared in the pit. The heat felt good on Tommy's face, which was numb with cold. "This man…Moolock…is a hero. He lured the rider who was following you to an old ski hut. There was a shootout. Moolock took two bullets."

Elahan and Tegan gasped.

"He's going to pull through. Moolock shot the other man. Fitch Drako. He's in bad shape. He hit Lelou on the head. He'll need stitches and some TLC. They've been airlifted to the hospital in Jackson."

"Moolock will be okay," Elahan repeated softly, as though to convince herself. She closed her eyes, lips moving silently in prayer. She touched her medicine bag beneath her dress and met Tommy's gaze. "The stones protected him."

Tommy touched his bag, too. "You gave Moolock one of your magic stones?"

"Yes." She steered the topic away from Moolock, shaking her head. "Fitch Drako is the man who wanted to hurt us. I knew he was wounded in his mind but I never thought he was this sick."

"No one knew. He was quiet. Kept to himself. Those are the ones to watch out for." Tommy cleared his throat. "We also caught Grisly. He wanted to kill Lelou."

Tegan's breath caught.

Tommy placed a hand on his son's shoulder. "Both men are in custody. Facing serious jail time. They'll never hurt anyone again."

The boy's shoulders slumped with relief.

"Why did you two take off like you did?" Tommy asked, a mild reprimand in his voice. "Why didn't you tell me what was going on?"

"No time," Elahan rasped. "Bad men were closing in. You would not have let us go. I knew you would come looking for us. You did. You brought others to help. You did your part, Tommy. We all did our part. We had Moolock's protection. The power of the stones kept us safe."

Elahan's inexplicable bond to this man, this stranger, at once angered and puzzled Tommy. She chose Moolock over him to protect her and Tegan when they were in imminent danger. Tommy took a deep breath to subdue a bitter slash of jealousy, and a feeling of betrayal, but his curiosity reached its limits. He blurted indignantly, "Who is this man? This Moolock? Why does he wear our family medicine bag?"

Elahan raised a veined hand to brush her white hair from her brow. She was a master at hiding her emotions, but not now. Her fingers trembled, and Tommy detected a flicker of fear, or shame, in her dark eyes. Tegan squirmed in his chair, a cautious look on his face. Tommy braced for bad news.

"Moolock is your uncle," Elahan said finally.

"My father had a brother? How can that be? Moolock's around my age."

"Just tell him, Nana," Tegan said impatiently.

Elahan stared at the floor for a long moment before her eyes found Tommy's, and he saw how hard this was for her. "Moolock is your age. He was born the same year as you. He's my son."

Tommy sat mute, feeling nothing. Then he struggled with a tangled thing inside his head, trying to make sense of her words.

"Moolock is your son? Who's his father? How come you never told me about him? Where's he been all these years?"

Elahan put up a hand for silence. "I will tell you everything." She sighed and began to share her story in a soft, quiet voice, beginning with her relationship with Moolock's father, a doctor, with whom she worked at the Lost River Reservation. Her face was radiant while reflecting on joyful times early in their relationship, but contorted with grief when relating her catastrophic losses. Forest died in the war, then her beautiful boy was ripped from her life, and she endured decades of separation from him. Elahan had an intensely emotional reunion with Moolock five years ago, and since then, he lived surreptitiously on the fringe of her life.

Feeling her sorrow like a physical pain, Tommy listened in silence, hungry to know these hidden details of her life, and the extraordinary man he met in the cabin. His grandmother had always been enshrouded in mystery. Suffering shimmered behind the veil of her dark eyes. Tommy now understood the lifelong estrangement that existed between Elahan and his father, Chac.

Tommy's heart tossed in a crosscurrent of emotions—feeling sympathy for Elahan, and fury at his father. Instead of supporting Elahan when she needed him most, Chac chastised her for having a baby with a married man. Chac had never hesitated to cast his strict moral values at his family like thunderbolts, which made Tommy's childhood challenging, and troubled. Tommy left home at eighteen to free himself from his father's reign of righteousness. Over the years, when Chac came to visit, Tommy was polite but distant, and Elahan generally kept herself busy in the garden or kitchen.

"I'm sorry Dad treated you so harshly, Nana," Tommy said. "At times, he's blind to everything except business and increasing his profit margin. He should've used his money to fight the Wainwrights in court. Instead, he made you feel ashamed. By doing nothing, he allowed them to steal your baby." Tommy looked at Elahan through glassy eyes and the words came out thick with emotion. "I've never been ashamed of you. Not for a second. Your presence in my life, and Tegan's, are my most precious gifts. I want to get to know my uncle. I want Moolock to know he's welcome. He's an important part of our family." Tommy leaned over and kissed Elahan on the forehead, realizing how miserly he'd been with his affection all these years.

Elahan's fingers twined through his, rough and warm. They locked eyes and her expression of tenderness pierced his heart.

"How do you like the cave, dad?"

"Moolock lives here?" Tommy took note of his surroundings for the first time—a drafty, ice-cold cavern encroached in shadow. Great for bats. Not humans. The man's horse lived in the same proximity as Moolock. Not a single frill or comfort. How could a man live this way?

"In cold weather. It's pretty cool, huh?" Tegan said.

"For Batman, maybe."

"I want to go home, Dad. I miss our house. I want to go see Moolock at the hospital."

Tommy smiled, roughing his son's hair. "We'll all go see Moolock. Let's pack up and hit the trail. Let's go home."

CHAPTER FORTY-FIVE

Three Days Later

Over coffee and pastries, Sidney's small staff sat around the conference table with bright eyes and alert faces—the exuberance of a job well done. Their appearance was much improved since the height of the recent crime spree. Putting their cases to rest, getting enough sleep, and returning to normal patrol duties had done wonders. Selena had been invited to join them this morning as a measure of gratitude for her contributions.

"I want to commend you all for the hard work you put into solving these cases," Sidney said. "We were scattered, working on different aspects of these crimes, and now I want to show you how all the parts fit together." Sidney pointed to their crime board, filled with photos of corpses, rape victims, the remnants of the burned barn, burglary suspects, and poachers.

"First the Stalker case." She tapped the photos of Lancer, Sander, and Grisly. "These three men poached hundreds, maybe thousands of animals. They also formed a successful crime gang that brazenly robbed residents of Two Creeks Village." She tapped Grisly's photo and a note of disgust entered her voice. "In addition, this man physically and sexually assaulted several women, including his two ex-wives. Grisly and Sander will not be seeing the light of day for years to come."

Next, she tapped photos of River and Jenna Menowa. "Nikah's death was an unfortunate accident but these two geniuses complicated matters by tampering with evidence and obstructing our investigation. They may be facing some jail time, hefty fines, and will certainly spend lots of money in court."

"What about Jenna's husband?" Darnell asked, frowning. "Her location has been released by the press. She thinks he'll try to kill her."

Sidney sighed. "Not much she can do. If a man is determined to harm a woman, a restraining order won't do much good. It's not bulletproof. Her husband's legal team has him coated in Teflon. Untouchable. Jenna's best bet is to leave Garnerville. Find anonymity somewhere else."

"A case of crime going unpunished," Amanda said angrily.

"It happens," Winnie said.

Turning back to the board, Sidney cleared her throat and continued, tapping the photo of Fitch Drako. "Here's another Prince Charming. I spoke with his doctor yesterday. Beating all odds, Drako survived a bullet wound to the head, and is conscious and recovering at the Jackson hospital. The bullet went through his cheek and out the back of his neck, missing his brain completely."

Eyes around the table widened with wonder.

"I didn't see that coming," Granger said.

"You saved his life. He was hanging by a thread when you patched him up."

Darnell slapped Granger on the back. "Good job. You saved the life of a total psycho."

"Good thing he did," Sidney said. "I spoke with Drako. Found out his mission. Why he was in pursuit of the Chetwoots."

That got the rapt attention of everyone in the room.

"He wanted to kidnap Tegan," Sidney said. "And hold him for ransom."

"No way," Selena said, eyes wide with shock.

"Christ," Granger added. "He was after the boy?"

Sidney nodded.

"Why pick on the Chetwoots? They don't seem to be swimming in money," Amanda said.

"Actually, they are," Sidney said. "Elahan's son, Chac, is part owner of the casino in Jackson. Every month, for years, he's deposited money in an account accessible to Elahan and Tommy, and a trust fund for Tegan. To their credit, the Chetwoots choose to live simply, but they could be living in a gleaming palace on a hill if they wanted to. Elahan and Chac aren't on the best terms. She uses the money to secretly pay the mortgages of some of the poorer people in the village, including Fitch Drako. He did some digging around and found out who his benefactor was, and their net worth. He was going to grab a bundle of greenbacks and head down to Mexico."

"A madman with a plan," Darnell snorted.

"Nice way to show his gratitude," Selena huffed.

"He feels he's been getting ripped off," Sidney said. "He said the profits from the casino should be going to everyone in the village, like on the reservations. He doesn't get that it's privately owned. Tucker Longtooth is the primary owner. It's not a tribal casino."

"Brain damage," Winnie said, circling her finger around her temple.

"So, who's this Moolock character?" Granger asked, his neon blues bright with curiosity. "Did you see him at the hospital?"

Sidney frowned. "Yes, I met with him. Caught him just in time. He checked himself out early, against doctor's orders, and was on his way out. The man's a hero, but he wants no recognition. He barely spoke to me, other than confirming everything you wrote in your report." Sidney felt a surge of sadness as she remembered the tall, striking man with the melancholic demeanor and haunted eyes. She detected his keen intelligence and hypersensitivity, cloaked in secrecy. He divulged nothing about his personal life and made no attempt to engage in polite conversation. "He also said that Drako tried to kill him in the woods a few days ago. Drako was also poaching, and Moolock was confiscating his traps. He kept the cartridges, which match Drako's rifle. One thing was crystal clear," Sidney continued. "The shootout at the cabin and the act of violence he committed toward another man, even in self-defense, distressed him deeply."

"Very mysterious. How does he know Elahan?" Winnie asked.

"He said they're old friends. Hospital records show his real name is Forest Wainwright the Fourth. I Googled him. He's a doctor from New England. Illustrious family. Was in the military. He and his wife worked at a base in Afghanistan as trauma doctors, but sadly, she was killed in a rocket attack. He came back to the states suffering from a TBI. Then he disappeared for the last five years, and now, he's popped up here."

"Impressive man," Granger said with admiration in his voice. "Tragic life."

"No good deed goes unpunished," Winnie said soberly.

"Poor man. How did he get mixed up in all of this?" Selena asked.

"Good question. For now, that remains a mystery. He said if I need him in the future, Elahan knows how to get hold of him." Sidney poured a mug of coffee from the carafe at the sidebar, blended in cream and sugar, took a sip, and turned back to the table. "By the way, a little bird told me we're all up for bonuses at the end of the year. Apparently, we have a very satisfied community. The mayor is beside himself with appreciation. Solving these cases in record time really made him look good."

"Pay raises would be nice," Winnie said with a wink.

"New patrol cars," Amanda added. "And more vacation time."

"Yeah, that ain't gonna happen," Darnell said.

"Curb your pessimism. Could be coming down the pike," Sidney teased. "You're all dismissed. Be safe out there."

Chairs pushed back from the table and everyone started filing out. Granger gave Selena's hand a quick squeeze as they walked out together. "We're still on for tomorrow night?" he asked.

"Dinner at seven." Selena beamed back at him, her cheeks coloring.

The two hadn't seen each other for the last few days. Tomorrow night was their first big date night. Sidney made arrangements to see a movie with David and his son, Dillon, so her sister could have privacy. She couldn't help but smile as she pulled on her parka. Could be an historic evening.

Officially not on duty until the evening shift, dressed in jeans and a turtleneck, Sidney crossed the lot to her Yukon. The temperature had stayed in the forties for the last few days, and the warmth of the sun felt good on her back. As she drove out of town, she saw melting snow shrinking into glistening islands on dormant lawns. Roofs were dripping, and rivulets of water gushed down gutters heading for storm drains.

Pleasant anticipation hummed in Sidney's veins as she turned off the highway and drove through the forest to David's house. Their afternoon liaisons had regrettably been put on hold, but one was about to start up in a few minutes. She parked in his driveway, scampered up the paved walkway, and rang the doorbell.

Grinning, David opened the door promptly and stepped aside with a wave of his hand. "Entre vous. I have lunch waiting."

She flashed him a naughty smile. "I'm starving."

He grinned.

She stepped past him and her midsection fluttered with a mix of attraction, affection, and excitement. He followed her into the kitchen, which was bright with sunshine. Something hidden in a covered pan on the stove smelled delicious. She viewed the brilliant blue lake through the window, then turned and got the intensity of David's full attention. He wore jeans and a denim work shirt, his dark hair was tousled, and there were tiny flecks of gold in his earnest brown eyes. The air heated up around them and for a moment the electric connection held her mute. His eyes held her in place as though they'd cast a spell over her.

"Let's loosen you up a little bit," he murmured. He pulled the elastic band from her hair and it fell heavy around her shoulders. David captured a lock and twisted it around his fingers. He gazed at her with longing, waiting for a signal from her to act on the physical yearning they both were feeling.

Eager to feel the hardness of his chest against the softness of her own, she slowly unbuttoned his shirt, slid her hands around his waist, and stroked his contoured muscles. He made a low noise and lifted her arms around his neck, then pulled her tight, his hands cupped around her bottom. They kissed softly, then deeply, and Sidney found herself vibrating like a plucked string, every nerve ending coming alive.

"The salmon's going to overcook," David murmured in her ear.

"Let's have dessert first," she murmured back.

With the barest hint of a smile, he took her hand and led her into the bedroom.

REVIEW THIS NOVEL and receive a FREE eBook by Linda Berry. Limited Supply. Contact Linda: lindaberrywriter@gmail.com

Also By Linda Berry

The Killing Woods
First Book in the Sidney Becker Mystery Series

Renowned Detective Sidney Becker is burned out. After years of homicide investigations in a big city, she's seen too many grisly crime scenes. Seeking balance, Sidney accepts the job of police chief in her hometown—a peaceful mountain community in Oregon.

Life is good. Beautiful scenery. Low crime. Close to family.

Then a beautiful young woman is found murdered in the woods. The staging of the body is chilling, and resembles another victim found in the same area years earlier. The case went cold. Now the killer has come out of hiding.

This man is meticulous and ruthless, and plans each murder to the smallest detail. No clues are found at the crime scene—except for an origami butterfly planted on each victim. Inside each is a handwritten message with an elusive meaning.

To outwit a killer more cunning than any she's faced before, Sidney must decode his cryptic messages and lure him into the open—before he strikes again.

CHAPTER ONE

BAILEY'S LOW, INSISTENT growls woke Ann from a dreamless sleep. She found herself sprawled on the overstuffed easy chair in the living room, feet propped on the ottoman, drool trickling down her chin. Half opening one eye, she peered at the antique clock on the mantle: 11:00 p.m.

She heard Bailey sniffing at the front door, and then the clicks of his claws traveled to the open window in the living room. She opened her other eye. The sable hound stood sifting the breeze through his muzzle with a sense of urgency. Ann knew what was coming next. Sure enough, Bailey trotted back to the front door and whimpered, gazing expectantly over one shoulder. Damn those big brown eyes.

Normally Ann would be in bed by now, but she had passed out after dinner, exhausted from carting her boxes of organic products to town at sunrise and standing for hours in her stall at the farmers market. By the time she loaded her truck and headed home, the pain in her calves had spread up her legs to her back and shoulders, and she felt every one of her forty-five years.

Bailey whined without let up. He knew how to play her. Ann looked longingly toward her bedroom before returning to the hound's pleading eyes. This was more urgent than a potty break.

No doubt, he had caught the scent of a deer or rabbit and wanted desperately to assail it with ferocious barking to assert his dominance over her small farm. Then he'd settle in for the night.

Since an unsolved murder rocked her town three years ago, Ann resisted going out late after dark. Still, she felt a pang of guilt. She and Bailey had missed their usual after dinner walk. If the spirited hound didn't exhaust his combustible energy, he'd be circling her bed at dawn, demanding that she rise.

"Okay, Bailey, you win." Ann heard the weariness in her voice as she heaved herself from the chair. Fatigue had settled into every part of her body and her limbs felt as heavy as flour sacks. "Only a half-mile up the highway and back."

Bailey sat at attention, tail vigorously thumping the floor.

Still dressed in jeans, a turtleneck sweater, and sturdy hiking shoes, Ann grabbed her Gor-Tex jacket from the coat rack, wrestled her arms through the sleeves, pulled Bailey's leash from a pocket, and snapped it onto his collar. The boards creaked softly as they stepped onto the covered front porch into the damp autumn chill. The moist air held the promise of the season's first frost. Her flashlight beam found the stone walkway, then the gravel driveway leading to the highway. A good rain had barreled through while she slept, and a strong wind unleashed the pungent fragrance of lavender and rosemary from her garden. Silvered in the moonlight, furrowed fields of tomatoes, herbs, and flowers sloped down to the shoreline of Lake Kalapuya, where her Tri-hull motorboat dipped and bobbed by the dock. A half-mile across the lurching waves, the lights of Garnerville shimmered through a tattered mist on the opposite shore.

Following the hound's tug on the leash, Ann picked up her pace, breathing deeply, her mind sharpening, muscles loosening. Steam rose off the asphalt. Scattered puddles reflected moonlight like pieces of glass. The thick forest of Douglas fir, red cedar, and big leaf maple engulfed both sides of the highway, surrendering to the occasional farm or ranch. Treetops swayed, branches dipped and waved, whispered and creaked. The night was alive with the sounds of frogs croaking and water dripping. The smell of apples perfumed the air as she trekked past her nearest neighbor's orchards. Miko's two-story clapboard farmhouse floated on a shallow sea of mist, windows black, yellow porch light fingering the darkness.

Ann didn't mingle with her neighbors, few as they were, and she took special pains to avoid Miko, whose wife had been the victim of the brutal murder in the woods adjacent to his property. The killer was never found, but an air of suspicion hovered over Miko ever since. Ann detested gossip and ignored it. She had her own reasons for avoiding Miko—and all other men, for that matter.

When they reached the narrow dirt road where they habitually turned to hike into the woods, Bailey froze, nose twitching, locked on a scent. He tugged hard at the leash, wanting her to follow.

"No," she said firmly, peering into the black mouth of the forest—a light-spangled paradise by day—black, damp, and ominous by night. "Let's go home."

Bailey trembled in his stance, growled with unusual intensity, and tugged harder. The hound had latched onto a rivulet of odor he wanted desperately to explore.

Ann jerked the leash. "Bailey, home!"

Normally obedient, Bailey ignored her. Using his seventy pounds of muscle as leverage, he yanked two, three times until the leash ripped from her fingers. Off he bounded, swallowed instantly by the darkness crouching beyond her feeble cone of light.

"Bailey! Come!"

No sound, just the incessant drip of water. Ann's beam probed the woods, jerking to the left, then the right. "Bailey!" She heard a steady, muffled, distant bark.

He's found what he's looking for. Bailey's barking abruptly ceased. Good. He's on his way back. She waited. No movement. No appearance of Bailey's big sable head emerging through the pitch.

Ann trembled as fear took possession of her senses. She bolted recklessly into the woods, her light beam bouncing along a trail that looked utterly foreign in the dark. Her feet crushed wet leaves and sloshed through puddles. Her left arm protected her face from the errant branch crossing her path. A second too late she saw the gnarled tree-root which seemed to jump out and snag her foot. She fell headlong, left hand breaking the fall, flashlight skidding beneath a carpet of leaves and pine needles. Blackness enveloped her. Shakily, she pulled herself to her feet, left wrist throbbing, trying to delineate shapes in the darkness, the moist scent of decay suffocating.

The forest was deathly still, seeming to hold its breath.

Soft rustling.

Silence.

Rustling again.

Something moved quietly and steadily through the underbrush. Adrenaline shot up her arms like electric shocks. Ann swept her hands beneath mounds of wet leaves, grasping roots and cones until her fingers closed around the shaft of her flashlight. She thumbed the switch and cut a slow swath from left to right, her light splintering between trees. Her beam froze on a hooded figure moving backward through the brush dragging a woman, her bare feet bumping through the tangled debris.

The man kept his face completely motionless, eyes fixed on hers in a chilling stare. The world became soaked in a hideous and wondrous slowness. He lowered the woman to the ground and hung his long arms at his side. He was quiet; so was Ann. He radiated stillness. The stillness of a tree. It was hypnotic.

Ann felt paralyzed. Tongue dry. Thoughts sluggish. Then threads of white-hot terror ripped through her chest and propelled her like a fired missile into motion. Switching off the beam, she turned and sprinted like a frightened doe back along the trail.

Buy: The Killing Woods https://amzn.to/2rEfIFR

ABOUT THE AUTHOR

Linda's love of art and literature led her to a twenty-five-year career as an award-winning copywriter and art director. Now retired, Linda writes mysteries and intense, fast-paced thrillers. She currently lives in Oregon with her husband and toy poodle.

To learn of new releases and discounts
add your name to Linda's mailing list:
www.lindaberry.net

Linda loves to hear from you. Follow her at:
Twitter: @lindaberry7272
Facebook: https://www.facebook.com/linda.berry.94617

Made in United States
North Haven, CT
11 October 2022

25299575R00202